DESCRIPTION OF A STRUGGLE
AND
THE GREAT WALL OF CHINA

Also by Franz Kafka

THE CASTLE
THE TRIAL
AMERICA
IN THE PENAL SETTLEMENT
WEDDING PREPARATIONS IN THE COUNTRY

LETTERS TO MILENA

FRANZ KAFKA

DESCRIPTION OF A STRUGGLE
AND
THE GREAT WALL OF CHINA

TRANSLATED BY
WILLA AND EDWIN MUIR
AND
TANIA AND JAMES STERN

LONDON
SECKER & WARBURG
1960

Made and printed in Great Britain by
Morrison & Gibb Ltd., London and Edinburgh
and first published 1960 by
Martin Secker & Warburg Ltd.
7 John Street, London, W.C.1.

404200-X

PUBLISHER'S NOTE

THIS volume completes, in the Definitive edition, the English translation of Kafka's fictional writings.

With the exception of four short pieces (*An Everyday Confusion, The Truth about Sancho Panza, The Silence of the Sirens* and *Prometheus*) and the *Reflections on Sin, Suffering, Hope, and the True Way*, which are now included in *Wedding Preparations*, it includes all the contents of *The Great Wall of China* translated by Willa and Edwin Muir (1933), together with a considerable amount of new material now translated for the first time by Tania and James Stern.

With the same exceptions this volume contains all the material in Volume V of the German Collected Edition, and the order of stories is the same as that in the German volume.

CONTENTS

Note : Pieces marked † are translated by Tania and James Stern. The remainder are translated by Willa and Edwin Muir.

7

8 CONTENTS

INTRODUCTION BY EDWIN MUIR TO
"THE GREAT WALL OF CHINA"

BEFORE he died Franz Kafka wrote a letter to his friend Max Brod, the novelist. "Dear Max," he wrote, "my last request is that all the writings I may leave behind me (in bookcases and drawers, in my rooms, in the office, or wherever any of them may have got to) ; everything in notebooks, manuscript sheets and letters, whether my own or other people's ; everything finished or in rough draft which you may have in your possession or can get hold of in my name—shall be burned at once unread. Letters which other people refuse to hand over they can at least promise to burn themselves."

After long consideration Herr Brod decided not to obey this injunction ; he has since set out his reasons for the course he took, a course that might easily have given rise to misunderstanding. It would be irrelevant to enter into those reasons here ; but it should be said that they completely vindicate his honour and his friendship, which he would have failed in if he had acted in any other way, knowing, as he did at the time, a great part of the writings he was asked to destroy. Among them were the three long allegorical novels, *The Castle*, *The Trial*, and *America*, and also the stories, allegories, fables and aphorisms in the present volume. That, however, does not still exhaust the great mass of written matter left by Kafka at his death ; and Herr Brod and Herr Schoeps, his German editors, are to follow up the present

9

volume with one of more personal and biographical interest.

The Castle has already appeared in English, and *The Trial*, Kafka's other long allegorical novel, is the natural companion to it. But I thought it expedient to interpose between these two books the present volume, which gives a more clear and general notion of Kafka's intentions as an artist and thinker than any of his other works. He is more explicit here than anywhere else ; the general outline of his thought and the world in which it moves can be clearly discerned. So it is hoped that any one who reads this volume will return to *The Castle* with a new understanding of many things that may have puzzled him in that strange heroic epic, and that he will start with an advantage when *The Trial* appears.

Little is publicly known of Kafka's life, for no biography of him has yet appeared.[1] There is, it is true, an imaginary portrait of him, under the name of Richard Garta, in Herr Brod's novel, *The Kingdom of Love*,[2] and the author tells me that the portrait is a faithful one, founded on biographical data ; but obviously it cannot be used except to indicate certain general traits of Kafka's character. The picture that emerges from Herr Brod's imaginary reconstruction and Kafka's own works is that of a man who, under a cover of deep reserve, concealed an almost absolute passion for rightness in all that he did. To take a trifling but characteristic example : the publication even of a short story or essay was for him always a matter involving long and difficult thought, and all that he actually published was at the urgent solicita-

[1] Since this Note was written Max Brod's *Life of Kafka* has appeared in German, and has been published in translations.
[2] London (Secker), 1930.

tion of his friends. This is one side of the picture : a scrupulousness that would seem pedantic if it were not the pushing of a virtue to its conclusion. On the other hand he had no trace of vanity where his writings were concerned, and habitually referred to them as " scribbles " ; and although the spiritual effort he made was probably without a parallel in his time he never ceased to regard it and himself with a sort of teasing humour. In any one else that might have been mistaken for disingenuousness ; but the whole temper of his work is the very opposite of disingenuous ; it is flawlessly honest and candid. He was faithful to himself and what he thought the right way of conduct in a singular and by ordinary standards fantastic degree. It is indeed clear from his writings that he himself was aware of the semblance of pedantry in which this sometimes involved him, and he actually emphasised it now and then to the point of caricature. But he saw so clearly that to strive for perfection was a human need, saw so clearly at the same time that all effort must end ludicrously short of the mark, that from the contrast was born a sense of proportion peculiarly his own, of which his humour—a humour of desperation—is the perfect expression. On the level where he lived and thought it was quite natural to him that he should ruthlessly exhaust his powers in striving for the right way of life, and just as natural that he should perceive the absurd inadequacy of the result. Yet this did not engender in him any trace of amused complaisance or philosophical laxity. His character seems paradoxical, but that is probably because it oper-ated uniformly on a higher level than that of ordinary men, while to himself it appeared perfectly ordinary and even obvious.

To a man so scrupulously resolved to think and act rightly in small matters as in great the ordinary business of life must have been unimaginably difficult. Herr Brod amusingly relates of Richard Garta—and it might have been a piece of comic characterisation out of *The Castle*—that he was almost always late for any appointment, not out of carelessness, but because of his very conscientiousness in making what he considered the necessary preparations, which, however, invariably took up more time than he had allowed for. His daily work —he was given a post in an insurance office after leaving the university, quite a usual procedure in Prague—must also have been full of extraordinary complications, acutely intensifying the feeling, which he would probably have had in any condition, that he had not found his right vocation in society. But these minor troubles were overshadowed by the disease from which he suffered for a long time, and of which he died. Traces of consumption appeared when he was quite a young man ; he was sent to a sanatorium and partially cured. Then he became involved in a disastrous love affair, and from Herr Brod's account of Richard Garta the course of love seems to have been just as full of insurmountable difficulties to him as the other business of life. After the affair was broken off he became very ill, and had once more to spend a long time recovering in sanatoriums and Bohemian mountain villages. The war came ; in Prague neither food nor coal was to be had except in scraps ; but the only record of that time that I have been able to find is the fantastic sketch entitled *The Bucket Rider* in the present volume, a reminiscence of the severe winter of 1917–1918, when there was a coal famine. Later, when he had set up house in Berlin with the woman who was to make him happy at last, the allied blockade was still in force though the war was over, food was bad and scarce, his disease returned more violently than ever, and he died in a sanatorium near Vienna in the summer of 1924, when he was only a little over forty.

That he must have suffered monstrously during some of those periods may be seen from certain of his earlier stories, particularly *The Country Doctor, In the Penal Settlement*, and *The Metamorphosis*, the last surely one of the most dreadful stories ever written. The mark of obsession is too clearly set on these tales to make them pleasant reading, and at times they touch the verge of actual madness. But the whole development of his art was towards proportion and clarity, and the difference between those earlier stories and the ones in this volume is very great. It may be, indeed, that something was lost to his work in the progress he made during the last few years of his life. In its serene and tender humour *Investigations of a Dog* (see this volume) is perfect; but the note of urgency which gave such a strange muffled power to his earlier and middle work has considerably weakened. One feels that the extreme tension of the conflict is over, and that he can contemplate it now almost as a memory, or with the eyes of one who will soon be delivered from it : the story seems to have been written in the last few months of his life. The atmosphere permeating it is as enigmatical in its own way as that of the plays attributed to Shakespeare's last period. The charged air which fills *The Castle* and *The Trial* has cleared ; the conflict and the passion have died away. There still remains a sense of vast and incomprehensible powers presiding over human destiny, but they no longer press upon the hero so stiflingly ; he is no longer face

to face with them as he once was, and consequently he
can see them more clearly. *The Castle* and *The Trial* are
undoubtedly Kafka's greatest works ; in temper, in
plan, in execution, they are heroic, and only to be compared, among modern works of fiction, with Hermann
Melville's *Moby Dick*. Yet he never wrote anything
more perfect in mood and more formally beautiful than
some of the stories in this volume, such as *Investigations
of a Dog*, *The Great Wall of China*, and *The Burrow*.

The problem with which all Kafka's work is concerned
is a moral and spiritual one. It is a twofold problem :
that of finding one's true vocation, one's true place,
whatever it may be, in the community ; and that of
acting in accordance with the will of heavenly powers.
But though it has those two aspects it was in his eyes a
single problem ; for a man's true place in the community is finally determined not by secular, but by
divine, law, and only when, by apparent chance or
deliberate effort, a man finds himself in his divinely
appointed place, can he live as he should. Many people
slip into their place without being aware of it ; others
are painfully conscious of the difficulty, the evident
impossibility, of finding any place at all ; and nobody
has been more clearly and deeply conscious of it, I think,
than Kafka. Two things no doubt exacerbated his feeling
of being shut out from the community : that he was of
Jewish blood, and that he was an invalid, and thus
doubly isolated. Yet it would be trivial to attach first
importance to these things, which did not give rise to
the problem, but merely accentuated it. For the problem
is an eternal one, eternal, that is, failing the realisation
of a perfect society, which is inconceivable. It is also a
problem that has become crucial in our time, where we

see tradition after tradition crumbling, and society itself
a chaos in which it is hard to find one's way, far less a
vocation that has a transcendent sanction.   The greatness of Kafka lies not in his having solved the problem,
which would be absurd, but rather in his having realised it
as it has never been realised before, illuminating it with a
power of imagination and thought unexampled in his time.

Roughly this seems to me to be the theme of all
Kafka's work, a theme in which is involved the mystery
of divine law and the mystery of human life, both of
which it touches simultaneously.   The full originality
of his imagination, the opulence of his invention, the
reader may be left to enjoy by himself.   There is no
other writer of his age—and it was the age of Rilke and
Proust—whose work carries so continuously, inevitably,
and naturally the mark of greatness ; and it would be
difficult to find in his mature work any lapse from uniform and easy power.   He has that complete integrity
which is like genius in that it seems something given
rather than acquired by effort.   And it is also his integrity
that makes all the artistic means he uses so infallibly right,
so absolutely suited to his purpose and what he has to say.

A few notes on the contents of this volume may be
useful.   Everything in it was written during the last
few years of Kafka's life, the earliest dating from 1917–
1919, the last from 1924, the year when he died.
Investigations of a Dog is by all indications the last story
he wrote, and it is virtually complete.   To understand
it properly one must assume that the human race are
invisible though still operatively present, roughly fulfilling towards the dog world the rôle of divine and
incomprehensible powers.   *The Burrow*, a description of
the shifts to which man is reduced in his isolation, and

the fatal imperfection of his most astute devices, is also one of Kafka's last works, written either before or after *Investigations of a Dog*, but in all probability before. It too is virtually finished, all that remained to be described being the appearance of the invisible enemy, to whom the hero was to succumb. *The Great Wall of China* was written earlier, in 1918 or 1919, and though apparently a fragment, is so perfect in itself that it may be read as a finished work. *The Giant Mole*, the one gravely incomplete story in the book, seems to belong to Kafka's later period, when his attention was turned for a while to science, on which the story is a deliciously ironical comment. The shorter stories and fables, all of them complete except one, *The Knock at the Manor Gate*, seem to belong to the years 1918–1922. The collection of aphorisms entitled " *He*," was written in 1920. The other aphorisms, to which the German editors have given the title they appear under, were carefully written out and numbered by Kafka himself on separate pieces of paper, and were found in a notebook bearing the date 1917–1919. Where two aphorisms have the same number they are written on the same sheet of paper. Those marked with an asterisk were scored out by Kafka, but not removed from their place in the sequence.

For the above information and for much enlightenment on other matters relating to Kafka I have to make the fullest and most grateful acknowledgments to Herr Max Brod and Herr Hans Joachim Schoeps, the editors of the German volume.

EDWIN MUIR.
(1933.)

DESCRIPTION OF A STRUGGLE

And people in their Sunday best
Stroll about, swaying over the gravel
Under this enormous sky
Which, from hills in the distance,
Stretches to distant hills.

I

AT about midnight a few people rose, bowed, shook
hands, said it had been a pleasant evening, and then
passed through the wide doorway into the vestibule,
to put on their coats. The hostess stood in the middle
of the room and made graceful bowing movements,
causing the dainty folds in her skirt to move up and
down.

I sat at a tiny table—it had three curved, thin legs—
sipping my third glass of benedictine, and while I drank
I surveyed my little store of pastries which I myself had
picked out and arranged in a pile.

Then I saw my new acquaintance, somewhat dishevelled
and out of shape, appear at the doorpost of an adjoining
room ; but I tried to look away for it was no concern
of mine. He, however, came towards me and, smiling
absentmindedly at my occupation, said : " Excuse me
for disturbing you, but until this very moment I've
been sitting alone with my girl in the room next door.
Ever since half-past ten. Lord, what an evening ! I
know it isn't right for me to be telling you this, for we
hardly know one another. We only met on the stairs

17

this evening and exchanged a few words as guests of the same house. And now—but you must forgive me, please—my happiness just cannot be contained, I can't help it. And since I have no other acquaintance here whom I can trust——"

I looked at him sadly—the piece of fruit cake which I had in my mouth did not taste particularly good—and said into his rather flushed face : " I'm glad of course that you consider me trustworthy, but displeased that you have confided in me. And you yourself, if you weren't in such a state, would know how improper it is to talk about an amorous girl to a man sitting alone drinking schnapps."

When I said this he sat down with a jolt, leaned back in his chair, and let his arms hang down. Then he pressed them back, his elbows pointed, and began talking in rather a loud voice : " Only a little while ago we were alone in that room, Annie and I. And I kissed her, I kissed her—her mouth, her ears, her shoulders. Oh, my Lord and Saviour ! "

A few guests, suspecting ours to be a rather more animated conversation, approached us closer, yawning. Whereupon I stood up and said so that all could hear : " All right then, if you insist, I'll go with you, but I repeat : it's ridiculous to climb up the Laurenziberg now, in winter and in the middle of the night. Besides, it's freezing, and as it has been snowing the roads out there are like skating rinks. Well, as you like——"

At first he gazed at me in astonishment and parted his wet lips ; but then, noticing the guests who had approached quite close, he laughed, stood up, and said : " I think the cold will do us good ; our clothes are full of heat and smoke ; what's more, I'm slightly tipsy without having drunk very much ; yes, let's say good-bye and go."

So we went to the hostess, and as he kissed her hand she said : " I am glad to see you looking so happy today."

Touched by the kindness of these words, he kissed her hand again ; whereupon she smiled. I had to drag him away. In the vestibule stood a housemaid, whom we hadn't seen before. She helped us into our coats and then took a small lantern to light us down the stairs. Her neck was bare save for a black velvet ribbon round her throat ; her loosely clothed body was stooped and kept lengthening as she went down the stairs before us, holding the lantern low. Her cheeks were flushed, for she had drunk some wine, and in the weak lamp-light which filled the whole stairwell, I could see her lips trembling.

At the foot of the stairs she put down the lantern, took a step towards my acquaintance, embraced him, kissed him, and remained in the embrace. Only when I pressed a coin into her hand did she drowsily detach her arms from him, slowly open the front door, and let us out into the night.

Over the deserted, evenly lit street stood a large moon in a slightly clouded, and therefore unusually extended, sky. On the frozen snow one had to take short steps.

Hardly were we outside when I evidently began to feel very gay. I raised my legs, let my joints crack, I shouted a name down the street as though a friend of mine had just vanished round the corner ; leaping, I threw my hat in the air and caught it boastfully.

My acquaintance, however, walked on beside me,

unconcerned. He held his head bent. He didn't even speak.

This surprised me, for I had calculated that he, once I had got him away from the party, would give vent to his joy. Now I too could calm down. No sooner had I given him an encouraging slap on the back than I suddenly no longer understood his mood, and withdrew my hand. Since I had no use for it, I stuck it in the pocket of my coat.

So we walked on in silence. Listening to the sound of our steps, I couldn't understand why I was incapable of keeping step with my acquaintance—especially since the air was clear and I could see his legs quite plainly. Here and there someone leaned out of a window and watched us.

On turning into the Ferdinandstrasse I realised that my acquaintance had begun to hum a melody from the *Dollar Princess*. It was low, but I could hear it distinctly. What did this mean? Was he trying to insult me? As for me, I was ready to do without not only this music, but the walk as well. Why wasn't he speaking to me, anyway? And if he didn't need me, why hadn't he left me in peace in the warm room with the benedictine and the pastries? It certainly wasn't I who had insisted on this walk. Besides, I could have gone for a walk on my own. I had merely been at a party, had saved an ungrateful young man from disgrace, and was now wandering about in the moonlight. That was all right, too. All day in the office, evenings at a party, at night in the streets, and nothing to excess. A way of life so natural that it borders on the excessive !

Yet my acquaintance was still behind me. Indeed, he even quickened his steps when he realised that he had fallen in the rear. No word was uttered, nor could it be said that we were running. But I wondered if it wouldn't be a good idea to turn down a side street; after all, I wasn't obliged to go on this walk with him. I could go home alone and no one could stop me. Then, secretly, I could watch my acquaintance pass the entrance to my street. Good-bye, dear acquaintance! On reaching my room I'll feel warm, I'll light the lamp in its iron stand on my table, and when I've done that I'll lie back in my armchair which stands on the torn oriental carpet. Pleasant prospects! Why not? But then? No then. The lamp will shine in the warm room, shine on my chest as I lie in the armchair. Then I'll cool off and spend hours alone between the painted walls and the floor which, reflected in the gilt-framed mirror hanging on the rear wall, appears slanted.

My legs were growing tired and I had already decided to go home and lie down, when I began to wonder if, before going away, I ought to say good-night to my acquaintance. But I was too timid to go away without a word and too weak to call to him out loud. So I stood still, leaned against the moonlit wall of a house, and waited.

My acquaintance came sailing along the pavement toward me as fast as though he expected me to catch him. He winked at me, suggesting some agreement which I had apparently forgotten.

" What's up ? " I asked.

" Oh, nothing," he said. " I only wanted to ask your opinion about that housemaid who kissed me on the staircase. Who is the girl ? Have you ever seen her before ? No ? Nor have I. Was she a housemaid at all ? I had meant to ask you this before, while she was walking down the stairs in front of us."

" I saw at once by her red hands that she's a house-maid, and not even the first housemaid, and when I gave her the money I felt her hard skin."

" But that merely proves that she has been some time in service, which no doubt is the case."

" You may be right about that. In that light one couldn't distinguish everything, but her face reminded me of the elder daughter of an officer I happen to know."

" Not me," he said.

" That won't stop me going home ; it's late and I have to be in the office early. One sleeps badly there." Whereupon I put out my hand to say good-bye to him.

" Whew, what a cold hand ! " he cried. " I wouldn't like to go home with a hand like that. You should have let yourself be kissed, too, my friend. That was an omission. Still, you can make up for it. But sleep ? On a night like this ? What an idea ! Just think how many thoughts a blanket smothers while one lies alone in bed, and how many unhappy dreams it keeps warm."

" I neither smother anything nor warm anything," I said.

" Oh, go on ! " he concluded, " you're a humorist ! "

At the same time he began walking again and I followed without realising it, for I was busy thinking of what he had said.

From these words I imagined that my acquaintance suspected in me something which, although it wasn't there, made me nevertheless rise in his estimation by his suspecting it. So it was just as well I hadn't gone home. Who knows, this man—thinking of housemaid affairs while walking beside me, his mouth steaming with cold—might be capable of bestowing on me in the eyes of the world a value without my having to work for it. Let's pray the girls won't spoil him ! By all means let them kiss and hug him, that's their duty and his right, but they mustn't carry him off. After all, when they kiss him they also kiss me a little—with the corners of their mouths, so to speak. But if they carry him off, then they steal him from me. And he must always remain with me, always. Who is to protect him, if not I ? And he's so stupid. Someone says to him in February : Come up the Laurenziberg—and off he goes. And suppose he falls down now, or catches cold ? Suppose some jealous man appears from the Postgasse and attacks him ? What will happen to me ? Am I to be just kicked out of the world ? I'll believe that when I see it ! No, he won't get rid of me.

Tomorrow he'll be talking to Fräulein Anna, about ordinary things at first, as is natural, but suddenly he won't be able to keep it from her any longer : Last night, Annie, after the party, you remember, I was with a man the like of whom you've certainly never seen. He looked—how can I describe him to you ?— like a stick dangling in the air, he looked, with a black-haired skull on top. His body was clad in a lot of small dull-yellow patches of cloth which covered him completely because they hung closely about him in the still air of last night. Well, Annie, does that spoil your appetite ? It does ? In that case it's my fault, then I told the whole thing badly. If only you'd seen him, walking timidly beside me, reading infatuation on my face (which wasn't very difficult) and going a long way ahead of me so as not to disturb me. I think, Annie, you'd have laughed a bit and been a bit afraid ;

but I was glad of his company. For where were you, Annie? You were in your bed, and your bed was far away—it might just as well have been in Africa. But sometimes I really felt as though the starry sky rose and fell with the gasping of his flat chest. You think I'm exaggerating? No, Annie. Upon my soul, no. Upon my soul which belongs to you, no.

And I didn't spare my acquaintance—we had just reached the first steps of the Franzensquai—the smallest fraction of the humiliation he must have felt at making such a speech. Save that my thoughts grew blurred at this moment, for the Moldau and the quarter of the town on the farther bank lay together in the dark. A number of lights burning there teased the eye.

We crossed the road in order to reach the railing along the river, and there we stood still. I found a tree to lean against. Because of the cold blowing up from the water, I put on my gloves, sighed for no good reason as one is inclined to do at night beside a river, but then I wanted to walk on. My acquaintance, however, was staring into the water, and didn't budge. Then he moved closer to the railing; his legs were already against the iron bar, he propped his elbows up and laid his forehead in his hands. What next? After all, I was shivering and had to put up the collar of my coat. My acquaintance stretched himself—his back, shoulders, neck—and held the upper half of his body, which rested on his taut arms, bent over the railing.

"Oh well, memories," said I. "Yes, even remembering in itself is sad, yet how much more its object! Don't let yourself in for things like that, it's not for you and not for me. It only weakens one's present position without strengthening the former one—nothing is more obvious—quite apart from the fact that the former one doesn't need strengthening. Do you think I have no memories? Oh, ten for every one of yours. Now, for instance, I could remember sitting on a bench in L. It was in the evening, also near a river. In summer, of course. And on such evenings it's my habit to pull up my legs and put my arms round them. I had leaned my head against the wooden back of the bench, and from there I watched the cloudlike mountains on the other bank. A violin was playing softly in the hotel by the river. Now and again on both banks trains chuffed by amidst shining smoke."

Turning suddenly round, my acquaintance interrupted me; he almost looked as though he were surprised to see me still here. "Oh, I could tell you much more," I said, nothing else.

"Just imagine," he began, "and it always happens like this. Today, as I was going downstairs to take a short walk before the evening party, I couldn't help being surprised by the way my hands were dangling about in my cuffs, and they were doing it so gaily. Which promptly made me think: Just wait, something's going to happen today. And it did, too." He said this while turning to go and looked at me smiling out of his big eyes.

So I had already got as far as that. He could tell me things like that and at the same time smile and look at me with big eyes. And I—I had to restrain myself from putting my arm round his shoulders and kissing him on the eyes as a reward for having absolutely no use for me. But the worst was that even that could no longer do any harm because it couldn't change anything, for now I had to go away, away at any price.

While I was still trying urgently to think of some means by which I could stay at least a little while longer with my acquaintance, it occurred to me that perhaps my long body displeased him by making him feel too small. And this thought—although it was late at night and we had hardly met a soul—tormented me so much that while walking I bent my back until my hands reached my knees. But in order to prevent my acquaintance from noticing my intentions I changed my position only very gradually, tried to divert his attention from myself, once even turning him towards the river, pointing out to him with outstretched hands the trees on the Schützeninsel and the way the bridge lamps were reflected in the river.

But wheeling suddenly round, he looked at me—I hadn't quite finished yet—and said : " What's this ? You're all crooked ! What on earth are you up to ? "

" Quite right. You're very observant," said I, my head on the seam of his trousers, which was why I couldn't look up properly.

" Enough of that ! Stand up straight ! What nonsense ! "

" No," I said, my face close to the ground, " I'll stay as I am."

" You really can annoy a person, I must say. Such a waste of time ! Come on, put an end to it."

" The way you shout ! In the quiet of the night ! " I said.

" Oh well, just as you like," he added, and after a while : " It's a quarter to one." He had evidently seen the time on the clock of the Mühlenturm.

I promptly stood up straight as though I'd been pulled up by the hair. For a while I kept my mouth open, to let my agitation escape. I understood : he was sending me away. There was no place for me near him, or if there were one, at least it could not be found. Why, by the way, was I so intent on staying with him ? No, I ought to go away—and this at once—to my relatives and friends who were waiting for me. But if I didn't have any relatives and friends then I must fend for myself (what was the good of complaining !), but I must leave here no less quickly. For in his eyes nothing could redeem me any longer, neither my length, my appetite, nor my cold hand. But if I were of the opinion that I had to remain with him, it was a dangerous opinion.

" I wasn't in need of your information," I said, which happened to be true.

" Thank God you're standing up straight again. All I said was that it's a quarter to one."

" That's all right," said I, and stuck two fingernails in the gaps between my chattering teeth. " If I didn't need your information, how much less do I need an explanation. The fact is, I need nothing but your mercy. Please, take back what you said just now ! "

" That it's a quarter to one ? But with pleasure, expecially since a quarter to one passed long ago."

He lifted his right arm, flicked his hand, and listened to the castanetlike sound of his cuff links.

Obviously, this is the time for the murder. I'll stay with him and slowly he'll draw the dagger—the handle of which he is already holding in his pocket—along his coat, and then plunge it into me. It's unlikely that he'll be surprised at the simplicity of it all—yet perhaps he will, who knows ? I won't scream, I'll just stare at him as long as my eyes can stand it.

" Well ? " he said.

In front of a distant coffee-house with black window-panes a policeman let himself glide over the pavement like a skater. His sword hampering him, he took it in his hand, and now he glided along for quite a while, finally ending up by almost describing a circle. At last he yodelled weakly and, melodies in his head, began once more to skate.

It wasn't until the arrival of this policeman—who, two hundred feet from an imminent murder, saw and heard only himself—that I began to feel a certain fear. I realised that whether I allowed myself to be stabbed or ran away, my end had come. Would it not be better, then, to run away and thus expose myself to a difficult and therefore more painful death? I could not immediately put my finger on the reasons in favour of this form of death, but I couldn't afford to spend my last remaining seconds looking for reasons. There would be time for that later provided I had the determination, and the determination I had.

I had to run away, it would be quite easy. At the turning to the left on to the Karlsbrücke I could jump to the right into the Karlsgasse. It was winding, there were dark doorways, and taverns still open ; I didn't need to despair.

As we stepped from under the arch at the end of the quay on to the Kreuzherrenplatz, I ran into that street with my arms raised. But in front of a small door in the Seminarkirche I fell, for there was a step which I had not expected. It made a little noise, the next street lamp was sufficiently far away, I lay in the dark.

From a tavern opposite came a fat woman with a lantern to see what had happened in the street. The piano within continued playing, but fainter, with only one hand, because the pianist had turned towards the door which, until now ajar, had been opened wide by a man in a high-buttoned coat. He spat and then hugged the woman so hard she was obliged to raise the lantern in order to protect it.

"Nothing's happened!" he shouted into the room, whereupon they both turned, went inside, and the door was closed.

When I tried to get up I fell down again. "Sheer ice," I said, and felt a pain in my knee. Yet I was glad that the people in the tavern hadn't seen me and that I could go on lying here peacefully until dawn.

My acquaintance had apparently walked on as far as the bridge without having noticed my disappearance, for it was some time before he joined me. I saw no signs of surprise as he bent down over me—lowering little more than his neck, exactly like a hyena—and stroked me with a soft hand. He passed it up and down my cheekbone and then laid his palm on my forehead. "You've hurt yourself, eh? Well, it's icy and one must be careful—didn't you tell me so yourself? Does your head ache? No? Oh, the knee. H'm. That's bad."

But it didn't occur to him to help me up. I supported my head with my right hand, my elbow on a cobblestone, and said: "Here we are together again." And as my fear was beginning to return, I pressed both hands against his shinbone in order to push him away. "Do go away," I said.

He had his hands in his pockets and looked up the empty street, then at the Seminarkirche, then up at the sky. At last, at the sound of a carriage in one of the near-by streets, he remembered me: "Why don't you

say something, my friend ? Do you feel sick ? Why
don't you get up ? Shall I look for a cab ? If you like,
I'll get you some wine from the tavern. In any case,
you mustn't lie here in the cold. Besides we wanted to
go up the Laurenziberg."

" Of course," said I, and got up on my own, but with
great pain. I began to sway, and had to look severely
at the statue of Karl IV to be sure of my position.
However, even this would not have helped me had I not
remembered that I was loved by a girl with a black
velvet ribbon round her neck, if not passionately, at
least faithfully. And it really was kind of the moon to
shine on me, too, and out of modesty I was about to
place myself under the arch of the tower bridge when it
occurred to me that the moon, of course, shone on
everything. So I happily spread out my arms in order
fully to enjoy the moon. And by making swimming
movements with my weary arms it was easy for me to
advance without pain or difficulty. To think that I
had never tried this before ! My head lay in the cool
air and it was my right knee that flew best ; I praised
it by patting it. And I remembered that once upon a
time I didn't altogether like an acquaintance, who was
probably still walking below me, and the only thing that
pleased me about the whole business was that my
memory was good enough to remember even a thing like
that. But I couldn't afford to do much thinking, for I
had to go on swimming to prevent myself from sinking
too low. However, to avoid being told later that anyone could swim on the pavement and that it wasn't worth
mentioning, I raised myself above the railing by increasing
my speed and swam in circles round the statue of every
saint I encountered. At the fifth—I was holding myself

just above the footpath by imperceptible flappings—my acquaintance gripped my hand. There I stood once more on the pavement and felt a pain in my knee.

" I've always admired," said my acquaintance, clutching me with one hand and pointing with the other at the statue of St. Ludmila, " I've always admired the hands of this angel here to the left. Just see how delicate they are ! Real angel's hands ! Have you ever seen anything like them ? You haven't, but I have, for this evening I kissed hands——"

But for me there was now a third possibility of perishing. I didn't have to let myself be stabbed, I didn't have to run away, I could simply throw myself into the air. Let him go up his Laurenziberg, I won't interfere with him, not even by running away will I interfere with him.

And now I shouted : " Out with your stories ! I no longer want to hear scraps. Tell me everything, from beginning to end. I won't listen to less, I warn you. But I'm burning to hear the whole thing." When he looked at me I stopped shouting so loud. " And you can count on my discretion ! Tell me everything that's on your mind. You've never had so discreet a listener as I."

And rather low, close to his ear, I said : " And you don't need to be afraid of me, that's quite unnecessary."

I heard him laugh.

" Yes, yes," I said. " I believe that. I don't doubt it," and so saying I pinched him in the calves—where they were exposed. But he didn't feel it. Whereupon I said to myself : " Why walk with this man ? You don't love him, nor do you hate him, because all he cares about is a girl and it's not even certain that she wears a white dress. So to you this man is indifferent—I repeat : indifferent. But he is also harmless, as has been proved. So walk on with him up the Laurenziberg, for you are already on your way, it's a beautiful night, but let him do the talking and enjoy yourself after your fashion, for this is the very best way (say it in a whisper) to protect yourself."

II

DIVERSIONS *or* PROOF THAT IT'S IMPOSSIBLE TO LIVE

I. A RIDE

AND now—with a flourish, as though it were not the first time—I leapt on to the shoulders of my acquaintance, and by digging my fists into his back I urged him into a trot. But since he stumped forward rather reluctantly and sometimes even stopped, I kicked him in the belly several times with my boots, to make him more lively. It worked and we came fast enough into the interior of a vast but as yet unfinished landscape.

The road on which I was riding was stony and rose considerably, but just this I liked and I let it become still stonier and steeper. As soon as my acquaintance stumbled I pulled him up by the collar and the moment he sighed I boxed his head. In doing so I felt how healthy this ride in the good air was for me, and in order to make him wilder I let a strong wind blow against us in long gusts.

Now I began to exaggerate my jumping movements on my acquaintance's broad shoulders, and gripping his neck tight with both hands I bent my head far back and contemplated the many and various clouds which, weaker than I, sailed clumsily with the wind. I laughed and trembled with courage. My coat spread out and gave me strength. I pressed my hands hard together and in doing so happened to make my acquaintance choke. Only when the sky became gradually hidden by the branches of the trees, which I let grow along the road, did I come to myself.

" I don't know," I cried without a sound, " I really don't know. If nobody comes, then nobody comes. I have done nobody any harm, nobody has done me any harm, but nobody will help me. A pack of nobodies. But it isn't quite like that. It's just that nobody helps me, otherwise a pack of nobodies would be nice, I would rather like (what do you think ?) to go on an excursion with a pack of nobodies. Into the mountains, of course, where else ? Just look at these nobodies pushing each other, all these arms stretched across or hooked into one another, these feet separated by tiny steps ! Everyone in frock coats, needless to say. We walk along so happily, a fine wind is whistling through the gaps made by us and our limbs. In the mountains our throats become free. It's a wonder we don't break into song."

Then my acquaintance collapsed, and when I examined him I discovered that he was badly wounded in the knee. Since he could no longer be of any use to me, I left him there on the stones without much regret and whistled down a few vultures which, obediently and with serious beaks settled down on him in order to guard him.

2. A WALK

I WALKED on, unperturbed. But since, as a pedestrian, I dreaded the effort of climbing the mountainous road, I let it become gradually flatter, let it slope down into a valley in the distance. The stones vanished at my will and the wind disappeared.

I walked at a brisk pace and since I was on my way down I raised my head, stiffened my body, and crossed my arms behind my head. Because I love pinewoods I went through woods of this kind, and since I like gazing silently up at the stars, the stars appeared slowly in the sky, as is their wont. I saw only a few fleecy clouds which a wind, blowing just at their height, pulled through the air, to the astonishment of the pedestrian.

Opposite and at some distance from my road, probably separated from it by a river as well, I caused to rise an enormously high mountain whose plateau, overgrown with brushwood, bordered on the sky. I could see quite clearly the little ramifications of the highest branches and their movements. This sight, ordinary as it may be, made me so happy that I, as a small bird on a twig of those distant scrubby bushes, forgot to let the moon come up. It lay already behind the mountain, no doubt angry at the delay.

But now the cool light which precedes the rising of the moon spread over the mountain and suddenly the moon itself appeared from beyond one of the restless bushes. I on the other hand had meanwhile been gazing in another direction, and when I now looked ahead of me and suddenly saw it glowing in its almost full roundness, I stood still with troubled eyes, for my precipitous road seemed to lead straight into this terrifying moon.

After a while, however, I grew accustomed to it and watched with composure the difficulty it had in rising, until finally, having approached one another a considerable part of the way, I felt overcome by an intense drowsiness caused, I assumed, by the fatigue of the walk to which I was unaccustomed. I wandered on for a while with closed eyes, keeping myself awake only by a loud and regular clapping of my hands.

But then, as the road threatened to slip away from under my feet and everything, as weary as I myself, began to vanish, I summoned my remaining strength and hastened to scale the slope to the right of the road in order to reach in time the high tangled pinewood where I planned to spend the night that probably lay ahead of us.

The haste was necessary. The stars were already fading and I noticed the moon sink feebly into the sky as though into troubled waters. The mountain already belonged to the darkness, the road crumbled away at the point where I had turned towards the slope, and from the interior of the forest I heard the approaching crashes of collapsing trees. Now I could have thrown myself down on the moss to sleep, but since I feared to sleep on the ground I crept—the trunk sliding quickly down the rings formed by my arms and legs—up a tree which was already reeling without wind. I lay down on a branch and, leaning my head against the trunk, went hastily to sleep while a squirrel of my whim sat stiff-tailed at the trembling end of the branch, and rocked itself.

My sleep was deep and dreamless. Neither the

waning moon nor the rising sun awoke me. And even
when I was about to wake up, I calmed myself by saying :
" You made a great effort yesterday, so spare your sleep,"
and went to sleep again.

Although I did not dream, my sleep was not free from
a continuous slight disturbance. All night long I heard
someone talking beside me. The words themselves I
could hardly hear—except isolated ones like " bench . . .
by the river," " cloudlike mountains," " trains . . .
amidst shining smoke " ; what I did hear was the special
kind of emphasis placed on them ; and I remember that
even in my sleep I rubbed my hands with pleasure at
not being obliged to recognise single words, since I was
asleep.

" Your life was monotonous," I said aloud in order to
convince myself, " it really was necessary for you to be
taken somewhere else. You ought to be content, it's
gay here. The sun's shining."

Whereupon the sun shone and the rain clouds grew
white and light and small in the blue sky. They sparkled
and billowed out. I saw a river in the valley.

" Yes, your life was monotonous, you deserve this
diversion," I continued as though compelled, " but was
it not also perilous ? " At that moment I heard someone
sigh terribly near.

I tried to climb down quickly, but since the branch
trembled as much as my hand I fell rigid from the top.
I did not fall heavily, not did I feel any pain, but I felt
so weak and unhappy that I buried my face in the ground :
I could not bear the strain of seeing around me the things
of the earth. I felt convinced that every movement
and every thought was forced, and that one had to be on
one's guard against them. Yet nothing seemed more

natural than to lie here on the grass, my arms beside my body, my face hidden. And I tried to persuade myself that I ought to be pleased to be already in this natural position, for otherwise many painful contortions, such as steps or words, would be required to arrive at it.

The river was wide and its noisy little waves reflected the light. On the other bank lay meadows which farther on merged into bushes behind which, at a great distance, one could see bright avenues of fruit trees leading to green hills.

Pleased by this sight, I lay down and, stopping my ears against the dread sound of sobs, I thought : Here I could be content. For here it is secluded and beautiful. It won't take much courage to live here. One will have to struggle here as anywhere else, but at least one won't have to do it with graceful movements. That won't be necessary. For there are only mountains and a wide river and I have sense enough to regard them as inanimate. Yes, when I totter alone up the steep path through the meadows in the evening I will be no more forsaken than the mountains, except that I will feel it. But I think that this, too, will pass.

Thus I toyed with my future life and tried stubbornly to forget. And all the time I blinked at that sky which was of an unusually promising colour. It was a long time since I'd seen it like this : I was moved and re-minded of certain days when I thought I had seen it in the same way. I took my hands from ears, spread out my arms, and let them fall in the grass.

I heard someone sob softly from afar. A wind sprang up and a great mass of leaves, which I had not seen before, rose rustling into the air. Unripe fruit thudded sense-lessly from the trees on to the ground. Ugly clouds rose from behind the mountain. The waves on the river creaked and receded from the wind.

I got up quickly. My heart hurt, for now it seemed impossible to escape from my suffering. I was already about to turn and leave this region and go back to my former way of life when the following idea occurred to me : " How strange it is that even in our time distinguished people are transported across a river in this complicated way. There's no other explanation than that it is in an old custom." I shook my head, for I was surprised.

3. THE FAT MAN

(a) An Address to the Landscape

FROM the thicket on the opposite bank four naked men strode vehemently forth, carrying on their shoulders a wooden litter. On this litter sat, oriental fashion, a monstrously fat man. Although carried through the thicket on an untrodden path, he did not push the thorny branches apart but simply let his motionless body thrust through them. His folds of fat were so carefully spread out that although they covered the whole litter and even hung down its side like the hem of a yellowish carpet, they did not hamper him. His hairless skull was small and gleamed yellow. His face bore the artless expression of a man who meditates and makes no effort to conceal it. From time to time he closed his eyes : on opening them again his chin became distorted.

" The landscape disturbs my thought," he said in a low voice. " It makes my reflections sway like suspen-

sion bridges in a furious current. It is beauti
for this reason wants to be looked at."

I close my eyes and say: You green mountain by t
with your rocks rolling against the water, you are beautiful.

But it is not satisfied; it wants me to open my eyes to it.

Then I might say to it with my eyes closed: " Mountain, I do not love you, for you remind me of the clouds,
of the sunset, of the rising sky, and these are things that
almost make me cry because one can never reach them
while being carried on a small litter. But when showing
me this, sly mountain, you block the distant view which
gladdens me, for it reveals the attainable at a glance.
That's why I do not love you, mountain by the water—
no, I do not love you."

But the mountain would be as indifferent to this speech
as to my former one so long as I did not talk with my
eyes open. This is the only way to please it.

And must we not keep it well disposed towards us in
order to keep it up at all—this mountain which has such
a capricious fondness for the pulp of our brains? It
might cast on me its jagged shadow, it might silently
thrust terrible bare walls in front of me and my bearers
would stumble over the little pebbles on the road.

But it is not only the mountain that is so vain, so
obtrusive and vindictive—everything else is, too. So I
must go on repeating with wide-open eyes—oh, how
they hurt!:

" Yes, mountain, you are beautiful and the forests on
your western slope delight me.—With you, flower, I am
also pleased, and your pink gladdens my soul.—You,
grass of the meadows, are already high and strong and
refreshing.—And you, exotic bushes, you prick so unexpectedly that our thoughts start leaping.—But with

you, river, I am so delighted that I will let myself be carried through your supple water."

After he had shouted this paean of praise ten times, accompanied by some humble shifting of his body, he let his head droop and said with closed eyes :

" But now—I implore you—mountain, flowers, grass, bush, and river, give me some room so that I may breathe.'

At that moment the surrounding mountains began to shift in hasty obedience, then withdrew behind a curtain of fog. Although the avenues stood firm for a while and guarded the width of the road, they soon merged into one another. In the sky in front of the sun lay a humid cloud with a delicately transparent edge in whose shade the country sank deeper and deeper while every-thing else lost its lovely outline.

The sound of the bearers' steps reached my side of the river and yet I could not distinguish any details in the dark square of their faces. I only saw them bending their heads sideways and arching their backs, for their burden was excessive. I was worried about them, for I realised that they were tired. So it was in suspense that I watched them step into the rushes, then walk through the wet sand, their strides still regular, until they finally sank into the muddy swamp where the two rear bearers bent even lower so as to keep the litter in its horizontal position. I pressed my hands together. By now they had to raise their feet high at every step until their bodies glistened with sweat in the cool air of this un-settled afternoon.

The fat man sat quiet, hands on his thighs ; the long pointed tips of the reeds grazed him as they flipped up in the wake of the bearers in front.

The bearers' movements grew more irregular the nearer

they came to the water. At times the litter swayed as though it were already on the waves. Small puddles in the rushes had to be jumped over or walked around, for they might possibly be deep.

At one moment wild ducks rose shrieking, mounting steeply into the rain cloud. It was then that I caught a glimpse of the fat man's face ; it looked alarmed. I got up and in hectic leaps I zigzagged over the stony slope separating me from the water. I paid no heed to the danger, was concerned only with helping the fat man should his servants no longer be able to carry him. I ran so recklessly that I couldn't stop, and was forced to dash into the splashing water, coming to a halt only when the water reached my knees.

Meanwhile the servants, with considerable distortions of their bodies, had carried the litter into the river, and holding themselves above the unruly water with one hand, they propped up the litter with four hairy arms, their muscles standing out in relief.

The water lapped against their chins, then rose to their mouths ; the bearers bent their heads back and the litter-handles fell on their shoulders. The water was already playing round the bridges of their noses, and yet they did not give up, although they had hardly reached the middle of the river. Then a low wave swept over the heads of those in front and the four men drowned in silence, their desperate hands pulling the litter down with them. Water gushed after them.

And now the evening sun's slanting rays broke forth from behind the rims of the great cloud and illuminated the hills and mountains as far as the eye could see, while the river and the region beneath the cloud lay in an uncertain light.

The fat man turned slowly in the direction of the flowing water and was carried down the river like a yellow wooden idol which had become useless and so had been cast into the river. He sailed along on the reflection of the rain cloud. Elongated clouds pulled and small hunched ones pushed him, creating considerable commotion the effect of which could even be noticed by the lapping of water against my knees and the stones on the bank.

I crept quickly up the slope so as to be able to accompany the fat man on his way, for I truly loved him. And perhaps I could learn something about the dangers of this apparently safe country. So I walked along a strip of sand to the narrowness of which one had to grow accustomed, hands in my pockets and my face turned at right angles to the river so that my chin rested almost on my shoulder.

Swallows perched on the stones by the shore.

The fat man said : " Dear sir on the bank, don't try to rescue me. This is the water's and the wind's revenge ; now I am lost. Yes, revenge it is, for how often have we attacked them, I and my friend the supplicant, amidst the singing of our swords, the flash of cymbals, the great splendour of trumpets, and the leaping blaze of drums ! "

A tiny mosquito with stretched wings flew straight through his belly without losing its speed.

The fat man continued :

(b) Beginning of a Conversation with the Supplicant

THERE was a time when I went to church day after day, for a girl I was in love with used to kneel there in prayer for half an hour every evening, which enabled me to watch her at my leisure.

Once when the girl failed to appear and in dismay I was watching the other people praying, my eye was caught by a young man who had flung his long emaciated figure on the ground. From time to time he clutched his skull with all his strength and, moaning loudly, beat it in the palms of his hands on the stone floor.

In the church there were only a few old women who kept turning their shawled heads sideways to glance at the praying man. This attention seemed to please him, for before each of his pious outbursts he let his eyes rove about to see how many people were watching him. Finding this unseemly, I decided to accost him on his way out of the church and ask him outright why he prayed in this manner. For since my arrival in this town clarity had become more important to me than anything else, even though at this moment I felt only annoyance at my girl's failure to appear.

Yet an hour passed before he stood up, brushed his trousers for such a long time that I felt like shouting : " Enough, enough ! We can all see that you have trousers on," crossed himself carefully, and with the lumbering gait of a sailor walked to the font of holy water.

I placed myself between the font and the door, determined not to let him pass without an explanation. I screwed up my mouth, this being the best preparation for resolute speech, and supported myself by standing on my right leg while resting the left one on its toes, for this position as I have often experienced gives me a sense of stability.

Now it is possible that this young man had already caught sight of me while sprinkling his face with holy water ; perhaps my stare had alarmed him even earlier, for he now quite unexpectedly rushed to the door and out. I involuntarily jumped to stop him. The glass door slammed. And when I passed through it a moment later I could not find him, for the narrow streets were numerous and the traffic considerable.

During the following days he failed to appear, but the girl came again and prayed in a corner of a side chapel. She wore a black dress with a transparent lace yoke—the crescent of her chemise could be seen through it—from the lower edge of which the silk hung down in a finely cut frill. And now that the girl had returned I was glad to forget about the young man, ignoring him even when he continued to appear regularly and to pray in his usual fashion.

Yet he always passed me by in sudden haste, his face averted. While praying, on the other hand, he kept glancing at me. It almost looked as though he were angry with me for not having accosted him earlier and was thinking that by my first attempt to talk to him I had actually taken upon me the duty to do so. One day as I was following the girl out as usual after a service, I ran into him in the semi-darkness and thought I saw him smile.

The duty to talk to him, needless to say, did not exist, nor had I much desire to do so any more. And even when I hurried up to the church one evening while the clock was striking seven and found, instead of the girl who of course had left long ago, only the young man exerting himself in front of the altar railings, I still hesitated.

At last I tiptoed to the door, slipped a coin to the blind beggar sitting there, and squeezed in beside him behind the open wing. And there for about half an hour

I looked forward to the surprise I was planning to spring upon the supplicant. But this feeling did not last. Before long I was morosely watching spiders creeping over my clothes and finding it tiresome to have to bend forward every time someone came breathing loud out of the darkness of the church.

But finally he came. The ringing of the great bells which had started a little while ago did not agree with him, I realised. Each time before taking a step he had to touch the ground lightly with his foot.

I straightened myself, took a long stride forward, and grabbed him. " Good evening," said I, and with my hand on his coat collar I pushed him down the steps on to the lighted square.

When we had reached ground level he turned towards me while I was still holding on to him from behind, so that we stood breast to breast.

" If only you'd let go of me ! " he said. " I don't know what you suspect me of, but I'm innocent." Then he repeated once more : " Of course I don't know what you suspect me of."

" There is no question here of suspicion or innocence. I ask you not to mention it again. We are strangers ; our acquaintance is no older than the church steps are high. What would happen if we were immediately to start discussing our innocence ? "

" Precisely what I think," he said. " As a matter of fact, you said ' our innocence.' Do you mean to suggest that if I had proved my innocence you would have to prove yours too ? Is that what you mean ? "

" That or something else," I said. " I accosted you only because I wanted to ask you something, remember that ! "

" I'd like to go home," he said, and made an effort to turn.

" I quite believe it. Would I have accosted you otherwise ? Don't get the idea that I accosted you on account of your beautiful eyes."

" Aren't you being a little too sincere ? "

" Must I repeat that there's no question of such things ? What has it to do with sincerity or insincerity ? I ask, you answer, and then good-bye. So far as I'm concerned you can even go home, and as fast as you like."

" Would it not be better to meet some other time ? At a more suitable hour ? Say in a coffee-house ? Besides, your fiancée left only a few minutes ago, you can easily catch her up, she has waited so long for you."

" No ! " I shouted into the noise of the passing tram. " You won't escape me. I like you more and more. You're a lucky catch. I congratulate myself."

To which he said : " Oh God, you have a sound heart, as they say, but a head of wood. You call me a lucky catch, how lucky you must be ! For my bad luck is precariously balanced and when touched it falls on to the questioner. And so : Good night."

" Fine," said I, surprised him and seized his right hand. " If you don't answer of your own accord, I'll force you. I'll follow you wherever you go, right or left, even up the stairs to your room, and in your room I'll sit down, wherever there's place. Go on then, keep staring at me, I can stand it. But how "—I stepped up close and because he was a head taller I spoke into his throat—" how are you going to summon up the courage to stop me ? "

Whereupon, stepping back, he kissed my hands in turn, and wetted them with his tears. " One cannot deny you anything. Just as you knew I want to go home, I knew even earlier that I cannot deny you anything. All I ask is that we go over there into the side street." I nodded and we went over. When a carriage separated us and I was left behind, he beckoned to me with both hands, to make me hurry.

But once there, not satisfied with the darkness of the street where the lamps were widely separated from one another and almost as high as the first floor, he led me into the low hallway of an old house and under a small lamp which hung dripping in front of the wooden stairs.

Spreading his handkerchief over the hollow in a worn step, he invited me to be seated : " It's easier for you to ask questions sitting down. I'll remain standing, it's easier for me to answer. But don't torment me ! "

I sat down because he took it all so seriously, but nevertheless felt I had to say : " You've led me to this hole as though we are conspirators, whereas I am bound to you simply by curiosity, you to me by fear. Actually, all I want to ask is why you pray like that in church. The way you carry on there ! Like an utter fool ! How ridiculous it all is, how unpleasant for the onlookers, how intolerable for the devout ! "

He had pressed his body against the wall, only his head moved slowly in space. " You're wrong ! The devout consider my behaviour natural, the others consider it devout."

" My annoyance proves you're mistaken."

" Your annoyance—assuming it's real—only proves that you belong neither to the devout nor to the others."

" You're right. I was exaggerating when I said your behaviour annoyed me ; no, it aroused my curiosity as

I stated correctly at first. But you, to which group do you belong ? "

" Oh, I just get fun out of people watching me, out of occasionally casting a shadow on the altar, so to speak."

" Fun ? " I asked, making a face.

" No, if you want to know. Don't be angry with me for expressing it wrongly. It's not fun, for me it's a need ; a need to let myself be nailed down for a brief hour by those eyes, while the whole town around me——"

" The things you say ! " I cried far too loud for the insignificant remark and the low hallway, but I was afraid of falling silent or of lowering my voice. " Really, the things you say ! Now I realise, by God, that I guessed from the very beginning the state you are in. Isn't it something like a fever, a seasickness on land, a kind of leprosy ? Don't you feel it's this very feverish-ness which is preventing you from being properly satis-fied with the real names of things, and that now, in your frantic haste, you're just pelting them with any old names ? You can't do it fast enough. But hardly have you run away from them when you've forgotten the names you gave them. The poplar in the fields, which you've called the ' Tower of Babel ' because you didn't want to know it was a poplar, sways again without a name, so you have to call it ' Noah in his cups.' "

He interrupted me : " I'm glad I haven't understood a word you've been saying."

Irritated, I said quickly : " Your being glad about it proves that you have understood it."

" Didn't I say so before ? One cannot deny you anything."

I put my hands on a step above me, leaned back, and

in this all but unassailable position, the wrestler's last resort, I asked : " Excuse me, but to throw back at me an explanation which I gave you is insincere."

At this he grew daring. To give his body unity he clasped his hands together and said with some reluctance : " You ruled out quarrels about insincerity from the very beginning. And truly, I'm no longer concerned with anything but to give you a proper explanation for my way of praying. Do you know why I pray like that ? "

He was putting me to the test. No, I didn't know, nor did I want to know. I hadn't even wanted to come here, I said to myself, but this creature had practically forced me to listen to him. So all I had to do was to shake my head and everything would be all right, but at the moment this was just what I couldn't do. The creature opposite me smiled. Then he crouched down on his knees and said with a sleepy expression : " Now I can tell you at last why I let you accost me. Out of curiosity, from hope. Your stare has been comforting me for a long time. And I hope to learn from you how things really are, why it is that around me things sink away like fallen snow, whereas for other people even a little liqueur glass stands on the table steady as a statue."

As I remained silent and only an involuntary twitching passed over my face, he asked : " So you don't believe this happens to other people ? You really don't ? Just listen, then. When as a child I opened my eyes after a brief afternoon nap, still not quite sure I was alive, I heard my mother up on the balcony asking in a natural tone of voice : ' What are you doing, my dear ? Goodness, isn't it hot ? ' From the garden a woman answered : ' Me, I'm having my tea on the lawn.' They spoke casually and not very distinctly, as though this woman had expected the question, my mother the answer."

Feeling that this required an answer, I put my hand in the hip pocket of my trousers as though I were looking for something. Actually I wasn't looking for anything, I just wished to change my appearance in order to show interest in the conversation. Finally I said I thought this a most remarkable incident and that I couldn't make head or tail of it. I also added that I didn't believe it was true and that it must have been invented for a special reason whose purpose wasn't clear to me just now. Then I closed my eyes so as to shut out the bad light.

" Well, isn't that encouraging ! For once you agree with me, and you accosted me to tell me that out of sheer unselfishness. I lose one hope and acquire another.

" Why, after all, should I feel ashamed of not walking upright and taking normal steps, of not tapping the pavement with my stick, and not touching the clothes of the people who pass noisily by ? Am I not rather entitled to complain bitterly at having to skip along the houses like a shadow without a clear outline, sometimes disappearing in the panes of the shop windows ?

" Oh, what dreadful days I have to live through ! Why is everything so badly built that high houses collapse every now and again for no apparent reason ? On these occasions I clamber over the rubble, asking everyone I meet : ' How could this have happened ? In our town—a new house—how many does that make today ?—Just think of it ! ' And no one can give me an answer.

" Frequently people fall in the street and lie there dead. Whereupon all the shop people open their doors laden with wares, hurry busily out, cart the dead into a house, come out again all smiles, then the chatter begins : ' Good morning—it's a dull day—I'm selling any amount of kerchiefs—ah yes, the war.' I rush into the house, and after raising my hand several times timidly with my finger crooked, I finally knock on the janitor's little window : ' Good morning,' I say, ' I understand a dead man was carried in here just now. Would you be kind enough to let me see him ? ' And when he shakes his head as though unable to make up his mind, I add : ' Take care, I'm a member of the secret police and insist on seeing the dead man at once ! ' Now he is no longer undecided. ' Out with you ! ' he shouts. ' This riffraff is getting in the habit of snooping about here every day. There's no dead man here. Perhaps next door.' I raise my hat and go.

" But then, on having to cross a large square, I forget everything. If people must build such huge squares from sheer wantonness, why don't they build a balustrade across them as well ? Today there's a southwest wind blowing. The spire of the Town Hall is moving in little circles. All the window-panes are rattling, and the lamp-posts are bending like bamboos. The Virgin Mary's cloak is coiling round her pillar and the wind is tugging at it. Does no one notice this ? The ladies and gentlemen who should be walking on the pavement are floating. When the wind falls they stand still, say a few words, and bow to one another, but when the wind rises again they are helpless, and all their feet leave the ground at the same time. Although obliged to hold on to their hats, their eyes twinkle gaily enough and no one has the slightest fault to find with the weather. I'm the only one who's afraid."

To which I was able to say : " That story you told me earlier about your mother and the woman in the garden I really don't find so remarkable. Not only have I heard and experienced many stories of this kind, I have even taken part in some. The whole thing is perfectly natural. Do you really mean to suggest that had I been on that balcony in the summer, I could not have asked the same question and given the same answer from the garden ? Quite an ordinary occurrence ! "

After I had said this, he seemed relieved at last. He told me I was well dressed and that he very much liked my tie. And what a fine complexion I had. And that confessions became most comprehensible when they were retracted.

(c) The Supplicant's Story

THEN he sat down beside me, for I had grown timid and, bending my head to one side, had made room for him. Nevertheless, it didn't escape my notice that he too was sitting there rather embarrassed, trying to keep some distance from me and speaking with difficulty :

" Oh, what dreadful days I have to live through ! Last night I was at a party. I was just bowing to a young lady in the gaslight and saying : ' I'm so glad winter's approaching '—I was just bowing with these words when to my annoyance I noticed that my right thigh had slipped out of joint. The knee-cap had also become a little loose.

" So I sat down, and as I always try to keep control over my sentences, I said : ' for winter's much less of an effort ; it's easier to comport oneself, one doesn't have to take so much trouble with one's words. Don't you agree, Fräulein ? I do hope I'm right about this.' My right leg was now giving me a lot of trouble. At first it seemed to have fallen apart completely, and only gradually did I manage to get it more or less back into shape by manipulation and careful rearrangement.

" Then I heard the girl who, out of sympathy, had also sat down, say in a low voice : ' No, you don't impress me at all because——'

" ' Just a moment,' I said, pleased and full of expectation, ' you mustn't waste so much as five minutes talking to me, dear Fräulein. Please eat something while you're talking, I implore you.'

" And stretching out my arm I took a large bunch of grapes hanging heavily from a bowl held up by a bronze winged cupid, dangled it for a moment in the air, and then laid it on a small blue plate which I handed to the girl, not without a certain elegance, I trust.

" ' You don't impress me at all,' she said, ' everything you say is boring and incomprehensible, but that alone doesn't make it true. What I really think, sir—why do you always call me dear Fräulein ?—is that you can't be bothered with the truth simply because it's too tiring.'

" God, how good that made me feel ! ' Yes, Fräulein, Fräulein ! ' I almost shouted, ' how right you are ! Dear Fräulein, if you only knew what a wild joy it is to find oneself so well understood—and without having made any effort ! '

" ' There's no doubt, sir, that for you the truth is too tiring. Just look at yourself ! The entire length of you is cut out of tissue paper, yellow tissue paper, like a silhouette, and when you walk one ought to hear you rustle. So one shouldn't get annoyed at your attitude or opinion, for you can't help bending to whatever draught happens to be in the room.'

" ' I don't understand that. True, several people are standing about here in this room. They lay their arms on the backs of chairs or they lean against the piano or they raise a glass tentatively to their mouths or they walk timidly into the next room, and having knocked their right shoulders against a cupboard in the dark, they stand breathing by the open window and think : There's Venus, the evening star. Yet here I am, among them. If there is a connection, I don't understand it. But I don't even know if there is a connection.—And you see, dear Fräulein, of all these people who behave so irresolutely, so absurdly as a result of their confusion, I alone seem worthy of hearing the truth about myself. And to make this truth more palatable you put it in a mocking way so that something concrete remains, like the outer walls of a house whose interior has been gutted. The eye is hardly obstructed ; by day the clouds and sky can be seen through the great window holes, and by night the stars. But the clouds are often hewn out of gray stones, and the stars form unnatural constellations—. How would it be if in return I were to tell you that one day everyone wanting to live will look like me—cut out of tissue paper, like silhouettes, as you pointed out— and when they walk they will be heard to rustle ? Not that they will be any different from what they are now, but that is what they will look like. Even you, dear Fräulein——'

" Then I noticed that the girl was no longer sitting beside me. She must have left soon after her last words, for now she was standing far away from me by a window, surrounded by three young men who were talking and laughing out of high white collars.

" So I happily drank a glass of wine and walked over to the pianist who, all alone and nodding to himself, happened to be playing something sad. I bent carefully down to his ear so as not to frighten him and whispered into the melody : ' Be so kind, sir, as to let me play now, for I'm just beginning to feel happy.'

" Since he paid no attention to me, I stood there for a while embarrassed, but then, overcoming my timidity, I went from one guest to another, saying casually : ' Today I'm going to play the piano. Yes.'

" Everyone seemed to know I couldn't play, but they smiled in a friendly way, pleased by the welcome interruption of their conversation. They paid proper attention to me only when I said to the pianist in a very loud voice : ' Do me the favour, sir, of letting me play now. After all, I'm just beginning to feel happy. A triumph is at stake.'

" Although the pianist stopped, he neither left his brown bench nor appeared to understand me. He sighed and covered his face with his long fingers.

" I felt a trifle sorry for him and was about to encourage him to continue playing when the hostess approached with a group of people.

" ' That's a funny coincidence,' they said and laughed aloud as though I were about to do something unnatural.

" The girl also joined them, looked at me contemptuously, and said : ' Please, madame, do let him play. Perhaps he wants to make some contribution to the entertainment. He ought to be encouraged. Please let him.'

" Everyone laughed, obviously thinking, as I did, that

it was meant ironically. Only the pianist was silent. Holding his head low, he stroked the wood of the bench with the forefinger of his left hand, as though he were making designs in sand. I began to tremble, and to hide it thrust my hands into my trouser pockets. Nor could I speak clearly any longer, for my whole face wanted to cry. Thus I had to choose the words in such a way that the thought of my wanting to cry would appear ludicrous to the listeners.

" ' Madame,' I said, ' I must play now because——' As I had forgotten the reason I abruptly sat down at the piano. And then I remembered again. The pianist stood up and stepped tactfully over the bench, for I was blocking his way. ' Please turn out the light. I can only play in the dark.' I straightened myself.

" At that moment two gentlemen seized the bench and, whistling a song and rocking me to and fro, carried me far away from the piano to the dining table.

" Everyone watched with approval and the girl said : ' You see, madame, he played quite well. I knew he would. And you were so worried.'

" I understood and thanked her with a bow, which I carried out well.

" They poured me some lemonade and a girl with red lips held my glass while I drank. The hostess offered me a meringue on a silver salver and a girl in a pure white dress put the meringue in my mouth. Another girl, voluptuous and with a mass of fair hair, held a bunch of grapes over me, and all I had to do was pluck them off with my lips while she gazed into my receding eyes.

" Since everyone was treating me so well I was a little surprised that they were so unanimous in holding me back when I tried to return to the piano.

" ' That's enough now,' said the host, whom I had not noticed before. He went out and promptly returned with an enormous top hat and a copper-brown overcoat with a flowery design. ' Here are your things.'

" They weren't my things, of course, but I didn't want to put him to the trouble of looking again. The host helped me into the overcoat which fitted beautifully, clinging lightly to my thin body. Bending over slowly, a lady with a kind face buttoned the coat all the way down.

" ' Good-bye,' said the hostess, ' and come back soon. You know you're always welcome.' Whereupon everyone bowed as though they thought it necessary. I tried to do likewise, but my coat was too tight. So I took my hat and, no doubt awkwardly, walked out of the room.

" But as I passed through the front door with short steps I was assaulted from the sky by moon and stars and a great vaulted expanse, and from the Ringplatz by the Town Hall, the Virgin's pillar, the church.

" I walked calmly from the shadow into the moonlight, unbuttoned my overcoat, and warmed myself ; then I put a stop to the humming of the night by raising my hands, and began to reflect as follows :

" ' What is it that makes you all behave as though you were real ? Are you trying to make me believe I'm unreal, standing here absurdly on the green pavement ? You, sky, surely it's a long time since you've been real, and as for you, Ringplatz, you never have been real.

" ' It's true, you're all still superior to me, but only when I leave you alone.

" ' Thank God, moon, you are no longer moon, but perhaps it's negligent of me to go on calling you so-called moon, moon. Why do your spirits fall when I call you

" forgotten paper lantern of a strange colour " ?   And why do you almost withdraw when I call you " the Virgin's pillar " ?   As for you, pillar of the Virgin Mary, I hardly recognise your threatening attitude when I call you " moon shedding yellow light ".

" ' It really seems to me that thinking about you doesn't do you any good ; you lose in courage and health.

" ' God, how much more profitable it would be if the Thinker could learn from the Drunk !

" ' Why has everything become so quiet ? I think the wind has dropped.   And the small houses which often used to roll across the square as though on little wheels are rooted to the spot—calm—calm—one can't even see the thin black line that used to separate them from the ground.'

" And I started to run.   I ran unimpeded three times round the great square, and as I didn't meet a drunk I ran on towards the Karlsgasse without slowing down and without any effort.   My shadow, often smaller than myself, ran beside me along the wall as though in a gorge between the wall and the street level.

" As I passed the fire station I heard a noise coming from the Kleiner Ring, and as I turned into it I saw a drunk standing by the iron railing of the fountain, his arms held out sideways and his feet in wooden shoes stamping the ground.

" Stopping to get my breath, I went up to him, raised my top hat, and introduced myself :

" ' Good evening, gentle nobleman, I am twenty-three years of age, but as yet I have no name.   But you, no doubt, hail from the great city of Paris—bearing extra-ordinary, well-nigh singable names.   You are surrounded by the quite unnatural odour of the dissolute Court of

France. No doubt your tinted eyes have beheld those great ladies standing on the high shining terrace ironically twisting their narrow waists while the ends of their decorated trains, spread over the steps, are still lying on the sand in the garden.—And surely, men servants in daringly cut grey tailcoats and white knee breeches climb tall poles, their legs hugging them but their torsos frequently bent back and to the side, for they have to raise enormous grey linen sheets off the ground with thick ropes and spread them in the air, because the great lady has expressed the wish for a misty morning.'

" When he belched I felt almost frightened. ' Is it really true, sir,' I said, ' that you hail from our Paris, from that tempestuous Paris—ah, from that luxuriant hailstorm ? '

" When he belched again, I said with embarrassment : ' I know, a great honour is being bestowed upon me.'

" And with nimble fingers I buttoned up my overcoat ; then with ardour and yet timidly I said : ' I know you do not consider me worthy of an answer, but if I did not ask you today my life would be spent in weeping. I ask you, much-bespangled sir, is it true what I have been told ? Are there people in Paris who consist of only sumptuous dresses, and are there houses that are only portals, and is it true that on summer days the sky over the city is a fleeting blue embellished only by little white clouds glued on to it, all in the shape of hearts ? And have they a highly popular panopticon there containing nothing but trees to which small plaques are fastened bearing the names of the most famous heroes, criminals, and lovers ?

" ' And then this other piece of news ! This clearly fabricated news ! These Paris streets, for instance, they

suddenly branch off, don't they ?   They're turbulent,
aren't they ?   Things are not always as they should be,
how could they be, after all ?   Sometimes there's an
accident, people gather together from the side streets
with that urban stride that hardly touches the pavement ;
they are all filled with curiosity, but also with fear of
disappointment ;   they breathe fast and stretch out their
little heads.   But when they touch one another they bow
low and apologise :   " I'm awfully sorry—I didn't mean
it—there's such a crowd :   forgive me, I beg you—it
was most clumsy of me, I admit.   My name is—my
name's Jerome Faroche, I'm a grocer in the rue de
Cabotin —allow me to invite you to lunch tomorrow—
my wife would also be delighted."

" ' So they go on talking while the street lies numb
and the smoke from the chimneys falls between the
houses.   That's how it is.   But it might happen that
two carriages stop on a crowded boulevard of a distinguished neighbourhood.   Serious-looking men servants
open the doors.   Eight elegant Siberian wolfhounds
come prancing out and jump barking across the boulevard.
And it's said that they are young Parisian dandies in
disguise.'

" His eyes were almost shut.   When I fell silent, he
stuck both hands in his mouth and tore at his lower jaw.
His clothes were covered with dirt.   Perhaps he had
been thrown out of some tavern and hadn't yet realised
it.

" Perhaps it was that short quiet lull between night
and day when our heads loll back unexpectedly, when
everything stands still without our knowing it, since
we are not looking at it, and then disappears ;   we remain
alone, our bodies bent, then look round but no longer see

anything, nor even feel any resistance in the air yet inwardly we cling to the memory that at a certain distance from us stand houses with roofs and with fortunately angular chimneys down which the darkness flows through garrets into various rooms. And it is fortunate that tomorrow will be a day on which, unlikely as it may seem, one will be able to see everything.

" Now the drunk jerked up his eyebrows so that a brightness appeared between them and his eyes, and he explained in fits and starts : ' It's like this, you see— I'm sleepy, you see, so that's why I'm going to sleep.— You see, I've a brother-in-law on the Wenzelsplatz— that's where I'm going, for I live there, for that's where I have my bed—so I'll be off—. But I don't know his name, you see, or where he lives—seems I've forgotten—but never mind, for I don't even know if I have a brother-in-law at all.—But I'll be off now, you see—. Do you think I'll find him ? '

" To which, without thinking, I said : ' That's certain. But you're coming from abroad and your servants don't happen to be with you. Allow me to show you the way.'

" He didn't answer. So I offered him my arm, to give him some support."

(d) Continued Conversation Between the Fat Man and the Supplicant

FOR some time already I had been trying to cheer myself up. I rubbed my body and said to myself : " It's time you spoke. You're becoming embarrassed. Do you feel oppressed ? Just wait ! You know these situations. Think it over at your leisure. Even the landscape will wait.

" It's the same as it was at the party last week. Someone is reading aloud from a manuscript. At his request I myself have copied one page. When I see my handwriting among the pages written by him, I take fright. It's without any stability. People are bending over it from three sides of the table. In tears, I swear it's not my handwriting."

" But what is the connection with today ? It's entirely up to you to start a sensible conversation. Everything's peaceful. Just make an effort, my friend !—You surely can find an objection. —You can say : ' I'm sleepy, I've a headache. Good-bye.' Quick then, quick ! Make yourself conspicuous !—What's that ? Again obstacles and more obstacles ? What does it remind you of ?— I remember a high plateau which rose against the wide sky as a shield to the earth. I saw it from a mountain and prepared myself to wander through it. I began to sing."

My lips were dry and disobedient as I said : " Ought it not to be possible to live differently ? "

" No," he said, questioning, smiling.

" But why do you pray in church every evening ? " I asked then, while everything between him and me, which until then I had been holding together as though in my sleep, collapsed.

" Oh, why should we talk about it ? People who live alone have no responsibility in the evenings. One fears a number of things—that one's body could vanish, that human beings may really be what they appear to be at twilight, that one might not be allowed to walk without a stick, that it might be a good idea to go to church and pray at the top of one's voice in order to be looked at and acquire a body."

Because he talked like that and then fell silent, I pulled my red handkerchief out of my pocket, bent my head, and wept.

He stood up, kissed me, and said : " What are you crying for ? You're tall, I like that ; you have long hands which all but obey your will ; why aren't you happy about it ? Always wear dark cuffs, that's my advice. —No—I flatter you and yet you cry ? I think you cope quite sensibly with the difficulty of living."

" We build useless war machines, towers, walls, curtains of silk, and we could marvel at all this a great deal if we had the time. We tremble in the balance, we don't fall, we flutter, even though we may be uglier than bats. And on a beautiful day hardly anyone can prevent us from saying : ' Oh God, today is a beautiful day,' for we are already established on this Earth and live by virtue of an agreement.

" For we are like tree trunks in the snow. They lie there apparently flat on the ground and it looks as though one could push them away with a slight kick. But no, one can't, for they are firmly stuck to the ground. So you see even this is only apparent."

The following thought prevented me from sobbing : "It is night and no one will reproach me tomorrow for what I might say now, for it could have been said in my sleep."

Then I said : " Yes, that's it, but what were we talking about ? We can't have been talking about the light in the sky because we are standing in the darkness of a hallway. No—we could have talked about it, nevertheless, for are we not free to say what we like in conversation ? After all, we're not aiming at any definite purpose or at the truth, but simply at making jokes and having a good time. Even so, couldn't you tell me the story of the woman in the garden once more? How admirable, how clever this woman is! We must follow her example. How fond I am of her! So it's a good thing I met you and waylaid you as I did. It has given me great pleasure to talk to you. I've learned several things that, perhaps intentionally, were hitherto unknown to me.—I'm grateful."

He looked pleased. And although contact with a human body is always repugnant to me, I couldn't help embracing him.

Then we stepped out of the hallway under the sky. My friend blew away a few bruised little clouds, allowing the uninterrupted surface of the stars to emerge. He walked with difficulty.

4. DROWNING OF THE FAT MAN

AND now everything was seized by speed and fell into the distance. The water of the river was dragged towards a precipice, tried to resist, whirled about a little at the crumbling edge, but then crashed in foaming smoke.

The fat man could not go on talking, he was forced to turn and disappear in the loud roar of the waterfall.

I, who had experienced so many pleasant diversions, stood on the bank and watched. "What are our lungs supposed to do?" I shouted. Shouted: "If they breathe fast they suffocate themselves from inner poisons; if they breathe slowly they suffocate from unbreathable air, from outraged things. But if they try to search for their own rhythm they perish from the mere search."

Meanwhile the banks of the river stretched beyond all bounds, and yet with the palm of my hand I touched the metal of a signpost which gleamed minutely in the far distance. This I really couldn't quite understand. After all I was small, almost smaller than usual, and a bush of white haws shaking itself very fast towered over me. This I saw, for a moment ago it had been close to me.

Nevertheless I was mistaken, for my arms were as huge as the clouds of a steady country rain, save that they were more hasty. I don't know why they were trying to crush my poor head. It was no larger than an ant's egg, but slightly damaged, and as a result no longer quite round. I made some beseeching, twisting movements with it, for the expression of my eyes could not have been noticed, they were so small.

But my legs, my impossible legs lay over the wooded mountains and gave shade to the village-studded valleys. They grew and grew! They already reached into the space that no longer owned any landscape, for some time their length had gone beyond my field of vision.

But no, it isn't like that—after all, I'm small, small for the time being—I'm rolling—I'm rolling—I'm an avalanche in the mountains! Please, passers-by, be so kind as to tell me how tall I am—just measure these arms, these legs.

III

" LET me think," said my acquaintance, who had accompanied me from the party and was walking quietly beside me on a path up the Laurenziberg. " Just stand still a moment so that I can get it clear.—I have

something to settle, you know. It's all such a strain—
the night is radiant, though rather cold, but this dis-
contented wind, it sometimes even seems to change the
position of those acacias."

The moon made the gardener's house cast a shadow
over the slightly humped path on which lay scanty
patches of snow. When I saw the bench that stood
beside the door, I pointed at it with a raised finger, and
as I was not brave and expected reproaches I laid my
left hand on my chest.

He sat down wearily, disregarding his beautiful
clothes, and astonished me by pressing his elbows against
his hips and laying his forehead on the tips of his
overstretched fingers.

"Yes, now I want to say this. You know, I live a
regular life. No fault can be found with it, everything I
do is considered correct and generally approved. Misfortune, as it is known in the society I frequent, has not
spared me, as my surroundings and I have realised with
satisfaction, and even the general good fortune has not
failed me and I myself have been able to talk about it in
a small circle of friends. True, until now I had never
been really in love. I regretted it occasionally, but
used the phrase when I needed it. And now I must confess : Yes, I am in love and quite beside myself with
excitement. I am an ardent lover, just what the girls
dream of. But ought I not to have considered that just
this former lack of mine gave an exceptional and gay,
an especially gay, twist to my circumstances ? "

"Calm yourself," I said without interest, thinking
only of myself. "Your loved one is beautiful, as I
couldn't help hearing."

"Yes, she is beautiful. While sitting next to her, all

I could think was : What an adventure—am I not daring !—there I go embarking on a sea voyage—drinking wine by the gallon. But when she laughs she doesn't show her teeth as one would expect ; instead, all one sees is the dark, narrow, curved opening of the mouth. Now this looks sly and senile, even though she throws back her head while laughing."

" I can't deny that," I said, sighing. " I've probably seen it, too, for it must be conspicuous. But it's not only that. It's the beauty of girls altogether. Often when I see dresses with manifold pleats, frills and flounces smoothly clinging to beautiful bodies, it occurs to me that they will not remain like this for long, that they will get creases that cannot be ironed out, dust will gather in the trimmings too thick to be removed, and that no one will make herself so miserable and ridiculous as every day to put on the same precious dress in the morning and take it off at night. And yet I see girls who are beautiful enough, displaying all kinds of attractive muscles and little bones and smooth skin and masses of fine hair, and who appear every day in the same natural fancy dress, always laying the same face in the same palm and letting it be reflected in the mirror. Only sometimes at night, on returning late from a party, this face stares out at them from the mirror worn out, swollen, already seen by too many people, hardly worth wearing any more."

" I've asked you several times on our walk whether you found my girl beautiful, but you always turned away without answering. Tell me, are you up to some mis-chief ? Why don't you comfort me ? "

I dug my feet into the shadow and said kindly : " You don't need to be comforted. After all, you're being loved." To avoid catching cold I held over my mouth a handkerchief with a design of blue grapes.

Now he turned towards me and leaned his fat face against the low back of the bench : " Actually I've still time, you know. I can still end this budding love affair at once, either by committing some misdeed, by unfaithfulness, or by going off to some distant land. For I've grave doubts about whether I should let myself in for all this excitement. Nothing is certain, no one can tell the direction or the duration for sure. If I go into a tavern with the intention of getting drunk, I know I'll be drunk that evening. But in this case ! In a week's time we're planning to go on an excursion with some friends. Imagine the storm this will create in the heart for the next fortnight ! Last night's kisses make me sleepy and prepare the way for savage dreams. I fight this by going for a walk at night, with the result that I'm in a permanent state of turmoil, my face goes hot and cold as though blown about by the wind, I have to keep fingering a pink ribbon in my pocket all the time, I'm filled with the gravest apprehensions about myself which I cannot follow up, and I can even stand your company, sir, whereas normally I would never spend so much time talking to you."

I was feeling very cold and the sky was already turning a whitish colour. " I'm afraid no misdeed, no unfaithfulness or departure to some distant land will be of any avail. You'll have to kill yourself," I said, adding a smile.

Opposite us on the other side of the avenue stood two bushes and down below these bushes was the town. There were still a few lights on.

" All right," he cried, and hit the bench with his

little tight fist which, however, he left lying there. " But you go on living. You don't kill yourself. No one loves you. You don't achieve anything. You can't cope with the next moment. Yet you dare to talk to me like that, you brute. You're incapable of loving, only fear excites you. Just take a look at my chest."

Whereupon he quickly opened his overcoat and waist-coat and his shirt. His chest was indeed broad and beautiful.

" Yes, such obstinate moods come over one sometimes," I began to say. " This summer I was in a village which lay by a river. I remember it well. I frequently sat on a bench by the shore in a twisted position. There was an hotel, and one often heard the sound of violins. Young healthy people sat in the garden at tables with beer and talked of hunting and adventures. And on the other bank were cloudlike mountains.

Then, with a limp, distorted mouth, I got up, stepped on to the lawn behind the bench, broke a few snow-covered twigs, and whispered into my acquaintance's ear : " I'm engaged, I confess it."

My acquaintance wasn't surprised that I had got up. " You're engaged ? " He sat there really quite ex-hausted, supported only by the back of the bench. Then he took off his hat and I saw his hair which, scented and beautifully combed, set off the round head on a fleshy neck in a sharp curving line, as was the fashion that winter.

I was pleased to have answered him so cleverly. " Just think," I said to myself, " how he moves in society with flexible neck and free-swinging arms. Keeping up an intelligent conversation, he can steer a lady right through a drawing room, and the fact that it's raining outside, that some timid man is standing about or some other wretched thing is happening, does not make him nervous. No, he goes on bowing with the same courtesy to the ladies. And there he sits now."

My acquaintance mopped his brow with a batiste handkerchief. " Please put your hand on my forehead," he said. " I beg you." When I didn't do so at once, he folded his hands.

As though our sorrow had darkened everything, we sat high up on the mountain as in a small room, although a little earlier we had already noticed the light and wind of the morning. We sat close together in spite of not liking one another at all, but we couldn't move far apart because the walls were firmly and definitely drawn. We could, however, behave absurdly and without human dignity, for we didn't have to be ashamed in the presence of the branches above us and the trees standing opposite us.

Then, without further ado, my acquaintance pulled a knife out of his pocket, opened it thoughtfully, and then, as though he were playing, he plunged it into his left upper arm, and didn't withdraw it. Blood promptly began to flow. His round cheeks grew pale. I pulled out the knife, cut up the sleeve of his overcoat and jacket, tore his shirt sleeve open. Then I ran a little way up and down the road to see if there was anyone who could help. All the branches were almost exaggeratedly visible and motionless. I sucked a little at the deep wound. Then I remembered the gardener's cottage. I ran up the steps leading to the upper lawn on the left side of the house, quickly examined the windows and doors, rang the bell furiously and stamped my feet, although I knew all the time that the house was uninhabited. Then I looked at the wound which was bleeding in a thin trickle. Having wetted his handkerchief in snow, I tied it clumsily round his arm.

" My dear, dear friend," said I, " you've wounded yourself for my sake. You're in such a good position, you're surrounded by well-meaning friends, you can go for a walk in broad daylight when any number of carefully dressed people can be seen far and near among tables or on mountain paths. Just think, in the spring we'll drive into the orchard—no, not we, that's unfortunately true—but you with your Annie will drive out at a happy trot. Oh yes, believe me, I beg you, and the sun will show you off to everyone at your best. Oh, there'll be music, the sound of horses from afar, no need to worry, there'll be shouting and barrel organs will be playing in the avenues."

" Oh God," he said, stood up, leaned on me and we went on, " oh God, that won't help. That won't make me happy. Excuse me. Is it late ? Perhaps I ought to do something in the morning. Oh God."

A lantern was burning close to the wall above ; it threw the shadows of the tree trunks across the road and the white snow, while on the slope the shadows of all the branches lay bent, as though broken.

THE GREAT WALL OF CHINA

THE Great Wall of China was finished off at its
northernmost corner. From the south-east and the
south-west it came up in two sections that finally con-
verged there. This principle of piecemeal construction
was also applied on a smaller scale by both of the two
great armies of labour, the eastern and the western. It
was done in this way : gangs of some twenty workers
were formed who had to accomplish a length, say of
five hundred yards of wall, while a similar gang built
another stretch of the same length to meet the first. But
after the junction had been made the construction of the
wall was not carried on from the point, let us say, where
this thousand yards ended ; instead the two groups of
workers were transferred to begin building again in quite
different neighbourhoods. Naturally in this way many
great gaps were left, which were only filled in gradually
and bit by bit, some, indeed, not till after the official
announcement that the wall was finished. In fact it is
said that there are gaps which have never been filled in
at all, an assertion, however, which is probably merely
one of the many legends to which the building of the
wall gave rise, and which cannot be verified, at least by
any single man with his own eyes and judgment, on
account of the extent of the structure.

Now on first thoughts one might conceive that it
would have been more advantageous in every way to
build the wall continuously, or at least continuously

within the two main divisions. After all the wall was intended, as was universally proclaimed and known, to be a protection against the peoples of the north. But how can a wall protect if it is not a continuous structure? Not only cannot such a wall protect, but what there is of it is in perpetual danger. These blocks of wall left standing in deserted regions could be easily pulled down again and again by the nomads, especially as these tribes, rendered apprehensive by the building operations, kept changing their encampments with incredible rapidity, like locusts, and so perhaps had a better general view of the progress of the wall than we, the builders. Nevertheless the task of construction probably could not have been carried out in any other way. To understand this we must take into account the following : The wall was to be a protection for centuries : accordingly the most scrupulous care in the building, the application of the architectural wisdom of all known ages and peoples, an unremitting sense of personal responsibility in the builders, were indispensable prerequisites for the work. True, for the more purely manual tasks ignorant day labourers from the populace, men, women and children who offered their services for good money, could be employed ; but for the supervision even of four-day labourers an expert versed in the art of building was required, a man who was capable of entering into and feeling with all his heart what was involved. And the higher the task, the greater the responsibility. And such men were actually to be had, if not indeed so abundantly as the work of construction could have absorbed, yet in great numbers.

For the work had not been undertaken without thought. Fifty years before the first stone was laid the art of architecture, and especially that of masonry, had been proclaimed as the most important branch of knowledge throughout the whole area of China that was to be walled round, and all other arts gained recognition only in so far as they had reference to it. I can still remember quite well us standing as small children, scarcely sure on our feet, in our teacher's garden, and being ordered to build a sort of wall out of pebbles ; and then the teacher, girding up his robe, ran full tilt against the wall, of course knocking it down, and scolded us so terribly for the shoddiness of our work that we ran weeping in all directions to our parents. A trivial incident, but significant of the spirit of the time.

I was lucky inasmuch as the building of the wall was just beginnning when, at twenty, I had passed the last examination of the lowest-grade school. I say lucky, for many who before my time had achieved the highest degree of culture available to them could find nothing year after year to do with their knowledge, and drifted uselessly about with the most splendid architectural plans in their heads, and sank by thousands into hopeless-ness. But those who finally came to be employed in the work as supervisors, even though it might be of the lowest rank, were truly worthy of their task. They were masons who had reflected much, and did not cease to reflect, on the building of the wall, men who with the first stone which they sank in the ground felt themselves a part of the wall. Masons of that kind, of course, had not only a desire to perform their work in the most thorough manner, but were also impatient to see the wall finished in its complete perfection. Day labourers have not this impatience, for they look only to their wages, and the higher supervisors, indeed even the supervisors of middle rank, could see enough of the manifold growth of the construction to keep their spirits confident and high. But to encourage the subordinate supervisors, intellectually so vastly superior to their apparently petty tasks, other measures must be taken. One could not, for instance, expect them to lay one stone on another for months or even years on end, in an uninhabited mountainous region, hundreds of miles from their homes ; the hopelessness of such hard toil which yet could not reach completion even in the longest lifetime, would have cast them into despair and above all made them less capable for the work. It was for this reason that the system of piecemeal building was decided on. Five hundred yards could be accomplished in about five years ; by that time, however, the supervisors were as a rule quite exhausted and had lost all faith in themselves, in the wall, in the world. Accordingly, while they were still exalted by the jubilant celebrations marking the completion of the thousand yards of wall, they were sent far, far away, saw on their journey finished sections of the wall rising here and there, came past the quarters of the high command and were presented with badges of honour, heard the rejoicings of new armies of labour streaming past from the depths of the land, saw forests being cut down to become supports for the wall, saw mountains being hewn into stones for the wall, heard at the holy shrines hymns rising in which the pious prayed for the completion of the wall. All this assuaged their impatience. The quiet life of their homes, where they rested some time, strengthened them ; the humble credulity with which their reports were listened to, the confidence with which the simple and peaceful burgher believed in the eventual completion of the wall, all this tightened up again the cords of the soul. Like eternally hopeful children they then said farewell to their homes ; the desire once more to labour on the wall of the nation became irresistible. They set off earlier than they needed ; half the village accompanied them for long distances. Groups of people with banners and scarfs waving were on all the roads ; never before had they seen how great and rich and beautiful and worthy of love their country was. Every fellow-countryman was a brother for whom one was building a wall of protection, and who would return lifelong thanks for it with all he had and did. Unity ! Unity ! Shoulder to shoulder, a ring of brothers, a current of blood no longer confined within the narrow circulation of one body, but sweetly rolling and yet ever returning throughout the endless leagues of China.

Thus, then, the system of piecemeal construction becomes comprehensible ; but there were still other reasons for it as well. Nor is there anything odd in my pausing over this question for so long ; it is one of the crucial problems in the whole building of the wall, unimportant as it may appear at first glance. If I am to convey and make understandable the ideas and feelings of that time I cannot go deeply enough into this very question.

First, then, it must be said that in those days things were achieved scarcely inferior to the construction of the Tower of Babel, although as regards divine approval, at least according to human reckoning, strongly at variance with that work. I say this because during the early days of building a scholar wrote a book in which he drew the comparison in the most exhaustive way. In it he tried to prove that the Tower of Babel failed to reach its goal, not because of the reasons universally advanced, or at least that among those recognised reasons the most important of all was not to be found. His proofs were drawn not merely from written documents and reports ; he also claimed to have made enquiries on the spot, and to have discovered that the tower failed and was bound to fail because of the weakness of the foundation. In this respect at any rate our age was vastly superior to that ancient one. Almost every educated man of our time was a mason by profession and infallible in the matter of laying foundations. That, however, was not what our scholar was concerned to prove ; for he maintained that the Great Wall alone would provide for the first time in the history of mankind a secure foundation for a new Tower of Babel. First the wall, therefore, and then the tower. His book was in everybody's hands at that time, but I admit that even today I cannot quite make out how he conceived this tower. How could the wall, which did not form even a circle, but only a sort of quarter or half-circle, provide the foundation for a tower ? That could obviously be meant only in a spiritual sense. But in that case why build the actual wall, which after all was something concrete, the result of the lifelong labour of multitudes of people ? And why were there in the book plans, somewhat nebulous plans, it must be admitted, of the tower, and proposals worked out in detail for mobilising the people's energies for the stupendous new work ?

There were many wild ideas in people's heads at that time—this scholar's book is only one example—perhaps simply because so many were trying to join forces as far as they could for the achievement of a single aim. Human nature, essentially changeable, unstable as the dust, can endure no restraint ; if it binds itself it soon

begins to tear madly at its bonds, until it rends everything asunder, the wall, the bonds and its very self.

It is possible that these very considerations, which
militated against the building of the wall at all, were
not left out of account by the high command when the
system of piecemeal construction was decided on. We
—and here I speak in the name of many people—did not
really know them ourselves until we had carefully
scrutinised the decrees of the high command, when we
discovered that without the high command neither our
book learning nor our human understanding would have
sufficed for the humble tasks which we performed in the
great whole. In the office of the command—where it
was and who sat there no one whom I have asked knew
then or knows now—in that office one may be certain
that all human thoughts and desires were revolved, and
counter to them all human aims and fulfilments. And
through the window the reflected splendours of divine
worlds fell on the hands of the leaders as they traced
their plans.

And for that reason the incorruptible observer must
hold that the command, if it had seriously desired it, could
also have overcome those difficulties which prevented a
system of continuous construction. There remains,
therefore, nothing but the conclusion that the command
deliberately chose the system of piecemeal construction.
But the piecemeal construction was only a makeshift
and therefore inexpedient. Remains the conclusion that
the command willed something inexpedient.—Strange
conclusion !—True, and yet in one respect it has much
to be said for it. One can perhaps safely discuss it now.
In those days many people, and among them the best,
had a secret maxim which ran : Try with all your might

to comprehend the decrees of the high command, but only up to a certain point ; then avoid further meditation. A very wise maxim, which moreover was elaborated in a parable that was later often quoted : Avoid further meditation, but not because it might be harmful ; it is not at all certain that it would be harmful. What is harmful or not harmful has nothing to do with the question. Consider rather the river in spring. It rises until it grows mightier and nourishes more richly the soil on the long stretch of its banks, still maintaining its own course until it reaches the sea, where it is all the more welcome because it is a worthier ally.—Thus far may you urge your meditations on the decrees of the high command.—But after that the river overflows its banks, loses outline and shape, slows down the speed of its current, tries to ignore its destiny by forming little seas in the interior of the land, damages the fields, and yet cannot maintain itself for long in its new expanse, but must run back between its banks again, must even dry up wretchedly in the hot season that presently follows.—Thus far may you not urge your meditations on the decrees of the high command.

Now though this parable may have had extraordinary point and force during the building of the wall, it has at most only a restricted relevance for my present essay. My enquiry is purely historical ; no lightning flashes any longer from the long since vanished thunder-clouds, and so I may venture to seek for an explanation of the system of piecemeal construction which goes farther than the one that contented people then. The limits which my capacity for thought imposes upon me are narrow enough, but the province to be traversed here is infinite. Against whom was the Great Wall to serve as a protection ?

Against the people of the north. Now, I come from the south-east of China. No northern people can menace us there. We read of them in the books of the ancients ; the cruelties which they commit in accordance with their nature make us sigh beneath our peaceful trees. The faithful representations of the artist show us these faces of the damned, their gaping mouths, their jaws furnished with great pointed teeth, their half-shut eyes that already seem to be seeking out the victim whom their jaws will rend and devour. When our children are unruly we show them these pictures, and at once they fly weeping into our arms. But nothing more than that do we know about these northerners. We have not seen them, and if we remain in our villages we shall never see them, even if on their wild horses they should ride as hard as they can straight towards us—the land is too vast and would not let them reach us, they would end their course in the empty air.

Why, then, since that is so, did we leave our homes, the stream with its bridges, our mothers and fathers, our weeping wives, our children who needed our care, and depart for the distant city to be trained there, while our thoughts journeyed still farther away to the wall in the north ? Why ? A question for the high command. Our leaders know us. They, absorbed in gigantic anxieties, know of us, know our petty pursuits, see us sitting together in our humble huts, and approve or disapprove the evening prayer which the father of the house recites in the midst of his family. And if I may be allowed to express such ideas about the high command, then I must say that in my opinion the high command has existed from old time, and was not assembled, say, like a gathering of mandarins summoned hastily to dis-

cuss somebody's fine dream in a conference as hastily
terminated, so that that very evening the people are
drummed out of their beds to carry out what has been
decided, even if it should be nothing but an illumination
in honour of a god who may have shown great favour to
their masters the day before, only to drive them into
some dark corner with cudgel blows tomorrow, almost
before the illuminations have died down. Far rather do
I believe that the high command has existed from all
eternity, and the decision to build the wall likewise.
Unwitting peoples of the north, who imagined they were
the cause of it! Honest, unwitting Emperor, who
imagined he decreed it! We builders of the wall know
that it was not so and hold our tongues.

*   *   *

During the building of the wall and ever since to this
very day I have occupied myself almost exclusively with
the comparative history of races—there are certain
questions which one can probe to the marrow, as it were,
only by this method—and I have discovered that we
Chinese possess certain folk and political institutions
that are unique in their clarity, others again unique in
their obscurity. The desire to trace the causes of these
phenomena, especially the latter, has always teased me
and teases me still, and the building of the wall is itself
essentially involved with these problems.

Now one of the most obscure of our institutions is that
of the empire itself. In Pekin, naturally, at the imperial
court, there is some clarity to be found on this subject,
though even that is more illusive than real. Also the
teachers of political law and history in the high schools
claim to be exactly informed on these matters, and to
be capable of passing on their knowledge to their

students. The farther one descends among the lower schools the more, naturally enough, does one find teachers' and pupils' doubts of their own knowledge vanishing, and a superficial culture mounting sky high round a few precepts that have been drilled into people's minds for centuries, precepts which, though they have lost nothing of their eternal truth, remain eternally invisible in this fog of confusion.

But it is precisely this question of the empire which in my opinion the common people should be asked to answer, since after all they are the empire's final support. Here, I must confess, I can only speak once more for my native place. Except for the nature gods and their ritual, which fills the whole year in such beautiful and rich alternation, we think only about the Emperor. But not about the present one ; or rather we would think about the present one if we knew who he was or knew anything definite about him. True—and it is the sole curiosity that fills us—we are always trying to get information on this subject, but, strange as it may sound, it is almost impossible to discover anything, either from pilgrims, though they have wandered through many lands, or from near or distant villages, or from sailors, though they have navigated not only our little stream, but also the sacred rivers. One hears a great many things, true, but can gather nothing definite.

So vast is our land that no fable could do justice to its vastness, the heavens can scarcely span it—and Pekin is only a dot in it, and the imperial palace less than a dot. The Emperor as such, on the other hand, is mighty throughout all the hierarchies of the world : admitted. But the existent Emperor, a man like us, lies much like us on a couch which is of generous proportions, perhaps, and yet very possibly may be quite narrow and short. Like us he sometimes stretches himself and when he is very tired yawns with his delicately cut mouth. But how should we know anything about that—thousands of miles away in the south—almost on the borders of the Tibetan Highlands ? And besides, any tidings, even if they did reach us, would arrive far too late, would have become obsolete long before they reached us. The Emperor is always surrounded by a brilliant and yet ambiguous throng of nobles and courtiers—malice and enmity in the guise of servants and friends—who form a counter-weight to the Imperial power and perpetually labour to unseat the ruler from his place with poisoned arrows. The Empire is immortal, but the Emperor himself totters and falls from his throne, yes, whole dynasties sink in the end and breathe their last in one death-rattle. Of these struggles and sufferings the people will never know ; like tardy arrivals, like strangers in a city, they stand at the end of some densely thronged side street peacefully munching the food they have brought with them, while far away in front, in the market square at the heart of the city, the execution of their ruler is proceeding.

There is a parable which describes this situation very well : The Emperor, so it runs, has sent a message to you, the humble subject, the insignificant shadow cowering in the remotest distance before the imperial sun ; the Emperor from his death-bed has sent a message to you alone. He has commanded the messenger to kneel down by the bed, and has whispered the message to him ; so much store did he lay on it that he ordered the messenger to whisper it back into his ear again. Then by a nod of the head he has confirmed that it is right. Yes, before the assembled spectators of his death—all the obstructing walls have been broken down, and on the spacious and loftily mounting open staircases stand in a ring the great princes of the Empire— before all these he has delivered his message. The messenger immediately sets out on his journey ; a powerful, an indefatigable man ; now pushing with his right arm, now with his left, he cleaves a way for himself through the throng ; if he encounters resistance he points to his breast, where the symbol of the sun glitters ; the way, too, is made easier for him than it would be for any other man. But the multitudes are so vast ; their numbers have no end. If he could reach the open fields how fast he would fly, and soon doubtless you would hear the welcome hammering of his fists on your door. But instead how vainly does he wear out his strength ; still he is only making his way through the chambers of the innermost palace ; never will he get to the end of them ; and if he succeeded in that nothing would be gained ; he must fight his way next down the stairs ; and if he succeeded in that nothing would be gained ; the courts would still have to be crossed ; and after the courts the second outer palace ; and once more stairs and courts ; and once more another palace ; and so on for thousands of years ; and if at last he should burst through the outermost gate—but never, never can that happen—the imperial capital would lie before him, the centre of the world, crammed to bursting with its own refuse. Nobody could fight his way through here even with a message from a dead man.—But you sit at your window when evening falls and dream it to yourself.

Just so, as hopelessly and as hopefully, do our people regard the Emperor. They do not know what emperor is reigning, and there exist doubts regarding even the name of the dynasty. In school a great deal is taught about the dynasties with the dates of succession, but the universal uncertainty on this matter is so great that even the best scholars are drawn into it. Long-dead emperors are set on the throne in our villages, and one that only lives in song recently had a proclamation of his read out by the priest before the altar. Battles that are old history are new to us, and one's neighbour rushes in with a jubilant face to tell the news. The wives of the emperors, pampered and overweening, seduced from noble custom by wily courtiers, swelling with ambition, vehement in their greed, uncontrollable in their lust, practise their abominations ever anew. The more deeply they are buried in time the more glaring are the colours in which their deeds are painted, and with a loud cry of woe our village eventually hears how an Empress drank her husband's blood in long draughts thousands of years ago.

Thus, then, do our people deal with departed emperors, but the living ruler they confuse among the dead. If once, only once in a man's lifetime, an imperial official on his tour of the provinces should arrive by chance at our village, make certain announcements in the name of the government, scrutinise the tax lists, examine the school children, enquire of the priest regarding our doings and affairs, and then, before he steps into his litter, should sum up his impressions in verbose admonitions to the assembled commune,—then a smile flits over every face, each man throws a stolen glance at his neighbour, and bends over his children so as not to be observed by the official. Why, they think to themselves, he's speaking of a dead man as if he were alive, this

Emperor of his died long ago, the dynasty is blotted out, the good official is having his joke with us, but we will behave as if we did not notice it, so as not to offend him. But we shall obey in earnest no one but our present ruler, for to do so would be a crime. And behind the departing litter of the official there arises in might as ruler of the village some figure fortuitously exalted from an urn already crumbled to dust.

Similarly our people are but little affected by revolutions in the state or contemporary wars. I recall an incident in my youth. A revolt had broken out in a neighbouring, but yet quite distant, province. What caused it I can no longer remember, nor is it of any importance now ; occasions for revolt can be found there any day, the people are an excitable people. Well, one day a leaflet published by the rebels was brought to my father's house by a beggar who had crossed that province. It happened to be a feast day, our rooms were filled with guests, the priest sat in the chief place and studied the sheet. Suddenly everybody started to laugh, in the confusion the sheet was torn, the beggar, who however had already received abundant alms, was driven out of the room with blows, the guests dispersed to enjoy the beautiful day. Why ? The dialect of this neighbouring province differs in some essential respects from ours, and this difference occurs also in certain turns of the written speech, which for us have an archaic character. Hardly had the priest read out two lines before we had already come to our decision. Ancient history told long ago, old sorrows long since healed. And though—so it seems to me in recollection—the gruesomeness of the living present was irrefutably conveyed by the beggar's words, we laughed and shook our heads and refused to listen any longer. So eager are our people to obliterate the present.

Is from such appearances any one should draw the conclusion that in reality we have no Emperor, he would not be far from the truth. Over and over again it must be repeated : There is perhaps no people more faithful to the Emperor than ours in the south, but the Emperor derives no advantage from our fidelity. True, the sacred dragon stands on the little column at the end of our village, and ever since the beginning of human memory it has breathed out its fiery breath in the direction of Pekin in token of homage—but Pekin itself is far stranger to the people in our village than the next world. Can there really be a village where the houses stand side by side, covering all the fields for a greater distance than one can see from our hills, and can there be dense crowds of people packed between these houses day and night ? We find it more difficult to picture such a city than to believe that Pekin and its Emperor are one, a cloud, say, peacefully voyaging beneath the sun in the course of the ages.

Now the result of holding such opinions is a life on the whole free and unconstrained. By no means immoral, however ; hardly ever have I found in my travels such pure morals as in my native village. But yet a life that is subject to no contemporary law, and attends only to the exhortations and warnings which come to us from olden times.

I guard against large generalisations, and do not assert that in all the countless villages in my province it is so, far less in all the five hundred provinces of China. Yet perhaps I may venture to assert on the basis of the many writings on this subject which I have read, as well as from my own observation—the building of the wall in particular, with its abundance of human material, provided a man of sensibility with the opportunity of traversing the souls of almost all the provinces—on the basis of all this, then, perhaps I may venture to assert that the prevailing attitude to the Emperor shows persistently and universally something fundamentally in common with that of our village. Now I have no wish whatever to represent this attitude as a virtue ; on the contrary. True, the essential responsibility for it lies with the government, which in the most ancient empire in the world has not yet succeeded in developing, or has neglected to develop, the institution of the empire to such precision that its workings extend directly and unceasingly to the farthest frontiers of the land. On the other hand, however, there is also involved a certain feebleness of faith and imaginative power on the part of the people, that prevents them from raising the empire out of its stagnation in Pekin and clasping it in all its palpable living reality to their own breasts, which yet desire nothing better than but once to feel that touch and then to die.

This attitude then is certainly no virtue. All the more remarkable is it that this very weakness should seem to be one of the greatest unifying influences among our people ; indeed, if one may dare to use the expression, the very ground on which we live. To set about establishing a fundamental defect here would mean undermining not only our consciences, but, what is far worse, our feet. And for that reason I shall not proceed any further at this stage with my enquiry into these questions.

THE REFUSAL

OUR little town does not lie on the frontier, no-where near ; it is so far from the frontier, in fact, that perhaps no one from our town has ever been there ; desolate highlands have to be crossed as well as wide fertile plains. To imagine even part of the road makes one tired, and more than part one just cannot imagine. There are also big towns on the road, each far larger than ours. Ten little towns like ours laid side by side, and ten more forced down from above, still would not produce one of these enormous, overcrowded towns. If one does not get lost on the way one is bound to lose oneself in these towns, and to avoid them is impossible on account of their size.

But what is even further from our town than the frontier, if such distances can be compared at all—it's like saying that a man of three hundred years is older than one of two hundred—what is even further than the frontier is the capital. Whereas we do get news of the frontier wars now and again, of the capital we learn next to nothing—we civilians that is, for of course the government officials have very good connections with the capital ; they can get news from there in as little as three months, so they claim at least.

Now it is remarkable and I am continually being surprised by the way we in our town humbly submit to all orders issued in the capital. For centuries no political change has been brought about by the citizens themselves.

In the capital great rulers have superseded each other—
indeed, even dynasties have been deposed or annihilated,
and new ones have started ; in the past century even the
capital itself was destroyed, a new one was founded far
away from it, later on this too was destroyed and the old
one rebuilt, yet none of this had any influence on our
little town. Our officials have always remained at their
posts ; the highest officials came from the capital, the
less high from other towns, and the lowest from among
ourselves—that is how it has always been and it has
suited us. The highest official is the chief tax-collector,
he has the rank of colonel, and is known as such. The
present one is an old man ; I've known him for years,
because he was already a colonel when I was a child. At
first he rose very fast in his career, but then he seems to
have advanced no further ; actually, for our little town
his rank is good enough, a higher rank would be out of
place. When I try to recall him I see him sitting on the
veranda of his house in the Market Square, leaning back,
pipe in mouth. Above him from the roof flutters the
imperial flag ; on the sides of the veranda, which is so
big that minor military manœuvres are sometimes held
there, washing hangs out to dry. His grandchildren, in
beautiful silk clothes, play around him ; they are not
allowed down in the Market Square, the children there
are considered unworthy of them, but the grandchildren
are attracted by the Square, so they thrust their heads
between the baluster and when the children below
begin to quarrel they join in the quarrel from above.

This colonel, then, commands the town. I don't
think he has ever produced a document entitling him to
this position ; very likely he does not possess such a
thing. Perhaps he really is chief tax-collector. But is

that all ? Does that entitle him to rule over all the other departments in the administration as well ? True, his office is very important for the government, but for the citizens it is hardly the most important. One is almost under the impression that the people here say : " Now that you've taken all we possess, please take us as well." In reality, of course, it was not he who seized the power, nor is he a tyrant. It has just come about over the years that the chief tax-collector is automatically the top official, and the colonel accepts the tradition just as we do.

Yet while he lives among us without laying too much stress on his official position, he is something quite different from the ordinary citizen. When a delegation comes to him with a request, he stands there like the wall of the world. Behind him is nothingness, one imagines hearing voices whispering in the background, but this is probably a delusion ; after all, he represents the end of all things, at least for us. At these receptions he really was worth seeing. Once as a child I was present when a delegation of citizens arrived to ask him for a government subsidy because the poorest quarter of the town had been burned to the ground. My father the blacksmith, a man well respected in the community, was a member of the delegation and had taken me along. There's nothing exceptional about this, everyone rushes to spectacles of this kind, one can hardly distinguish the actual delegation from the crowd. Since these receptions usually take place on the veranda, there are even people who climb up by ladder from the Market Square and take part in the goings-on from over the balustrade. On this occasion about a quarter of the veranda had been reserved for the colonel, the crowd filling the rest of it. A few soldiers kept watch, some of them standing round him in a semicircle. Actually a single soldier would have been quite enough, such is our fear of them. I don't know exactly where these soldiers come from, in any case from a long way off, they all look very much alike, they wouldn't even need a uniform. They are small, not strong but agile people, the most striking thing about them is the prominence of their teeth which almost overcrowd their mouths, and a certain restless twitching of their small narrow eyes. This makes them the terror of the children, but also their delight, for again and again the children long to be frightened by these teeth, these eyes, so as to be able to run away in horror. Even grown-ups probably never quite lose this childish terror, at least it continues to have an effect. There are, of course, other factors contributing to it. The soldiers speak a dialect utterly incomprehensible to us, and they can hardly get used to ours—all of which produces a certain shut-off, unapproachable quality corresponding, as it happens, to their character, for they are silent, serious and rigid. They don't actually do anything evil, and yet they are almost unbearable in an evil sense. A soldier, for example, enters a shop, buys some trifling object, and stays there leaning against the counter ; he listens to the conversations, probably does not understand them, and yet gives the impression of understanding; he himself does not say a word, just stares blankly at the speaker, then back at the listeners, all the while keeping his hand on the hilt of the long knife in his belt. This is revolting, one loses the desire to talk, the customers start leaving the shop, and only when it is quite empty does the soldier also leave. Thus wherever the soldiers appear, our lively people grow silent. That's what happened this time, too. As on all solemn occasions the colonel stood upright, holding in front of him two poles of bamboo in his outstretched hands. This is an ancient custom implying more or less that he supports the law, and the law supports him. Now everyone knows, of course, what to expect up on the veranda, and yet each time people take fright all over again. On this occasion, too, the man chosen to speak could not begin ; he was already standing opposite the colonel when his courage failed him and, muttering a few excuses, he pushed his way back into the crowd. No other suitable person willing to speak could be found, albeit several unsuitable ones offered themselves ; a great commotion ensued and messengers were sent in search of various citizens who were well-known speakers. During all this time the colonel stood there motionless, only his chest moving visibly up and down to his breathing. Not that he breathed with difficulty, it was just that he breathed so conspicuously, much as frogs breathe—except that with them it is normal, while here it was exceptional. I squeezed myself through the grown-ups and watched him through a gap between two soldiers, until one of them kicked me away with his knee. Meanwhile the man originally chosen to speak had regained his composure and, firmly held up by two fellow citizens, was delivering his address. It was touching to see him smile throughout this solemn speech describing a grievous misfortune—a most humble smile which strove in vain to elicit some slight reaction on the colonel's face. Finally he formulated the request—I think he was only asking for a year's tax exemption, but possibly also for timber from the imperial forests at a reduced price. Then he bowed low, remaining in this position for some time, as did everyone else except the colonel, the soldiers and a number of officials in the background. To the child it seemed ridiculous that the people on the ladders should climb down a few rungs so as not to be seen during the significant pause and now and again peer inquisitively over the floor of the veranda. After this had lasted quite a while an official, a little man, stepped up to the colonel and tried to reach the latter's height by standing on his toes. The colonel, still motionless save for his deep breathing, whispered something in his ear, whereupon the little man clapped his hands and everyone rose. " The petition has been refused," he announced. " You may go." An undeniable sense of relief passed through the crowd, everyone surged out, hardly a soul paying any special attention to the colonel who, as it were, had turned once more into a human being like the rest of us. I still caught one last glimpse of him as he wearily let go of the poles, which fell to the ground, then sank into an armchair produced by some officials, and promptly put his pipe in his mouth.

This whole occurrence is not isolated, it's in the general run of things. Indeed, it does happen now and again that minor petitions are granted, but then it invariably looks as though the colonel had done it as a powerful private person on his own responsibility, and it had to be kept all but a secret from the government—not explicitly of course, but that is what it feels like. No doubt in our little town the colonel's eyes, so far as we know, are also the eyes of the government, and yet there is a difference which it is impossible to comprehend completely.

In all important matters, however, the citizens can always count on a refusal. And now the strange fact is that without this refusal one simply cannot get along, yet at the same time these official occasions designed to receive the refusal are by no means a formality. Time after time one goes there full of expectation and in all seriousness and then one returns, if not exactly strengthened or happy, nevertheless not disappointed or tired. About these things I do not have to ask the opinion of anyone else, I feel them in myself, as everyone does ; nor do I have any great desire to find out how these things are connected.

As a matter of fact there is, so far as my observations go, a certain age group that is not content—these are the young people roughly between seventeen and twenty. Quite young fellows, in fact, who are utterly incapable of foreseeing the consequences of even the least significant, far less a revolutionary, idea. And it is among just them that discontent creeps in.

THE PROBLEM OF OUR LAWS

OUR laws are not generally known ; they are kept secret by the small group of nobles who rule us. We are convinced that these ancient laws are scrupulously administered ; nevertheless it is an extremely painful thing to be ruled by laws that one does not know. I am not thinking of possible discrepancies that may arise in the interpretation of the laws, or of the disadvantages involved when only a few and not the whole people are allowed to have a say in their interpretation. These disadvantages are perhaps of no great importance. For the laws are very ancient ; their interpretation has been the work of centuries, and has itself doubtless acquired the status of law ; and though there is still a possible freedom of interpretation left, it has now become very restricted. Moreover the nobles have obviously no cause to be influenced in their interpretation by personal interests inimical to us, for the laws were made to the advantage of the nobles from the very beginning, they themselves stand above the laws, and that seems to be why the laws were entrusted exclusively into their hands. Of course, there is wisdom in that—who doubts the wisdom of the ancient laws ?—but also hardship for us ; probably that is unavoidable.

The very existence of these laws, however, is at most a matter of presumption. There is a tradition that they exist and that they are a mystery confided to the nobility, but it is not and cannot be more than a mere tradition sanctioned by age, for the essence of a secret code is that it should remain a mystery. Some of us among the people have attentively scrutinised the doings of the nobility since the earliest times and possess records made by our forefathers—records which we have conscientiously continued—and claim to recognise amid the countless number of facts certain main tendencies which permit of this or that historical formulation ; but when in accordance with these scrupulously tested and logically ordered conclusions we seek to orient ourselves somewhat towards the present or the future, everything becomes uncertain, and our work seems only an intellectual game, for perhaps these laws that we are trying to unravel do not exist at all. There is a small party who are actually of this opinion and who try to show that, if any law exists, it can only be this : The Law is whatever the nobles do. This party see everywhere only the arbitrary acts of the nobility, and reject the popular tradition, which according to them possesses only certain trifling and incidental advantages that do not offset its heavy drawbacks, for it gives the people a false, deceptive and over-confident security in confronting coming events. This cannot be gainsaid, but the overwhelming majority of our people account for it by the fact that the tradition is far from complete and must be more fully enquired into, that the material available, prodigious as it looks, is still too meagre, and that several centuries will have to pass before it becomes really adequate. This view, so comfortless as far as the present is concerned, is lightened only by the belief that a time will eventually come when the tradition and our research into it will jointly reach their conclusion, and as it were gain a breathing space, when everything will have become clear, the law will belong to the people, and the nobility will vanish. This is not maintained in any spirit of hatred against the nobility ; not at all, and by no one. We are more inclined to hate ourselves, because we have not yet shown ourselves worthy of being entrusted with the laws. And that is the real reason why the party which believes that there is no law has remained so small—although its doctrine is in certain ways so attractive, for it unequivocally recognises the nobility and its right to go on existing.

Actually one can express the problem only in a sort of paradox : Any party which would repudiate, not only all belief in the laws, but the nobility as well, would have the whole people behind it ; yet no such party can come into existence, for nobody would dare to repudiate the nobility. We live on this razor edge. A writer once summed the matter up in this way : The sole visible and indubitable law that is imposed upon us is the nobility, and must we ourselves deprive ourselves of that one law ?

THE CITY COAT OF ARMS

AT first all the arrangements for building the Tower of Babel were characterised by fairly good order, indeed the order was perhaps too perfect ; too much thought was taken for guides, interpreters, accommodation for the workmen and roads of communication, as if there were centuries before one to do the work in. In fact the general opinion at that time was that one simply could not build too slowly ; a very little insistence on this would have sufficed to make one hesitate to lay the foundations at all. People argued in this way : The essential thing in the whole business is the idea of building a tower that will reach to heaven. In comparison with that idea everything else is secondary. The idea, once seized in its magnitude, can never vanish again ; so long as there are men on the earth there will be also the irresistible desire to complete the building. That being so, however, one need have no anxiety about the future ; on the contrary, human knowledge is increasing, the art of building has made progress and will make further progress, a piece of work which takes us a year may perhaps be done in half the time in another hundred years, and better done, too, more enduringly. So why exert oneself to the extreme limit of one's present powers ? There would be some sense in doing that only if it were likely that the tower could be completed in one generation. But that is beyond all hope. It is far more likely that the next generation with their perfected knowledge will find the work of their predecessors bad, and tear down what has been built so as to begin anew. Such thoughts paralysed people's powers, and so they troubled less about the tower than the construction of a city for the workmen. Every nationality wanted the finest quarter for itself, and this gave rise to disputes, which developed into bloody conflicts. These conflicts never came to an end ; to the leaders they were a new proof that, in the absence of the necessary unity, the building of the tower must be done very slowly, or indeed preferably postponed until universal peace was declared. But the time was spent not only in conflict ; the town was embellished in the intervals, and this unfortunately enough evoked fresh envy and fresh conflict. In this fashion the age of the first generation passed away, but none of the succeeding ones showed any difference ; except that technical skill increased and with it occasion for conflict. To this must be added that the second or third generation had already recognised the senselessness of building a heaven-reaching tower ; but by that time everybody was too deeply involved to leave the city. All the legends and songs that came to birth in that city are filled with longing for a prophesied day when the city would be destroyed by five successive blows from a gigantic fist. It is for that reason too that the city has a closed fist on its coat of arms.

ON PARABLES

MANY complain that the words of the wise are always merely parables and of no use in daily life, which is the only life we have. When the sage says : " Go over," he does not mean that we should cross to some actual place, which we could do anyhow if the labour were worth it ; he means some fabulous yonder, something unknown to us, something too that he cannot designate more precisely, and therefore cannot help us here in the very least. All these parables really set out to say merely that the incomprehensible is incomprehensible, and we know that already. But the cares we have to struggle with every day : that is a different matter.

Concerning this a man once said : Why such reluctance ? If you only followed the parables you yourselves would become parables and with that rid of all your daily cares.

Another said : I bet that is also a parable.

The first said. You have won.

The second said : But unfortunately only in parable.

The first said : No, in reality : in parable you have lost.

POSEIDON

POSEIDON sat at his desk, going over the accounts.
The administration of all the waters gave him endless
work. He could have had as many assistants as he
wanted, and indeed he had quite a number, but since he
took his job very seriously he insisted on going through
all the accounts again himself, and so his assistants were
of little help to him. It cannot be said that he enjoyed
the work; he carried it out simply because it was
assigned to him; indeed he had frequently applied for
what he called more cheerful work, but whenever
various suggestions were put to him it turned out that
nothing suited him so well as his present employment.
Needless to say, it was very difficult to find him another
job. After all, he could not possibly be put in charge of
one particular ocean. Quite apart from the fact that in
this case the work involved would not be less, only more
petty, the great Poseidon could hold only a superior
position. And when he was offered a post unrelated to
the waters, the very idea made him feel sick, his divine
breath came short and his brazen chest began to heave.
As a matter of fact, no one took his troubles very
seriously; when a mighty man complains one must
pretend to yield, however hopeless the case may seem.
No one ever really considered relieving Poseidon of his
position; he had been destined to be God of the Seas
since time immemorial, and that was how it had to
remain.

What annoyed him most—and this was the chief cause of discontent with his job—was to learn of the rumours that were circulating about him ; for instance, that he was constantly cruising through the waves with his trident. Instead of which here he was sitting in the depths of the world's ocean, endlessly going over the accounts, an occasional journey to Jupiter being the only interruption of the monotony, a journey moreover from which he usually returned in a furious temper. As a result he had hardly seen the oceans, save fleetingly during his hasty ascent to Olympus, and had never really sailed upon them. He used to say that he was postponing this until the end of the world, for then there might come a quiet moment when, just before the end and having gone through his last account, he could still make a quick little tour.

THE HUNTER GRACCHUS

TWO boys were sitting on the harbour wall playing with dice. A man was reading a newspaper on the steps of the monument, resting in the shadow of a hero who was flourishing his sword on high. A girl was filling her bucket at the fountain. A fruit-seller was lying beside his scales, staring out to sea. Through the vacant window and door openings of a café one could see two men quite at the back drinking their wine. The proprietor was sitting at a table in front and dozing. A bark was silently making for the little harbour, as if borne by invisible means over the water. A man in a blue blouse climbed ashore and drew the rope through a ring. Behind the boatman two other men in dark coats with silver buttons carried a bier, on which, beneath a great flower-patterned tasselled silk cloth, a man was apparently lying.

Nobody on the quay troubled about the newcomers; even when they lowered the bier to wait for the boatman, who was still occupied with his rope, nobody went nearer, nobody asked them a question, nobody accorded them an inquisitive glance.

The pilot was still further detained by a woman who, a child at her breast, now appeared with loosened hair on the deck of the boat. Then he advanced and indicated a yellowish two-storeyed house that rose abruptly on the left beside the sea; the bearers took up their burden and bore it to the low but gracefully pillared door. A little boy opened a window just in time to see the party vanishing into the house, then hastily shut the window again. The door too was now shut; it was of black oak, and very strongly made. A flock of doves which had been flying round the belfry alighted in the street before the house. As if their food were stored within, they assembled in front of the door. One of them flew up to the first storey and pecked at the window-pane. They were bright-hued, well-tended, beautiful birds. The woman on the boat flung grain to them in a wide sweep; they ate it up and flew across to the woman.

A man in a top-hat tied with a band of crêpe now descended one of the narrow and very steep lanes that led to the harbour. He glanced round vigilantly, everything seemed to displease him, his mouth twisted at the sight of some offal in a corner. Fruit skins were lying on the steps of the monument; he swept them off in passing with his stick. He rapped at the house door, at the same time taking his top-hat from his head with his black-gloved hand. The door was opened at once, and some fifty little boys appeared in two rows in the long entry-hall, and bowed to him.

The boatman descended the stairs, greeted the gentleman in black, conducted him up to the first storey, led him round the bright elegant and loggia which encircled the courtyard, and both of them entered, while the boys pressed after them at a respectful distance, a cool spacious room looking towards the back, from whose window no habitation, but only a bare, blackish grey rocky wall was to be seen. The bearers were busied in setting up and lighting several long candles at the head of the bier, yet these did not give light, but only scared away the shadows which had been immobile till then, and made them flicker over the walls. The cloth covering the bier had been thrown back. Lying on it was a man with wildly matted hair, who looked somewhat like a hunter. He lay without motion and, it seemed, without breathing, his eyes closed ; yet only his trappings indicated that this man was probably dead.

The gentleman stepped up to the bier, laid his hand on the brow of the man lying upon it, then knelt down and prayed. The boatman made a sign to the bearers to leave the room ; they went out, drove away the boys who had gathered outside, and shut the door. But even that did not seem to satisfy the gentleman. He glanced at the boatman ; the boatman understood, and vanished through a side door into the next room. At once the man on the bier opened his eyes, turned his face painfully towards the gentleman, and said : " Who are you ? " Without any mark of surprise the gentleman rose from his kneeling posture and answered : " The Burgomaster of Riva."

The man on the bier nodded, indicated a chair with a feeble movement of his arm, and said, after the Burgomaster had accepted his invitation : " I knew that, of course, Burgomaster, but in the first moments of returning consciousness I always forget, everything goes round before my eyes, and it is best to ask about anything even if I know. You too probably know that I am the hunter Gracchus."

" Certainly," said the Burgomaster. " Your arrival was announced to me during the night. We had been asleep for a good while. Then towards midnight my wife cried : ' Salvatore '—that's my name—' look at that dove at the window.' It was really a dove, but as big as a cock. It flew over to me and said in my ear : ' Tomorrow the dead hunter Gracchus is coming ; receive him in the name of the city '."

The hunter nodded and licked his lips with the tip of his tongue : " Yes, the doves flew here before me. But do you believe, Burgomaster, that I shall remain in Riva ? "

" I cannot say that yet," replied the Burgomaster. " Are you dead ? "

" Yes," said the hunter, " as you see. Many years ago, yes, it must be a great many years ago. I fell from a precipice in the Black Forest—that is in Germany—when I was hunting a chamois. Since then I have been dead."

" But you are alive too," said the Burgomaster.

" In a certain sense," said the hunter, " in a certain sense I am alive too. My death ship lost its way ; a wrong turn of the wheel, a moment's absence of mind on the pilot's part, a longing to turn aside towards my lovely native country, I cannot tell what it was ; I only know this, that I remained on earth and that ever since my ship has sailed earthly waters. So I, who asked for nothing better than to live among my mountains, travel after my death through all the lands of the earth."

" And you have no part in the other world ? " asked the Burgomaster, knitting his brow.

" I am for ever," replied the hunter, " on the great stair that leads up to it. On that infinitely wide and spacious stair I clamber about, sometimes up, sometimes down, sometimes on the right, sometimes on the left, always in motion. The hunter has been turned into a butterfly. Do not laugh."

" I am not laughing," said the Burgomaster in self-defence.

" That is very good of you," said the hunter. " I am always in motion. But when I make a supreme flight and see the gate actually shining before me I awaken presently on my old ship, still stranded forlornly in some earthly sea or other. The fundamental error of my one-time death grins at me as I lie in my cabin. Julia, the wife of the pilot, knocks at the door and brings me on my bier the morning drink of the land whose coasts we chance to be passing. I lie on a wooden board, I wear—it cannot be a pleasure to look at me—a filthy winding sheet, my hair and beard, black tinged with grey, have grown together inextricably, my limbs are covered with a great flower-patterned woman's shawl with long fringes. A sacramental candle stands at my head and lights me. On the wall opposite me is a little picture, evidently of a Bushman who is aiming his spear at me and taking cover as best he can behind a beautifully painted shield. On shipboard one is often a prey to stupid imaginations, but that is the stupidest of them all. Otherwise my wooden cage is quite empty. Through a hole in the side wall come in the warm airs of the southern night, and I hear the water slapping against the old boat.

" I have lain here ever since the time, when as the hunter Gracchus living in the Black Forest, I followed a chamois and fell from a precipice. Everything happened in good order. I pursued, I fell, bled to death in a ravine, died, and this ship should have conveyed me to the next world. I can still remember how gladly I stretched myself out on this board for the first time. Never did the mountains listen to such songs from me as these shadowy walls did then.

" I had been glad to live and I was glad to die. Before I stepped aboard, I joyfully flung away my wretched load of ammunition, my knapsack, my hunting rifle that I had always been proud to carry, and I slipped into my winding sheet like a girl into her marriage dress. I lay and waited. Then came the mishap."

"A terrible fate," said the Burgomaster, raising his hand defensively. "And you bear no blame for it?"

"None," said the hunter. "I was a hunter; was there any sin in that? I followed my calling as a hunter in the Black Forest, where there were still wolves in those days. I lay in ambush, shot, hit my mark, flayed the skins from my victims: was there any sin in that? My labours were blessed. 'The great hunter of the Black Forest' was the name I was given. Was there any sin in that?"

"I am not called upon to decide that," said the Burgomaster, "yet to me also there seems to be no sin in such things. But then, whose is the guilt?"

"The boatman's," said the hunter. "Nobody will read what I say here, no one will come to help me; even if all the people were commanded to help me, every door and window would remain shut, everyone would take to bed and draw the bedclothes over his head, the whole earth would become an inn for the night. And there is sense in that, for nobody knows of me, and if anyone knew he would not know where I could be found, and if he knew where I could be found he would not know how to deal with me, he would not know how to help me. The thought of helping me is an illness that has to be cured by taking to one's bed.

"I know that, and so I do not shout to summon help, even though at moments—when I lose control over myself, as I have done just now, for instance—I think seriously of it. But to drive out such thoughts I need only look

round me and verify where I am, and—I can safely assert
—have been for hundreds of years.''

" Extraordinary,'' said the Burgomaster, " extraordinary.—And now do you think of staying here in Riva
with us ? ''

" I think not,'' said the hunter with a smile, and, to
excuse himself, he laid his hand on the Burgomaster's
knee. " I am here, more than that I do not know,
further than that I cannot go. My ship has no rudder,
and it is driven by the wind that blows in the undermost
regions of death.''

THE KNOCK AT THE MANOR GATE

IT was summer, a hot day. With my sister I was passing the gate of a great house on our way home. I cannot tell now whether she knocked on the gate out of mischief or out of absence of mind, or merely threatened it with her hand and did not knock at all. A hundred paces farther on along the road, which here turned to the left, began the village. We did not know it very well, but no sooner had we passed the first house when people appeared and made friendly or warning signs to us ; they were themselves apparently terrified, bowed down with terror. They pointed towards the manor house that we had passed and reminded us of the knock on the gate. The proprietor of the manor would charge us with it, the interrogation would begin immediately. I remained quite calm and also tried to calm my sister's fears. Probably she had not struck the door at all, and if she had it could never be proved. I tried to make this clear to the people around us ; they listened to me but refrained from passing any opinion. Later they told me that not only my sister, but I too, as her brother, would be charged. I nodded and smiled. We all gazed back at the manor, as one watches a distant smoke-cloud and waits for the flames to appear. And right enough we presently saw horsemen riding in through the wide-open gate. Dust rose, concealing everything, only the tops of the tall spears glittered. And hardly had the troop vanished into the manor courtyard before they seemed to have turned their horses again, for they were already on their way to us. I urged my sister to leave me, I myself would set everything right. She refused to leave me. I told her that she should at least change, so as to appear in better clothes before these gentlemen. At last she obeyed and set out on the long road to our home. Already the horsemen were beside us, and even before dismounting they enquired after my sister. She wasn't here at the moment, was the apprehensive reply, but she would come later. The answer was received with indifference ; the important thing seemed their having found me. The chief members of the party appeared to be a young lively fellow, who was a judge, and his silent assistant, who was called Assmann. I was commanded to enter the village inn. Shaking my head and hitching up my trousers I slowly began my statement, while the sharp eyes of the party scrutinised me. I still half believed that a word would be enough to free me, a city man, and with honour too, from this peasant folk. But when I had stepped over the threshold of the inn the judge, who had hastened in front and was already awaiting me, said : " I'm really sorry for this man." And it was beyond all possibility of doubt that by this he did not mean my present state, but something that was to happen to me. The room looked more like a prison cell than an inn parlour. Great stone flags on the floor, dark, quite bare walls, into one of which an iron rung was fixed, in the middle something that looked half a pallet, half an operating table.

Could I endure any other air than prison air now ? That is the great question, or rather it would be if I still had any prospect of release.

A CROSSBREED

I HAVE a curious animal, half-cat, half-lamb. It is a legacy from my father. But it only developed in my time ; formerly it was far more lamb than cat. Now it is both in about equal parts. From the cat it takes its head and claws, from the lamb its size and shape ; from both its eyes, which are wild and changing, its hair, which is soft, lying close to its body, its movements, which partake both of skipping and slinking. Lying on the window-sill in the sun it curls itself up in a ball and purrs ; out in the meadow it rushes about as if mad and is scarcely to be caught. It flies from cats and makes to attack lambs. On moonlight nights its favourite promenade is the tiles. It cannot mew and it loathes rats. Beside the hen-coop it can lie for hours in ambush, but it has never yet seized an opportunity for murder.

I feed it on milk ; that seems to suit it best. In long draughts it sucks the milk into it through its teeth of a beast of prey. Naturally it is a great source of entertainment for children. Sunday morning is the visiting hour. I sit with the little beast on my knees, and the children of the whole neighbourhood stand round me.

Then the strangest questions are asked, which no human being could answer : Why there is only one such animal, why I rather than anybody else should own it, whether there was ever an animal like it before and what would happen if it died, whether it feels lonely, why it has no children, what it is called, etc.

I never trouble to answer, but confine myself without further explanation to exhibiting my possession. Sometimes the children bring cats with them ; once they actually brought two lambs. But against all their hopes there was no scene of recognition. The animals gazed calmly at each other with their animal eyes, and obviously accepted their reciprocal existence as a divine fact.

Sitting on my knees the beast knows neither fear nor lust of pursuit. Pressed against me it is happiest. It remains faithful to the family that brought it up. In that there is certainly no extraordinary mark of fidelity, but merely the true instinct of an animal which, though it has countless step-relations in the world, has perhaps not a single blood relation, and to which consequently the protection it has found with us is sacred.

Sometimes I cannot help laughing when it sniffs round me and winds itself between my legs and simply will not be parted from me. Not content with being lamb and cat, it almost insists on being a dog as well. Once when, as may happen to any one, I could see no way out of my business difficulties and all that depends on such things, and had resolved to let everything go, and in this mood was lying in my rocking-chair in my room, the beast on my knees, I happened to glance down and saw tears dropping from its huge whiskers. Were they mine, or were they the animal's ? Had this cat, along with the soul of a lamb, the ambitions of a human being ? I did not inherit much from my father, but this legacy is worth looking at.

It has the restlessness of both beasts, that of the cat and that of the lamb, diverse as they are. For that reason its skin feels too narrow for it. Sometimes it jumps up on the armchair beside me, plants its front legs on my shoulder, and puts its muzzle to my ear. It is as if it were saying something to me, and as a matter of fact it turns its head afterwards and gazes in my face to see the impression its communication has made. And to oblige it I behave as if I had understood and nod. Then it jumps to the floor and dances about with joy.

Perhaps the knife of the butcher would be a release for this animal ; but as it is a legacy I must deny it that. So it must wait until the breath voluntarily leaves its body, even though it sometimes gazes at me with a look of human understanding, challenging me to do the thing of which both of us are thinking.

THE BRIDGE

I WAS stiff and cold, I was a bridge, I lay over a ravine. My toes on one side, my fingers clutching the other, I had clamped myself fast into the crumbling clay, the tails of my coat fluttered at my sides. Far below brawled the icy trout stream. No tourist strayed to this impassable height, the bridge was not yet traced on any map. So I lay and waited ; I could only wait. Without falling no bridge, once spanned, can cease to be a bridge.

It was towards evening one day—was it the first, was it the thousandth ? I cannot tell—my thoughts were always in confusion and perpetually moving in a circle. It was towards evening in summer, the roar of the stream had grown deeper, when I heard the sound of a human step! To me, to me. Straighten yourself, bridge, make ready, railless beams, to hold up the passenger entrusted to you. If his steps are uncertain steady them unobtrusively, but if he stumbles show what you are made of and like a mountain god hurl him across to land.

He came, he tapped me with the iron point of his stick, then he lifted my coat-tails with it and put them in order upon me. He plunged the point of his stick into my bushy hair and let it lie there for a long time, forgetting me no doubt while he wildly gazed round him. But then—I was just following him in thought over mountain and valley—he jumped with both feet on the middle of my body. I shuddered with wild pain, not

knowing what was happening. Who was it? A child?
A dream? A wayfarer? A suicide? A tempter? A
destroyer? And I turned round so as to see him. A
bridge to turn round! I had not yet turned quite round
when I already began to fall. I fell and in a moment I
was torn and transpierced by the sharp rocks which had
always gazed up at me so peacefully from the rushing
water.

THE VULTURE

A VULTURE was hacking at my feet. It had already torn my boots and stockings to shreds, now it was hacking at the feet themselves. Again and again it struck at them, then circled several times restlessly round me, then returned to continue its work. A gentleman passed by, looked on for a while, then asked me why I suffered the vulture. "I'm helpless," I said. "When it came and began to attack me, I of course tried to drive it away, even to strangle it, but these animals are very strong, it was about to spring at my face, but I preferred to sacrifice my feet. Now they are almost torn to bits." "Fancy letting yourself be tortured like this!" said the gentleman. "One shot and that's the end of the vulture." "Really?" I said. "And would you do that?" "With pleasure," said the gentleman, "I've only got to go home and get my gun. Could you wait another half hour?" "I'm not sure about that," said I, and stood for a moment rigid with pain. Then I said: "Do try it in any case, please." "Very well," said the gentleman, "I'll be as quick as I can." During this conversation the vulture had been calmly listening, letting its eye rove between me and the gentleman. Now I realised that it had understood everything; it took wing, leaned far back to gain impetus, and then, like a javelin thrower, thrust its beak through my mouth, deep into me. Falling back, I was relieved to feel him drowning irretrievably in my blood, which was filling every depth, flooding every shore.

THE DEPARTURE

I ORDERED my horse to be brought from the stables.
The servant did not understand my orders. So I went
to the stables myself, saddled my horse, and mounted.
In the distance I heard the sound of a trumpet, and I
asked the servant what it meant. He knew nothing
and had heard nothing. At the gate he stopped me and
asked: " Where is the master going?" " I don't know,"
I said, "just out of here, just out of here. Out of here,
nothing else, it's the only way I can reach my goal." " So
you know your goal?" he asked. " Yes," I replied,
" I've just told you. Out of here—that's my goal."

GIVE IT UP !

IT was very early in the morning, the streets clean and deserted, I was on my way to the station. As I compared the tower clock with my watch I realised it was much later than I had thought and that I had to hurry ; the shock of this discovery made me feel uncertain of the way, I wasn't very well acquainted with the town as yet ; fortunately, there was a policeman at hand, I ran to him and breathlessly asked him the way. He smiled and said : " You asking me the way ? " " Yes," I said, " since I can't find it myself." " Give it up ! Give it up ! " said he, and turned with a sudden jerk, like someone who wants to be alone with his laughter.

AT NIGHT

DEEPLY lost in the night. Just as one sometimes lowers one's head to reflect, thus to be utterly lost in the night. All around people are asleep. It's just play acting, an innocent self-deception, that they sleep in houses, in safe beds, under a safe roof, stretched out or curled up on mattresses, in sheets, under blankets; in reality they have flocked together as they had once upon a time and again later in a deserted region, a camp in the open, a countless number of men, an army, a people, under a cold sky on cold earth, collapsed where once they had stood, forehead pressed on the arm, face to the ground, breathing quietly. And you are watching, are one of the watchmen, you find the next one by brandishing a burning stick from the brushwood pile beside you. Why are you watching? Someone must watch, it is said. Someone must be there.

THE HELMSMAN

" AM I not the helmsman here?" I called out. "You?"
asked a tall dark man and passed his hands over
his eyes as though to banish a dream. I had been standing
at the helm in the dark night, a feeble lantern burning
over my head, and now this man had come and tried to
push me aside. And as I would not yield, he put his
foot on my chest and slowly crushed me while I still
clung to the hub of the helm, wrenching it round in
falling. But the man seized it, pulled it back in place,
and pushed me away. I soon collected myself, however,
ran to the hatchway which gave on to the mess quarters,
and cried out : " Men ! Comrades ! Come here,
quick ! A stranger has driven me away from the helm ! "
Slowly they came up, climbing the companion ladder,
tired, swaying, powerful figures. " Am I the helmsman ? " I asked. They nodded, but they had eyes only
for the stranger, stood round him in a semicircle, and
when, in a commanding voice, he said : " Don't disturb
me ! " they gathered together, nodded at me, and withdrew
down the companion ladder. What kind of people are
these ? Do they ever think, or do they only shuffle
pointlessly over the earth ?

THE TOP

A CERTAIN philosopher used to hang about wherever children were at play. And whenever he saw a boy with a top, he would lie in wait. As soon as the top began to spin the philosopher went in pursuit and tried to catch it. He was not perturbed when the children noisily protested and tried to keep him away from their toy ; so long as he could catch the top while it was still spinning, he was happy, but only for a moment; then he threw it to the ground and walked away. For he believed that the understanding of any detail, that of a spinning top, for instance, was sufficient for the understanding of all things. For this reason he did not busy himself with great problems, it seemed to him uneconomical. Once the smallest detail was understood, then everything was understood, which was why he busied himself only with the spinning top. And whenever preparations were being made for the spinning of the top, he hoped that this time it would succeed : as soon as the top began to spin and he was running breathlessly after it, the hope would turn to certainty, but when he held the silly piece of wood in his hand, he felt nauseated. The screaming of the children, which hitherto he had not heard and which now suddenly pierced his ears, chased him away, and he tottered like a top under a clumsy whip.

A LITTLE FABLE

"ALAS," said the mouse, "the world is growing smaller every day. At the beginning it was so big that I was afraid, I kept running and running, and I was glad when at last I saw walls far away to the right and left, but these long walls have narrowed so quickly that I am in the last chamber already, and there in the corner stands the trap that I must run into." "You only need to change your direction," said the cat, and ate it up.

THE BUCKET RIDER

COAL all spent ; the bucket empty ; the shovel useless ; the stove breathing out cold ; the room freezing ; the leaves outside the window rigid, covered with rime ; the sky a silver shield against any one who looks for help from it. I must have coal ; I cannot freeze to death ; behind me is the pitiless stove, before me the pitiless sky, so I must ride out between them and on my journey seek aid from the coal-dealer. But he has already grown deaf to ordinary appeals ; I must prove irrefutably to him that I have not a single grain of coal left, and that he means to me the very sun in the firmament. I must approach like a beggar, who, with the death-rattle already in his throat, insists on dying on the doorstep, and to whom the gentlefolk's cook accordingly decides to give the dregs of the coffee-pot ; just so must the coal-dealer, filled with rage, but acknowledging the command, " Thou shalt not kill," fling a shovelful of coal into my bucket.

My mode of arrival must decide the matter ; so I ride off on the bucket. Seated on the bucket, my hands on the handle, the simplest kind of bridle, I propel myself with difficulty down the stairs ; but once down below my bucket ascends, superbly, superbly ; camels humbly squatting on the ground do not rise with more dignity, shaking themselves under the sticks of their drivers. Through the hard frozen streets we go at a regular canter ; often I am upraised as high as the first storey of a house ; never do I sink as low as the house doors. And at last I float at an extraordinary height above the vaulted cellar of the dealer, whom I see far below crouching over his table, where he is writing ; he has opened the door to let out the excessive heat.

" Coal-dealer ! " I cry in a voice burned hollow by the frost and muffled in the cloud made by my breath, " please, coal-dealer, give me a little coal. My bucket is so light that I can ride on it. Be kind. When I can I'll pay you."

The dealer puts his hand to his ear. " Do I hear rightly ? " he throws the question over his shoulder to his wife. " Do I hear rightly ? A customer."

" I hear nothing," says his wife, breathing in and out peacefully while she knits on, her back pleasantly warmed by the heat.

" Oh, yes, you must hear," I cry. " It's me ; an old customer ; faithful and true ; only without means at the moment."

" Wife," says the dealer, " it's someone, it must be ; my ears can't have deceived me so much as that ; it must be an old, a very old customer, that can move me so deeply."

" What ails you, man ? " says his wife, ceasing from her work for a moment and pressing her knitting to her bosom. " It's nobody, the street is empty, all our customers are provided for ; we could close down the shop for several days and take a rest."

" But I'm sitting up here on the bucket," I cry, and unfeeling frozen tears dim my eyes, " please look up here, just once ; you'll see me directly ; I beg you, just a shovelful ; and if you give me more it'll make me so happy that I won't know what to do. All the other

customers are provided for. Oh, if I could only hear
the coal clattering into the bucket ! "

" I'm coming," says the coal-dealer, and on his short
legs he makes to climb the steps of the cellar, but his
wife is already beside him, holds him back by the arm
and says : " You stay here ; seeing you persist in your
fancies I'll go myself. Think of the bad fit of coughing
you had during the night. But for a piece of business,
even if it's one you've only fancied in your head, you're
prepared to forget your wife and child and sacrifice your
lungs. I'll go."

" Then be sure to tell him all the kinds of coal we
have in stock ; I'll shout out the prices after you."

" Right," says his wife, climbing up to the street.
Naturally she sees me at once. " Frau Coal-dealer," I
cry, " my humblest greetings ; just one shovelful of
coal ; here in my bucket ; I'll carry it home myself.
One shovelful of the worst you have. I'll pay you in full
for it, of course, but not just now, not just now."
What a knell-like sound the words " not just now "
have, and how bewilderingly they mingle with the
evening chimes that fall from the church steeple near by !

" Well, what does he want ? " shouts the dealer.
" Nothing," his wife shouts back, " there's nothing
here ; I see nothing, I hear nothing ; only six striking,
and now we must shut up the shop. The cold is terrible ;
tomorrow we'll likely have lots to do again."

She sees nothing and hears nothing ; but all the same
she loosens her apron-strings and waves her apron to waft
me away. She succeeds, unluckily. My bucket has all
the virtues of a good steed except powers of resistance,
which it has not ; it is too light ; a woman's apron can
make it fly through the air.

" You bad woman ! " I shout back, while she, turning into the shop, half-contemptuous, half-reassured, flour-ishes her fist in the air. " You bad woman ! I begged you for a shovelful of the worst coal and you would not give it me." And with that I ascend into the regions of the ice mountains and am lost for ever.

THE MARRIED COUPLE

BUSINESS in general is so bad that sometimes, when my work in the office leaves me a little time, I myself pick up the case of samples and call on my customers personally. Long since I had intended to visit some time, among others, N., with whom once I had constant business relations, which, however, during the last year have almost completely lapsed for some reason unknown to me. Besides, there need not always be real reasons for such misfortunes; in the present unstable state of affairs often a mere nothing, a word, will turn the scale, and in the same way a mere nothing, a word, can put things right again. To gain admittance to N., however, is a somewhat ticklish business; he is an old man, grown somewhat infirm too of late, and though he still insists on attending to business matters himself, he is hardly ever to be seen in his office; if you want to speak to him you have to go to his house, and one gladly puts off a business call of that kind.

Last evening after six I nevertheless set out for his house; it was really no time for paying calls, but my visit after all was a business, not a social one, and might be regarded accordingly. I was in luck. N. was in; he had just come back with his wife from a walk, the servant told me, and was now in the bedroom of his son, who was unwell and confined to his bed. I was requested to go there; at first I hesitated, but then the desire to get my disagreeable visit over as quickly as possible turned the scale, and I allowed myself to be conducted as I was, in my overcoat and hat and with my case of samples, through a dark room into a faintly lit one, where a small company was gathered.

My first glance fell, probably by instinct, on an agent only too well known to me, a trade rival of my own in some respects. So he had stolen a march on me, it seemed. He was sitting comfortably by the bed of the sick man, just as if he were a doctor; he sat brazenly there in his beautiful ample overcoat, which was un-buttoned; the sick man too probably had his own thoughts as he lay there with his cheeks faintly flushed with fever, now and then glancing at his visitor. He was no longer young either, N.'s son, a man of about my own age with a short beard, somewhat unkempt on account of his illness. Old N., a tall, broad-shouldered man, but to my astonishment grown very thin because of some creeping malady, bent and infirm, was still wearing the fur coat in which he had entered, and mumbling some-thing to his son. His wife, small and frail, but im-mensely vivacious, yet only when she spoke to him—us others she scarcely noticed—was occupied in helping him to take off his overcoat, which, considering the great difference in their height, was a matter of some difficulty, but at last was achieved. Perhaps, indeed, the real difficulty was caused by N.'s impatience, for with restless hands he kept on feeling for the easy chair, which his wife, after the overcoat was off, quickly pushed forward for him. She herself then took up the fur coat, beneath which she almost vanished, and carried it out.

Now at last, it seemed to me, my moment had come, or rather it had not come and probably would never come; yet if I was to attempt anything it must be done at once, for I felt that here the conditions for a business interview could only become increasingly unfavourable ; and to plant myself down here for all time, as the agent apparently intended, was not my way ; besides, I did not want to take the slightest notice of him. So I began without ceremony to state my business, although I saw that N. would have liked at that moment to have a chat with his son. Unfortunately I have a habit when I have worked myself up—and that takes a very short time, and on this occasion took a shorter time than usual—of getting up and walking about while I am talking. Though a very good arrangement in one's own office, in a strange house it may be somewhat burdensome. But I could not restrain myself, particularly as I was feeling the lack of my usual cigarette. Well, every man has his bad habits, yet I can congratulate myself on mine when I think of the agent's. For what is to be said of his behaviour, of the fact, for instance, that every now and then he would suddenly and quite unexpectedly clap his hat on his head ; he had been holding it on his knee until then, slowly pushing it up and down there. True, he took it off again immediately, as if he had made a blunder, but he had had it on his head nevertheless for a second or two, and besides he repeated this performance again and again every few minutes. Surely such conduct must be called unpardonable. It did not disturb me, however. I walked up and down, completely absorbed in my own proposals, and ignored him ; but there are people whom that trick with the hat might have put off completely. However, when I am thoroughly worked up I disregard not only such annoyances as these, but everything. I see, it is true, all that is going on, but do not admit it, so to speak, to my consciousness until I am finished, or until some objection has been raised. Thus I noticed quite well, for instance, that N. was by no means in a receptive state ; holding on to the arms of his chair, he twisted about uncomfortably, never even glanced up at me, but gazed blankly, as if searching for something, into vacancy, and his face was so impassive that one might have thought no syllable of what I was saying, indeed no awareness of my presence, had penetrated to him. Yes, his whole bearing, the bearing of a sick man, in itself inauspicious for me, I took in quite well ; nevertheless I talked on as if I had still some prospect of putting everything right again by my talk, by the advantageous offers I made—I was myself alarmed by the concessions I granted, concessions that had not even been asked for. It gave me a certain satisfaction also to notice that the agent, as I verified by a fleeting glance, had at last left his hat in peace and folded his arms across his chest ; my performance, which was partly, I must confess, intended for him, seemed to have given a severe blow to his designs. And in the elation produced by this result I might perhaps have gone on talking for a long time still, if the son, whom until now I had regarded as a secondary factor in my plans, had not suddenly raised himself in his bed and pulled me up by shaking his fist. Obviously he wanted to say something, to point out something, but he had not strength enough. At first I thought that his mind was wandering, but then I involuntarily glanced at old N. I understood better.

N. sat with wide-open, glassy, bulging eyes, which seemed on the point of failing ; he was trembling and his body was bent forward as if someone were holding him down or striking him on the shoulders ; his lower lip, indeed the lower jaw itself with the exposed gums, hung down helplessly ; his whole face seemed out of drawing ; he still breathed, though with difficulty ; but then, as if delivered, he fell back against the back of his chair, closed his eyes, the mark of some great strain passed over his face and vanished, and all was over. I sprang to him and seized his lifeless hand, which was so cold that it sent a chill through me ; no pulse beat there now. So it was all over. Still, he was a very old man. We would be fortunate if we all had such an easy death. But how much there was to be done ! And what should one do first ? I looked round for help ; but the son had drawn the bedclothes over his head, and I could hear his wild sobbing ; the agent, cold as a fish, sat immovably on his chair, two steps from N., and was obviously resolved to do nothing, to wait for what time would bring ; so I, only I was left to do something, and the hardest thing that anyone could be asked to do, that was to tell the news to his wife in some bearable form, in a form that did not exist, in other words. And already I could hear her eager shuffling steps in the next room.

Still wearing her outdoor clothes—she had not found time to change—she bore in a night-shirt that she had warmed before the fire for her husband to put on. " He's fallen asleep," she said, smiling and shaking her head, when she found us sitting so still. And with the infinite trustfulness of the innocent she took up the same hand that I had held a moment before with such fear and repugnance, kissed it playfully, and—how could we three others have borne the sight ?—N. moved, yawned loudly, allowed his night-shirt to be put on, endured with a mixture of annoyance and irony his wife's tender reproaches for having overstrained himself by taking such a long walk, and strangely enough said in reply, to provide no doubt a different explanation for his having fallen asleep, something about feeling bored. Then, so as not to catch cold by going through the draughty passage into a different room, he lay down for the time being in his son's bed ; a pillow was made beside his son's feet with two cushions hastily brought by his wife. After all that had gone before I found nothing particularly odd in that. Then he asked for the evening paper, opened it without paying any attention to his guests, but did not read it, only glancing through it here and there, and made several very unpleasant observations on our offers, observations which showed astonishing shrewdness, while he waved his free hand disdainfully, and clicking his tongue indicated that our business methods had left a bad taste in his mouth. The agent could not refrain from making one or two untimely remarks, no doubt he felt in his insensitive way that some compensation was due to him after what had happened, but his way of securing it was the worst he could have chosen. I said good-bye as soon as I could, I felt almost grateful to the agent ; if he had not been there I would not have had the resolution to leave so soon.

In the lobby I met Frau N. again. At the sight of that pathetic figure I said impulsively that she reminded me a little of my mother. And as she remained silent I added : " Whatever people say, she could do wonders. Things that we destroyed she could make whole again. I lost her when I was still a child." I had spoken with deliberate slowness and distinctness, for I assumed the old lady was hard of hearing. But she must have been quite deaf, for she asked without transition : " And what does my husband intend to do about your offer ? "

From a few parting words I noticed, moreover, that she confused me with the agent ; I like to think that otherwise she would have been more forthcoming.

Then I descended the stairs. The descent was more tiring than the ascent had been, and not even that had been easy. Oh, how many business calls come to nothing, and yet one must keep going.

MY NEIGHBOUR

MY business rests entirely on my own shoulders. Two girl clerks with typewriters and ledgers in the front office, my own room with writing-desk, safe, consulting-table, easy chair and telephone : such is my entire working apparatus. So simple to control, so easy to direct. I'm quite young, and a lot of business comes my way. I don't complain, I don't complain.

At the beginning of the year a young man snapped up the empty premises next to mine, which very foolishly I hesitated to close with until too late. They also consist of a room and a front room, with a kitchen, however, thrown in—a room and a front room I would certainly have found some use for, my two girls clerk feel somewhat overdriven as it is—but what use would a kitchen have been to me ? This petty consideration was solely responsible for my allowing the premises to be snatched from under my nose. Now that young man sits there. Harras, his name is. What he actually does there I have no idea. On the door there is a plate : " Harras Bureau." I have made enquiries and I am told it is a business similar to mine. One can't exactly warn people against giving the fellow credit, for after all he is a young and pushing man who probably has a future ; yet one can't advise people to trust him either, for by all appearances he has no assets so far. The usual thing said by people who don't know.

Sometimes I meet Harras on the stairs ; he seems

always to be in an extraordinary hurry, for he literally shoots past me. I have never got a good look at him yet, for his office key is always in his hand when he passes me. In a tick he has the door open. Like the tail of a rat he has slipped through and I'm left standing again before the plate " Harras Bureau," which I have read already far oftener than it deserves.

The wretchedly thin walls betray the honourable and capable man, but shield the dishonest. My telephone is fixed to the wall that separates me from my neighbour. But I single that out merely as a particularly ironical circumstance. For even if it hung on the opposite wall, everything could be heard in the next room. I have accustomed myself to refrain from naming the names of my customers when speaking on the telephone to them. But of course it does not need much skill to guess the names from characteristic but unavoidable turns of the conversation. Sometimes I absolutely dance with apprehension round the telephone, the receiver at my ear, and yet can't help divulging the secret.

Because of all this my business decisions have naturally become unsure, my voice nervous. What is Harras doing while I'm telephoning? If I wanted to exaggerate —and one must often do that so as to make things clear in one's mind—I might assert that Harras does not require a telephone, he uses mine, he pushes his sofa against the wall and listens ; while I at the other side must fly to the telephone, listen to all the requests of my customers, come to difficult and grave decisions, carry out long calculations—but worst of all, during all this time, involuntarily give Harras valuable information through the wall.

Perhaps he doesn't even wait for the end of the conversation, but gets up at the point where the matter has become clear to him, flies through the town with his usual haste, and before I have hung up the receiver, is already at his goal working against me.

THE TEST

I AM a servant, but there is no work for me. I am
timid and don't push myself to the fore, indeed I don't
even push myself into line with the others, but that is
only one reason for my non-employment, it's even
possible that it has nothing to do with my non-employment,
in any case the main thing is that I am not called upon
to serve, others have been called yet they have not tried
harder than I, indeed perhaps they have not even felt the
desire to be called, whereas I, at least sometimes, have
felt it very strongly.

So I lie on the pallet in the servants' hall, stare at the
beams in the ceiling, fall asleep, wake up and promptly
fall asleep again. Occasionally I walk over to the tavern
where they sell a sour beer, occasionally I have even
poured away a glass in disgust, but at other times I
drink it. I like sitting there because from behind the
closed little window, without the possibility of being
discovered, I can see across to the windows of our house.
Not that one sees very much there, to my knowledge
only the windows of the corridors look out on the street,
and moreover not even those of the corridors leading to
my employers' apartments. But it is also possible that
I am mistaken ; someone, without my having asked him,
once said so, and the general impression of this house
front confirms this. Only rarely are the windows
opened, and when this does occur it is done by a servant
who may lean against the balustrade to look down for a

while. It follows therefore that these are corridors where he cannot be taken by surprise. As a matter of fact I am not personally acquainted with these servants ; those who are permanently employed upstairs sleep elsewhere, not in my room.

Once when I arrived at the tavern, a guest was sitting at my observation post. I did not dare look at him closely and was about to turn round in the door and leave. The guest, however, called me over, and it turned out that he too was a servant whom I had once seen somewhere before, but without having spoken to him.

" Why do you want to run away ? Sit down and have a drink ! I'll pay." So I sat down. He asked me several things, but I couldn't answer, indeed I didn't even understand his questions. So I said : " Perhaps you are sorry now that you invited me, so I'd better go," and I was about to get up. But he stretched his hand out over the table and pressed me down. " Stay," he said, " that was only a test. He who does not answer the questions has passed the test."

ADVOCATES

I WAS not at all certain whether I had any advocates, I could not find out anything definite about it, every face was unfriendly, most people who came towards me and whom I kept meeting in the corridors looked like fat old women ; they had huge blue and white striped aprons covering their entire bodies, kept stroking their stomachs and swaying awkwardly to and fro. I could not even find out whether we were in a law court. Some facts spoke for it, others against. What reminded me of a law court more than all the details was a droning noise which could be heard incessantly in the distance ; one could not tell from which direction it came, it filled every room to such an extent that one had to assume it came from everywhere or, what seemed more likely, that just the place where one happened to be standing was the very place where the droning originated, but this was probably an illusion, for it came from a distance. These corridors, narrow and austerely vaulted, turning in gradual curves with high, sparsely decorated doors, seemed to have been created specially for profound silence ; they were the corridors of a museum or a library. Yet if it were not a law court, why was I searching for an advocate here ? Because I was searching for an advocate everywhere ; he is needed everywhere, if anything less in court than elsewhere, for a court, one assumes, passes judgment according to the law. If one were to assume that this was being done unfairly or frivolously, then

life would not be possible ; one must have confidence
that the court allows the majesty of the law its full scope,
for this is its sole duty. Within the law all is accusation,
advocacy, and verdict ; any interference by an individual
here would be a crime. It is different, however, in the
case of the verdict itself ; this is based on inquiries
being made here and there, from relatives and strangers,
from friends and enemies, in the family and public life,
in town and village—in short, everywhere. Here it is
most necessary to have advocates, advocates galore, the
best possible advocates, one next to the other, a living
wall, for advocates are by nature hard to set in motion ;
the plaintiffs, however, those sly foxes, those slinking
weasels, those little mice, they slip through the tiniest
gaps, scuttle through the legs of the advocates. So look
out ! That's why I am here, I'm collecting advocates.
But I have not found any as yet, only those old women
keep on coming and going ; if I were not on my search
it would put me to sleep. I'm not in the right place—
alas, I cannot rid myself of the feeling that I'm not in
the right place. I ought to be in a place where all kinds
of people meet, from various parts of the country, from
every class, every profession, of all ages ; I ought to
have an opportunity of choosing carefully out of a crowd
those who are kind, those who are able, and those who
have an eye for me. Perhaps the most suitable place for
this would be a huge fair-ground ; instead of which I
am hanging about in these corridors where only these old
women are to be seen, and not even many of them, and
always the same ones, and even those few will not let
themselves be cornered, despite their slowness ; they
slip away from me, float about like rain clouds, and are
completely absorbed by unknown activities. Why is it

then that I run headlong into a house without reading
the sign over the door, promptly find myself in these
corridors, and settle here with such obstinacy that I
cannot even remember ever having been in front of the
house, ever having run up the stairs ! But back I cannot
go, this waste of time, this admission of having been on
the wrong track would be unbearable for me. What ?
Run downstairs in this brief, hurried life accompanied as
it is by that impatient droning ? Impossible. The time
allotted to you is so short that if you lose one second you
have already lost your whole life, for it is no longer, it is
always just as long as the time you lose. So if you have
started out on a walk, continue it whatever happens ;
you can only gain, you run no risk, in the end you may
fall over a precipice perhaps, but had you turned back
after the first steps and run downstairs you would have
fallen at once—and not perhaps, but for certain. So if
you find nothing in the corridors open the doors, if you
find nothing behind these doors there are more floors,
and if you find nothing up there, don't worry, just leap
up another flight of stairs. As long as you don't stop
climbing the stairs won't end, under your climbing feet
they will go on growing upwards.

HOME-COMING

I HAVE returned, I have passed under the arch and I am looking round. It's my father's old yard. The puddle in the middle. Old, useless tools, jumbled together, block the way to the attic stairs. The cat lurks on the banister. A torn piece of cloth, once wound round a stick in a game, flutters in the breeze. I have arrived. Who is going to receive me? Who is waiting behind the kitchen door? Smoke is rising from the chimney, coffee is being made for supper. Do you feel you belong, do you feel at home? I don't know, I feel most uncertain. My father's house it is, but each object stands cold beside the next, as though preoccupied with its own affairs, which I have partly forgotten, partly never known. What use can I be to them, what do I mean to them, even though I am the son of my father, the old farmer? And I don't dare knock at the kitchen door, I only listen from a distance, I only listen from a distance, standing up, in such a way that I cannot be taken by surprise as an eavesdropper. And since I am listening from a distance, I hear nothing but a faint striking of the clock passing over from childhood days, but perhaps I only think I hear it. Whatever else is going on in the kitchen is the secret of those sitting there, a secret they are keeping from me. The longer one hesitates before the door, the more estranged one becomes. What would happen if someone were to open the door now and ask me a question? Would not I myself then behave like one who wants to keep his secret?

FELLOWSHIP

WE are five friends, one day we came out of a house one after the other, first one came and placed himself beside the gate, then the second came, or rather he glided through the gate like a ball of quicksilver, and placed himself near the first one, then came the third, then the fourth, then the fifth. Finally we all stood in a row. People began to notice us, they pointed at us and said : Those five just came out of that house. Since then we have been living together ; it would be a peaceful life if it weren't for a sixth one continually trying to interfere. He doesn't do us any harm, but he annoys us, and that is harm enough ; why does he intrude where he is not wanted ? We don't know him and don't want him to join us. There was a time, of course, when the five of us did not know one another, either ; and it could be said that we still don't know one another, but what is possible and can be tolerated by the five of us is not possible and cannot be tolerated with this sixth one. In any case, we are five and don't want to be six. And what is the point of this continual being together anyhow ? It is also pointless for the five of us, but here we are together and will remain together ; a new combination, however, we do not want, just because of our experiences. But how is one to make all this clear to the sixth one ? Long explanations would almost amount to accepting him in our circle, so we prefer not to explain and not to accept him. No matter how he pouts his lips we push him away with our elbows, but however much we push him away, back he comes.

BLUMFELD, AN ELDERLY BACHELOR

ONE evening Blumfeld, an elderly bachelor, was climbing up to his apartment—a laborious undertaking, for he lived on the sixth floor. While climbing up he thought, as he had so often recently, how unpleasant this utterly lonely life was : to reach his empty rooms he had to climb these six floors almost in secret, there put his dressing gown on, again almost in secret, light his pipe, read a little of the French magazine to which he had been subscribing for years, at the same time sip at a homemade kirsch, and finally, after half an hour, go to bed, but not before having completely rearranged his bedclothes which the unteachable charwoman would insist on arranging in her own way. Some companion, someone to witness these activities, would have been very welcome to Blumfeld. He had already been wondering whether he shouldn't acquire a little dog. These animals are gay and above all grateful and loyal ; one of Blumfeld's colleagues has a dog of this kind ; it follows no one but its master and when it hasn't seen him for a few moments it greets him at once with loud barkings, by which it is evidently trying to express its joy at once more finding that extraordinary benefactor, its master. True, a dog also has its drawbacks. However well kept it may be, it is bound to dirty the room. This just cannot be avoided ; one cannot give it a hot bath each time before letting it into the room ; besides, its health couldn't stand that. Blumfeld, on the other hand, can't stand dirt in his room. To him cleanliness is essential, and several times a week he is obliged to have words with his charwoman, who is unfortunately not very painstaking in this respect. Since she is hard of hearing he usually drags her by the arm to those spots in the room which he finds lacking in cleanliness. By this strict discipline he has achieved in his room a neatness more or less commensurate with his wishes. By acquiring a dog, however, he would be almost deliberately introducing into his room the dirt which hitherto he had been so careful to avoid. Fleas, the dog's constant companions, would appear. And once fleas were there, it would not be long before Blumfeld would be abandoning his comfortable room to the dog and looking for another one. Uncleanliness, however, is but one of the drawbacks of dogs. Dogs also fall ill and no one really understands dogs' diseases. Then the animal sits in a corner or limps about, whimpers, coughs, chokes from some pain ; one wraps it in a rug, whistles a little melody, offers it milk—in short, one nurses it in the hope that this, as indeed is possible, is a passing sickness while it may be a serious, disgusting, and contagious disease. And even if the dog remains healthy, one day it will grow old, one won't have the heart to get rid of the faithful animal in time, and then comes the moment when one's own age peers out at one from the dog's oozing eyes. Then one has to cope with the half-blind, weak-lunged animal all but immobile with fat, and in this way pay dearly for the pleasures the dog once had given. Much as Blumfeld would like to have a dog at this moment, he would rather go on climbing the stairs alone for another thirty years than be burdened later on by such an old dog which, sighing louder than he, would drag itself up, step by step.

So Blumfeld will remain alone, after all ; he really feels none of the old maid's longing to have around her some submissive living creature that she can protect, lavish her affection upon, and continue to serve—for which purpose a cat, a canary, even a goldfish would suffice—or, if this cannot be, rest content with flowers on the windowsill. Blumfeld only wants a companion, an animal to which he doesn't have to pay much attention, which doesn't mind an occasional kick, which even, in an emergency, can spend the night in the street, but which nevertheless, when Blumfeld feels like it, is promptly at his disposal with its barking, jumping, and licking of hands. This is what Blumfeld wants, but since, as he realises, it cannot be had without serious drawbacks, he renounces it, and yet—in accordance with his thoroughgoing disposition—the idea from time to time, this evening, for instance, occurs to him again.

While taking the key from his pocket outside his room, he is startled by a sound coming from within. A peculiar rattling sound, very lively but very regular. Since Blumfeld has just been thinking of dogs, it reminds him of the sounds produced by paws pattering one after the other over a floor. But paws don't rattle, so it can't be paws. He quickly unlocks the door and switches on the light. He is not prepared for what he sees. For this is magic—two small white celluloid balls with blue stripes jumping up and down side by side on the parquet ; when one of them touches the floor the other is in the air, a game they continue ceaselessly to play. At school one day Blumfeld had seen some little pellets jumping about like this during a well-known electrical experiment, but these are comparatively large balls jumping freely about in the room and no electrical experiment is being made. Blumfeld bends down to get a good look at them. They are undoubtedly ordinary balls, they probably contain several smaller balls, and it is these which produce the rattling sound. Blumfeld gropes in the air to find out whether they are hanging from some threads—no, they are moving entirely on their own. A pity Blumfeld isn't a small child, two balls like these would have been a happy surprise for him, whereas now the whole thing gives him rather an unpleasant feeling. It's not quite pointless after all to live in secret as an unnoticed bachelor, now someone, no matter who, has penetrated this secret and sent him these two strange balls.

He tries to catch one but they retreat before him, thus luring him on to follow them through the room. It's really too silly, he thinks, running after balls like this ; he stands still and realises that the moment he abandons the pursuit, they too remain on the same spot. I will try to catch them all the same, he thinks again, and hurries towards them. They immediately run away, but Blumfeld, his legs apart, forces them into a corner of the room, and there, in front of a trunk, he manages to catch one ball. It's a small cool ball, and it turns in his hand, clearly anxious to slip away. And the other ball, too, as though aware of its comrade's distress, jumps higher than before, extending the leaps until it touches Blumfeld's hand. It beats against his hand, beats in ever faster leaps, alters its angle of attack, then, powerless against the hand which encloses the ball so completely, springs even higher and is probably trying to reach Blumfeld's face. Blumfeld could catch this ball too, and lock them both up somewhere, but at the moment it strikes him as too humiliating to take such measures against two little balls. Besides, it's fun owning these balls, and soon enough they'll grow tired, roll under the cupboard, and be quiet. Despite this deliberation, however, Blumfeld, near to anger, flings the ball to the ground, and it is a miracle that in doing so the delicate, all but transparent celluloid cover doesn't break. Without hesitation the two balls resume their former low, well-coördinated jumps.

Blumfeld undresses calmly, arranges his clothes in the wardrobe which he always inspects carefully to make sure the charwoman has left everything in order. Once or twice he glances over his shoulder at the balls which, unpursued, seem to be pursuing him ; they have followed him and are now jumping close behind him. Blumfeld puts on his dressing gown and sets out for the opposite wall to fetch one of the pipes which are hanging in a rack. Before turning round he instinctively kicks his foot out backwards, but the balls know how to get out of its way and remain untouched. As Blumfeld goes off to fetch the pipe the balls at once follow close behind him ; he shuffles along in his slippers, taking irregular steps, yet each step is followed almost without pause by the sound of the balls ; they are keeping pace with him. To see how the balls manage to do this, Blumfeld turns suddenly round. But hardly has he turned when the balls describe a semicircle and are already behind him again, and this they repeat every time he turns. Like submissive companions, they try to avoid appearing in front of Blumfeld. Up to the present they have evidently dared to do so only in order to introduce themselves ; now, however, it seems they have actually entered into his service.

Hitherto, when faced with situations he couldn't master, Blumfeld had always chosen to behave as though he hadn't noticed anything. It had often helped and usually improved the situation. This, then, is what he does now ; he takes up a position in front of the pipe rack and, puffing out his lips, chooses a pipe, fills it with particular care from the tobacco pouch close at hand, and allows the balls to continue their jumping behind him. But he hesitates to approach the table, for to hear the sound of the jumps coinciding with that of his own steps almost hurts him. So there he stands, and while taking an unnecessarily long time to fill his pipe he measures the distance separating him from the table. At last, however, he overcomes his faintheartedness and covers the distance with such stamping of feet that he cannot hear the balls. But the moment he is seated he can hear them jumping up and down behind his chair as distinctly as ever.

Above the table, within reach, a shelf is nailed to the wall on which stands the bottle of kirsch surrounded by little glasses. Beside it, in a pile, lie several copies of the French magazine. (This very day the latest issue has arrived and Blumfeld takes it down. He quite forgets the kirsch ; he even has the feeling that today he is proceeding with his usual activities only to console himself, for he feels no genuine desire to read. Contrary to his usual habit of carefully turning one page after the other, he opens the magazine at random and there finds a large photograph. He forces himself to examine it in detail. It shows a meeting between the Czar of Russia and the President of France. This takes place on a ship. All about as far as can be seen are many other ships, the smoke from their funnels vanishing in the bright sky.

Both Czar and President have rushed towards each other with long strides and are clasping one another by the hand. Behind the Czar as well as behind the President stand two men. By comparison with the gay faces of the Czar and the President, the faces of their attendants are very solemn, the eyes of each group focused on their master. Lower down—the scene evidently takes place on the top deck—stand long lines of saluting sailors cut off by the margin. Gradually Blumfeld contemplates the picture with more interest, then holds it a little further away and looks at it with blinking eyes. He has always had a taste for such imposing scenes. The way the chief personages clasp each other's hand so naturally, so cordially and lightheartedly, this he finds most lifelike. And it's just as appropriate that the attendants—high-ranking gentlemen, of course, with their names printed beneath—express in their bearing the solemnity of the historical moment.)

And instead of helping himself to everything he needs, Blumfeld sits there tense, staring at the bowl of his still unlit pipe. He is lying in wait. Suddenly, quite unexpectedly, his numbness leaves him and with a jerk he turns round in his chair. But the balls, equally alert, or perhaps automatically following the law governing them, also change their position the moment Blumfeld turns, and hide behind his back. Blumfeld now sits with his back to the table, the cold pipe in his hand. And now the balls jump under the table and, since there's a rug there, they are less audible. This is a great advantage: only faint, hollow noises can be heard, one has to pay great attention to catch their sound. Blumfeld, however, does pay great attention, and hears them distinctly. But this is so only for the moment, in a little while he probably won't hear them any more. The fact that they cannot make themselves more audible on the rug strikes Blumfeld as a great weakness on the part of the balls. What one has to do is lay one or even better two rugs under them and they are all but powerless. Admittedly only for a limited time, and besides, their very existence wields a certain power.

Just now Blumfeld could have made good use of a dog, a wild young animal would soon have dealt with these balls ; he imagines this dog trying to catch them with its paws, chasing them from their positions, hunting them all over the room, and finally getting hold of them between its teeth. It's quite possible that before long Blumfeld will acquire a dog.

For the moment, however, the balls have no one to fear but Blumfeld, and he has no desire to destroy them just now, perhaps he lacks the necessary determination. He comes home in the evening tired from work and just when he is in need of some rest he is faced with this surprise. Only now does he realise how tired he really is. No doubt he will destroy the balls, and that in the near future, but not just yet, probably not until tomorrow. If one looks at the whole thing with an unprejudiced eye, the balls behave modestly enough. From time to time, for instance, they could jump into the foreground, show themselves, and then return again to their positions, or they could jump higher so as to beat against the table top in order to compensate themselves for the muffling effect of the rug. But this they don't do, they don't want to irritate Blumfeld unduly, they are evidently confining themselves to what is absolutely necessary.

Even this measured necessity, however, is quite sufficient to spoil Blumfeld's rest at the table. He has

been sitting there only a few minutes and is already
contemplating going to bed. One of his motives for this
is that he can't smoke here, for he has left the matches
on his bedside table. Thus he would have to fetch these
matches, but once having reached the bedside table he
might as well stay there and lie down. For this he has
an ulterior motive : he thinks that the balls, with their
mania for keeping behind him, will jump on to the bed
and that there, in lying down, on purpose or not, he
will squash them. The objection, that what would then
remain of the balls could still go on jumping, he dis-
misses. Even the unusual must have its limits. Complete balls jump anyway, even if not incessantly, but
fragments of balls never jump, and consequently will
not jump in this case, either. " Up ! " he shouts,
having grown almost reckless from this reflection and,
the balls still behind him, he stamps off to bed. His
hope seems to be confirmed, for when he purposely takes
up a position quite near the bed, one ball promptly
springs on to it. Then, however, the unexpected occurs :
the other ball disappears under the bed. The possibility
that the balls could jump under the bed as well had not
occurred to Blumfeld. He is outraged about the one
ball, although he is aware how unjust this is, for by
jumping under the bed the ball fulfils its duty perhaps
better than the ball on the bed. Now everything depends
on which place the balls decide to choose, for Blumfeld
does not believe that they can work separately for any
length of time. And sure enough a moment later the
ball on the floor also jumps on to the bed. Now I've
got them, thinks Blumfeld, hot with joy, and tears his
dressing gown from his body to throw himself into bed.
At that moment, however, the very same ball jumps

back under the bed.   Overwhelmed with disappointment, Blumfeld almost collapses.   Very likely the ball just took a good look round up there and decided it didn't like it.   And now the other one has followed, too, and of course remains, for it's better down there.   " Now I'll have these drummers with me all night," thinks Blumfeld, biting his lips and nodding his head.

He feels gloomy, without actually knowing what harm the balls could do him in the night.   He is a good sleeper, he will easily be able to ignore so slight a noise. To make quite sure of this and mindful of his past experience, he lays two rugs on the floor.   It's as if he owned a little dog for which he wants to make a soft bed.   And as though the balls had also grown tired and sleepy, their jumping has become lower and slower than before.   As Blumfeld kneels beside the bed, lamp in hand, he thinks for a moment that the balls might come to rest on the rug—they fall so weakly, roll so slowly along.   Then, however, they dutifully rise again.   Yet it is quite possible that in the morning when Blumfeld looks under the bed he'll find there two quiet, harmless children's balls.

But it seems that they may not even be able to keep up their jumping until the morning, for as soon as Blumfeld is in bed he doesn't hear them any more.   He strains his ears, leans out of bed to listen—not a sound. The effect of the rugs can't be as strong as that ;   the only explanation is that the balls are no longer jumping, either because they aren't able to bounce themselves off the rug and have therefore abandoned jumping for the time being or, which is more likely, they will never jump again.   Blumfeld could get up and see exactly what's going on, but in his relief at finding peace at last he

prefers to remain where he is. He would rather not
risk disturbing the pacified balls even with his eyes.
Even smoking he happily renounces, turns over on his
side, and promptly goes to sleep.

But he does not remain undisturbed; as usual he
sleeps without dreaming, but very restlessly. Innumerable times during the night he is startled by the delusion
that someone is knocking at his door. He knows quite
well that no one is knocking; who would knock at night
and at his lonely bachelor's door? Yet although he
knows this for certain, he is startled again and again and
each time glances in suspense at the door, his mouth
open, eyes wide, a strand of hair trembling over his
damp forehead. He tries to count how many times he
has been woken but, dizzy from the huge numbers he
arrives at, he falls back to sleep again. He thinks he
knows where the knocking comes from; not from the
door, but somewhere quite different; being heavy with
sleep, however, he cannot quite remember on what his
suspicions are based. All he knows is that innumerable
tiny unpleasant sounds accumulate before producing the
great strong knocking. He would happily suffer all the
unpleasantness of the small sounds if he could be spared
the actual knocking, but for some reason it's too late;
he cannot interfere, the moment has passed, he can't
even speak, his mouth opens but all that comes out is a
silent yawn, and furious at this he thrusts his face into
the pillows. Thus the night passes.

In the morning he is awakened by the charwoman's
knocking; with a sigh of relief he welcomes the gentle
tap on the door whose inaudibility has in the past always
been one of his sources of complaint. He is about to
shout " Come in ! " when he hears another lively, faint,

yet all but belligerent knocking. It's the balls under the bed. Have they woken up? Have they, unlike him, gathered new strength overnight? " Just a moment," shouts Blumfeld to the charwoman, jumps out of bed and, taking great care to keep the balls behind him, throws himself on the floor, his back still towards them ; then, twisting his head over his shoulder, he glances at the balls and—nearly lets out a curse. Like children pushing away blankets that annoy them at night, the balls have apparently spent all night pushing the rugs, with tiny twitching movements, so far away from under the bed that they are now once more on the parquet, where they can continue making their noise. " Back on to the rugs ! " says Blumfeld with an angry face, and only when the balls, thanks to the rugs, have become quiet again, does he call in the charwoman. While she —a fat, dull-witted, stiff-backed woman—is laying the breakfast on the table and doing the few necessary chores, Blumfeld stands motionless in his dressing gown by his bed so as to keep the balls in their place. With his eyes he follows the charwoman to see whether she notices anything. This, since she is hard of hearing, is very unlikely, and the fact that Blumfeld thinks he sees the charwoman stopping here and there, holding on to some furniture and listening with raised eyebrows, he puts down to his overwrought condition caused by a bad night's sleep. It would relieve him if he could persuade the charwoman to speed up her work, but if anything she is slower than usual. She loads herself laboriously with Blumfeld's clothes and shuffles out with them into the corridor, stays away a long time, and the din she makes beating the clothes echoes in his ears with slow, monotonous thuds. And during all this time Blumfeld has to remain on the bed, cannot move for fear of drawing the balls behind him, has to let the coffee—which he likes to drink as hot as possible—get cold, and can do nothing but stare at the drawn blinds behind which the day is dimly dawning. At last the charwoman has finished, bids him good morning, and is about to leave ; but before she actually goes she hesitates by the door, moves her lips a little, and takes a long look at Blumfeld. Blumfeld is about to remonstrate when she at last departs. Blumfeld longs to fling the door open and shout after her that she is a stupid, idiotic old woman. However, when he reflects on what he actually has against her, he can only think of the paradox of her having clearly noticed nothing and yet trying to give the impression that she has. How confused his thoughts have become ! And all on account of a bad night. Some explanation for his poor sleep he finds in the fact that last night he deviated from his usual habits by not smoking or drinking any schnapps. When for once I don't smoke or drink schnapps—and this is the result of his reflections—I sleep badly.

From now on he is going to take better care of his health, and he begins by fetching some cotton wool from his medicine chest which hangs over his bedside table and putting two little wads of it into his ears. Then he stands up and takes a trial step. Although the balls do follow he can hardly hear them ; the addition of another wad makes them quite inaudible. Blumfeld takes a few more steps ; nothing particularly unpleasant happens. Everyone for himself, Blumfeld as well as the balls, and although they are bound to one another they don't disturb each other. Only once, when Blumfeld turns round rather suddenly and one ball fails to make the counter-movement fast enough, does he touch it with his knee.

But this is the only incident. Otherwise Blumfeld calmly drinks his coffee ; he is as hungry as though, instead of sleeping last night, he had gone for a long walk ; he washes in cold, exceedingly refreshing water, and puts on his clothes. He still hasn't pulled up the blinds ; rather, as a precaution, he has preferred to remain in semi-darkness ; he has no wish for the balls to be seen by other eyes. But now that he is ready to go he has somehow to provide for the balls in case they should dare— not that he thinks they will—to follow him into the street. He thinks of a good solution, opens the large wardrobe, and places himself with his back to it. As though divining his intention, the balls steer clear of the wardrobe's interior, taking advantage of every inch of space between Blumfeld and the wardrobe ; when there's no other alternative they jump into the wardrobe for a moment, but when faced by the dark out they promptly jump again. Rather than be lured over the edge further into the wardrobe, they neglect their duty and stay by Blumfeld's side. But their little ruses avail them nothing, for now Blumfeld himself climbs backward into the wardrobe and they have to follow him. And with this their fate has been sealed, for on the floor of the wardrobe lie various smallish objects such as boots, boxes, small trunks which, although carefully arranged—Blumfeld now regrets this—nevertheless considerably hamper the balls. And when Blumfeld, having by now pulled the door almost to, jumps out of it with an enormous leap such as he has not made for years, slams the door and turns the key, the balls are imprisoned. " Well, that worked," thinks Blumfeld, wiping the sweat from his face. What a din the balls are making in the wardrobe ! It sounds as though they are desperate. Blumfeld, on the other hand, is very contented. He leaves the room and already the deserted corridor has a soothing effect on him. He takes the wool out of his ears and is enchanted by the countless sounds of the waking house. Few people are to be seen, it's still very early.

Downstairs in the hall in front of the low door leading to the charwoman's basement apartment stands that woman's ten-year-old son. The image of his mother, not one feature of the woman has been omitted in this child's face. Bandy-legged, hands in his trouser pockets, he stands there wheezing, for he already has a goitre and can breathe only with difficulty. But whereas Blumfeld, whenever the boy crosses his path, usually quickens his step to spare himself the spectacle, today he almost feels like pausing for a moment. Even if the boy has been brought into the world by this woman and shows every sign of his origin, he is nevertheless a child, the thoughts of a child still dwell in this shapeless head, and if one were to speak to him sensibly and ask him something, he would very likely answer in a bright voice, innocent and reverential, and after some inner struggle one could bring oneself to pat these cheeks. Although this is what Blumfeld thinks, he nevertheless passes him by. In the street he realises that the weather is pleasanter than he had suspected from his room. The morning mist has dispersed and patches of blue sky have appeared, brushed by a strong wind. Blumfeld has the balls to thank for his having left his room much earlier than usual ; even the paper he has left unread on the table ; in any case he has saved a great deal of time and can now afford to walk slowly. It is remarkable how little he worries about the balls now that he is separated from them. So long as

they were following him they could have been considered
as something belonging to him, something which, in
passing judgment on his person, had somehow to be
taken into consideration. Now, however, they were mere
toys in his wardrobe at home. And it occurs to Blumfeld
that the best way of rendering the balls harmless would
be to put them to their original use. There in the hall
stands the boy ; Blumfeld will give him the balls, not
lend them, but actually present them to him, which is
surely tantamount to ordering their destruction. And
even if they were to remain intact they would mean even
less in the boy's hands than in the wardrobe, the whole
house would watch the boy playing with them, other
children would join in, and the general opinion that the
balls are things to play with and in no way life companions of Blumfeld would be firmly and irrefutably
established. Blumfeld runs back into the house. The
boy has just gone down the basement stairs and is about
to open the door. So Blumfeld has to call the boy and
pronounce his name, a name that to him seems as ludicrous as everything else connected with the child.
" Alfred ! Alfred ! " he shouts. The boy hesitates for
a long time. " Come here ! " shouts Blumfeld. " I've
got something for you." The janitor's two little girls
appear from the door opposite and, full of curiosity,
take up positions on either side of Blumfeld. They
grasp the situation much more quickly than the boy and
cannot understand why he doesn't come at once. Without taking their eyes off Blumfeld they beckon to the
boy, but cannot fathom what kind of present is awaiting
Alfred. Tortured with curiosity, they hop from one
foot to the other. Blumfeld laughs at them as well as
at the boy. Then latter seems to have figured it all out

D.S.—6

and climbs stiffly, clumsily up the steps. Not even in his gait can he manage to belie his mother, who, incidentally, has appeared in the basement doorway. To make sure that the charwoman also understands and in the hope that she will supervise the carrying out of his instructions, should it be necessary, Blumfeld shouts excessively loud. "Up in my room," says Blumfeld, "I have two lovely balls. Would you like to have them?" Not knowing how to behave, the boy simply screws up his mouth, turns round and looks inquiringly down at his mother. The girls, however, promptly begin to jump around Blumfeld and ask him for the balls. "You will be allowed to play with them too," Blumfeld tells them, but waits for the boy's answer. He could of course give the balls to the girls, but they strike him as too unreliable and for the moment he has more confidence in the boy. Meanwhile the latter, without having exchanged a word, has taken counsel with his mother and nods his assent to Blumfeld's repeated question. "Then listen," says Blumfeld, who is quite prepared to receive no thanks for his gift. "Your mother has the key of my door, you must borrow it from her. But here is the key to my wardrobe, and in the wardrobe you will find the balls. Take good care to lock the wardrobe and the room again. But with the balls you can do what you like and you don't have to bring them back. Have you understood me?" Unfortunately, the boy has not understood. Blumfeld has tried to make everything particularly clear to this hopelessly dense creature, but for this very reason has repeated everything too often, has in turn too often mentioned keys, room, and wardrobe, and as a result the boy stares at him as though he were rather a seducer than his benefactor. The girls, on the other hand, have understood everything immediately, press against Blumfeld, and stretch out their hands for the key. "Wait a moment," says Blumfeld, by now annoyed with them all. Time, moreover, is passing, he can't stand about much longer. If only the mother would say that she has understood him and take matters in hand for the boy! Instead of which she still stands down by the door, smiles with the affectation of the bashful deaf, and is probably under the impression that Blumfeld up there has suddenly fallen for the boy and is hearing him his lessons. Blumfeld on the other hand can't very well climb down the basement stairs and shout into the charwoman's ear to make her son for God's sake relieve him of the balls! It had required enough of his self-control as it was to entrust the key of his wardrobe for a whole day to this family. It is certainly not in order to save himself trouble that he is handing the key to the boy rather than himself leading the boy up and there giving him the balls. But he can't very well first give the balls away and then immediately deprive the boy of them by—as would be bound to happen—drawing them after him as his followers. "So you still don't understand me?" asks Blumfeld almost wistfully after having started a fresh explanation which, however, he immediately interrupts at sight of the boy's vacant stare. So vacant a stare renders one helpless. It could tempt one into saying more than one intends, if only to fill the vacancy with sense. Whereupon "We'll fetch the balls for him!" shout the girls. They are shrewd and have realised that they can obtain the balls only through using the boy as an intermediary, but that they themselves have to bring about this mediation. From the janitor's room a clock strikes, warning

Blumfeld to hurry. " Well, then, take the key," says Blumfeld, and the key is more snatched from his hand than given by him. He would have handed it to the boy with infinitely more confidence. " The key to the room you'll have to get from the woman," Blumfeld adds. " And when you return with the balls you must hand both keys to her." " Yes, yes ! " shout the girls and run down the steps. They know everything, absolutely everything ; and as though Blumfeld were infected by the boy's denseness, he is unable to understand how they could have grasped everything so quickly from his explanations.

Now they are already tugging at the charwoman's skirt but, tempting as it would be, Blumfeld cannot afford to watch them carrying out their task, not only because it's already late, but also because he has no desire to be present at the liberation of the balls. He would in fact far prefer to be several streets away when the girls first open the door of his room. After all, how does he know what else he might have to expect from these balls ! And so for the second time this morning he leaves the house. He has one last glimpse of the charwoman defending herself against the girls, and of the boy stirring his bandy legs to come to his mother's assistance. It's beyond Blumfeld's comprehension why a creature like this servant should prosper and propagate in this world.

While on his way to the linen factory, where Blumfeld is employed, thoughts about his work gradually get the upper hand. He quickens his step and, despite the delay caused by the boy, he is the first to arrive in his office. The office is a glass-enclosed room containing a writing desk for Blumfeld and two standing desks for the two assistants subordinate to him. Although these standing desks are so small and narrow as to suggest they are meant for school children, this office is very crowded and the assistants cannot sit down, for then there would no place for Blumfeld's chair. As a result they stand all day, pressed against their desks. For them of course this is very uncomfortable, but it also makes it very difficult for Blumfeld to keep an eye on them. They often press eagerly against their desks not so much in order to work as to whisper to one another or even to take forty winks. They give Blumfeld a great deal of trouble ; they don't help him sufficiently with the enormous amount of work that is imposed on him. This work involves supervising the whole distribution of fabrics and cash among the women homeworkers who are employed by the factory for the manufacture of certain fancy commodities. To appreciate the magnitude of this task an intimate knowledge of the general conditions is necessary. But since Blumfeld's immediate superior has died some years ago, no one any longer possesses this knowledge, which is also why Blumfeld cannot grant anyone the right to pronounce an opinion on his work. The manufacturer, Herr Ottomar, for instance, clearly underestimates Blumfeld's work ; no doubt he recognises that in the course of twenty years Blumfeld has deserved well of the factory, and this he acknowledges not only because he is obliged to, but also because he respects Blumfeld as a loyal, trustworthy person.—He under-estimates his work, nevertheless, for he believes it could be conducted by methods more simple and therefore in every respect more profitable than those employed by Blumfeld. It is said, and it is probably not incorrect, that Ottomar shows himself so rarely in Blumfeld's department

simply to spare himself the annoyance which the
sight of Blumfeld's working methods causes him.   To
be so unappreciated is undoubtedly sad for Blumfeld,
but there is no remedy, for he cannot very well compel
Ottomar to spend let us say a whole month on end in
Blumfeld's department in order to study the great
variety of work being accomplished there, to apply his
own allegedly better methods, and to let himself be
convinced of Blumfeld's soundness by the collapse of the
department—which would be the inevitable result.   And
so Blumfeld carries on his work undeterred as before,
gives a little start whenever Ottomar appears after a long
absence, then with the subordinate's sense of duty makes
a feeble effort to explain to Ottomar this or that arrangement, whereupon the latter, his eyes lowered and giving
a silent nod, passes on.   But what worries Blumfeld more
than this lack of appreciation is the thought that one day
he will be compelled to leave his job, the immediate
consequence of which will be pandemonium, a confusion
no one will be able to straighten out because so far as he
knows there isn't a single soul in the factory capable of
replacing him and of carrying on his job in a manner that
could be relied upon to prevent months of the most
serious interruptions.   Needless to say, if the boss under-
estimates an employee the latter's colleagues try their
best to surpass him in this respect.   In consequence
everyone underestimates Blumfeld's work ; no one con-
siders it necessary to spend any time training in Blumfeld's department, and when new employees are hired
not one of them is ever assigned to Blumfeld.   As a result
Blumfeld's department lacks a younger generation to
carry on.   When Blumfeld, who up to then had been
managing the entire department with the help of only

one servant, demanded an assistant, weeks of bitter
fighting ensued.   Almost every day Blumfeld appeared
in Ottomar's office and explained to him calmly and in
minute detail why an assistant was needed in his department.   He was needed not by any means because Blumfeld wished to spare himself, Blumfeld had no intention
of sparing himself, he was doing more than his share of
work and this he had no desire to change, but would
Herr Ottomar please consider how in the course of time
the business had grown, how every department had been
correspondingly enlarged, with the exception of Blumfeld's department, which was invariably forgotten !   And
would he consider too how the work had increased just
there !   When Blumfeld had entered the firm, a time
Herr Ottomar could probably not remember, they had
employed some ten seamstresses, today the number
varied between fifty and sixty.   Such a job requires great
energy ;   Blumfeld could guarantee that he was completely
wearing himself out in this work, but that he will continue to master it completely he can henceforth no
longer guarantee.   True, Herr Ottomar had never flatly
refused Blumfeld's requests, this was something he
could not do to an old employee, but the manner in which
he hardly listened, in which he talked to others over
Blumfeld's head, made halfhearted promises and had
forgotten everything in a few days—this behaviour was
insulting to say the least.   Not actually to Blumfeld.
Blumfeld is no romantic, pleasant as honour and recognition may be, Blumfeld can do without them, in spite
of everything he will stick to his desk as long as it is at
all possible, in any case he is in the right, and right, even
though on occasion it may take a long time, must prevail
in the end.   True, Blumfeld has at last been given two

assistants, but what assistants ! One might have thought Ottomar had realised he could express his contempt for the department even better by granting rather than by refusing it these assistants. It was even possible that Ottomar had kept Blumfeld waiting so long because he was looking for two assistants just like these, and—as may be imagined—took a long time to find them. And now of course Blumfeld could no longer complain ; if he did, the answer could easily be foreseen : after all, he had asked for one assistant and had been given two, that's how cleverly Ottomar had arranged things. Needless to say, Blumfeld complained just the same, but only because his predicament all but forced him to do so, not because he still hoped for any redress. Nor did he complain emphatically, but only by the way, whenever the occasion arose. Nevertheless, among his spiteful colleagues the rumour soon spread that someone had asked Ottomar if it were really possible that Blumfeld, who after all had been given such unusual aid, was still complaining. To which Ottomar answered that this was correct. Blumfeld was still complaining, and rightly so. He, Ottomar, had at last realised this and he intended gradually to assign to Blumfeld one assistant for each seamstress, in other words some sixty in all. In case this number should prove insufficient, however, he would let him have even more and would not cease until the bedlam, which had been developing for years in Blumfeld's department, was complete. Now it cannot be denied that in this remark Ottomar's manner of speech had been cleverly imitated, but Blumfeld had no doubts whatever that Ottomar would not dream of speaking about him in such a way. The whole thing was a fabrication of the loafers in the offices on the first floor.

Blumfeld ignored it—if only he could as calmly have
ignored the presence of the assistants ! But there they
stood, and could not be spirited away. Pale, weak
children. According to their credentials they had already
passed school age, but in reality this was difficult to
believe. In fact their rightful place was so clearly at
their mother's knee that one would hardly have dared to
entrust them to a teacher. They still couldn't even
move properly ; standing up for any length of time tired
them inordinately, especially when they first arrived.
When left to themselves they promptly doubled up in
their weakness, standing hunched and crooked in their
corner. Blumfeld tried to point out to them that if
they went on giving in to their indolence they would
become cripples for life. To ask the assistants to make
the slightest move was to take a risk ; once when one of
them had been ordered to carry something a short
distance, he had run so eagerly that he had banged his
knee against a desk. The room had been full of seamstresses, the desks covered in merchandise, but Blumfeld
had been obliged to neglect everything and take the
sobbing assistant into the office and there bandage his
wound. Yet even this zeal on the part of the assistant
was superficial ; like actual children they tried once in
a while to excel, but far more often—indeed almost always
—they tried to divert their superior's attention and to
cheat him. Once, at a time of the most intensive work,
Blumfeld had rushed past them, dripping with sweat,
and had observed them secretly swapping stamps among
the bales of merchandise. He had felt like banging
them on the head with his fists, it would have been the
only possible punishment for such behaviour, but they
were after all only children and Blumfeld could not very

well knock children down. And so he continued to put up with them. Originally he had imagined that the assistants would help him with the essential chores which at the moment of the distribution of goods required so much effort and vigilance. He had imagined himself standing in the centre behind his desk, keeping an eye on everything and making the entries in the books while the assistants ran to and fro, distributing everything according to his orders. He had imagined that his supervision which, sharp as it was, could not cope with such a crowd, would be complemented by the assistants' attention ; he had hoped that these assistants would gradually acquire experience, cease depending entirely on his orders, and finally learn to discriminate on their own between the seamstresses as to their trustworthiness and requirements. Blumfeld soon realised that all these hopes had been in vain and that he could not afford to let them even talk to the seamstresses. From the beginning they had ignored some of the seamstresses, either from fear or dislike ; others to whom they felt partial they would sometimes run to meet at the door. To them the assistants would bring whatever the women wanted, pressing it almost secretly into their hands, although the seamstresses were perfectly entitled to receive it, would collect on a bare shelf for these favourites various cuttings, worthless remnants, but also a few still useful odds and ends, waving them blissfully at the women behind Blumfeld's back and in return having sweets popped into their mouths. Blumfeld of course soon put an end to this mischief and the moment the seamstresses arrived he ordered the assistants back into their glass-enclosed cubicles. But for a long time they considered this to be a grave injustice, they sulked, wilfully broke their nibs, and sometimes, although not daring to raise their heads, even knocked loudly against the glass panes in order to attract the seamstresses' attention to the bad treatment which in their opinion they were suffering at Blumfeld's hands.

The wrong they do themselves the assistants cannot see. For instance, they almost always arrive late at the office. Blumfeld, their superior, who from his earliest youth has considered it natural to arrive half an hour before the office opens—not from ambition or an exaggerated sense of duty but simply from a certain feeling of decency—often has to wait more than an hour for his assistants. Chewing his breakfast roll he stands behind his desk, looking through the accounts in the seamstresses' little books. Soon he is immersed in his work and thinking of nothing else when suddenly he receives such a shock that his pen continues to tremble in his hand for some while afterwards. One of the assistants has dashed in, looking as though he is about to collapse ; he is holding on to something with one hand while the other is pressed against his heaving chest. All this, however, simply means that he is making excuses for being late, excuses so absurd that Blumfeld purposely ignores them, for if he didn't he would have to give the young man a well-deserved thrashing. As it is, he just glances at him for a moment, points with outstretched hand at the cubicle, and turns back to his work. Now one really might expect the assistant to appreciate his superior's kindness and hurry to his place. No, he doesn't hurry, he dawdles about, he walks on tiptoe, slowly placing one foot in front of the other. Is he trying to ridicule his superior ? No. Again it's just that mixture of fear and self-complacency against which one is powerless. How else explain the fact that even today Blumfeld, who has himself arrived unusually late in the office and now after a long wait—he doesn't feel like checking the books—sees, through the clouds of dust raised by the stupid servant with his broom, the two assistants sauntering peacefully along the street? Arm in arm, they appear to be telling one another important things which, however, are sure to have only the remotest and very likely irreverent connections with the office. The nearer they approach the glass door, the slower they walk. One of them seizes the door handle but fails to turn it; they just go on talking, listening, laughing. " Hurry out and open the door for our gentlemen ! " shouts Blumfeld at the servant, throwing up his hands. But when the assistants come in, Blumfeld no longer feels like quarrelling, ignores their greetings, and goes to his desk. He starts doing his accounts, but now and again glances up to see what his assistants are up to. One of them seems to be very tired and rubs his eyes. When hanging up his overcoat he takes the opportunity to lean against the wall. In the street he seemed lively enough, but the proximity of work tires him. The other assistant, however, is eager to work, but only work of a certain kind. For a long time it has been his wish to be allowed to sweep. But this is work to which he is not entitled ; sweeping is exclusively the servant's job ; in itself Blumfeld would have nothing against the assistant sweeping, let the assistant sweep, he can't make a worse job of it than the servant, but if the assistant wants to sweep then he must come earlier, before the servant begins to sweep, and not spend on it time that is reserved exclusively for office work. But since the young man is totally deaf to any sensible argument, at least the servant

—that half-blind old buffer whom the boss would certainly not tolerate in any department but Blumfeld's and who is still alive only by the grace of the boss and God—at least the servant might be sensible and hand the broom for a moment to the young man who, being clumsy, would soon lose his interest and run after the servant with the broom in order to persuade him to go on sweeping. It appears, however, that the servant feels especially responsible for the sweeping; one can see how he, the moment the young man approaches him, tries to grasp the broom more firmly with his trembling hands; he even stands still and stops sweeping so as to direct his full attention to the ownership of the broom. The assistant doesn't actually plead in words, for he is afraid of Blumfeld, who is ostensibly doing his accounts; moreover, ordinary speech is useless, since the servant can be made to hear only by excessive shouting. So at first the assistant tugs the servant by the sleeve. The servant knows, of course, what it is about, glowers at the assistant, shakes his head and pulls the broom nearer, up to his chest. Whereupon the assistant folds his hands and pleads. Actually, he has no hope of achieving anything by pleading, but the pleading amuses him and so he pleads. The other assistant follows the goings-on with low laughter and seems to think, heaven knows why, that Blumfeld can't hear him. The pleading makes not the slightest impression on the servant, who turns round and thinks he can safely use the broom again. The assistant, however, has skipped after him on tiptoe and, rubbing his hands together imploringly, now pleads from another side. This turning of the one and skipping of the other is repeated several times. Finally the servant feels cut off from all sides and realises—something which, had

he been slightly less stupid, he might have realised from
the beginning—that he will be tired out long before the
assistant. So, looking for help elsewhere, he wags his
finger at the assistant and points at Blumfeld, suggesting
that he will lodge a complaint if the assistant refuses to
desist. The assistant realises that if he is to get the broom
at all he'll have to hurry, so he impudently makes a
grab for it. An involuntary scream from the other
assistant heralds the imminent decision. The servant
saves the broom once more by taking a step back and
dragging it after him. But now the assistant is up in
arms : with open mouth and flashing eyes he leaps forward, the servant tries to escape, but his old legs wobble
rather than run, the assistant tugs at the broom and
though he doesn't succeed in getting it he nevertheless
causes it to drop and in this way it is lost to the servant.
Also apparently to the assistant for, the moment the
broom falls, all three, the two assistants and the servant,
are paralysed, for now Blumfeld is bound to discover
everything. And sure enough Blumfeld at his peephole
glances up as though taking in the situation only now.
He stares at each one with a stern and searching eye,
even the broom on the floor does not escape his notice.
Perhaps the silence has lasted too long or perhaps the
assistant can no longer suppress his desire to sweep, in
any case he bends down—albeit very carefully, as though
about to grab an animal rather than a broom—seizes it,
passes it over the floor, but, when Blumfeld jumps up
and steps out of his cubicle, promptly casts it aside in
alarm. " Both of you back to work ! And not another
sound out of you ! " shouts Blumfeld, and with an
outstretched hand he directs the two assistants back to
their desks. They obey at once, but not shamefaced or

with lowered heads, rather they squeeze themselves stiffly past Blumfeld, staring him straight in the eye as though trying in this way to stop him from beating them. Yet they might have learned from experience that Blumfeld on principle never beats anyone. But they are over-apprehensive, and without any tact keep trying to protect their real or imaginary rights.

THE BURROW

I HAVE completed the construction of my burrow and it seems to be successful. All that can be seen from the outside is a big hole; that, however, really leads nowhere; if you take a few steps you strike against natural firm rock. I can make no boast of having contrived this ruse intentionally; it is simply the remains of one of my many abortive building attempts, but finally it seemed to me advisable to leave this one hole without filling it in. True, some ruses are so subtle that they defeat themselves, I know that better than any one, and it is certainly a risk to draw attention by this hole to the fact that there may be something in the vicinity worth enquiring into. But you do not know me if you think I am afraid, or that I built my burrow simply out of fear. At a distance of some thousand paces from this hole lies, covered by a movable layer of moss, the real entrance to the burrow; it is secured as safely as anything in this world can be secured; yet someone could step on the moss or break through it, and then my burrow would lie open, and anybody who liked—please note, however, that quite uncommon abilities would also be required—could make his way in and utterly destroy everything. I know that very well, and even now when I am better off than ever before I can scarcely pass an hour in complete tranquillity; at that one point in the dark moss I am vulnerable, and in my dreams I often see a greedy muzzle sniffing round it persistently. It will be objected that I could quite well have filled in the entrance too, with a thin layer of hard earth on top and with loose soil further down, so that it would not cost me much trouble to dig my way out again whenever I liked. But that plan is impossible ; prudence itself demands that I should have a way of leaving at a moment's notice if necessary, prudence itself demands, as alas ! so often, the element of risk in life. All this involves very laborious calculation, and the sheer pleasure of the mind in its own keenness is often the sole reason why one keeps it up. I must have a way of leaving at a moment's notice, for, despite all my vigilance, may I not be attacked from some quite unexpected quarter ? I live in peace in the inmost chamber of my house, and meanwhile the enemy may be burrowing his way slowly and stealthily towards me. I do not say that he has a better scent than I ; probably he knows as little about me as I of him. But there are insatiable robbers who burrow blindly through the ground, and to whom the very size of my house gives the hope of hitting by chance on some of its far-flung passages. I certainly have the advantage of being in my own house and knowing all the passages and how they run. A robber may very easily become my victim and a succulent one too. But I am growing old ; I am not as strong as many others, and my enemies are countless ; it could well happen that in flying from one enemy I might run into the jaws of another. Anything might happen ! In any case I must have the confident knowledge that somewhere there is an exit easy to reach and quite free, where I have to do nothing whatever to get out, so that I might never—Heaven shield us !—suddenly feel the teeth of the pursuer in my flank while I am desperately burrowing away, even if it is at loose easy soil. And it is not only by external enemies that I am threatened. There are also enemies in the bowels of the earth. I have never seen them, but legend tells of them and I firmly believe in them. They are creatures of the inner earth ; not even legend can describe them. Their very victims can scarcely have seen them ; they come, you hear the scratching of their claws just under you in the ground, which is their element, and already you are lost. Here it is of no avail to console yourself with the thought that you are in your own house ; far rather are you in theirs. Not even my exit could save me from them; indeed in all probability it would not save me in any case, but rather betray me ; yet it is a hope, and I cannot live without it. Apart from this main exit I am also connected with the outer world by quite narrow, tolerably safe passages which provide me with good fresh air to breathe. They are the work of the field mice. I have made judicious use of them, transforming them into an organic part of my burrow. They also give me the possibility of scenting things from afar, and thus serve as a protection. All sorts of small fry, too, come running through them, and I devour these ; so I can have a certain amount of subterranean hunting, sufficient for a modest way of life, without leaving my burrow at all ; and that is naturally a great advantage.

But the most beautiful thing about my burrow is the stillness. Of course, that is deceitful. At any moment it may be shattered and then all will be over. For the time being, however, the silence is still with me. For hours I can stroll through my passages and hear nothing except the rustling of some little creature, which I immediately reduce to silence between my jaws, or the pattering of soil, which draws my attention to the need for repair ; otherwise all is still. The fragrance of the woods floats in ; the place feels both warm and cool. Sometimes I lie down and roll about in the passage with pure joy. When autumn sets in, to possess a burrow like mine, and a roof over your head, is great good fortune for any one getting on in years. Every hundred yards I have widened the passages into little round cells ; there I can curl myself up in comfort and lie warm. There I sleep the sweet sleep of tranquillity, of satisfied desire, of achieved ambition ; for I possess a house. I do not know whether it is a habit that still persists from former days, or whether the perils even of this house of mine are great enough to awaken me ; but invariably every now and then I start up out of profound sleep and listen, listen into the stillness which reigns here un-changed day and night, smile contentedly and then sink with loosened limbs into still profounder sleep. Poor homeless wanderers in the roads and woods, creeping for warmth into a heap of leaves or a herd of their comrades, delivered into all the perils of heaven and earth ! I lie here in a room secured on every side—there are more than fifty such rooms in my burrow—and pass as much time as I choose between dozing and unconscious sleep.

Not quite in the centre of the burrow, carefully chosen to serve as a refuge in case of extreme danger from siege if not from immediate pursuit, lies the chief cell. While all the rest of the burrow is the outcome rather of intense intellectual than of physical labour, this Castle Keep was fashioned by the most arduous labour of my whole body. Several times, in the despair brought on by physical exhaustion, I was on the point of giving up the whole business, flung myself down panting and cursed the burrow, dragged myself outside and left the place lying open to all the world. I could afford to do that, for I had no longer any wish to return to it, until at last, after hours or days, back I went repentantly, and when I saw that the burrow was unharmed I could almost have raised a hymn of thanksgiving, and in sincere gladness of heart started on the work anew. My labours on the Castle Keep were also made harder, and unnecessarily so (unnecessarily in that the burrow derived no real benefit from those labours) by the fact that just at the place where, according to my calculations, the Castle Keep should be, the soil was very loose and sandy and had literally to be hammered and pounded into a firm state to serve as a wall for the beautifully vaulted chamber. But for such tasks the only tool I possess is my forehead. So I had to run with my forehead thousands and thousands of times, for whole days and nights, against the ground, and I was glad when the blood came, for that was a proof that the walls were beginning to harden ; and in that way, as everybody must admit, I richly paid for my Castle Keep.

In the Castle Keep I assemble my stores ; everything over and above my daily wants that I capture inside the burrow, and everything I bring back with me from my hunting expeditions outside, I pile up here. The place is so spacious that food for half a year scarcely fills it. Consequently I can divide up my stores, walk about among them, play with them, enjoy their plenty and their various smells, and reckon up exactly how much they represent. That done, I can always arrange accordingly, and make my calculations and hunting plans for the future, taking into account the season of the year. There are times when I am so well provided for that in my indifference to food I never even touch the smaller fry

that scuttle about the burrow, which, however, is probably imprudent of me. My constant preoccupation with
defensive measures involves a frequent alteration or
modification, though within narrow limits, of my views
on how the building can best be organised for that end.
Then it sometimes seems risky to make the Castle Keep
the basis of defence ; the ramifications of the burrow
present me with manifold possibilities, and it seems more
in accordance with prudence to divide up my stores
somewhat, and put part of them in certain of the smaller
rooms ; thereupon I mark off every third room, let us
say, as a reserve storeroom, or every fourth room as a
main and every second as an auxiliary storeroom, and so
forth. Or I ignore certain passages altogether and store
no food in them, so as to throw any enemy off the scent,
or I choose quite at random a very few rooms according
to their distance from the main exit. Each of these new
plans involves of course heavy work ; I have to make my
calculations and then carry my stores to their new places.
True, I can do that at my leisure and without any hurry,
and it is not at all unpleasant to carry such good food
in your jaws, to lie down and rest whenever you like,
and, which is an actual pleasure, to have an occasional
nibble. But it is not so pleasant when, as sometimes
happens, you suddenly fancy, starting up from your sleep,
that the present distribution of your stores is completely
and totally wrong, capable of leading to great dangers,
and must be set right at once, no matter how tired or
sleepy you may be ; then I rush, then I fly, then I have
no time for calculation ; as I am burning to execute my
perfectly new, perfectly satisfactory plan, I seize whatever
my teeth hit upon and drag it or carry it away, sighing,
groaning, stumbling, and nothing will content me but

some radical alteration of the present state of things, which seems imminently dangerous. Until little by little full wakefulness sobers me, and I can hardly understand my panic haste, breathe in deeply the tranquillity of my house, which I myself have disturbed, return to my resting-place, fall asleep at once in new-won exhaustion, and on awakening find hanging from my jaws, say, a rat, as indubitable proof of night labours which already seem almost unreal. Then again there are times when the storing of all my food in one place seems the best plan of all. Of what use to me could my stores in the smaller rooms be, how much could I store there in any case? And whatever I put there would block the passage, and be a greater hindrance than help to me if I were pursued and had to fly. Besides, it is stupid but true that one's self-conceit suffers if one cannot see all one's stores together, and so at one glance know how much one possesses. And in dividing up my food in those various ways might not a great deal get lost? I can't be always scouring through all my passages and cross-passages so as to make sure that everything is in order. The idea of dividing up my stores is of course a good one, but only if one had several rooms similar to my Castle Keep. Several such rooms! Indeed! And who is to build them? In any case they could not be worked into the general plan of my burrow at this late stage. But I will admit that that is a fault in my burrow; it is always a fault to have only one model of anything. And I confess too that during the whole time I was constructing the burrow a vague divination that I should have more than one keep stirred in my mind, vaguely, yet clearly enough if I had only welcomed it; I did not yield to it, I felt too feeble for the enormous labour it would involve, more, I felt too feeble even to admit to myself the necessity for that labour, and comforted myself as best I could with the vague hope that a building which in any other case would clearly be inadequate, would in my own unique, exceptional, favoured case suffice, presumably, because providence was interested in the preservation of my forehead, that unique instrument. So I have only one Castle Keep, but my dark premonitions that one would not suffice have faded. However that may be I must content myself with the one big chamber, the smaller ones are simply no substitute for it, and so, when this conviction has grown on me, I begin once more to haul all my stores back from them to the Castle Keep. For some time afterwards I find a certain comfort in having all the passages and rooms free, in seeing my stores growing in the Castle Keep and emitting their variegated and mingled smells, each of which delights me in its own fashion, and every one of which I can distinguish even at a distance, as far as the very remotest passages. Then I usually enjoy periods of particular tranquillity, in which I change my sleeping-place by stages, always working in towards the centre of the burrow, always steeping myself more profoundly in the mingled smells, until at last I can no longer restrain myself and one night rush into the Castle Keep, mightily fling myself upon my stores, and glut myself with the best that I can seize until I am completely gorged. Happy, but dangerous hours ; any one who knew how to exploit them could destroy me with ease and without any risk. Here too the absence of a second or third large storeroom works to my detriment ; for it is the single huge accumulated mass of food that seduces me. I try to guard myself in various ways against this danger ; the distribution of

my stores in the smaller rooms is really one of these
expedients ; but unfortunately, like other such expedients, it leads through renunciation to still greater
greed, which, overruling my intelligence, makes me
arbitrarily alter my plans of defence to suit its ends.

To regain my composure after such lapses I make a
practice of reviewing the burrow, and after the necessary
improvements have been carried out, frequently leave it,
though only for a short spell. At such moments the hardship of renouncing it for a long time seems too punitive,
even to myself, yet I recognise clearly the need for my
occasional short excursions. It is always with a certain
solemnity that I approach the exit again. During my
spells of home life I avoid it, steer clear even of the
outer windings of the corridor that leads to it ; besides,
it is no easy job to wander about there, for I have contrived there a whole little maze of passages ; it was there
that I began my burrow, at a time when I had no hope
of ever completing it according to my plans ; I began,
half in play, at that corner, and so my first joy in labour
found riotous satisfaction there in a labyrinthine burrow
which at the time seemed to me the crown of all burrows,
but which I judge today, perhaps with more justice, to
be too much of an idle *tour de force*, not really worthy of
the rest of the burrow, and though perhaps theoretically
brilliant—here is my main entrance, I said in those days,
ironically addressing my invisible enemies and seeing
them all already caught and stifled in the outer labyrinth
—is in reality a flimsy piece of jugglery that would hardly
withstand a serious attack or the struggles of an enemy
fighting for his life. Should I reconstruct this part of
my burrow ? I keep on postponing the decision, and
the labyrinth will probably remain as it is. Apart from

the sheer hard work that I should have to face, the task would also be the most dangerous imaginable. When I began the burrow I could work away at it in comparative peace of mind, the risk wasn't much greater than any other risk ; but to attempt that today would be to draw the whole world's attention, and gratuitously, to my burrow ; today the whole thing is impossible. I am almost glad of that, for I still have a certain sentiment about this first achievement of mine. And if a serious attack were attempted, could any kind of entrance design save me ? An entrance can deceive, can lead astray, can give the attacker no end of worry, and the present one too can do that at a pinch. But a really serious attack has to be met by an instantaneous mobilisation of all the resources in the burrow and all the forces of my body and soul—that, of course, is self-evident. So this entrance can very well remain where it is. The burrow has so many unavoidable defects imposed by natural causes that it can surely stand this one defect for which I am responsible, and which I recognise as a defect, even if only after the event. In spite of that, however, I do not deny that this fault worries me from time to time, indeed always. If on my customary rounds I avoid this part of the burrow, the fundamental reason is because the sight of it is painful to me, because I don't want to be perpetually reminded of a defect in my house, even if that defect is only too disturbingly present in my mind. Let it continue to exist ineradicably at the entrance ; I can at least refuse to look at it as long as that is possible. If I merely walk in the direction of the entrance, even though I may be separated from it by several passages and rooms, I find myself sensing an atmosphere of great danger, actually as if my hair were growing thin and in a moment

might fly off and leave me bare and shivering, exposed to
the howls of my enemies. Yes, the mere thought of the
entrance door brings such feelings with it, yet it is the
labyrinth leading up to it that torments me most of all.
Sometimes I dream that I have reconstructed it, trans-
formed it completely, quickly, in a night, with a giant's
strength, nobody having noticed, and now it is impreg-
nable ; the nights in which such dreams come to me are
the sweetest I know, tears of joy and deliverance still
glisten on my beard when I awaken.

So I must thread the tormenting complications of this
labyrinth physically as well as mentally whenever I go
out, and I am both exasperated and touched when, as
sometimes happens, I lose myself for a moment in my
own maze, and the work of my hands seems to be still
doing its best to prove its sufficiency to me, its maker,
whose final judgment has long since been passed on it.
But then I find myself beneath the mossy covering, which
has been left untouched for so long—since I stay for long
spells in my house—that it has grown fast to the soil
round it, and now only a little push with my head is
needed and I am in the upper world. For a long time I
do not dare to make that little movement, and if it were
not that I should have to traverse the labyrinth once
more I would certainly leave the matter for the time
being and turn back again. Just think. Your house is
protected and self-sufficient. You live in peace, warm,
well-nourished, master, sole master of all your manifold
passages and rooms, and all this you are prepared, it
appears, not merely to give up, but actually to abandon ;
you nurse the confident hope, certainly, that you will
regain it again ; yet is it not a dangerous, a far too
dangerous stake that you are playing for ? Can there be

any reasonable grounds for such a step ? No, for such acts as these there can be no reasonable grounds. But all the same I then cautiously raise the trap-door and slip outside, let it softly fall back again, and fly as fast as I can from the treacherous spot.

Yet I am not really free. True, I am no longer confined by narrow passages, but rush through the open woods, and feel new powers awakening in my body for which there was no room, as it were, in the burrow, not even in the Castle Keep, though it had been ten times as big. The food too is better up here ; though hunting is more difficult, success more rare, the results are more valuable from every point of view ; I do not deny all this ; I appreciate it and take advantage of it as fully as most animals, and probably more fully, for I do not hunt like a vagrant out of mere idleness or desperation, but calmly and methodically. Also I am not permanently doomed to this free life, for I know that my term is measured, that I do not have to hunt here for ever, and that, whenever I am weary of this life and wish to leave it, Someone, whose invitation I shall not be able to withstand, will, so to speak, summon me to him. And so I can pass my time here quite without care and in complete enjoyment, or rather I could, and yet I cannot. My burrow takes up too much of my thoughts. I fled from the entrance fast enough, but soon I am back at it again. I seek out a good hiding-place and keep watch on the entrance of my house—this time from outside— for whole days and nights. Call it foolish if you like ; it gives me infinite pleasure and reassures me. At such times it is as if I were not so much looking at my house as at myself sleeping, and had the joy of being in a profound slumber and simultaneously of keeping vigilant guard over myself. I am privileged, as it were, not only to dream about the spectres of the night in all the help- lessness and blind trust of sleep, but also at the same time to confront them in actuality with the calm judg- ment of the fully awake. And strangely enough I discover that my situation is not so bad as I had often thought, and will probably think again when I return to my house. In this respect—it may be in others too, but in this one especially—these excursions of mine are truly indispensable. Carefully as I have chosen an out-of-the- way place for my door, the traffic that passes it is never- theless, if one takes a week's observations, very great ; but so it is, no doubt, in all inhabited regions, and prob- ably it is actually better to hazard risks of dense traffic, whose very impetus carries it past, than to be delivered in complete solitude to the first persistently searching intruder. Here enemies are numerous and their allies and accomplices still more numerous, but they fight one another, and while thus employed rush pass my burrow without noticing it. In all my time I have never seen any one investigating the actual door of my house, which is fortunate both for me and for him, for I would certainly have launched myself at his throat, forgetting everything else in my anxiety for the burrow. True, intruders come in whose neighbourhood I dare not remain, and from whom I have to fly as soon as I scent them in the distance ; on their attitude to the burrow I really can't pronounce with certainty, but it is at least a reassurance than when I presently return I never find any of them there, and the entrance is undamaged. There have been happy periods in which I could almost assure myself that the enmity of the world towards me had ceased or been assuaged, or that the strength of the burrow had raised

me above the destructive struggle of former times. The
burrow has probably protected me in more ways than I
thought or dared think while I was inside it. This fancy
used to have such a hold over me that sometimes I have
been seized by the childish desire never to return to the
burrow again, but to settle down somewhere close to the
entrance, to pass my life watching it, and gloat perpetually upon the reflection—and in that find my happiness
—how steadfast a protection my burrow would be if I
were inside it. Well, one is soon roughly awakened from
childish dreams. What does this protection which I am
looking at here from the outside amount to after all ?
Dare I estimate the danger which I run inside the burrow
from observations which I make when outside ? Can
my enemies, to begin with, have any proper awareness
of me if I am not in my burrow ? A certain awareness
of me they certainly have, but not full awareness. And
is not that full awareness the real definition of a state of
danger ? So the experiments I attempt here are only
half-experiments or even less, calculated merely to re-
assure my fears and by giving me false reassurance to lay
me open to great perils. No, I do not watch over my
own sleep, as I imagined ; rather it is I who sleep, while
the destroyer watches. Perhaps he is one of those who
pass the entrance without seeming to notice it, concerned
merely to ascertain, just like myself, that the door is
still untouched and waits for their attack, and only pass
because they know that the master of the house is out,
or because they are quite aware that he is guilelessly
lying on the watch in the bushes close by. And I leave
my post of observation and find I have had enough of this
outside life ; I feel that there is nothing more that I can
learn here, either now or at any time. And I long to say

a last good-bye to everything up here, to go down into
my burrow never to return again, let things take their
course, and not try to retard them with my profitless
vigils. But after watching for such a long time everything that happens round the entrance, I find great
difficulty in summoning the resolution to carry out the
actual descent, which might easily draw any one's
attention, and without knowing what is happening
behind my back and behind the door after it is fastened.
I take advantage of stormy nights to get over the necessary
preliminaries, and quickly bundle in my spoil ; that seems
to have come off, but whether it has really come off will
only be known when I myself have made the descent ;
it will be known, but not by me, or by me, but too late.
So I give up the attempt and do not make the descent.
I dig an experimental burrow, naturally at a good distance
from the real entrance, a burrow just as long as myself,
and seal it also with a covering of moss. I creep into my
hole, close it after me, wait patiently, keep vigil for long
or short spells, and at various hours of the day, then
fling off the moss, issue from my hole, and summarise
my observations. These are extremely heterogeneous,
and both good and bad ; but I have never been able to
discover a universal principle or an infallible method of
descent. In consequence of all this I have not yet
summoned the resolution to make my actual descent,
and am thrown into despair at the necessity of doing it
soon. I almost screw myself to the point of deciding
to emigrate to distant parts and take up my old comfortless
life again, which had no security whatever, but was one
indiscriminate succession of perils, yet in consequence
prevented me from perceiving and fearing particular
perils, as I am constantly reminded by comparing my

secure burrow with ordinary life. Certainly such a
decision would be an arrant piece of folly, produced
simply by living too long in senseless freedom ; the
burrow is still mine, I have only to take a single step
and I am safe. And I tear myself free from all my doubts
and by broad daylight rush to the door, quite resolved
to raise it now ; but I cannot, I rush past it and fling
myself into a thorn bush, deliberately, as a punishment,
a punishment for some sin I do not know of. Then, at
the last moment, I am forced to admit to myself that I
was right after all, and that it is really impossible to
go down into the burrow without leaving the thing I
love best, for a little while at least, at the mercy of all
my enemies, on the ground, in the trees, in the air.
And the danger is by no means a fanciful one, but very
real. It need not be any particular enemy that is pro-
voked to pursue me, it may very well be some chance
innocent little creature, some disgusting little beast which
follows me out of curiosity, and thus, without knowing
it, becomes the leader of all the world against me ; nor
need it be even that, it may be—and that would be just
as bad, indeed in some respects worse—it may be someone
of my own kind, a connoisseur and prizer of burrows, a
hermit, a lover of peace, but all the same a filthy scoundrel
who wishes to be housed where he has not built. If he
were actually to arrive now, if in his obscene lust he
were to discover the entrance and set about working at
it, lifting the moss ; if he were actually to succeed, if
he were actually to wriggle his way down in my stead,
until only his hindquarters still showed ; if all this were
actually to happen, so that at last, casting all prudence
to the winds, I might in my blind rage leap on him,
maul him, tear the flesh from his bones, destroy him,

drink his blood, and fling his corpse among the rest of
my spoil, but above all—that is the main thing—were at
last back in my burrow once more, I would have it in
my heart to greet the labyrinth itself with rapture ; yet
first I would draw the moss covering over me, and I
would want to rest, it seems to me, for all the remainder
of my life.   But nobody comes and I am left to my own
resources.   Perpetually obsessed by the sheer difficulty of
the attempt, I lose much of my timidity, I no longer
attempt even to appear to avoid the entrance, but make a
hobby of prowling round it ; by now it is almost as if I
were the enemy spying out a suitable opportunity for
successfully breaking in.   If I only had someone I could
trust to keep watch at my post of observation ; then of
course I could descend in perfect peace of mind.   I
should make an agreement with this trusty confederate
of mine that he would keep a careful note of the state
of things during my descent and for quite a long time
afterwards, and if he saw any sign of danger knock on
the moss covering, and if he saw nothing do nothing.
With that a clean sweep would be made of all my fears,
no residue would be left, or at most my confidant.   For
would he not demand some counterservice from me ;
would he not at least want to see the burrow ?   That in
itself, to let any one freely into my burrow, would be
exquisitely painful to me.   I built it for myself, not for
visitors, and I think I would refuse to admit him ; not
even though he alone made it possible for me to get into
the burrow would I let him in.   But I simply could not
admit him, for either I must let him go in first by himself, which is simply unimaginable, or we must both
descend at the same time, in which case the advantage I
am supposed to derive from him, that of being kept

watch over, would be lost.   And what trust can I really
put in him ?   Can I trust one whom I have had under
my eyes just as fully when I can't see him, and the moss
covering separates us ?   It is comparatively easy to trust
any one if you are supervising him or at least can supervise him ;   perhaps it is possible even to trust someone
at a distance ;   but completely to trust someone outside
the burrow when you are inside the burrow, that is in a
different world, that, it seems to me, is impossible.   But
such considerations are not in the least necessary ;   the
mere reflection is enough that during or after my descent
one of the countless accidents of existence might prevent
my confidant from fulfilling his duty, and what incal-
culable results might not the smallest accident of that
kind have for me ?   No, if one takes it by and large, I
have no right to complain that I am alone and have
nobody that I can trust.   I certainly lose nothing by
that and probably spare myself trouble.   I can only trust
myself and my burrow.   I should have thought of that
before and taken measures to meet the difficulty that
worries me so much now.   When I began the burrow it
would at least have been partly possible.   I should have
so constructed the first passage that it had two entrances
at a moderate distance from each other, so that after
descending through the one entrance with that slowness
which is unavoidable, I might rush at once through the
passage to the second entrance, slightly raise the moss
covering, which would be so arranged as to make that
easy, and from there keep watch on the position for
several days and nights.   That would have been the only
right way of doing it.   True, the two entrances would
double the risk, but that consideration need not delay
me, for one of the entrances, serving merely as a post of

observation, could be quite narrow. And with that I lose myself in a maze of technical speculations, I begin once more to dream my dream of a completely perfect burrow, and that somewhat calms me ; with closed eyes I behold with delight perfect or almost perfect structural devices for enabling me to slip out and in unobserved. While I lie there thinking such things I admire these devices very greatly, but only as technical achievements, not as real advantages ; for this freedom to slip out and in at will, what does it amount to ? It is the mark of a restless nature, of inner uncertainty, disreputable desires, evil propensities that seem still worse when one thinks of the burrow, which is there at one's hand and can flood one with peace if one only remains quite open and receptive to it. For the present, however, I am outside it seeking some possibility of returning, and for that the necessary technical devices would be very desirable. But perhaps not so very desirable after all. Is it not a very grave injustice to the burrow to regard it in moments of nervous panic as a mere hole into which one can creep and be safe ? Certainly it is a hole among other things, and a safe one, or should be, and when I picture myself in the midst of danger, then I insist with clenched teeth and all my will that the burrow should be nothing but a hole set apart to save me, and that it should fulfil that clearly defined function with the greatest possible efficiency, and I am ready to absolve it from every other duty. Now the truth of the matter—and one has no eye for that in times of great peril, and only by a great effort even in times when danger is threatening—is that in reality the burrow does provide a considerable degree of security, but by no means enough, for is one ever free from anxieties inside it ? These anxieties are different from ordinary ones, prouder, richer in content, often long repressed, but in their destructive effects they are perhaps much the same as the anxieties that existence in the outer world gives rise to. Had I constructed the burrow exclusively to assure my safety I would not have been disappointed, it is true ; nevertheless the relation between the enormous labour involved and the actual security it would provide, at least in so far as I could feel it and profit by it, would not have been in my favour. It is extremely painful to have to admit such things to oneself, but one is forced to do it, confronted by that entrance over there which now literally locks and bars itself against me, the builder and possessor. Yet the burrow is not a mere hole for taking refuge in. When I stand in the Castle Keep surrounded by my piled-up stores, surveying the ten passages which begin there, raised and sunken passages, vertical and rounded passages, wide and narrow passages, as the general plan dictates, and all alike still and empty, ready by their various routes to conduct me to all the other rooms, which are also still and empty—then all thought of mere safety is far from my mind, then I know that here is my castle, which I have wrested from the refractory soil with tooth and claw, with pounding and hammering blows, my castle which can never belong to any one else, and is so essentially mine that I can calmly accept in it even my enemy's mortal stroke at the final hour, for my blood will ebb away here in my own soil and not be lost. And what but that is the meaning of the blissful hours which I pass, now peacefully slumbering, now happily keeping watch, in these passages, these passages which suit me so well, where one can stretch oneself out in comfort, roll about in childish delight, lie and dream, or sink into blissful sleep. And the smaller rooms, each familiar to me, so familiar that in spite of their complete similarity I can clearly distinguish one from the other with my eyes shut by the mere feel of the wall : they enclose me more peacefully and warmly than a bird is enclosed in its nest. And all, all still and empty.

But if that is the case, why do I hang back? Why do I dread the thought of the intruding enemy more than the possibility of never seeing my burrow again? Well, the latter alternative is fortunately an impossibility ; there is no need for me even to take thought to know what the burrow means to me ; I and the burrow belong so indissolubly together that in spite of all my fears I could make myself quite comfortable out here, and not even need to overcome my repugnance and open the door ; I could be quite content to wait here passively, for nothing can part us for long, and somehow or other I shall quite certainly find myself in my burrow again. But on the other hand how much time may pass before then, and how many things may happen in that time, up here no less than down there? And it lies with me solely to curtail that interval and to do what is necessary at once.

And then, too exhausted to be any longer capable of thought, my head hanging, my legs trembling with fatigue, half-asleep, feeling my way rather than walking, I approach the entrance, slowly raise the moss covering, slowly descend, leaving the door open in my distraction for a needlessly long time, and presently remember my omission, and get out again to make it good—but what need was there to get out for that? All that was needed was to draw to the moss covering ; right ; so I creep in again and now at last draw to the moss covering. Only in this state, and in this state alone, can I achieve my

descent.—So at last I lie down beneath the moss on the
top of my blood-stained soil and can now enjoy my
longed-for sleep.   Nothing disturbs me, no one has
tracked me down, above the moss everything seems to be
quiet thus far at least, but even if all were not quiet I
question whether I could stop to keep watch now ;   I
have changed my place, I have left the upper world and
am in my burrow, and I feel its effect at once.   It is a
new world, endowing me with new powers, and what I
felt as fatigue up there is no longer that here.   I have
returned from a journey, dog-tired with my wanderings,
but the sight of the old house, the thought of all the
things that are waiting to be done, the necessity at least
to cast a glance at all the rooms, but above all to make
my way immediately to the Castle Keep ;   all this trans-
forms my fatigue into ardent zeal ;   it is as though at the
moment when I set foot in the burrow I had wakened
from a long and profound sleep.   My first task is a very
laborious one and requires all my attention ;   I mean
getting my spoil through the narrow and thin-walled
passages of the labyrinth.   I shove with all my might,
and the work gets done too, but far too slowly for me ;   to
hasten it I drag part of my flesh supply back again and
push my way over it and through it ;   now I have only
a portion of my spoil before me and it is easier to make
progress ;   but my road is so blocked by all this flesh in
these narrow passages, through which it is not always
easy for me to make my way when I am alone, that I
could quite easily smother among my own stores ;   sometimes I can only rescue myself from their pressure by
eating and drinking a clear space for myself.   But the
work of transport is successful, I finish it in quite a
reasonable time, the labyrinth is behind me, I reach an

ordinary passage and breathe freely, push my spoil
through a communication passage into a main passage
expressly designed for the purpose, a passage sloping
down steeply to the Castle Keep. What is left to be
done is not really work at all ; my whole load rolls and
flows down the passage almost of itself. The Castle
Keep at last ! At last I can dare to rest. Everything is
unchanged, no great mishap seems to have occurred, the
few little defects that I note at a first glance can soon be
repaired ; first, however, I must go my long round of all
the passages, but that is no hardship, that is merely to
commune again with friends, as I often did in the old
days or—I am not so very old yet, but my memory of
many things is already quite confused—as I often did,
or as I have often imagined I did. I begin with the
second passage, deliberately restraining myself, for once
having seen the Castle Keep I have infinite time—within
the burrow I always have infinite time—since everything
I do there is valuable and important and satisfies me to a
certain extent. I begin with the second passage, but
break off in the middle and turn into the third passage
and let it take me back again to the Castle Keep, and
now of course I have to begin at the second passage once
more, and so I play with my task and lengthen it out and
smile to myself and congratulate myself and become
quite dazed with all the work in front of me, but never
think of turning aside from it. It is for your sake, ye
passages and rooms, and you, Castle Keep, above all,
that I have come back, counting my own life as nothing
in the balance, after stupidly trembling for it for so long,
and postponing my return to you. What do I care for
danger now that I am with you ? You belong to me,
I to you, we are united ; what can harm us ? What if

my foes should be assembling even now up above there
and their muzzles be preparing to break through the
moss ? And with its silence and emptiness the burrow
answers me, confirming my words.—But now a feeling
of lassitude overcomes me and in some favourite room
I curl myself up tentatively, I have not yet surveyed
everything by a long way, though still resolved to examine everything to the very end ; I have no intention
of sleeping here, I have merely yielded to the temptation
of making myself comfortable and pretending I want to
sleep, I merely wish to find out if this is as good a place
for sleeping in as it used to be. It is, but it is a better
place for sleep than for wakening, and I remain lying
where I am in deep slumber.

I must have slept for a long time. I was only wakened
when I had reached the last light sleep which dissolves of
itself, and it must have been very light, for it was an
almost inaudible whistling noise that wakened me. I
recognised what it was immediately ; the smaller fry,
whom I had allowed far too much latitude, had burrowed a
new channel somewhere during my absence, this channel
must have chanced to intersect an older one, the air was
caught there, and that produced the whistling noise.
What an indefatigably busy lot these smaller fry are, and
what a nuisance their diligence can be ! First I shall
have to listen at the walls of my passages and locate the
place of disturbance by experimental excavations, and
only then will I be able to get rid of the noise. However,
this new channel may be quite welcome as a further
means of ventilation, if it can be fitted into the plan of
the burrow. But after this I shall keep a much sharper
eye on the small fry than I used to ; I shall spare none
of them.

As I have a good deal of experience in investigations of this kind the work probably will not take me long and I can start upon it at once ; there are other jobs awaiting me, it is true, but this is the most urgent ; I must have silence in my passages. This noise, however, is a comparatively innocent one ; I did not hear it at all when I first arrived, although it must certainly have been there ; I must first feel quite at home before I could hear it ; it is, so to speak, audible only to the ear of the householder. And it is not even constant, as such noises usually are ; there are long pauses, obviously caused by stoppages of the current of air. I start on my investigations, but I can't find the right place to begin at, and though I cut a few trenches I do it at random ; naturally that has no effect, and the hard work of digging and the still harder work of filling the trenches up again and beating the earth firm is so much labour lost. I don't seem to be getting any nearer to the place where the noise is, it goes on always on the same thin note, with regular pauses, now a sort of whistling, but again like a kind of piping. Now I could leave it to itself for the time being ; it is very disturbing, certainly, but there can hardly be any doubt that its origin is what I took it to be at first ; so it can scarcely become louder, on the contrary such noises may quite well—though until now I have never had to wait so long for that to happen—may quite well vanish of themselves in the course of time through the continued labours of these little burrowers ; and apart from that often chance itself puts one on the track of the disturbance, where systematic investigation has failed for a long time. In such ways I comfort myself, and resolve simply to continue my tour of the passages, and visit the rooms, many of which I have not even seen yet since my return, and enjoy myself contemplating the Castle Keep now and then between times ; but my anxiety will not let me, and I must go on with my search. These little creatures take up much, far too much, time that could be better employed. In such cases as the present it is usually the technical problem that attracts me ; for example, from the noise, which my ear can distinguish in all its finest shades, so that it has a perfectly clear outline to me, I deduce its cause, and now I am on fire to discover whether my conclusion is valid. And with good reason, for as long as that is not established I cannot feel safe, even if it were merely a matter of discovering where a grain of sand that had fallen from one of the walls had rolled to. And even a noise such as this is by no means a trifling matter, regarded from that angle. But whether trifling or important, I can find nothing, no matter how hard I search, or it may be that I find too much. This had to happen just in my favourite room, I think to myself, and I walk a fair good distance away from it, almost half-way along the passage leading to the next room ; but I do this merely as a joke, pretending to myself that my favourite room is not alone to blame, but that there are disturbances elsewhere as well, and with a smile on my face I begin to listen ; but soon I stop smiling, for, right enough, the same whistling meets me here, too. It is really nothing to worry about ; sometimes I think that nobody but myself would hear it ; it is true, I hear it now more and more distinctly, for my ear has grown keener through practice ; though in reality it is exactly the same noise wherever I may hear it, as I have convinced myself by comparing my impressions. Nor is it growing louder ; I recognise this when I listen in the middle of the passage instead of pressing my ear

against the wall. Then it is only by straining my ears,
indeed by lowering my head as well, that I can more
guess at than hear the merest trace of a noise now and
then. But it is this very uniformity of the noise everywhere that disturbs me most, for it cannot be made to
agree with my original assumption. Had I rightly
divined the cause of the noise, then it must have issued
with greatest force from some given place, which it would
be my task to discover, and after that have grown fainter
and fainter. But if my hypothesis does not meet the
case, what can the explanation be ? There still remains
the possibility that there are two noises, that up to now
I have been listening at a good distance from the two
centres, and that while its noise increases, when I draw
near to one of them, the total result remains approxi-
mately the same for the ear in consequence of the lessening
volume of sound from the other centre. Already I have
almost fancied sometimes, when I have listened carefully,
that I could distinguish, if very indistinctly, differences of
tone which support this new assumption. In any case I
must extend my sphere of investigation far farther than
I have done. Accordingly I descend the passage to the
Castle Keep and begin to listen there. Strange, the same
noise there, too. Now it is a noise produced by the
burrowing of some species of small fry who have in-
famously exploited my absence ; in any case they have
no intention of doing me harm, they are simply busied
with their own work, and so long as no obstacle comes
in their way they will keep on in the direction they have
taken ; I know all this, yet that they should have dared
to approach the very Castle Keep itself is incomprehensible
to me and fills me with agitation, and confuses the
faculties which I need so urgently for the work before

me. Here I have no wish to discover whether it is the
unusual depth at which the Castle Keep lies, or its great
extent and correspondingly powerful air suction, calculated to scare burrowing creatures away, or the mere
fact that it is the Castle Keep, that by some channel or
other has penetrated to their dull minds. In any case I
have never noticed any sign of burrowing in the walls of
the Castle Keep until now. Crowds of little beasts have
come here, it is true, attracted by the powerful smells ;
here I have had a constant hunting-ground, but my quarry
has always burrowed a way through in the upper passages,
and come running down here, somewhat fearfully, but
unable to withstand such a temptation. But now, it
seems, they are burrowing in all the passages. If I had
only carried out the best of the grand plans I thought out
in my youth and early manhood, or rather, if I had only
had the strength to carry them out, for there would have
been no lack of will. One of these favourite plans of
mine was to isolate the Castle Keep from its surroundings,
that is to say, to restrict the thickness of its walls to
about my own height, and leave a free space of about the
same width all round the Castle Keep, except for a
narrow foundation, which unfortunately would have to be
left to bear up the whole. I had always pictured this
free space, and not without reason, as the loveliest
imaginable haunt. What a joy to lie pressed against the
rounded outer wall, pull oneself up, let oneself slide
down again, miss one's footing and find oneself on firm
earth, and play all those games literally upon the Castle
Keep and not inside it ; to avoid the Castle Keep, to
rest one's eyes from it whenever one wanted, to postpone
the joy of seeing it until later and yet not have to do
without it, but literally hold it safe between one's

claws, a thing that is impossible if you have only an
ordinary open entrance to it ; but above all to be able to
stand guard over it, and in that way to be so completely
compensated for renouncing the actual sight of it that,
if one had to choose between staying all one's life in the
Castle Keep or in the free space outside it, one would
choose the latter, content to wander up and down there
all one's days and keep guard over the Castle Keep.   Then
there would be no noises in the walls, no insolent burrowing up to the very Keep itself ; then peace would be
assured there and I would be its guardian ; then I would
not have to listen with loathing to the burrowing of the
small fry, but with delight to something that I cannot hear
now at all : the murmurous silence of the Castle Keep.

But that beautiful dream is past and I must set to
work, almost glad that now my work has a direct connection with the Castle Keep, for that wings it.   Certainly
as I can see more and more clearly, I need all my energies
for this task, which at first seemed quite a trifling one.
I listen now at the walls of the Castle Keep, and wherever
I listen, high or low, at the roof or the floor, at the
entrance or in the corners, everywhere, everywhere, I
hear the same noise.   And how much time, how much
care must be wasted in listening to that noise, with its
regular pauses.   One can, if one wishes, find a tiny
deceitful comfort in the fact that here in the Castle
Keep, because of its vastness, one hears nothing at all,
as distinguished from the passages, when one stands back
from the walls.   Simply as a rest and a means to regain
my composure I often make this experiment, listen in-
tently and am overjoyed when I hear nothing.   But the
question still remains, what can have happened ?   Confronted with this phenomenon my original explanation

completely falls to the ground. But I must also reject
other explanations which present themselves to me. One
could assume, for instance, that the noise I hear is simply
that of the small fry themselves at their work. But all
my experience contradicts this ; I cannot suddenly begin
to hear now a thing that I have never heard before though
it was always there. My sensitiveness to disturbances
in the burrow has perhaps become greater with the years,
yet my hearing has by no means grown keener. It is of
the very nature of small fry not to be heard. Would I
have tolerated them otherwise ? Even at the risk of
starvation I would have exterminated them. But perhaps
—this idea now insinuates itself—I am concerned here
with some animal unknown to me. That is possible.
True, I have observed the life down here long and carefully enough, but the world is full of diversity and is
never wanting in painful surprises. Yet it cannot be a
single animal, it must be a whole swarm that has suddenly
fallen upon my domain, a huge swarm of little creatures,
which as they are audible, must certainly be bigger than
the small fry, but yet cannot be very much bigger, for
the sound of their labours is itself very faint. It may be,
then, a swarm of unknown creatures on their wanderings,
who happen to be passing by my way, who disturb me,
but will presently cease to do so. So I could really wait
for them to pass, and need not put myself to the trouble
of work that will be needless in the end. Yet if these
creatures are strangers, why is it that I never see any of
them ? I have already dug a host of trenches, hoping to
catch one of them, but I can find not a single one. Then
it occurs to me that they may be quite tiny creatures,
far tinier than any I am acquainted with, and that it is
only the noise they make that is greater. Accordingly I

investigate the soil I have dug up, I cast the lumps into
the air so that they break into quite small particles, but
the noise-makers are not among them. Slowly I come
to realise that by digging such small fortuitous trenches
I achieve nothing ; in doing that I merely disfigure the
walls of my burrow, scratching hastily here and there
without taking time to fill up the holes again ; at many
places already there are heaps of earth which block my
way and my view. Still, that is only a secondary worry ;
for now I can neither wander about my house, nor review
it, nor rest ; often already I have fallen asleep at my work
in some hole or other, with one paw clutching the soil
above me, from which in a semi-stupor I have been trying to tear a lump. I intend now to alter my methods. I
shall dig a wide and carefully constructed trench in the
direction of the noise and not cease from digging until,
independent of all theories, I find the real cause of the
noise. Then I shall eradicate it, if that is within my
power, and if it is not, at least I shall know the truth.
That truth will bring me either peace or despair, but
whether the one or the other, it will be beyond doubt or
question. This decision strengthens me. All that I have
done till now seems to me far too hasty ; in the excitement of my return, while I had not yet shaken myself
free from the cares of the upper world, and was not yet
completely penetrated by the peace of the burrow, but
rather hypersensitive at having had to renounce it for
such a long time, I was thrown into complete confusion of
mind by an unfamiliar noise. And what was it ? A
faint whistling, audible only at long intervals, a mere
nothing to which I don't say that one could actually get
used, for no one could get used to it, but which one
could, without actually doing anything about it at once,

observe for a while, that is, listen every two hours, let us say, and patiently register the results, instead of, as I had done, keeping one's ear fixed to the wall and at every hint of noise tearing out a lump of earth, not really hoping to find anything, but simply so as to do something to give expression to one's inward agitation. All that will be changed now, I hope. And then, with furious shut eyes, I have to admit to myself that I hope nothing of the kind, for I am still trembling with agitation just as I was hours ago, and if my reason did not restrain me I would probably like nothing better than to start stubbornly and defiantly digging, simply for the sake of digging, at some place or other, whether I heard anything there or not ; almost like the small fry, who burrow either without any object at all or simply because they eat the soil. My new and reasonable plan both tempts me and leaves me cold. There is nothing in it to object to, I at least know of no objection ; it is bound, so far as I can see, to achieve my aim. And yet at bottom I do not believe in it ; I believe in it so little that I do not even fear the terrors which its success may well bring. I do not believe even in a dreadful denouement ; indeed it seems to me that I have been thinking ever since the first appearance of the noise of such a methodical trench, and have not begun upon it until now simply because I put no trust in it. In spite of that I shall of course start on the trench ; I have no other alternative ; but I shall not start at once, but postpone the task for a little while. If reason is to be reinstated on the throne again, it must be completely reinstated ; I shall not rush blindly into my task. In any case I shall first repair the damage that I have done to the burrow with my wild digging ; that will take a good long time, but it is necessary ; if the

new trench is really to reach its goal it will probably be
long, and if it should lead to nothing at all it will be
endless ; in any case this task means a longish absence
from the burrow, though an absence by no means so
painful as an absence in the upper world, for I can interrupt my work whenever I like and pay a visit to my house ;
and even if I should not do that the air of the Castle
Keep will be wafted to me and surround me while I
work ; nevertheless it means leaving the burrow and
surrendering myself to an uncertain fate, and consequently
I want to leave the burrow in good order behind me ; it
shall not be said that I, who am fighting for its peace,
have myself destroyed that peace without reinstating it
at once. So I begin by shovelling the soil back into the
holes from which it was taken, a kind of work I am familiar
with, that I have done countless times almost without
regarding it as work, and at which, particularly as
regards the final pressing and smoothing down—and this
is no empty boast, but the simple truth—I am unbeatable.
But this time everything seems difficult, I am too dis-
tracted, every now and then, in the middle of my work,
I press my ear to the wall and listen, and without taking
any notice let the soil that I have just lifted trickle back
into the passage again. The final embellishments, which
demand a stricter attention, I can hardly achieve at all.
Hideous protuberances, disturbing cracks remain, not to
speak of the fact that the old buoyancy simply cannot be
restored again to a wall patched up in such a way. I try
to comfort myself with the reflection that my present
work is only temporary. When I return after peace has
been restored I shall repair everything properly : work
will be mere play to me then. Oh yes, work is mere
play in fairy tales, and this comfort of mine belongs to

the realm of fairy tales too. It would be far better to
do the work thoroughly now, at once, far more reasonable than perpetually to interrupt it and wander off
through the passages to discover new sources of noise,
which is easy enough, all that is needed being to stop at
any point one likes and listen. And that is not the end
of my useless discoveries. Sometimes I fancy that the
noise has stopped, for it makes long pauses ; sometimes
such a faint whistling escapes notice, one's own blood is
pounding all too loudly in one's ears ; then two pauses
come one after another, and for a while one thinks that
the whistling has stopped for ever. I listen no longer, I
jump up, all life is transfigured ; it is as if the fountains
from which flows the silence of the burrow were un-
sealed. I refrain from verifying my discovery at once, I
want first to find someone to whom in all good faith I
can confide it, so I rush to the Castle Keep, I remember,
for I and everything in me has awakened to new life,
that I have eaten nothing for a long time, I snatch something or other from among my store of food half buried
under debris and hurriedly begin to swallow it while I
hurry back to the place where I made my incredible
discovery, I only want to assure myself about it incidentally, perfunctorily, while I am eating ; I listen, but the
most perfunctory listening shows at once that I was shame-
fully deceived : away there in the distance the whistling
still remains unshaken. And I spit out my food, and
would like to trample it underfoot, and go back to my
task, not caring which I take up ; at any place where it
seems to be needed, and there are enough places like that,
I mechanically start on something or other, just as if the
overseer had appeared and I must make a pretence of
working for his benefit. But hardly have I well begun in

this fashion when it may happen that I make a new discovery. The noise seems to have become louder, not
much louder, of course—here it is always a matter of the
subtlest shades—but all the same sufficiently louder for
the ear to recognise it clearly. And this growing-louder
is like a coming-nearer ; still more distinctly than you
hear the increasing loudness of the noise you can literally
see the step that brings it closer to you. You leap back
from the wall, you try to grasp at once all the possible
consequences that this discovery will bring with it. You
feel as if you had never really organised the burrow for
defence against attack ; you had intended to do so, but
despite all your experience of life the danger of an
attack, and consequently the need to organise the place
for defence, seemed remote—or rather not remote (how
could it possibly be !)—but infinitely less important than
the need to put it in a state where one could live peacefully ; and so that consideration was given priority in
everything relating to the burrow. Many things in this
direction might have been done without affecting the
plan of the whole ; most incomprehensibly they have
been neglected. I have had a great deal of luck all those
years, luck has spoilt me ; I have had anxieties, but
anxiety leads to nothing when you have luck to back you.

The thing to do, really to do now, would be to go carefully over the burrow and consider every possible means
of defending it, work out a plan of defence and a corresponding plan of construction, and then start on the work
at once with the vigour of youth. That is the work that
would really be needed, for which, I need not say, it is
now far too late in the day ; yet that is what would really
be needed, and not the digging of a grand experimental
trench, whose only real result would be to deliver me

hand and foot to the search for danger, out of the foolish
fear that it will not arrive quickly enough of itself.
Suddenly I cannot comprehend my former plan. I can
find no slightest trace of reason in what had seemed so
reasonable ; once more I lay beside by work and even my
listening ; I have no wish to discover any further signs
that the noise is growing louder ; I have had enough of
discoveries ; I let everything slide ; I would be quite
content if I could only still the conflict going on within
me.   Once more I let my passages lead me where they
will, I come to more and more remote ones that I have
not yet seen since my return, and that are quite unsullied
by my scratching paws, and whose silence rises up to
meet me and sinks into me. I do not surrender to it, I
hurry on, I do not know what I want, probably simply to
put off the hour. I stray so far that I find myself at the
labyrinth ; the idea of listening beneath the moss covering
tempts me ; such distant things, distant for the moment,
chain my interest. I push my way up and listen. Deep
stillness ; how lovely it is here, outside there nobody
troubles about my burrow, everybody has his own affairs,
which have no connection with me ; how have I managed
to achieve this state of things with all my calculations ?
Here under the moss covering is perhaps the only place
in my burrow now where I can listen for hours and hear
nothing. A complete reversal of things in the burrow ;
what was once the place of danger has become a place of
tranquillity, while the Castle Keep has been plunged into
the bustle of the world and all its perils. Still worse,
even here there is no peace in reality, here nothing has
changed ; silent or vociferous, danger lies in ambush as
before above the moss, but I have grown insensitive to it,
my mind is far too much taken up with the whistling

in my walls. Is my mind really taken up with it? It grows louder, it comes nearer, but I wriggle my way through the labyrinth and make a couch for myself up here under the moss; it is almost as if I were already leaving the house to the whistler, content if I can only have a little peace up here. To the whistler? Have I come, then, to a new conclusion concerning the cause of the noise? But surely the noise is caused by the channels bored by the small fry? Is not that my considered opinion? It seems to me that I have not retreated from it thus far. And if the noise is not caused directly by these channels, it is indirectly. And even if it should have no connection with them whatever, one is not at liberty to make *a priori* assumptions, but must wait until one finds the cause, or it reveals itself. One could play with hypotheses, of course, even at this stage; for instance it is possible that there has been a water burst at some distance away, and that what seems a piping or whistling to me is in reality a gurgling. But apart from the fact that I have no experience in that sphere—the groundwater that I found at the start I drained away at once, and in this sandy soil it has never returned—apart from this fact the noise is undeniably a whistling and simply not to be translated into a gurgling. But what avails all exhortations to be calm; my imagination will not rest, and I have actually come to believe—it is useless to deny it to myself—that the whistling is made by some beast, and moreover not by a great many small ones, but by a single great one. Many signs contradict this. The noise can be heard everywhere and always at the same strength, and moreover uniformly, both by day and night. At first, therefore, one cannot but incline to the hypothesis of a great number of little animals; but as I must have found some of them during my digging and I have found nothing, it only remains for me to assume the existence of a great beast, especially as the things that seem to contradict the hypothesis are merely things which make the beast, not so much impossible, as merely dangerous beyond all one's powers of conception. For that reason alone have I stuck out against this hypothesis. I shall cease from this self-deception. For a long time already I have played with the idea that the beast can be heard at such a great distance because it works so furiously ; it burrows as fast through the ground as another animal can walk on the open road ; the ground still trembles at its burrowing when it has ceased ; this reverberation and the noise of the boring itself unite into one sound at such a great distance, and I, as I hear only the last dying ebb of that sound, hear it always at the same uniform strength. It follows from this also that the beast is not making for me, seeing that the noise never changes ; more likely it has a plan in view whose purpose I cannot decipher ; I merely assume that the beast—and I make no claim whatever that it knows of my existence—is encircling me ; it has probably made several circles round my burrow already since I began to observe it. The nature of the noise, the piping or whistling, gives me much food for thought. When I scratch and scrape in the soil in my own fashion the sound is quite different. I can explain the whistling only in this way : that the beast's chief means of burrowing is not its claws, which it probably employs merely as a secondary resource, but its snout or its muzzle, which, of course, apart from its enormous strength, must also be fairly sharp at the point. It probably bores its snout into the earth with one mighty push and tears out a great lump ; while it is doing that I hear nothing ; that is the pause ; but then it draws in the air for a new push. This indrawal of its breath, which must be an earth-shaking noise, not only because of the beast's strength, but of its haste, its furious lust for work as well : this noise I hear then as a faint whistling. But quite incomprehensible remains the beast's capacity to work without stopping ; perhaps the short pauses provide also the opportunity of snatching a moment's rest ; but apparently the beast has never yet allowed itself a really long rest, day and night it goes on burrowing, always with the same freshness and vigour, always thinking of its object, which must be achieved with the utmost expedition, and which it has the ability to achieve with ease. Now I could not have foreseen such an opponent. But apart altogether from the beast's peculiar character-istics, what is happening now is only something which I should really have feared all the time, something against which I should have been constantly prepared : the fact that someone would come. By what chance can every-thing have flowed on so quietly and happily for such a long time ? Who can have diverted my enemies from their path, and forced them to make a wide detour round my property ? Why have I been spared for so long, only to be delivered to such terrors now ? Compared with this, what are all the petty dangers in brooding over which I have spent my life ! As owner of the burrow I had hoped to be in a stronger position than any enemy who might chance to appear. But simply by virtue of being owner of this great vulnerable edifice I am obviously defenceless against any serious attack. The joy of possessing it has spoilt me, the vulnerability of the burrow has made me vulnerable ; any wound to it hurts me as

if I myself were hit.   It is precisely this that I should have
foreseen ;   instead of thinking only of my own defence—
and how perfunctorily and vainly I have done even that—
I should have thought of the defence of the burrow.
Above all, provision should have been made for cutting
off sections of the burrow, and as many as possible of
them, from the endangered sections when they are
attacked ;   this should have been done by means of impro-
vised land-slides, calculated to operate at a moment's
notice ;   moreover these should have been so thick, and
have provided such an effectual barrier, that the attacker
would not even guess that the real burrow only began
at the other side.   More, these land-slides should have
been so devised that they not only concealed the burrow,
but also entombed the attacker.   Not the slightest
attampt have I made to carry out such a plan, nothing at
all has been done in this direction, I have been as thoughtless as a child, I have passed my manhood's years in
childish games, I have done nothing but play even with
the thought of danger, I have shirked really taking thought
for actual danger.   And there has been no lack of warning.

Nothing, of course, approaching the present situation
has happened before ;   nevertheless there was an incident
not unlike it when the burrow was only beginning.   The
main difference between that time and this is simply that
the burrow was only beginning then. . . . In those days
I was literally nothing more than a humble apprentice
in his first year, the labyrinth was only sketched out in
rough outline, I had already dug a little room, but the
proportions and the execution of the walls were sadly
bungled ;   in short everything was so tentative that it
could only be regarded as an experiment, as something
which, if one lost patience some day, one could leave

lying as it was without much regret. Then one day as
I lay on a heap of earth resting from my labours—I have
rested far too often from my labours all my life—suddenly I heard a noise in the distance. Being young at
the time, I was less frightened than curious. I left my
work to look after itself and set myself to listen ; I
listened and listened, and had no wish to fly up to my
moss covering and stretch myself out there so that I
might not hear. I did listen, at least. I could clearly
recognise that the noise came from some kind of burrowing similar to my own ; it was somewhat fainter, of
course, but how much of that might be put down to the
distance one could not tell. I was intensely interested,
but otherwise calm and cool. Perhaps I am in somebody's
else's burrow, I thought to myself, and now the owner
is boring his way towards me. If that assumption had
proved to be correct I would have gone away, for I have
never had any desire for conquest or bloodshed, and
begun building somewhere else. But after all I was still
young and still without a burrow, so I could remain
quite cool. Besides, the further course of the noise
brought no real cause for apprehension, except that it was
not easy to explain. If whoever was boring there was
really making for me, because he had heard me boring,
then if he changed his direction, as now actually happened, it could not be told whether he did this because
my pause for rest had deprived him of any definite point
to make towards, or because—which was more plausible
—he had himself changed his plans. But perhaps I had
been deceived altogether, and he had never been actually
making in my direction ; at any rate the noise grew
louder for a while as if he were drawing nearer, and
being young at that time I probably would not have been

displeased to see the burrower suddenly rising from the ground ; but nothing of that kind happened, at a certain point the sound of boring began to weaken, it grew fainter and fainter, as if the burrower were gradually diverging from his first route, and suddenly it broke off altogether, as if he had decided now to take the diametrically opposite direction and were making straight away from me into the distance. For a long time I still went on listening for him in the silence, before I returned once more to my work. Now that warning was definite enough, but I soon forgot it, and it scarcely influenced my building plans.

Between that day and this lie my years of maturity, but is it not as if there were no interval at all between them ? I still take long rests from my labours and listen at the wall, and the burrower has changed his intention anew, he has turned back, he is returning from his journey, thinking he has given me ample time in the interval to prepare for his reception. But on my side everything is worse prepared for than it was then ; the great burrow stands defenceless, and I am no longer a young apprentice, but an old architect, and the powers I still have fail me when the decisive hour comes ; yet old as I am it seems to me that I would gladly be still older, so old that I should never be able to rise again from my resting-place under the moss. For to be honest I cannot endure the place, I rise up and rush, as if I had filled myself up there with new anxieties instead of peace, down into the house again. What was the state of things the last time I was here ? Had the whistling grown fainter ? No, it had grown louder. I listen at ten places choses at random and definitely note my own disappointment ; the whistling is just the same as ever, nothing has altered. Up there under the moss no change touches one, there one is at peace, uplifted above time ; but here every instant frets and gnaws at the listener. I go once more the long road to the Castle Keep, all my surroundings seem filled with agitation, seem to be looking at me, and then look away again so as not to annoy me, yet cannot refrain the very next moment from trying to read the saving solution from my expression. I shake my head, I have not yet found any solution. Nor do I go to the Castle Keep in pursuance of any plan. I pass the spot where I had intended to begin the experimental trench, I look it over once more, it would have been an admirable place to begin at, the trench's course would have been in the direction where lay the majority of the tiny ventilation holes, which would have greatly lightened my labours ; perhaps I should not have had to dig very far, should not even have had to dig to the source of the noise ; perhaps if I had listened at the ventilation holes it would have been enough. But no consideration is potent enough to animate me to this labour of digging. This trench will bring me certainty, you say ? I have reached the stage where I no longer wish to have certainty. In the Castle Keep I choose a lovely piece of flayed red flesh and creep with it into one of the heaps of earth ; there I shall have silence at least, such silence, at any rate, as still can be said to exist here. I munch and nibble at the flesh, think of the strange beast going its own road in the distance, and then again that I should enjoy my store of food as fully as possible, while I still have the chance. This last is probably the sole plan I have left that I can carry out. For the rest I try to unriddle the beast's plans. Is it on its wanderings, or is it working on its own burrow ? If it is on its wanderings then perhaps an understanding with it might be possible. If it should really break through to the burrow I shall give it some of my store and it will go on its way again. It will go its way again, a fine story. Lying on my heap of earth I can naturally dream of all sorts of things, even of an understanding with the beast, though I know well enough that no such thing can happen, and that at the instant when we see each other, more, at the moment when we merely guess at each other's presence, we shall both blindly bare our claws and teeth, neither of us a second before or after the other, both of us filled with a new and different hunger, even if we should already be gorged to bursting. And with entire justice, for who, even if he were merely on his wanderings, would not change his itinerary and his plans for the future on catching sight of the burrow ? But perhaps the beast is digging in its own burrow, in which case I cannot even dream of an understanding. Even if it should be such a peculiar beast as to be able to tolerate a neighbour near its burrow, it could not tolerate my burrow, it would not tolerate in any case a neighbour who could be clearly heard. Now actually the beast seems to be a great distance away : if it would only withdraw a little farther the noise, too, would probably disappear ; perhaps in that case everything would be peaceful again as in the old days ; all this would then become a painful but salutary lesson, spurring me on to make the most diverse improvements on the burrow ; if I have peace, and danger does not immediately threaten me, I am still quite fit for all sorts of hard work ; perhaps, considering the enormous possibilities which its powers of work open before it, the beast has given up the idea of extending its burrow in my direction, and is compensating itself for that in some other one. That consummation also cannot, of course, be brought about by negotiation but only by the beast itself, or by some compulsion exercised from my side. In both cases the decisive factor will be whether the beast knows about me, and if so what it knows. The more I reflect upon it the more improbable does it seem to me that the beast has even heard of me ; it is possible, though unimaginable, that it can have received news of me through some other channel, but it has certainly never heard me. So long as I still knew nothing about it, it simply cannot have heard me, for at that time I kept very quiet, nothing could be more quiet than my return to the burrow ; afterwards, when I dug the experimental trenches, perhaps it could have heard me, though my style of digging makes very little noise ; but if it had heard me I must have noticed some sign of it, the beast must at least have stopped its work every now and then to listen. But all remained unchanged.

THE GIANT MOLE

THOSE, and I am one of them, who find even a small ordinary sized mole disgusting, would probably have died of disgust if they had seen the great mole that a few years back was observed in the neighbourhood of one of our villages, which achieved a certain transitory celebrity on account of the incident. Today it has long since sunk back into oblivion again, and in that only shares the obscurity of the whole incident, which has remained quite inexplicable, but which people, it must be confessed, have also taken no great pains to explain ; and so, as the result of an incomprehensible apathy in those very circles which should have concerned themselves with it, and who in fact have shown enthusiastic interest in far more trifling matters, the affair has been forgotten without ever being adequately investigated. In any case the fact that the village could not be reached by the railroad was no excuse. Many people came from great distances out of pure curiosity, there were even foreigners among them ; it was only those who should have shown something more than curiosity that refrained from coming. In fact, if a few quite simple people, people whose daily work gave them hardly a moment of leisure—if these people had not quite disinterestedly taken up the affair, the rumour of this natural phenomenon would probably have never spread beyond the locality. Indeed, rumour itself, which usually cannot be held within bounds, was actually sluggish in this

case ; if it had not literally been given a shove it would
not have spread. But even that was no valid reason for
refusing to enquire into the affair ; on the contrary this
second phenomenon should have been investigated as
well. Instead the old village teacher was left to write
the sole account in black and white of the incident, and
though he was an excellent man in his own professional
his abilities and his equipment alike rendered it impossible for him to produce an exhaustive description
that could be used as a foundation by others, far less,
therefore, an actual explanation of the occurrence. His
little pamphlet was printed, and a good few copies were
sold to visitors to the village about that time ; it also
received some public recognition, but the teacher was
wise enough to perceive that his fragmentary labours,
in which no one supported him, were at bottom without
value. If in spite of that he did not relax in them, and
made the question his life work, though it naturally
became more hopeless from year to year, that only shows
on the one hand how powerful an effect the appearance
of the great mole was capable of producing, and on the
other how much laborious effort and fidelity to his convictions may be found in an old and obscure village
teacher. But that he suffered deeply from the cold attitude of the recognised authorities is proved by a brief
brochure with which he followed up his pamphlet several
years later, by which time hardly any one could remember
what it was all about. In this brochure he complained
of the lack of understanding that he had encountered in
people where it was least to be expected ; complaints
which carried conviction less by the skill with which
they were expressed than by their honesty. Of such
people he said very appositely : " It is not I, but they,

who talk like old village teachers." And among other things he adduced the pronouncement of a scholar to whom he had gone expressly about his affair. The name of the scholar was not mentioned, but from various circumstances we could guess who it was. After the teacher had managed with great difficulty to secure admittance, he perceived at once from the very way in which he was greeted that the savant had already acquired a rooted prejudice against the matter. The absence with which he listened to the long report which the teacher, pamphlet in hand, delivered to him, can be gauged from a remark that he let fall after a pause for ostensible reflection : " The soil in your neighbourhood is particularly black and rich. Consequently it provides the moles with particularly rich nourishment, and so they grow to an unusual size."

" But not to such a size as that ! " exclaimed the teacher, and he measured off two yards on the wall, somewhat exaggerating the length of the mole in his exasperation. " Oh, and why not ? " replied the scholar, who obviously looked upon the whole affair as a great joke. With this verdict the teacher had to return to his home. He tells how his wife and six children were waiting for him by the roadside in the snow, and how he had to admit to them the final collapse of his hopes.

When I read of the scholar's attitude towards the old man I was not yet acquainted with the teacher's pamphlet. But I at once resolved myself to collect and correlate all the information I could discover regarding the case. If I could not employ physical force against the scholar, I could at least write a defence of the teacher, or more exactly, of the good intentions of an honest but uninfluential man. I admit that I rued this decision later, for I soon saw that its execution was bound to involve me in a very strange predicament. On the one hand my own influence was far from sufficient to effect a change in learned or even public opinion in the teacher's favour, while on the other the teacher was bound to notice that I was less concerned with his main object, which was to prove that the great mole had actually been seen, than to defend his honesty, which must naturally be self-evident to him and in need of no defence. Accordingly, what was bound to happen was this : I would be mis-understood by the teacher, though I wanted to collaborate with him, and instead of helping him I myself would probably require support, which was unlikely to be given. Besides, my decision would impose a great burden of work upon me. If I wanted to convince people I could not invoke the teacher, since he himself had not been able to convince them. To read his pamphlet could only have led me astray, and so I refrained from reading it until I should have finished my own labours. More, I did not even get in touch with the teacher. True, he heard of my enquiries through intermediaries, but he did not know whether I was working for him or against him. In fact he probably assumed the latter, though he denied it later on ; for I have proof of the fact that he put various obstacles in my way. It was quite easy for him to do that, for of course I was com-pelled to undertake anew all the enquiries he had already made, and so he could always steal a march on me. But that was the only objection that could be justly made to my method, an unavoidable reproach, moreover, which the caution and self-abnegation with which I drew my conclusions palliated still more. But for the rest my pamphlet was quite influenced by the teacher, perhaps

on this point, indeed, I showed all too great a scrupu-
losity ; from my words one might have thought nobody
whatever had enquired into the case before, and I was
the first to interrogate those who had seen or heard of
the mole, the first to correlate the evidence, the first to
draw conclusions. When later I read the teacher's
pamphlet—it had a very circumstantial title : " A mole,
larger in size than any ever seen before "—I found that
we actually did not agree on certain important points,
though we both believed we had proved our main point,
namely, the existence of the mole. These differences
prevented the establishment of the friendly relations
with the teacher that I had been looking forward to in
spite of everything. On his side there developed a feeling
almost of hostility. True, he was always modest and
humble in his bearing towards me, but that only made
his real feelings the more obvious. In other words, he
was of the opinion that I had merely damaged his credit,
and that my belief that I had been or could be of assistance to him was simplicity at best, but more likely
presumption or artifice. He was particularly fond of
saying that all his previous enemies had shown their
hostility either not at all, or in private, or at most by
word of mouth, while I had considered it necessary to
have my censures straightway published. Moreover, the
few opponents of his who had really occupied themselves
with the subject, if but superficially, had at least listened
to his, the teacher's views, before they had given expression to their own ; while I, on the strength of unsys-
tematically assembled and in part misunderstood evidence,
had published conclusions which, even if they were
correct as regarded the main point, must evoke incredulity,
and among the public no less than the educated. But

the faintest hint that the existence of the mole was
unworthy of credence was the worst thing that could
happen in this case.

To these reproaches, veiled as they were, I could easily
have found an answer—for instance, that his own
pamphlet achieved the very summit of the incredible—
it was less easy, however, to make headway against his
continual suspicion, and that was the reason why I was
very reserved in my dealings with him. For in his heart
he was convinced that I wanted to rob him of the fame of
being the first man publicly to vindicate the mole. Now
of course he really enjoyed no fame whatever, but only
an absurd notoriety that was shrinking more and more,
and for which I had certainly no desire to compete.
Besides, in the foreword to my pamphlet I had expressly
declared that the teacher must stand for all time as the
discoverer of the mole—and he was not even that—and
that only my sympathy with his unfortunate fate had
spurred me on to write. "It is the aim of this pamphlet"
—so I ended up all too melodramatically, but it corres-
ponded with my feelings at that time—" to help in
giving the teacher's book the wide publicity it deserves.
If I succeed in that, then may my name, which I regard
as only transiently and indirectly associated with this
question, be blotted from it at once." Thus I dis-
claimed expressly any major participation in the affair;
it was almost as if I had foreseen in some manner the
teacher's unbelievable reproaches. Nevertheless he found
in that very passage a handle against me, and I do not
deny that there was a faint show of justice in what he
said or rather hinted; indeed I was often struck by the
fact that he showed almost a keener penetration where I
was concerned than he had done in his pamphlet. For

he maintained that my foreword was double-faced. If
I was really concerned solely to give publicity to his
pamphlet, why had I not occupied myself exclusively with
him and his pamplet, why had I not pointed out its virtues,
its irrefutability, why had I not confined myself to insist-
ing on the significance of the discovery and making that
clear, why had I instead tackled the discovery itself,
while completely ignoring the pamphlet ? Had not the
discovery been made already ? Was there still anything
left to be done in that direction ? But if I really thought
that it was necessary for me to make the discovery all
over again, why had I emphasised the original discovery
so solemnly in my foreword ? One might put that down
to false modesty, but it was something worse. I was
trying to belittle the discovery, I was drawing attention
to it merely for the purpose of depreciating it, while he
on the other hand had enquired into and finally established
it. Perhaps the affair had sunk somewhat into oblivion ;
now I had made a noise about it again, but at the same
time I had made the teacher's position more difficult
than ever. What did he care whether his honesty was
vindicated or not ? All that he was concerned with was
the thing itself, and with that alone. But I was only of
disservice to it, for I did not understand it, I did not
prize it at its true value, I had not real feeling for it.
It was infinitely above my intellectual capacity. He sat
before me and looked at me, his old wrinkled face quite
composed, and yet this was what he was thinking. Yet
it was not true that he was only concerned with the
thing itself : actually he was very greedy for fame, and
wanted to make money out of the business too, which,
however, considering his large family, was very understandable. Nevertheless my interest in the affair seemed

so trivial compared with his own, that he felt he could claim to be completely disinterested without deviating very seriously from the truth. And indeed my inner doubts refused to be quite calmed by my telling myself that the man's reproaches were really due to the fact that he clung to his mole, so to speak, with both hands, and was bound to look upon any one who laid even a finger on it as a traitor. For that was not true ; his attitude was not to be explained by greed, or at any rate by greed alone, but rather by the touchiness which his great labours and their complete unsuccess had bred in him. Yet even his touchiness did not explain everything. Perhaps my interest in the affair was really too trivial. The teacher was used to lack of interest in strangers. He regarded it as a universal evil, but no longer suffered from its individual manifestations. Now a man had appeared who, strangely enough, took up the affair and even he did not understand it. Attacked from this side I can make no defence. I am no zoologist ; yet perhaps I would have thrown myself into the case with my whole heart if I had discovered it ; but I had not discovered it. Such a gigantic mole is certainly a prodigy, yet one cannot expect the continuous and un-divided attention of the whole world to be accorded it, particularly if its existence is not completely and irrefut-ably established, and in any case it cannot be produced. And I admit too that even if I had been the discoverer I would probably never have come forward so gladly and voluntarily in defence of the mole as I had in that of the teacher.

Now the misunderstanding between me and the teacher would probably have quickly cleared up if my pamphlet had achieved success. But success was not forthcoming.

Perhaps the book was not well enough written, not persuasive enough ; I am a business man, it may be that the composition of such a pamphlet was still further beyond my limited powers than those of the teacher, though in the kind of knowledge required I was greatly superior to him.   Besides, my unsuccess may be explicable in other ways ; the time at which the pamphlet appeared may have been inauspicious.   The discovery of the mole, which had failed to penetrate to a wide public at the time it took place, was not so long past on the one hand as to be completely forgotten, and thus capable of being brought alive again by my pamphlet, while on the other hand enough time had elapsed quite to exhaust the trivial interest that had originally existed.   Those who took my pamphlet at all seriously told themselves, in that bored tone which from the first had characterised the debate, that now the old useless labours on this wearisome question were to begin all over again ; and some even confused my pamphlet with the teacher's. In a leading agricultural journal appeared the following comment, fortunately at the very end, and in small print : " The pamphlet on the giant mole has once more been sent to us. Years ago we remember having had a hearty laugh over it. Since then it has not become more intelligible, not we more hard of understanding. But we simply refuse to laugh at it a second time. Instead, we would ask our teaching associations whether more useful work cannot be found for our village teachers than hunting out giant moles."   An unpardonable confusion of identity.   They had read neither the first nor the second pamphlet, and the two perfunctorily scanned expressions, " giant mole " and " village teacher," were sufficient for these gentlemen, as representatives of

publicly esteemed interests, to pronounce on the subject.
Against this attack measures might have been attempted
and with success, but the lack of understanding between
the teacher and myself kept me from venturing upon
them. I tried instead to keep the review from his knowledge as long as I could. But he very soon discovered it,
as I recognised from a sentence in one of his letters, in
which he announced his intention of visiting me for the
Christmas holidays. He wrote : " The world is full
of malice, and people smooth the path for it," by which
he wished to convey that I was one of the malicious,
but, not content with my own innate malice, wished also
to make the world's path smooth for it : in other words,
was acting in such a way as to arouse the general malice
and help it to victory. Well, I summoned the resolution
I required, and was able to await him calmly, and calmly
greet him when he arrived, this time a shade less polite
in his bearing than usual ; he carefully drew out the
journal from the breast-pocket of his old-fashioned
padded overcoat, and opening it handed it to me. " I've
seen it," I replied, handing the journal back unread.
" You've seen it," he said with a sigh ; he had the old
teacher's habit of repeating unwelcome answers. "Of
course I won't take this lying down ! " he went on,
tapping the journal excitedly with his finger and glancing
up sharply at me, as if I were of a different mind ; he
certainly had some idea of what I was about to say, for I
think I have noticed, not so much from his words as
from other indications, that he often has a genuine
intuition of my wishes, though he never yields to them
or lets himself be diverted from his aims. What I said
to him I can set down almost word for word, for I took
a note of it shortly after our interview. " Do what you

like," I said, "our ways part from this moment. I fancy that that is neither unexpected nor unwelcome news to you. The review in this journal is not the real reason for my decision ; it has merely finally confirmed it. The real reason is this : originally I thought my intervention might be of some use to you, while now I cannot but recognise that I have damaged you in every direction. Why it has turned out so I cannot say ; the causes of success and unsuccess are always ambiguous ; but don't look for the sole explanation in my short-comings. Consider ; you too had the best intentions, and yet, if one regards the matter objectively, you failed. I don't intend it as a joke, for it would be a joke against myself, when I say that your connection with me must unfortunately be counted among your failures. It is neither cowardice nor treachery, if I withdraw from the affair now. Actually it involves a certain degree of self-renunciation ; my pamphlet itself proves how much I respect you personally, in a certain sense you have become my teacher, and I have almost grown fond of the mole itself. Nevertheless I have decided to step aside ; you are the discoverer, and all that I can do is to prevent you from gaining possible fame, while I attract failure and pass it on to you. At least that is your own opinion. Enough of that. The sole expiation that I can make is to beg your forgiveness and, should you require it, to publish openly, that is, in this journal, the admission I have just made to yourself."

These were my words ; they were not entirely sincere, but the sincerity in them was obvious enough. My explanation had the effect upon him that I had roughly anticipated. Most old people have something deceitful, something perfidious, in their dealing with people

younger than themselves ; you live at peace with them,
imagine you are on the best of terms with them, know
their ruling prejudices, receive continual assurances of
amity, take the whole thing for granted ; and when
something decisive happens and those peaceful relations,
so long nourished, should come into effective operation,
suddenly these old people rise before you like strangers,
show that they have deeper and stronger convictions,
and now for the first time literally unfurl their banner,
and with terror you read upon it the new decree. The
reason for this terror lies chiefly in the fact that what
the old say now is really far more just and sensible than
what they said before ; it is as if even the self-evident
had degrees of validity, and their words now were more
self-evident than ever. But the final deceit that lies in
their words consists in this, that at bottom they have
always said what they are saying now. I must have
probed deeply into the teacher, seeing that his next words
did not entirely take me by surprise. " Child," he said,
laying his hand on mine and patting it gently, " how
did you ever take it into your head to go into this affair ?
—The very first I heard of it I talked it over with my
wife." He pushed his chair back from the table, got
up, spread out his arms, and stared at the floor, as if his
tiny little wife were standing there and he were speaking
to her. " We've struggled on alone," he said to her,
" for many years ; now, it seems, a noble protector has
risen for us in the city, a fine business man, Mr. So-and-
so. We should congratulate ourselves, shouldn't we ?
A business man in the city isn't to be sniffed at ; when
an ignorant peasant believes us and says so it doesn't
help us, for what a peasant may say or do is of no
account ; whether he says the old village teacher is

right, or spits to show his contempt, the net result is
the same. And if instead of one peasant ten thousand
should stand up for us, the result, if possible, would
only be still worse. A business man in the city, on the
other hand, is quite a different pair of shoes ; a man like
that has connections, things he says in passing, as it
were, are taken up and repeated, new patrons interest
themselves in the question, one of them, it may be,
remarks : ' You can learn even from old village teachers,'
and next day whole crowds of people are saying it to
one another, people you would never imagine saying such
things, to look at them. Next money is found to finance
the business, one gentlemen goes round collecting for it
and the others shower subscriptions on him ; they decide
that the village teacher must be dragged from his
obscurity ; they arrive, they don't bother about his
external appearance, but take him to their bosoms, and
since his wife and children depend on him, they accept
them too. Have you ever watched city people ? They
chatter without stopping. When there's a whole lot of
them together you can hear their chatter running from
right to left and back again, and up and down, this way
and that. And so, chattering away, they push us into
the coach, so that we've hardly time to bow to everybody.
The gentleman on the driver's seat puts his glasses
straight, flourishes his whip, and off we go. They all
wave a parting greeting to the village, as if we were still
there and not sitting among them. The more important
city people drive out in carriages to meet us. As we
approach they get up from their seats and crane their
necks. The gentleman who collected the money arranges
everything methodically and in order. When we drive
into the city we are a long procession of carriages. We

think the public welcome is over ; but it really only
begins when we reach our hotel. A great crowd gathers
as soon as our arrival is announced. What interests
one interests all the rest immediately. They take their
views from one another and promptly make those views
their own. All the people who haven't managed to
drive out and meet us in carriages, are waiting in front
of the hotel ; others could have driven out, but they
were too self-conscious. They're waiting too. It's
extraordinary, the way that the gentleman who collected
the money keeps his eye on everything and directs
everything."

I had listened coolly to him, indeed I had grown cooler
and cooler while he went on. On the table I had piled
up all the copies of my pamphlet in my possession. Only
a few were missing, for during the past week I had sent
out a circular demanding the return of all the copies
distributed, and had received most of them back. True,
from several quarters I had got very polite notes saying
that So-and-so could not remember having received such
a pamphlet, and that, if it had actually arrived, he was
sorry to confess that he must have lost it. Even that was
gratifying ; in my heart I desired nothing better. Only
one reader begged me to let him keep the pamphlet as a
curiosity, pledging himself, in accordance with the spirit
of my circular, to show it to no one for twenty years.
The village teacher had not yet seen my circular. I was
glad that his words made it so easy for me to show it him.
I could do that without anxiety in any case, however, as
I had drawn it up very circumspectly, keeping his
interests in mind the whole time. The crucial passage
in the circular ran as follows : " I do not ask for the
return of the pamphlet because I retract in any way the

opinions defended there or wish them to be regarded as erroneous or even undemonstrable on any point. My request has purely personal and moreover very urgent grounds ; but no conclusion whatever must be drawn from it as regards my attitude to the whole matter. I beg to draw your particular attention to this, and would be glad also if you would make the fact better known."

For the time being I kept my hand over the circular and said : " You reproach me in your heart because things have not turned out as you hoped. Why do that ? Don't let us embitter our last moments together. And do try to see that, though you've made a discovery, it isn't necessarily greater than every other discovery, and consequently the injustice you suffer under any greater than other injustices. I don't know the ways of learned societies, but I can't believe that in the most favourable circumstances you would have been given a reception even remotely resembling the one you seem to have described to your wife. While I myself still hoped that something might come of my pamphlet, the most I expected was that perhaps the attention of a professor might be drawn to our case, that he might commission some young student to enquire into it, that this student might visit you and check in his own fashion your and my enquiries once more on the spot, and that finally, if the results seemed to him worth consideration—we must not forget that all young students are full of scepticism— he might bring out a pamphlet of his own in which your discoveries would be put on a scientific basis. All the same, even if that hope had been realised nothing very much would still have been achieved. The student's pamphlet, supporting such queer opinions, would prob- ably be held up to ridicule. If you take this agricultural journal as a sample, you can see how easily that may happen ; and scientific periodicals are still more un-scrupulous in such matters. And that's quite under-standable ; professors bear a great responsibility towards themselves, towards science, towards posterity ; they can't take every new discovery to their bosoms straight away. We others have the advantage of them there. But I'll leave that out of account and assume that the student's pamphlet has found acceptance. What would happen next ? You would probably receive honourable mention, the fact that you are a teacher possibly would go in your favour ; people would say : ' Our village teachers have sharp eyes ' ; and this journal, if journals have a memory or a conscience, would be forced to make you a public apology ; also some well-intentioned professor would be found to secure a scholarship for you ; it's possible they might even get you to come to the city, find a post for you in some school, and so give you a chance of using the scientific resources of a city so as to improve yourself. But if I am to be quite frank, I think they would content themselves with merely trying to do all this. They would summon you and you would appear, but only as an ordinary petitioner like hundreds of others, and not in solemn state ; they would talk to you and praise your honest efforts, but they would see at the same time that you were an old man, that it was hopeless for any one to begin to study science at such an age, and moreover that you had hit upon your discovery more by chance than by design, and had besides no ambition to extend your labours beyond this one case. For these reasons they would probably send you back to your village again. Your discovery, of course, would be carried further, for it is not so trifling that, once having achieved recognition, it could be forgotten again. But you would not hear much more about it, and what you heard you would scarcely understand. Every new discovery is assumed at once into the sum-total of knowledge, and with that ceases in a sense to be a discovery; it dissolves into the whole and disappears, and one must have a trained scientific eye even to recognise it after that. For it is related to fundamental axioms of whose existence we don't even know, and in the debates of science it is raised on these axioms into the very clouds. How can we expect to understand such things? Often as we listen to some learned discussion we may be under the impression that it is about your discovery, when it is about something quite different, and the next time, when we think it is about something else, and not about your discovery at all, it may turn out to be about that and that alone.

"Don't you see that? You would remain in your village, you would be able with the extra money to feed and clothe your family a little better; but your discovery would be taken out of your hands, and without your being able with any show of justice to object; for only in the city could it be given its final seal. And people wouldn't be altogether ungrateful to you, they might build a little museum on the spot where the discovery was made, it would become one of the sights of the village, you would be given the keys to keep, and, so that you shouldn't lack some outward token of honour, they could give you a little medal to wear on the breast of your coat, like those worn by attendants in scientific institutions. All this might have been possible; but was it what you wanted?"

Without stopping to consider his answer he turned on

me and said : " And so that's what you wanted to achieve for me ? "

" Probably," I said, " I didn't consider what I was doing carefully enough at the time to be able to answer that clearly now. I wanted to help you, but that was a failure, and the worst failure I have ever had. That's why I want to withdraw now and undo what I've done as far as I'm able."

" Well and good," said the teacher, taking out his pipe and beginning to fill it with the tobacco that he carried loose in all his pockets. " You took up this thankless business of your own free will, and now of your own free will you withdraw. So that's all right."

" I'm not an obstinate man," I said. " Do you find anything to object to in my proposal ? "

" No, absolutely nothing," said the teacher, and his pipe was already going. I could not bear the stink of his tobacco, and so I rose and began to walk up and down the room. From previous encounters I was used to the teacher's extreme taciturnity, and to the fact that in spite of it he never seemed to have any desire to stir from my room once he was in it. That had often disturbed me before. He wants something more, I always thought at such times, and I would offer him money, which indeed he invariably accepted. Yet he never went away before it suited his convenience. Generally his pipe was smoked out by that time, then he would ceremoniously and respectfully push his chair in to the table, make a detour round it, seize his ash plant standing in the corner, press my hand warmly, and go. But today his silent presence as he sat there was an actual torture to me. When one has bidden a last farewell to someone, as I had done, a farewell accepted in good faith, surely the mutual formalities that remain should be got over as quickly as possible, and one should not burden one's host purposelessly with one's silent presence. As I contemplated the stubborn little old fellow from behind, while he sat at the table, it seemed an impossible idea ever to show him the door.

INVESTIGATIONS OF A DOG

HOW much my life has changed, and yet how unchanged it has remained at bottom ! When I think back and recall the time when I was still a member of the canine community, sharing in all its preoccupations, a dog among dogs, I find on closer examination that from the very beginning I sensed some discrepancy, some little maladjustment, causing a slight feeling of discomfort which not even the most decorous public functions could eliminate ; more, that sometimes, no, not sometimes, but very often, the mere look of some fellow-dog of my own circle that I was fond of, the mere look of him, as if I had just caught it for the first time, would fill me with helpless embarrassment and fear, even with despair. I tried to quiet my apprehensions as best I could ; friends, to whom I divulged them, helped me ; more peaceful times came—times, it is true, in which these sudden surprises were not lacking, but in which they were accepted with more philosophy, fitted into my life with more philosophy, inducing a certain melancholy and lethargy, it may be, but nevertheless allowing me to carry on as a somewhat cold, reserved, shy and calculating, but, all things considered, normal enough dog. How, indeed, without these intervals of convalescence, could I have reached the age that I enjoy at present ; how could I have fought my way through to the serenity with which I contemplate the terrors of youth and endure the terrors of age ; how could I have

come to the point where I am able to draw the consequences of my admittedly unhappy, or, to put it more
moderately, not very happy position, and live almost
entirely in accordance with them ? Solitary and with-
drawn, with nothing to occupy me save my hopeless but,
as far as I am concerned, indispensable little investigations, that is how I live ; yet in my distant isolation I
have not lost sight of my people, news often penetrates
to me, and now and then I even let news of myself reach
them. The others treat me with respect but do not
understand my way of life ; yet they bear me no grudge,
and even young dogs whom I sometimes see passing in
the distance, a new generation of whose childhood I have
only a vague memory, do not deny me a reverential
greeting.

For it must not be assumed that, for all my peculiarities,
which lie open to the day, I am in the least exempt from
the laws of my species. Indeed when I reflect on it—
and I have time and disposition and capacity enough for
that—I see that dogdom is in every way a marvellous
institution. Apart from us dogs there are all sorts of
creatures in the world, wretched, limited, dumb creatures
who have no language but mechanical cries : many of us
dogs study them, having given them names, try to help
them, educate them, uplift them, and so on. For my
part I am quite indifferent to them except when they
try to disturb me, I confuse them with one another, I
ignore them. But one thing is too obvious to have
escaped me ; namely, how little inclined they are, compared with us dogs, to stick together, how silently and
unfamiliarly and with what a curious hostility they pass
each other by, how mean are the interests that suffice to
bind them together for a little in ostensible union, and

how often these very interests give rise to hatred and
conflict. Consider us dogs, on the other hand! One
can safely say that we all live together in a literal heap,
all of us, different as we are from one another on account
of numberless and profound modifications which have
arisen in the course of time. All in one heap! We
are drawn to each other and nothing can prevent us from
satisfying that communal impulse ; all our laws and
institutions, the few that I still know and the many that
I have forgotten, go back to this longing for the greatest
bliss we are capable of, the warm comfort of being together. But now consider the other side of the picture.
No creatures to my knowledge live in such wide disper-
sion as we dogs, none have so many distinctions of class,
of kind, of occupation, distinctions too numerous to
review at a glance ; we, whose one desire is to stick
together—and again and again we succeed at transcendent
moments in spite of everything—we above all others are
compelled to live separated from one another by strange
vocations that are often incomprehensible even to our
canine neighbours, holding firmly to laws that are not
those of the dog world, but are actually directed against
it. How baffling these questions are, questions on which
one would prefer not to touch—I understand that stand-
point too, even better than my own—and yet questions
to which I have completely capitulated. Why do I not
do as the others : live in harmony with my people and
accept in silence whatever disturbs the harmony, ignoring
it as a small error in the great account, always keeping
in mind the things that bind us happily together, not
those that drive us again and again, although by sheer
force, out of our social circle ?

I can recall an incident in my youth ; I was at the

time in one of those inexplicable blissful states of exaltation which every one must have experienced as a child ; I was still quite a puppy, everything pleased me, everything was my concern, I believed that great things were going on around me of which I was the leader and to which I must lend my voice, things which must be wretchedly thrown aside if I did not run for them and wag my tail for them—childish fantasies that fled with riper years. But at the time their power was very great, I was completely under their spell, and presently something actually did happen, something so extraordinary that it seemed to justify my wild expectations. In itself it was nothing very extraordinary, for I have seen many such things, and more remarkable things too, often enough since, but at the time it struck me with all the force of a first impression, one of those impressions which can never be erased and influence much of one's later conduct. I encountered, in short, a little company of dogs, or rather I did not encounter them, they appeared before me. Before that I had been running along in darkness for some time, filled with a premonition of great things—a premonition that may well have been delusive, for I always had it. I had run in darkness for a long time, up and down, blind and deaf to everything, led on by nothing but a vague desire, and now I suddenly came to a stop with the feeling that I was in the right place, and looking up saw that it was bright day, only a little hazy, and everywhere a blending and confusion of the most intoxicating smells ; I greeted the morning with an uncertain barking, when—as if I had conjured them up—out of some place of darkness, to the accompaniment of terrible sounds such as I had never heard before, seven dogs stepped into the light. Had I not

distinctly seen that they were dogs and that they themselves brought the sound with them—though I could not
recognise how they produced it—I would have run away
at once ; but as it was I stayed. At that time I still
knew hardly anything of the creative gift for music with
which the canine race alone is endowed, it had naturally
enough escaped my but slowly developing powers of
observation ; for though music had surrounded me as a
perfectly natural and indispensable element of existence
ever since I was a suckling, an element which nothing
impelled me to distinguish from the rest of existence, my
elders had drawn my attention to it only by such hints
as were suitable for a childish understanding ; all the
more astonishing, then, indeed devastating, were these
seven great musical artists to me. They did not speak,
they did not sing, they remained, all of them, silent,
almost determinedly silent ; but from the empty air
they conjured music. Everything was music, the lifting
and setting down of their feet, certain turns of the head,
their running and their standing still, the positions they
took up in relation to one another, the symmetrical
patterns which they produced by one dog setting his
front paws on the back of another and the rest following
suit until the first bore the weight of the other six, or
lying flat on the ground and then crawling through complicated concerted evolutions ; and none made a false
move, not even the last dog, though he was a little unsure,
did not always establish contact at once with the others,
sometimes hesitated, as it were, on the stroke of the
beat, but yet was unsure only by comparison with the
superb sureness of the others, and even if he had been
much more unsure, indeed quite unsure, would not have
been able to do any harm, the others, great masters all

of them keeping the rhythm so unshakably. But it is too much to say that I saw them clearly, that I actually even saw them. They appeared from somewhere, I inwardly greeted them as dogs, and although I was profoundly confused by the sounds that accompanied them, yet they were dogs nevertheless, dogs like you and me ; I regarded them by force of habit simply as dogs I had happened to meet on my road, and felt a wish to approach them and exchange greetings ; they were quite near too, dogs much older than me, certainly, and not of my woolly, long-haired kind, but yet not so very alien in size and shape, indeed quite familiar to me, for I had already seen many such or similar dogs ; but while I was still involved in these reflections the music insensibly got the upper hand, literally knocked the breath out of me and swept me far away from those actual little dogs, and quite against my will, while I howled as if some pain were being inflicted upon me, my mind could attend to nothing but this blast of music which seemed to come from all sides, from the heights, from the deeps, from everywhere, seizing the listener by the middle, overwhelming him, crushing him, and over his swooning body still blowing fanfares so near that they seemed far away and almost inaudible. And then a respite came, for one was already too exhausted, too annulled, too feeble to listen any longer ; a respite came and I beheld again the seven little dogs carrying out their evolutions, making their leaps ; I longed to shout to them in spite of their aloofness, to beg them to enlighten me, to ask them what they were doing—I was a child and believed I could ask anybody about anything—but hardly had I begun, hardly did I feel on good and familiar doggish terms with the seven, when the music started again,

robbed me of my wits, whirled me round in its circles
as if I myself were one of the musicians instead of being
only their victim, cast me hither and thither, no matter
how much I begged for mercy, and rescued me finally
from its own violence by driving me into a labyrinth of
wooden bars which rose round that place, though I had
not noticed it before, but which now firmly caught me,
kept my head pressed to the ground, and though the
music still resounded in the open space behind me, gave
me a little time to get my breath back. I must admit
that I was less surprised by the artistry of the seven dogs
—it was incomprehensible to me, and also quite definitely
beyond my capacities—than by their courage in facing
so openly the music of their own making, and their
power to endure it calmly without collapsing. But now
from my hiding-place I saw, on looking more closely,
that it was not so much coolness as the most extreme
tension that characterised their performance ; these
limbs apparently so sure in their movements quivered
at every step with a perpetual apprehensive twitching ;
as if rigid with despair the dogs kept their eyes fixed on
one another, and their tongues, whenever the tension
weakened for a moment, hung wearily from their jowls.
It could not be fear of failure that agitated them so
deeply ; dogs that could dare and achieve such things
had no need to fear that. Then why were they afraid ?
Who then forced them to do what they were doing ?
And I could no longer restrain myself, particularly as
they now seemed in some incomprehensible way in need
of help, and so through all the din of the music I shouted
out my questions loudly and challengingly. But they—
incredible ! incredible !—they never replied, behaved as
if I were not there. Dogs who make no reply to the

greeting of other dogs are guilty of an offence against good manners which the humblest dog would never pardon any more than the greatest. Perhaps they were not dogs at all ? But how should they not be dogs ? Could I not actually hear on listening more closely the subdued cries with which they encouraged each other, drew each other's attention to difficulties, warned each other against errors ; could I not see the last and youngest dog, to whom most of those cries were addressed, often stealing a glance at me as if he would have dearly wished to reply, but refrained because it was not allowed ? But why should it not be allowed, why should the very thing which our laws unconditionally command not be allowed in this one case ? I became indignant at the thought and almost forgot the music. Those dogs were violating the law. Great magicians they might be, but the law was valid for them too ; I knew that quite well though I was a child. And having recognised that I now noticed something else. They had good grounds for remaining silent, that is, assuming that they remained silent from a sense of shame. For how were they conducting themselves ? Because of all the music I had not noticed it before, but they had flung away all shame, the wretched creatures were doing the very thing which is both most ridiculous and indecent in our eyes ; they were walking on their hind legs. Fie on them ! They were uncovering their nakedness, blatantly making a show of their nakedness, they were doing that as though it were a meritorious act, and when, obeying their better instincts for a moment, they happened to let their front paws fall, they were literally appalled as if at an error, as if Nature were an error, hastily raised their legs again, and their eyes seemed to be begging forgiveness for having been forced

to cease momentarily from their abomination. Was the
world standing on its head ? Where could I be ? What
could have happened ? If only for my own sake I dared
not hesitate any longer now, I dislodged myself from
the tangle of bars, took one leap into the open and made
towards the dogs—I, the younger scholar, must be the
teacher now, must make them understand what they
were doing, must keep them from committing further
sin. " And old dogs too ! And old dogs too ! " I
kept on saying to myself. But scarcely was I free and
only a leap or two away from the dogs, when the music
again had me in its power. Perhaps in my ardour I
might even have managed to withstand it, for I knew it
better now, if in the midst of all its majestic amplitude,
which was terrifying, but still not unconquerable, a
clear, piercing, continuous note which came without
variation literally from the remotest distance—perhaps
the real melody in the midst of the music—had not now
rung out, forcing me to my knees. Oh, the music these
dogs made almost drove me out of my senses ! I could
not move a step farther, I no longer wanted to instruct
them ; they could go on raising their front legs, committing sin and seducing others to the sin of silently
regarding them ; I was such a young dog—who could
demand such a difficult task from me ? I made myself
still more insignificant than I was, I whimpered, and if
the dogs had asked me now what I thought of their
performance, probably I would have had not a word to
say against it. Besides it was not long before the dogs
vanished with all their music and their radiance into
the darkness from which they had emerged.

As I have already said, this whole episode contains
nothing of much note ; in the course of a long life one

encounters all sorts of things which, taken from their context and seen through the eyes of a child, might well seem far more astonishing. Besides, one may, of course —in the pungent popular phrase—have " got it all wrong," as well as everything connected with it ; then it could be demonstrated that this was simply a case where seven musicians had assembled to practise their art in the morning stillness, that a very young dog had strayed to the place, a burdensome intruder whom they had tried to drive away by particularly terrifying or lofty music, unfortunately without success. He pestered them with his questions ; were they, already disturbed enough by the mere presence of the stranger, to be expected to attend to his distracting interruptions as well and make them worse by responding to them ? Even if the law commands us to reply to everybody, was such a tiny stray dog in truth a somebody worth regarding ? And perhaps they did not even understand him, for likely enough he barked his questions very indistinctly. Or perhaps they did understand him and with great self-control answered his questions, but he, a mere puppy unaccustomed to music, could not distinguish the answer from the music. And as for walking on their hind legs, perhaps, unlike other dogs, they actually used only these for walking ; if it was a sin, well it was a sin. But they were alone, seven friends together, an intimate gathering within their own four walls so to speak, quite private so to speak ; for one's friends, after all, are not the public, and where the public is not present an inquisitive little street dog is certainly not capable of constituting it ; but, granting this, is it not as if nothing at all had happened ? It is not quite so, but very nearly so, and parents should not let their children run about so freely, and had much better teach them to hold their tongues and respect the aged.

If all this is admitted, then it disposes of the whole case. But many things that are disposed of in the minds of grown-ups are not yet settled in the minds of the young. I rushed about, told my story, asked questions, made accusations and investigations, tried to drag others to the place where all this had happened, and burned to show everybody where I had stood and where the seven had stood, and where and how they had danced and made their music ; and if any one had come with me, instead of shaking me off and laughing at me, I would probably have sacrificed my innocence and tried myself to stand on my hind legs so as to reconstruct the scene clearly. Now children are blamed for all they do, but also in the last resort forgiven for all they do. And I have preserved my childish qualities, and in spite of that have grown to be an old dog. Well, just as at that time I kept on unceasingly discussing the foregoing incident—which today I must confess I lay far less importance upon—analysing it into its constituent parts, arguing it with my listeners without regard to the company I found myself in, devoting my whole time to the problem, which I found as wearisome as everybody else, but which—that was the difference—for that very reason I was resolved to pursue indefatigably until I solved it, so that I might be left free to regain the ordinary, calm, happy life of every day : just so have I, though with less childish means—yet the difference is not so very great— laboured in the years since and go on labouring today.

But it began with that concert. I do not blame the concert ; it is my innate disposition that has driven me on, and it would certainly have found some other opportunity of coming into action had the concert never taken place. Yet the fact that it happened so soon used to make me feel sorry for myself ; it robbed me of a great part of my childhood ; the blissful life of the young dog, which many can spin out for years, in my case lasted for only a few short months. So be it. There are more important things than childhood. And perhaps I have the prospect of far more childish happiness, earned by a life of hard work, in my old age than any actual child would have the strength to bear, but which then I shall possess.

I began my enquiries with the simplest things ; there was no lack of material ; it is the actual superabundance, unfortunately, that casts me into despair in my darker hours. I began to enquire into the question : What the canine race nourished itself upon ? Now that is, if you like, by no means a simple question, of course ; it has occupied us since the dawn of time, it is the chief object of all our meditation, countless observations and essays and views on this subject have been published, it has grown into a province of knowledge which in its prodigious compass is not only beyond the comprehension of any single scholar, but of all our scholars collectively, a burden which cannot be borne except by the whole of the dog community, and even then not without difficulty and only in part ; for it ever and again crumbles away like a neglected ancestral inheritance and must laboriously be rehabilitated anew—not to speak at all of the difficulties and almost unfulfillable conditions of my investigation. No one need point all this out to me, I know it all as well as any average sensual dog can do ; I have no ambition to meddle with real scientific matters, I have all the respect for knowledge that it deserves, but to increase knowledge I lack the equipment, the diligence, the leisure, and—not least, and particularly during the past few years—the desire as well. I swallow down my food, but the slightest preliminary methodical politico-economical observation of it does not seem to me worth while. In this connection the essence of all knowledge is enough for me, the simple rule with which the mother weans her young ones from her teats and sends them out into the world: "Water the ground as much as you can." And is not almost everything contained in that? What has scientific enquiry, ever since our first fathers inaugurated it, of decisive importance to add to it? Mere details, mere details, and how uncertain they are: but this rule will remain as long as we are dogs. It concerns our staple food: true, we have also other resources, but only at a pinch, and if the year is not too bad we could live on this staple food; we find it in the earth, but the earth needs our water to nourish it and only at that price provides us with our food, the emergence of which, however, and this should not be forgotten, can also be hastened by certain spells, songs, and ritual movements. But in my opinion that is all; there is nothing else that is fundamental to be said on the question. In this opinion, moreover, I am at one with the vast majority of the dog community, and must firmly dissociate myself from all heretical views on this point. Quite honestly I have no ambition to be peculiar, or to pose as being in the right against the majority; I am only too happy when I can agree with my comrades, as I do in this case. My own enquiries, however, are in another direction. My personal observation tells me that the earth, when it is watered and scratched according to the rules of science, extrudes nourishment, and moreover in such quality, in such abundance, in such ways, in such places, at such hours, as the laws partially or completely established by science demand. I accept all this ; my question, however, is the following : " Whence does the earth procure this food ? " A question which people in general pretend not to understand, and to which the best answer they can give is : " If you haven't enough to eat, we'll give you some of ours." Now consider this answer. I know that it is not one of the virtues of dogdom to share with others food that one has once gained possession of. Life is hard, the earth stubborn, science rich in knowledge but poor in practical results : any one who has food keeps it to himself ; that is not selfishness, but the opposite, dog law, the unanimous decision of the people, the outcome of their victory over egoism, for the possessors are always in a minority. And for that reason this answer : " If you haven't enough to eat, we'll give you some of ours " is merely a way of speaking, a jest, a form of raillery. I have not forgotten that. But all the more significant did it seem to me, when I was rushing about everywhere with my questions during those days, that they put the jest aside as far as I was concerned ; true, they did not actually give me anything to eat— where could they have found it at a moment's notice ?— and even if any one chanced to have some food, naturally he forgot everything else in the fury of his hunger ; yet they all seriously meant what they said when they made the offer, and here and there, right enough, I was presently allowed some slight trifle if I was only smart enough to snatch it quickly. How came it that people treated me so strangely, pampered me, favoured me ? Because I was a lean dog, badly fed and neglectful of my needs ? But there were countless badly fed dogs running

about, and the others snatched even the wretchedest scrap
from under their noses whenever they could, and not
often from greed, but generally on principle. No, they
treated me with special favour ; I cannot give much
detailed proof of this, but I have a firm conviction that
it was so. Was it my questions, then, that pleased them,
and that they regarded as so clever ? No, my questions
did not please them and were generally looked on as
stupid. And yet it could only have been my questions
that won me their attention. It was as if they would
rather do the impossible, that is stop my mouth with
food—they did not do it, but they would have liked to
do it—than endure my questions. But in that case they
would have done better to drive me away and refuse to
listen to my questions. No, they did not want to do
that ; they did not indeed want to listen to my questions,
but it was because I asked questions that they did not
want to drive me away. That was the time—much as I
was ridiculed and treated as a silly puppy, and pushed
here and pushed there—the time when I actually enjoyed
most public esteem ; never again was I to enjoy anything
like it ; I had free entry everywhere, no obstacle was
put in my way, I was actually flattered, though the
flattery was disguised as rudeness. And all really because
of my questions, my impatience, my thirst for knowledge.
Did they want to lull me to sleep, to divert me, without
violence, almost lovingly, from a path that was false, yet
not so completely false that violence was permissible ?—
also a certain respect and fear kept them from employing
violence. I divined even in those days something of this ;
today I know it quite well, far better than those who
actually practised it at the time : what they wanted to do
was really to divert me from my path. They did not

succeed ; they achieved the opposite ; my vigilance was sharpened. More, it became clear to me that it was I who was trying to seduce the others, and that I was actually successful up to a certain point. Only with the assistance of the whole dog world could I begin to understand my own questions. For instance when I asked : " Whence does the earth procure this food ? " was I troubled, as appearances might quite well indicate, about the earth ; was I troubled about the labours of the earth ? Not in the least ; that, as I very soon recognised, was far from my mind ; all that I cared for was the race of dogs, that and nothing else. For what is there actually except our own species ? To whom else can one appeal in the wide and empty world ? All knowledge, the totality of all questions and all answers, is contained in the dog. If one could but realise this knowledge, if one could but bring it into the light of day, if we dogs would but own that we know infinitely more than we admit to ourselves ! Even the most loquacious dog is more secretive of his knowledge than of the places where good food can be found. Trembling with desire, whipping yourself with your own tail, you steal cautiously upon your fellow-dog, you ask, you beg, you howl, you bite, and achieve— and achieve what you could have achieved just as well without any effort : amiable attention, friendly contiguity, honest acceptance, ardent embraces, barks that mingle as one : everything is directed towards achieving an ecstasy, a forgetting and finding again ; but the one thing that you long to win above all, the admission of knowledge, remains denied to you. To such prayers, whether silent or loud, the only answer you get, even after you have employed your powers of seduction to the utmost, are vacant stares, averted glances, troubled and veiled eyes. It is much the same as it was when, a mere puppy, I shouted to the dog musicians and they remained silent.

Now one might say : " You torment yourself because of your fellow-dogs, because of their silence on crucial questions ; you assert that they know more than they admit, more than they will allow to be valid, and that this silence, the mysterious reason for which is also, of course, tacitly concealed, poisons existence and makes it unendurable for you, so that you must either alter it or have done with it ; that may be ; but you are yourself a dog, you have also the dog knowledge ; well, bring it out, not merely in the form of a question, but as an answer. If you utter it, who will think of opposing you ? The great choir of dogdom will join in as if it had been waiting for you. Then you will have clarity, truth, avowal, as much of them as you desire. The roof of this wretched life, of which you say so many hard things, will burst open, and all of us, shoulder to shoulder, will ascend into the lofty realm of freedom. And if we should not achieve that final consummation, if things should become worse than before, if the whole truth should be more insupportable than the half, if it should be proved that the silent are in the right as the guardians of existence, if the faint hope that we still possess should give way to complete hopelessness, the attempt is still worth the trial, since you do not desire to live as you are compelled to live. Well, then, why do you make it a reproach against the others that they are silent, and remain silent your-self ? " Easy to answer : Because I am a dog ; in essentials just as locked in silence as the others, stubbornly resisting my own questions, dour out of fear. To be precise, is it in the hope that they might answer me that

I have questioned my fellow-dogs, at least since my adult years? Have I any such foolish hope? Can I contemplate the foundations of our existence, divine their profundity, watch the labour of their construction, that dark labour, and expect all this to be forsaken, neglected, undone, simply because I ask a question? No, that I truly expect no longer. I understand my fellow-dogs, am flesh of their flesh, of their miserable ever-renewed, ever desirous flesh. Yet it is not merely flesh and blood that we have in common, but knowledge also, and not only knowledge, but the key to it as well. I do not possess that key except in common with all the others; I cannot grasp it without their help. The hardest bones, containing the richest marrow, can be conquered only by a united crunching of all the teeth of all dogs. That, of course, is only a figure of speech and exaggerated; if all teeth were but ready they would not need even to bite, the bones would crack themselves and the marrow would be freely accessible to the feeblest of dogs. If I remain faithful to this metaphor, then the goal of my aims, my questions, my enquiries, appears monstrous, it is true. For I want to compel all dogs thus to assemble together, I want the bones to crack open under the pressure of their collective preparedness, and then I want to dismiss them to the ordinary life that they love, while all by myself, quite alone, I lap up the marrow. That sounds monstrous, almost as if I wanted to feed on the marrow, not merely of a bone, but of the whole canine race itself. But it is only a metaphor. The marrow that I am discussing here is no food; on the contrary, it is a poison.

My questions only serve as a goad to myself; I only want to be stimulated by the silence which rises up around me as the ultimate answer. "How long will you be able to endure the fact that the world of dogs, as your researches make more and more evident, is pledged to silence and always will be ? How long will you be able to endure it ? " That is the real great question of my life, before which all smaller ones sink into insignificance ; it is put to myself alone and concerns no one else. Unfortunately I can answer it more easily than the smaller, specific questions : I shall probably hold out till my natural end ; the calm of old age will put up a greater and greater resistance to all disturbing questions. I shall very likely die in silence and surrounded by silence, indeed almost peacefully, and I look forward to that with composure. An admirably strong heart, lungs that it is impossible to use up before their time, have been given to us dogs as if in malice ; we survive all questions, even our own, bulwarks of silence that we are.

Recently I have taken more and more to examining my life, looking for the decisive, the fundamental, error that I must surely have made ; and I cannot find it. And yet I must have made it, for if I had not made it and yet were unable by the diligent labour of a long life to achieve my desire, that would prove that my desire is impossible, and complete hopelessness must follow. Behold, then, the work of a lifetime. First of all my enquiries into the question : Whence does the earth procure the food it gives us ? A young dog, at bottom naturally greedy for life, I renounced all enjoyments, apprehensively avoided all pleasures, buried my head between my front paws when I was confronted by temptation, and addressed myself to my task. I was no scholar, neither in the information I acquired, nor in method, nor in intention. That was probably a defect, but it could not have been a decisive one. I had had little schooling, for I left my mother's care at an early age, soon got used to independence, led a free life ; and premature independence is inimical to systematic learning. But I have seen much, listened to much, spoken with dogs of all sorts and conditions, understood everything, I believe, fairly intelligently, and correlated my particular observations fairly intelligently : that has compensated somewhat for my lack of scholarship, not to mention that independence, if it is a disadvantage in learning things, is an actual advantage when one is making one's own enquiries. In my case it was all the more necessary as I was not able to employ the real method of science, to avail myself, that is, of the labours of my predecessors, and establish contact with contemporary investigators. I was entirely cast on my own resources, began at the very beginning, and with the consciousness, inspiriting to youth, but utterly crushing to age, that the fortuitous point to which I carried my labours must also be the final one. Was I really so alone in my enquiries, at the beginning and up to now? Yes and no. It is inconceivable that there must not always have been and that there are not today individual dogs in the same case as myself. I cannot be so accursed as that. I do not deviate from the dog nature by a hairbreadth. Every dog has like me the impulse to question, and I have like every dog the impulse not to answer. Every one has the impulse to question. How otherwise could my questions have affected my hearers in the slightest—and they were often affected, to my ecstatic delight, an exaggerated delight, I must confess— and how otherwise could I have been prevented from achieving much more than I have done? And that I have the compulsion to remain silent needs unfortunately no particular proof. I am at bottom, then, no different from any other dog ; everybody, no matter how he may differ in opinion from me and reject my views, will gladly admit that, and I in turn will admit as much of any other dog. Only the mixture of the elements is different, a difference very important for the individual, significant for the race. And how can one credit that the composition of these available elements has never chanced through all the past and present to result in a mixture similar to mine, one, moreover, if mine be regarded as unfortunate, more unfortunate still ? To think so would be contrary to all experience. We dogs are all engaged in the strangest occupations, occupations in which one would refuse to believe if one had not the most reliable information concerning them. The best example I can quote is that of the hovering dog. The first time I heard of one I laughed and simply refused to believe it. What ? One was asked to believe that there was a very tiny species of dog, not much bigger than my head even when it was full grown, and this dog, who must of course be a feeble creature, an artificial, weedy, brushed and curled fop by all accounts, incapable of making an honest jump, this dog was supposed, according to people's stories, to remain for the most part high up in the air, apparently doing nothing at all but simply resting there ? No, to try to make me swallow such things was exploiting the simplicity of a young dog too outrageously, I told myself. But shortly afterwards I heard from another source an account of another hovering dog. Could there be a conspiracy to fool me ? But after that I saw the dog musicians with my own eyes, and from that day I considered everything possible, no prejudices fettered my powers of apprehension, I investigated the most senseless rumours, following them as far as they could take me, and the most senseless seemed to me in this senseless world more probable than the sensible, and moreover particularly fertile for investigation. So it was too with the hovering dogs. I discovered a great many things about them ; true, I have succeeded to this day in seeing none of them, but their existence I have been firmly convinced for a long time, and they occupy an important place in my picture of the world. As usual it is not, of course, their technique that chiefly gives me to think. It is wonderful—who can gainsay it ? —that these dogs should be able to float in the air : in my amazed admiration for that I am at one with my fellow-dogs. But far more strange to my mind is the senselessness, the senselessness of these existences. They have no relation whatever to the general life of the community, they hover in the air, and that is all, and life goes on its usual way ; someone now and then refers to art and artists, but there it ends. But why, my good dogs, why on earth do these dogs float in the air ? What sense is there in their occupation ? Why can one get no word of explanation regarding them ? Why do they hover up there, letting their legs, the pride of dogs, fall into desuetude, preserving a detachment from the nourishing earth, reaping without having sowed ? being particularly well provided for as I hear, and at the cost of the dog community too. I can flatter myself that my enquiries into these matters made some stir. People began to investigate after a fashion, to collect data ; they made a beginning, at least, although they are never likely to go farther. But after all that is something. And though the truth will not be discovered by such means —never can that stage be reached—yet they throw light

on some of the profounder ramifications of falsehood.
For all the senseless phenomena of our existence, and the
most senseless most of all, are susceptible of investigation.
Not completely, of course—that is the diabolical jest—
but sufficiently to spare one painful questions. Take the
hovering dogs once more as an example ; they are not
haughty as one might imagine at first, but rather particularly dependent upon their fellow-dogs ; if one tries
to put oneself in their place one will see that. For they
must do what they can to obtain pardon, and not openly
—that would be a violation of the obligation to keep
silence—they must do what they can to obtain pardon
for their way of life, or else divert attention from it so
that it may be forgotten—and they do this, I have been
told, by means of an almost unendurable volubility.
They are perpetually talking, partly of their philosophical
reflections, with which, seeing that they have completely
renounced bodily exertion, they can continuously occupy
themselves, partly of the observations which they have
made from their exalted stations ; and although, as is
very understandable considering their lazy existence, they
are not much distinguished for intellectual power, and
their philosophy is as worthless as their observations, and
science can make hardly any use of their utterances, and
besides is not reduced to draw assistance from such
wretched sources, nevertheless if one asks what the
hovering dogs are really doing one will invariably receive
the reply that they contribute a great deal to knowledge.
" That is true," remarks someone, " but their contri-
butions are worthless and wearisome." The reply to
that is a shrug, or a change of the subject, or annoyance,
or laughter, and in a little while, when you ask again,
you learn once more that they contribute to knowledge,

and finally when you are asked the question you yourself will reply—if you are not careful—to the same effect. And perhaps indeed it is well not to be too obstinate, but to yield to public sentiment, to accept the extant hovering dogs, and without recognising their right to existence, which cannot be done, yet to tolerate them. But more than this must not be required ; that would be going too far, and yet the demand is made. We are perpetually being asked to put up with new hovering dogs who are always appearing. One does not even know where they come from. Do these dogs multiply by propagation ? Have they actually the strength for that ? —for they are nothing much more than a beautiful coat of hair, and what is there in that to propagate ? But even if that improbable contingency were possible, when could it take place? For they are invariably seen alone, self-complacently floating high up in the air, and if for once in a while they descend to take a run, it lasts only for a minute or two, a few mincing struts and once more they are back in strict solitude, absorbed in what is supposed to be profound thought, from which, even when they exert themselves to the utmost, they cannot tear themselves free, or at least so they say. But if they do not propagate their kind, is it credible that there can be dogs who voluntarily give up life on the solid ground, voluntarily become hovering dogs, and merely for the sake of the comfort and a certain technical accomplishment choose that empty life on cushions up there ? It is unthinkable ; neither propagation nor voluntary transition is thinkable. The facts, however, show that there are always new hovering dogs in evidence ; from which one must conclude that, in spite of obstacles which appear insurmountable to our understanding, no dog species, however curious, ever dies out, once it exists, or, at least, not without a tough struggle, not without being capable of putting up a successful defence for a long time.

But if that is valid for such an out-of-the-way, externally odd, inefficient species as the hovering dog, must I not also accept it as valid for mine ? Besides, I am not in the least queer outwardly ; an ordinary middle-class dog such as is very prevalent, in this neighbourhood, at least, I am neither particularly exceptional in any way, nor particularly repellent in any way ; and in my youth and to some extent also in maturity, so long as I attended to my appearance and had lots of exercise, I was actually considered a very handsome dog. My front view was particularly admired, my slim legs, the fine set of my head ; but my silvery white and yellow coat, which curled only at the hair tips, was very pleasing too ; in all that there was nothing strange ; the only strange thing about me is my nature, yet even that, as I am always careful to remember, has its foundation in universal dog nature. Now if not even the hovering dogs live in isolation, but invariably manage to encounter their fellows somewhere or other in the great dog world, and even to conjure new generations of themselves out of nothingness, then I too can live in the confidence that I am not quite forlorn. Certainly the fate of types like mine must be a strange one, and the existence of my colleagues can never be of visible help to me, if for no other reason than that I should scarcely ever be able to recognise them. We are the dogs who are crushed by the silence, who long to break through it, literally to get a breath of fresh air ; the others seem to thrive on silence : true, that is only so in appearance, as in the case of the musical dogs, who ostensibly were quite calm when they played, but in reality were in a state of intense excitement ; nevertheless the illusion is very strong, one tries to make a breach in it, but it mocks every attempt. What help, then, do my colleagues find ? What kind of attempts do they make to manage to go on living in spite of everything ? These attempts may be of various kinds. My own bout of questioning while I was young was one. So I thought that perhaps if I associated with those who asked many questions I might find my real comrades. Well, I did so for some time, with great self-control, a self-control made necessary by the annoyance I felt when I was interrupted by perpetual questions that I mostly could not answer myself : for the only thing that concerns me is to obtain answers. Moreover, who is not eager to ask questions when he is young, and how, when so many questions are going about, are you to pick out the right questions ? One question sounds like another ; it is the intention that counts, but that is often hidden even from the questioner. And besides it is a peculiarity of dogs to be always asking questions, they ask them confusedly all together ; it is as if in doing that they were trying to obliterate every trace of the genuine questions. No, my real colleagues are not to be found among the youthful questioners, and just as little among the old and silent, to whom I now belong. But what good are all these questions, for they have failed me completely ; apparently my colleagues are cleverer dogs than I, and have recourse to other excellent methods that enable them to bear this life, methods which, nevertheless, as I can tell from my own experience, though they may perhaps help at a pinch, though they may calm, lull to rest, distract, are yet on the whole as impotent as my own, for, no matter where I look, I can see no sign of their success. I am afraid that the last thing by which I can hope to recognise my real colleagues is their success. But where, then, are my real colleagues ? Yes, that is the burden of my complaint ; that is the kernel of it. Where are they ? Everywhere and nowhere. Perhaps my next-door neighbour, only three jumps away, is one of them ; we often bark across to each other, he calls on me some-times too, though I do not call on him. Is he my real colleague ? I do not know, I certainly see no sign of it in him, but it is possible. It is possible, but all the same nothing is more improbable. When he is away I can amuse myself, drawing on my fancy, by discovering in him many things that have a suspicious resemblance to myself ; but once he stands before me all my fancies become ridiculous. An old dog, a little smaller even than myself—and I am hardly medium size—brown, short-haired, with a tired hang of the head and a shuffling gait ; on the top of all this he trails his left hind leg behind him a little because of some disease. For a long time now I have been more intimate with him than with anybody else ; I am glad to say that I can still get on tolerably well with him, and when he goes away I shout the most friendly greetings after him, though not out of affection, but in anger at myself ; for if I follow him I find him just as disgusting again, slinking along there with his trailing leg and his much too low hindquarters. Sometimes it seems to me as if I were trying to humiliate myself by privately calling him my colleague. Nor in our talks does he betray any trace of similarity of thought ; true, he is clever and cultured enough as these things go here, and I could learn much from him ; but is it for cleverness and culture that I am looking ? We con-verse usually about local questions, and I am astonished

—my isolation has made me more clear-sighted in such matters—how much intelligence is needed even by an ordinary dog, even in average and not unfavourable circumstances, if he is to live out his life and defend himself against the greater of life's customary dangers. True, knowledge provides the rules one must follow, but even to grasp them imperfectly and in rough outline is by no means easy, and when one has actually grasped them the real difficulty still remains, namely to apply them to local conditions—here almost nobody can help, almost every hour brings new tasks, and every new patch of earth its specific problems ; no one can maintain that he has settled everything for good and that henceforth his life will go on, so to speak, of itself, not even I myself, though my needs shrink literally from day to day.   And all this ceaseless labour—to what end ? Merely to entomb oneself deeper and deeper in silence, it seems, so deep that one can never be dragged out of it again by anybody.

People often cry up the universal progress made by the dog community throughout the ages, and probably mean by that more particularly the progress in knowledge. Certainly knowledge is progressing, its advance is irresistible, it actually progresses at an accelerating speed, always faster, but what is there to praise in that ? It is as if one were to praise someone because with the years he grows older, and in consequence comes nearer and nearer to death with increasing speed. That is a natural and moreover an ugly process in which I find nothing to praise. I can only see decline everywhere, in saying which, however, I do not mean that earlier generations were essentially better than ours, but only younger ; that was their great advantage, their memory was not so overburdened as ours today, it was easier to get them to speak out, and even if nobody actually succeeded in doing that, the possibility of it was greater, and it is indeed this greater sense of possibility that moves us so deeply when we listen to those old and strangely simple stories. Here and there we catch a curiously significant phrase and we would almost like to leap to our feet, if we did not feel the weight of centuries upon us. No, whatever objection I may have to my age, former generations were not better, indeed in a sense they were far worse, far weaker. Even in those days wonders did not openly walk the streets for any one to seize ; but all the same dogs—I cannot put it in any other way—had not yet become so doggish as today, the edifice of dogdom was still loosely put together, the true Word could still have intervened, planning or replanning the structure, changing it at will, transforming it into its opposite ; and the Word was there, was very near at least, on the tip of everybody's tongue, any one might have hit upon it. And what has become of it today ? Today one may pluck out one's very heart and not find it. Our generation is lost, it may be, but it is more blameless than those earlier ones. I can understand the hesitation of my generation, indeed it is no longer mere hesitation ; it is the thousandth forgetting of a dream dreamt a thousand times and forgotten a thousand times ; and who can damn us merely for forgetting for the thousandth time ? But I fancy I understand the hesitation of our forefathers too, we would probably have acted just as they did ; indeed I could almost say : Well for us that it was not we who had to take the guilt upon us, that instead we can hasten in almost guiltless silence towards death in a world darkened by others. When our first fathers

strayed they had doubtless scarcely any notion that their
aberration was to be an endless one, they could still
literally see the cross-roads, it seemed an easy matter to
turn back whenever they pleased, and if they hesitated
to turn back it was merely because they wanted to enjoy
a dog's life for a little while longer; it was not yet a
genuine dog's life, and already it seemed intoxicatingly
beautiful to them, so what must it become in a little
while, a very little while, and so they strayed farther.
They did not know what we can now guess at, contemplating the course of history : that change begins in the
soul before it appears in ordinary existence, and that,
when they began to enjoy a dog's life, they must already
have possessed real old dogs' souls, and were by no means
so near their starting-point as they thought, or as their
eyes feasting on all doggish joys tried to persuade them.
But who can speak of youth at this time of day ? These
were the really young dogs, but their sole ambition unfortunately was to become old dogs, truly a thing which
they could not fail to achieve, as all succeeding generations
show, and ours, the last, most clearly of all.

Naturally I do not talk to my neighbour of these things,
yet often I cannot but think of them when I am sitting
opposite him—that typical old dog—or bury my nose
in his coat, which already has a whiff of the smell of
cast-off hides. To talk to him, or even to any of the
others, about such things, would be pointless. I know
what course the conversation would take. He would
urge a slight objection now and then, but finally he
would agree—agreement is the best weapon of defence—
and the matter would be buried : why indeed trouble
to exhume it at all ? And in spite of this there is a profound understanding between my neighbours and me,

going deeper than mere words. I shall never cease to maintain that, though I have no proof of it and perhaps am merely suffering from an ordinary delusion, caused by the fact that for a long time this dog has been the only one with whom I have held any communication, and so I am bound to cling to him. " Are you after all my colleague in your own fashion ? And ashamed because everything has miscarried with you ? Look, the same fate has been mine. When I am alone I weep over it ; come, it is sweeter to weep in company." I often have such thoughts as these and then I give him a prolonged look. He does not lower his glance, but neither can one read anything afrom it ; he gazes at me dully, wondering why I am silent and why I have broken off the conversation. But perhaps that very glance is his way of questioning me, and I disappoint him just as he disappoints me. In my youth, if other problems had not been more important to me then, and I had not been perfectly satisfied with my own company, I would probably have asked him straight out and received an answer flatly agreeing with me, and that would have been worse even than today's silence. But is not everybody silent in exactly the same way ? What is there to prevent me from believing that every one is my colleague instead of thinking that I have only one or two fellow-enquirers—lost and forgotten along with their petty achievements, so that I can never reach them by any road through the darkness of ages or the confused throng of the present : why not believe that all dogs from the beginning of time have been my colleagues, all diligent in their own way, all unsuccessful in their own way, all silent or falsely garrulous in their own way, as hopeless research is apt to make one ? But in that case I need not have severed myself from my fellows at all, I could have remained quietly among the others, I had no need to fight my way out like a stubborn child through the closed ranks of the grown-ups, who indeed wanted as much as I to find a way out, and who seemed incomprehensible to me simply because of their knowledge, which told them that nobody could ever escape and that it was stupid to use force.

Such ideas, however, are definitely due to the influence of my neighbour ; he confuses me, he fills me with dejection ; and yet in himself he is happy enough, at least when he is in his own quarters I often hear him shouting and singing ; it is really unbearable. It would be a good thing to renounce this last tie also, to cease giving way to the vague dreams which all contact with dogs unavoidably provokes, no matter how hardened one may consider oneself, and to employ the short time that still remains for me exclusively in prosecuting my researches. The next time he comes I shall slip away, or pretend I am asleep, and keep up the pretence until he stops visiting me.

Also my researches have become intermittent, I relax, I grow weary, I trot mechanically where once I raced enthusiastically. I think of the time when I began to enquire into the question : " Whence does the earth procure this food ? " Then indeed I really lived among the people, I pushed my way where the crowd was thickest, wanted everybody to know my work and be my audience, and my audience was even more essential to me than my work ; I still expected to produce some effect or other, and that naturally gave me a great impetus, which now that I am solitary is gone. But in those days I was so full of strength that I achieved

something unprecedented, something at variance with all
our principles, and that every contemporary eye-witness
assuredly recalls now as an uncanny feat. Our scientific
knowledge, which generally makes for an extreme
specialisation, is remarkably simple in one province. I
mean where it teaches that the earth engenders our food,
and then, after having laid down this hypothesis, gives
the methods by which the different foods may be obtained
in their best kinds and greatest abundance. Now it is
of course true that the earth brings forth all food, of that
there can be no doubt : but as simple as people generally
imagine it to be the matter is not ; and their belief that
it is simple prevents further enquiry. Take an ordinary
occurrence that happens every day. If we were to be
quite inactive, as I am almost completely now, and after
a perfunctory scratching and watering of the soil lay
down and waited for what was to come, then we should
find the food on the ground, assuming, that is, that a
result of some kind is inevitable. Nevertheless that is
not what usually happens. Those who have preserved
even a little freedom of judgment on scientific matters—
and their numbers are truly small, for science draws a
wider and wider circle round itself—will easily see,
without having to make any specific experiment, that
the main part of the food that is discovered on the ground
in such cases comes from above ; indeed customarily we
snap up most of our food, according to our dexterity and
greed, before it has reached the ground at all. In saying
that, however, I am saying nothing against science ; the
earth, of course, brings forth this kind of food too.
Whether the earth draws one kind of food out of itself
and calls down another kind from the skies perhaps makes
no essential difference, and science, which has established

that in both cases it is necessary to prepare the ground, need not perhaps concern itself with such distinctions, for does it not say : " If you have food in your jaws you have solved all questions for the time being." But it seems to me that science nevertheless takes a veiled interest, at least to some extent, in these matters, inasmuch as it recognises two chief methods of procuring food ; namely, the actual preparation of the ground, and secondly the auxiliary perfecting processes of incantation, dance, and song. I find here a distinction in accordance with the one I have myself made ; not a definitive distinction, perhaps, but yet clear enough. The scratching and watering of the ground, in my opinion, serves to produce both kinds of food, and remains indispensable ; incantation, dance, and song, however, are concerned less with the ground food in the narrower sense, and serve principally to attract the food from above. Tradition fortifies me in this interpretation. The ordinary dogs themselves set science right here without knowing it, and without science being able to venture a word in reply. If, as science claims, these ceremonies minister only to the soil, giving it the potency, let us say, to attract food from the air, then logically they should be directed exclusively to the soil ; it is the soil that the incantations must be whispered to, the soil that must be danced to. And to the best of my knowledge science ordains nothing else than this. But now comes the remarkable thing ; the people in all their ceremonies gaze upwards. This is no insult to science, since science does not forbid it, but leaves the husbandman complete freedom in this respect ; in its teaching it takes only the soil into account, and if the husbandman carries out its instructions concerning the preparation of the ground it

is content ; yet, in my opinion, it should really demand
more than this if it is logical. And, though I have never
been deeply initiated into science, I simply cannot conceive how the learned can bear to let our people, unruly
and passionate as they are, chant their incantations with
their faces turned upwards, wail our ancient folk songs
into the air, and spring high in their dances as though,
forgetting the ground, they wished to take flight from
it for ever. I took this contradiction as my starting-point
and whenever, according to the teachings of science, the
harvest time was approaching, I restricted my attention
to the ground, it was the ground that I scratched in the
dance, and I almost gave myself a crick in the neck
keeping my head as close to the ground as I could. Later
I dug a hole for my nose, and sang and declaimed into
it so that only the ground might hear, and nobody else
beside or above me.

The results of my experiment were meagre. Sometimes the food did not appear, and I was already preparing
to rejoice at this proof, but then the food would appear ;
it was exactly as if my strange performance had caused
some confusion at first, but had shown itself later to
possess advantages, so that in my case the usual barking
and leaping could be dispensed with. Often, indeed,
the food appeared in greater abundance than formerly,
but then again it would stay away altogether. With a
diligence hitherto unknown in a young dog I drew up
exact reports of all my experiments, fancied that here
and there I was on a scent that might lead me further,
but then it lost itself again in obscurity. My inadequate
grounding in science also undoubtedly held me up here.
What guarantee had I, for instance, that the absence of
the food was not caused by unscientific preparation of

the ground rather than by my experiments, and if that should be so, then all my conclusions were invalid. In certain circumstances I might have been able to achieve an almost scrupulously exact experiment : namely, if I had succeeded only once in bringing down food by an upward incantation without preparing the ground at all, and then had failed to extract food by an incantation directed exclusively to the ground. I attempted indeed something of this kind, but without any real belief in it and without conditions being quite perfect ; for it is my fixed opinion that a certain amount of ground-preparation is always necessary, and even if the heretics who deny this are right, their theory can never be proved in any case, seeing that the watering of the ground is done under a kind of compulsion, and within certain limits simply cannot be avoided. Another and somewhat tangential experiment succeeded better and aroused some public attention. Arguing from the customary method of snatching food while still in the air, I decided to allow the food to fall to the ground, but to make no effort to snatch it. Accordingly I always made a small jump in the air when the food appeared, but timed it so that it might always fail of its object ; in the majority of instances the food fell dully and indifferently to the ground in spite of this, and I flung myself furiously upon it, with the fury both of hunger and of disappointment. But in isolated cases something else happened, something really strange ; the food did not fall but followed me through the air ; the food pursued the hungry. That never went on for long, always for only a short stretch, then the food fell after all, or vanished completely, or—the most common case—my greed put a premature end to the experiment and I swallowed down the tempting bait. All the same I was happy at that time, a stir of curiosity ran through my neighbourhood, I attracted uneasy attention, I found my acquaintances more accessible to my questions, I could see in their eyes a gleam that seemed like an appeal for help ; and even if it was only the reflection of my own glance I asked for nothing more, I was satisfied. Until at last I discovered —and the others discovered it simultaneously—that this experiment of mine was a commonplace of science, had already succeeded with others far more brilliantly than with me, and though it had not been attempted for a long time on account of the extreme self-control it required, had also no need to be repeated, for scientifically it had no value at all. It only proved what was already known, that the ground not only attracts food vertically from above, but also at a slant, indeed sometimes in spirals. So there I was left with my experiment, but I was not discouraged, I was too young for that ; on the contrary, this disappointment braced me to attempt perhaps the greatest achievement of my life. I did not believe the scientists' depreciations of my experiment, yet belief was of no avail here, but only proof, and I resolved to set about establishing that and thus raise my experiment from its original irrelevance and set it in the very centre of the field of research. I wished to prove that when I retreated before the food it was not the ground that attracted it at a slant, but I who drew it after me. This first experiment, it is true, I could not carry any further ; to see the food before one and experiment in a scientific spirit at the same time—one cannot keep that up indefinitely. But I decided to do something else ; I resolved to fast completely as long as I could stand it, and at the same time avoid all sight of food, all temptation. If I were to withdraw myself in this manner, remain lying day and night with closed eyes, trouble myself neither to snatch food from the air nor to lift it from the ground, and if, as I dared not expect, yet faintly hoped, without taking any of the customary measures, and merely in response to the unavoidable irrational watering of the ground and the quiet recitation of the incantations and songs (the dance I wished to omit, so as not to weaken my powers) the food were to come of itself from above, and without going near the ground were to knock at my teeth for admittance—if that were to happen, then, even if science was not confuted, for it has enough elasticity to admit exceptions and isolated cases—I asked myself what would the other dogs say, who fortunately do not possess such extreme elasticity? For this would be no exceptional case like those handed down by history, such as the incident, let us say, of the dog who refuses, because of bodily illness or trouble of mind, to prepare the ground, to track down and seize his food, upon which the whole dog community recite magical formulæ and by this means succeed in making the food deviate from its customary route into the jaws of the invalid. I, on the contrary, was perfectly sound and at the height of my powers, my appetite so splendid that it prevented me all day from thinking of anything but itself ; I submitted, moreover, whether it be credited or not, voluntarily to my period of fasting, was myself quite able to conjure down my own supply of food and wished also to do so, and so I asked no assistance from the dog community, and indeed rejected it in the most determined manner.

I sought a suitable place for myself in an outlying clump of bushes, where I would have to listen to no talk of food, no sound of munching jaws and bones being gnawed ; I ate my fill for the last time and laid me down. As far as possible I wanted to pass my whole time with closed eyes ; until the food came it would be perpetual night for me, even though my vigil might last for days or weeks. During that time, however, I dared not sleep much, better indeed if I did not sleep at all—and that made everything much harder—for I must not only conjure the food down from the air, but also be on my guard lest I should be asleep when it arrived ; yet on the other hand sleep would be very welcome to me, for I would manage to fast much longer asleep than awake. For those reasons I decided to arrange my time prudently and sleep a great deal, but always in short snatches. I achieved this by always resting my head while I slept on some frail twig, which soon snapped and so awoke me. So there I lay, sleeping or keeping watch, dreaming or singing quietly to myself. My first vigils passed uneventfully ; perhaps in the place whence the food came no one had yet noticed that I was lying there in resistance to the normal course of things, and so there was no sign. I was a little disturbed in my concentration by the fear that the other dogs might miss me, presently find me, and attempt something or other against me. A second fear was that at the mere wetting of the ground, though it was unfruitful ground according to the findings of science, some chance nourishment might appear and seduce me by its smell. But for a time nothing of that kind happened and I could go on fasting. Apart from such fears I was more calm during this first stage than I could remember ever having been before. Although in reality I was labouring to annul the findings of science, I felt within me a deep reassurance, indeed almost the proverbial serenity of the scientific worker. In my thoughts I begged forgiveness of science ; there must be room in it for my researches too ; consolingly in my ears rang the assurance that no matter how great the effect of my enquiries might be, and indeed the greater the better, I would not be lost to ordinary dog life ; science regarded my attempts with benevolence, it itself would undertake the interpretation of my discoveries, and that promise already meant fulfilment ; while until now I had felt outlawed in my innermost heart and had run my head against the traditional walls of my species like a savage, I would now be accepted with great honour, the long-yearned-for warmth of assembled canine bodies would lap me round, I would ride uplifted high on the shoulders of my fellows. Remarkable effects of my first hunger. My achievement seemed so great to me that I began to weep with emotion and self-pity there among the quiet bushes, which it must be confessed was not very understandable, for when I was looking forward to my well-earned reward why should I weep ? Probably out of pure happiness. It is always when I am happy, and that is seldom enough, that I weep. After that, however, these feelings soon passed. My beautiful fancies fled one by one before the increasing urgency of my hunger ; a little longer and I was, after an abrupt farewell to all my imaginations and my sublime feelings, totally alone with the hunger burning in my entrails. " That is my hunger," I told myself countless times during this stage, as if I wanted to convince myself that my hunger and I were still two things and I could shake it off like a burdensome lover ; but in reality we were very painfully one, and when I explained to myself : " That is my hunger," it was really my hunger that was speaking and having its joke at my expense. A bad, bad time ! I still shudder to think of it, and not merely, please note this, on account of the suffering I endured then, but because I know I was insufficiently equipped then and consequently shall have to live through that suffering once more if I am ever to achieve anything ; for today I still hold fasting to be the final and most potent weapon of research. The way goes through fasting ; the highest, if it is attainable, is attainable only by the highest effort, and the highest effort among us is voluntary fasting. So when I think of those times—and I would gladly pass my life in brooding over them—I cannot help thinking also of the time that still threatens me. It seems to me that it takes almost a lifetime to recuperate from such an attempt ; my whole life as an adult lies between me and that fast, and I have not recovered yet. When I begin upon my next fast I shall perhaps have more resolution than the first time, because of my greater experience and deeper insight into the need for the attempt, but my powers are still enfeebled by that first essay, and so I shall probably begin to fail at the mere approach of these familiar horrors. My weaker appetite will not help me ; it will reduce the value of the attempt only by a very little, and will, indeed, probably force me to fast longer than was necessary the first time. I think I am clear on these and many other matters, the long interval has not been wanting in trial attempts, often enough I have literally got my teeth into hunger ; but I was not still strong enough for the ultimate effort, and now the unspoilt ardour of youth is of course gone for ever. It vanished in the great privations of that first fast. All sorts of thoughts tormented me. Our forefathers appeared threateningly before me. True, I held them responsible for everything, even if I dared not say so openly ; it was they who involved our dog life in guilt, and so I could easily have responded to their menaces with counter-menaces ; but I bow before their knowledge, it came from sources of which we know no longer, and for that reason, much as I may feel compelled to oppose them, I shall never actually overstep their laws, but content myself with wriggling out through the gaps, for which I have a particularly good nose. On the question of fasting I appealed to the well-known dialogue in the course of which one of our sages once expressed the intention of forbidding fasting, but was dissuaded by a second with the words : " But who would ever think of fasting ? " whereupon the first sage allowed himself to be persuaded and withdrew the prohibition. But now arises the question : " Is not fasting really forbidden after all ? " The great majority of commentators deny this and regard fasting as freely permitted, and holding as they think with the second sage do not worry in the least about the evil consequences that may result from erroneous interpretations. I had naturally assured myself on this point before I began my fast. But now that I was twisted with the pangs of hunger, and in my distress of mind sought relief in my own hind legs, despairingly licking and gnawing at them up to the very buttocks, the universal interpretation of this dialogue seemed to me entirely and completely false, I cursed the commentators' science, I cursed myself for having been led astray by it ; for the dialogue contained, as any child could see, more than merely one prohibition of fasting ; the first sage wished to forbid fasting ; what a sage wishes is already done, so fasting was forbidden ; as for the second sage, he not only agreed with the first, but actually considered fasting impossible, piled therefore on the first prohibition a second, that of dog nature itself ; the first sage saw this and thereupon withdrew the explicit prohibition, that was to say, he imposed upon all dogs, the matter being now settled, the obligation to know themselves and to make their own prohibitions regarding fasting. So here was a threefold prohibition instead of merely one, and I had violated it. Now I could at least have obeyed at this point, though tardily, but in the midst of pain I felt a longing to go on fasting, and I followed it as greedily as if it were a strange dog. I could not stop ; perhaps too I was already too weak to get up and seek safety for myself in familiar scenes. I tossed about on the fallen forest leaves, I could no longer sleep, I heard noises on every side ; the world, which had been asleep during my life hitherto, seemed to have been awakened by my fasting, I was tortured by the fancy that I would never be able to eat again, and I must eat so as to reduce to silence this world rioting so noisily round me, and I would never be able to do so ; but the greatest noise of all came from my own belly, I often laid my ear against it with startled eyes, for I could hardly believe what I heard. And now that things were becoming unendurable my very nature seemed to be seized by the general frenzy, and made senseless attempts to save itself ; the smell of food began to assail me, delicious dainties that I had long since forgotten, delights of my childhood ; yes, I could smell the very fragrance of my mother's teats ; I forgot my resolution to resist all smells, or rather I did not forget it ; I dragged myself to and fro, never for more than a few yards, and sniffed as if that were in accordance with my resolution, as if I were looking for food simply to be on my guard against it.

The fact that I found nothing did not disappoint me ; the food must be there, only it was always a few steps away, my legs failed me before I could reach it. But simultaneously I knew that nothing was there, and that I made those feeble movements simply out of fear lest I might collapse in this place and never be able to leave it. My last hopes, my last dreams vanished ; I would perish here miserably ; of what use were my researches ? —childish attempts undertaken in childish and far happier days ; here and now was the hour of deadly earnest, here my enquiries should have shown their value, but where had they vanished ? Only a dog lay here helplessly snapping at the empty air, a dog who, though he still watered the ground with convulsive haste at short intervals and without being aware of it, could not remember even the shortest of the countless incantations stored in his memory, not even the little rhyme which the newly born puppy says when it snuggles under its mother. It seemed to me as if I were separated from all my fellows not by a quite short stretch, but by an infinite distance, and as if I would die less of hunger than of neglect. For it was clear that nobody troubled about me, nobody beneath the earth, on it, or above it ; I was dying of their indifference ; they said indifferently : " He is dying," and it would actually come to pass. And did I not myself assent ? Did I not say the same thing ? Had I not wanted to be forsaken like this ? Yes, brothers, but not so as to perish in that place, but to achieve truth and escape from this world of falsehood, where there is no one from whom you can learn the truth, not even from me, born as I am a citizen of falsehood. Perhaps the truth was not so very far off, and I not so forsaken, therefore, as I thought ; or I may have been forsaken less by my fellows than by myself, in yielding and consenting to die.

But one does not die so easily as a nervous dog imagines. I merely fainted, and when I came to and raised my eyes a strange hound was standing before me. I did not feel hungry, but rather filled with strength, and my limbs, it seemed to me, were light and agile, though I made no attempt to prove this by getting to my feet. My visual faculties in themselves were no keener than usual ; a beautiful but not at all extraordinary hound stood before me ; I could see that, and that was all, and yet it seemed to me that I saw something more in him. There was blood under me, at first I took it for food ; but I recognised it immediately as blood that I had vomited. I turned my eyes from it to the strange hound. He was lean, long-legged, brown with a patch of white here and there, and had a fine, strong, piercing glance. "What are you doing here ? " he asked. "You must leave this place." "I can't leave it just now," I said, without trying to explain, for how could I explain everything to him ; besides, he seemed to be in a hurry. "Please go away," he said, impatiently lifting his feet and setting them down again. "Let me be," I said, "leave me to myself and don't worry about me ; the others don't." "I ask you to go for your own sake," he said. "You can ask for any reason you like," I replied. "I can't go even if I wanted to." "You need have no fear of that," he said, smiling. "You can go all right. It's because you seem to be feeble that I ask you to go now, and you can go slowly if you like ; if you linger now you'll have to race off later on." "That's my affair," I replied. "It's mine too," he said, saddened by my stubbornness, yet obviously resolved to let me lie for the time being, but at the same time to seize the opportunity of paying court to me. At any other time I would gladly have submitted to the blandishments of such a beautiful creature, but at that moment, why, I cannot tell, the thought filled me with terror. " Get out ! " I screamed, and all the louder as I had no other means of protecting myself. " All right, I'll leave you then," he said, slowly retreating. " You're wonderful. Don't I please you ? " " You'll please me by going away and leaving me in peace," I said, but I was no longer so sure of myself as I tried to make him think. My senses, sharpened by fasting, suddenly seemed to see or hear something about him ; it was just beginning, it was growing, it came nearer, and I knew that this hound had the power to drive me away, even if I could not imagine to myself at the moment how I was ever to get to my feet. And I gazed at him— he had merely shaken his head sadly at my rough answer —with ever-mounting desire. " Who are you ? " I asked. " I'm a hunter," he replied. " And why won't you let me lie here ? " I asked. " You disturb me," he said. " I can't hunt while you're here." " Try," I said, " perhaps you'll be able to hunt after all." " No," he said, " I'm sorry, but you must go." " Don't hunt for this one day ! " I implored him. " No," he said, " I must hunt." " I must go ; you must hunt," I said, " nothing but musts. Can you explain to me why we must ? " " No," replied he, " but there's nothing that needs to be explained, these are natural, self-evident things." " Not quite self-evident as all that," I said, " you're sorry that you must drive me away, and yet you do it." " That's so," he replied. " That's so," I echoed him crossly, " that isn't an answer. Which sacrifice would you rather make : to give up your hunting or give up driving me away?" "To give up my hunting," he said without hesitation. "There!" said I, "don't you see that you're contradicting yourself?" "How am I contradicting myself?" he replied. "My dear little dog, can it be that you really don't understand that I must? Don't you understand the most self-evident fact?" I made no answer, for I noticed—a new life ran through me, life such as terror gives—I noticed from almost invisible indications, which perhaps nobody but myself could have noticed, that in the depths of his chest the hound was preparing to upraise a song. "You're going to sing," I said. "Yes," he replied gravely, "I'm going to sing, soon, but not yet." "You're beginning already," I said. "No," he said, "not yet. But be prepared." "I can hear it already, though you deny it," I said, trembling. He was silent, and then I thought I saw something such as no dog before me had ever seen, at least there is no slightest hint of it in our tradition, and I hastily bowed my head in infinite fear and shame in the pool of blood lying before me. I thought I saw that the hound was already singing without knowing it nay, more, that the melody, separated from him, was floating on the air in accordance with its own laws, and, as though he had no part in it, was moving towards me, towards me alone. Today, of course, I deny the validity of all such perceptions and ascribe them to my over-excitation at that time, but even if it was an error it had nevertheless a sort of grandeur, and is the sole, even if delusive, reality that I have carried over into this world from my period of fasting, and shows at least how far we can go when we are beyond ourselves. And I was actually quite beyond myself. In ordinary circumstances I would have been very ill, incapable of moving;

but the melody, which the hound soon seemed to acknowledge as his, was quite irresistible. It grew stronger and stronger ; its waxing power seemed to have no limits, and already almost burst my ear-drums. But the worst was that it seemed to exist solely for my sake, this voice before whose sublimity the woods fell silent to exist solely for my sake ; who was I, that I could dare to remain here, lying brazenly before it in my pool of blood and filth. I tottered to my feet and looked down at myself ; this wretched body can never run, I still had time to think, but already, spurred on by the melody, I was careering from the spot in splendid style. I said nothing to my friends ; probably I could have told them all when I first arrived, but I was too feeble, and later it seemed to me that such things could not be told. Hints which I could not refrain from occasionally dropping were quite lost in the general conversation. For the rest I recovered physically in a few hours, but spiritually I still suffer from the effects of that experiment.

Nevertheless, I next carried my researches into music. True, science had not been idle in this sphere either ; the science of music, if I am correctly informed, is perhaps still more comprehensive than that of nurture, and in any case established on a firmer basis. That may be explained by the fact that this province admits of more objective enquiry than the other, and its knowledge is more a matter of pure observation and systematisation, while in the province of food the main object is to achieve practical results. That is the reason why the science of music is accorded greater esteem than that of nurture, but also why the former has never penetrated so deeply into the life of the people. I myself felt less attracted to the science of music than to any other until I heard that

voice in the forest. My experience with the musical
dogs had indeed drawn my attention to music, but I was
still too young at that time. Nor is it by any means easy
even to come to grips with that science ; it is regarded
as very esoteric and politely excludes the crowd. Besides,
although what struck me most deeply at first about these
dogs was their music, their silence seemed to me still
more significant ; as for their affrighting music, probably
it was quite unique, so that I could leave it out of account ;
but thenceforth their silence confronted me everywhere
and in all the dogs I met. So for penetrating into real
dog nature research into food seemed to me the best
method, calculated to lead me to my goal by the straightest
path. Perhaps I was mistaken. A border region between
these two sciences, however, had already attracted my
attention. I mean the theory of incantation, by which food
is called down. Here again it is very much against me
that I have never seriously tackled the science of music
and in this sphere cannot even count myself among the
half-educated, the class on whom science looks down
most of all. This fact I cannot get away from. I could
not—I have proof of that, unfortunately—I could not
pass even the most elementary scientific examination set
by an authority on the subject. Of course, quite apart
from the circumstances already mentioned, the reason for
that can be found in my incapacity for scientific investigation, my limited powers of thought, my bad memory,
but above all in my inability to keep my scientific aim
continuously before my eyes. All this I frankly admit,
even with a certain degree of pleasure. For the more
profound cause of my scientific incapacity seems to me
to be an instinct, and indeed by no means a bad one. If
I wanted to brag I might say that it was this very instinct

that invalidated my scientific capacities, for it would surely be a very extraordinary thing if one who shows a tolerable degree of intelligence in dealing with the ordinary daily business of life, which certainly cannot be called simple, and moreover one whose findings have been checked and verified, where that was possible, by individual scientists if not by science itself, should *a priori* be incapable of planting his paw even on the first rung of the ladder of science. It was this instinct that made me—and perhaps for the sake of science itself, but a different science from that of today, an ultimate science —prize freedom higher than everything else. Freedom ! Certainly such freedom as is possible today is a wretched business. But nevertheless freedom, nevertheless a possession.

APHORISMS

" HE "

NOTES FROM THE YEAR 1920

HE is never quite ready for any contingency, yet he cannot even blame himself for that, for when in this life, which insists so mercilessly that we must be ready at every moment, can one ever find time in which to make oneself ready? and even if there were time how can one make ready before knowing the task; in other words, can one ever be equal to a natural task, a spontaneous task that has not merely been artificially concocted? So he has long since fallen under the wheels; a contingency for which, strangely enough, but also comfortingly enough, he was least ready of all.

*   *   *

All that he does seems to him, it is true, extraordinarily new, but also, because of the incredible spate of new things, extraordinarily amateurish, indeed scarcely tolerable, incapable of becoming history, breaking short the chain of the generations, cutting off for the first time at its most profound source the music of the world, which before him could at least be divined. Sometimes in his arrogance he has more anxiety for the world than for himself.

He could have resigned himself to a prison. To end as a prisoner—that could be a life's ambition. But it was a barred cage that he was in. Calmly and insolently, as if at home, the din of the world streamed out and in through the bars, the prisoner was really free, he could take part in everything, nothing that went on outside escaped him, he could simply have left the cage, the bars were yards apart, he was not even a prisoner.

He has the feeling that merely by being alive he is blocking his own way. From this sense of hindrance, again, he deduces the proof that he is alive.

* * *

The bony structure of his own forehead blocks his way ; he batters himself bloody against his own forehead.

* * *

He feels imprisoned on this earth, he feels constricted ; the melancholy, the impotence, the sickness, the feverish fancies of the captive afflict him ; no comfort can comfort him, since it is merely comfort, gentle head-splitting comfort glozing the brutal fact of imprisonment. But if he is asked what he actually wants he cannot reply, for —that is one of his strongest proofs—he has no conception of freedom.

* * *

Some deny the existence of misery by pointing to the sun ; he denies the existence of the sun by pointing to misery.

* * *

The sluggish, self-torturing, wavelike motion of all life, whether of other life or his own, which often seems to stagnate for a long time but in reality never ceases, tortures

him because it brings with it the never-ceasing compulsion
to think.   Sometimes it seems to him that this torture
heralds events.   When he hears that a married friend of
his is waiting the birth of his first child he recognises
that in thought he has already paid the price of that
birth.

*   *   *

He sees in two ways : the first is a calm contemplation,
consideration, investigation, an overflow of life inevitably
involving a certain sensation of comfort.   The possible
manifestations of this process are infinite, for though
even a wood-louse needs a relatively large crevice in
which to accommodate itself, no space whatever is
required for such labours ; even where not the smallest
crack can be found they may exist in tens of thousands,
mutually interpenetrating one another.   That is the first
stage.   The second is the moment when he is called upon
to render an account of all this, finds himself incapable
of uttering a sound, is flung back again on contemplation,
etc., but now, knowing the hopelessness of it all, can
no longer dabble about in it, and so makes his body
heavy and sinks with a curse.

*   *   *

This is the problem : Many years ago I sat one day,
in a sad enough mood, on the slopes of the Laurenziberg.
I went over the wishes that I wanted to realise in life.   I
found that the most important or the most delightful
was the wish to attain a view of life (and—this was
necessarily bound up with it—to convince others of it
in writing), in which life, while still retaining its natural
full-bodied rise and fall, would simultaneously be recognised no less clearly as a nothing, a dream, a dim hovering.

A beautiful wish, perhaps, if I had wished it rightly. Considered as a wish, somewhat as if one were to hammer together a table with painful and methodical technical efficiency, and simultaneously do nothing at all, and not in such a way that people could say : " Hammering a table together is nothing to him," but rather " Hammering a table together is really hammering a table together to him, but at the same time it is nothing," whereby certainly the hammering would have become still bolder, still surer, still more real and, if you will, still more senseless.

But he could not wish in this fashion, for his wish was not a wish, but only a vindication of nothingness, a justification of non-entity, a rouch of animation which he wanted to lend to nonentity, in which at that time he had scarcely taken his first few conscious steps, but which he already felt as his element. It was a sort of farewell that he took from the illusive world of youth ; although youth had never directly deceived him, but only caused him to be deceived by the utterances of all the authorities he had around him. So is explained the necessity of his " wish."

* * *

He proves nothing but himself, his sole proof is himself, all his opponents overcome him at once, but not by refuting him (he is irrefutable), but by proving themselves.

* * *

Human associations rest on this, that someone by superior force of life gives the appearance of having refuted other individuals in themselves irrefutable. The result is sweet and comforting for those individuals, but it is deficient in truth and invariably therefore in permanence.

He was once part of a monumental group. Round some elevated figure or other in the centre were ranged in carefully thought-out order symbolical images of the military caste, the arts, the sciences, the handicrafts. He was one of those many figures. Now the group is long since dispersed, or at least he has left it and makes his way through life alone. He no longer has even his old vocation, indeed he has actually forgotten what he once represented. Probably it is this very forgetting that gives rise to a certain melancholy, uncertainty, unrest, a certain longing for vanished ages, darkening the present. And yet this longing is an essential element in human effort, perhaps indeed human effort itself.

*   *   *

He does not live for the sake of his personal life ; he does not think for the sake of his personal thoughts. It seems to him that he lives and thinks under the compulsion of a family, which, it is true, is itself superabundant in life and thought, but for which he constitutes, in obedience to some law unknown to him, a formal necessity. Because of this unknown family and this unknown law he cannot be exempted.

*   *   *

The original sin, the ancient wrong committed by man, consists in the complaint, which man makes and never ceases making, that a wrong has been done to him, that the original sin was once committed upon him.

*   *   *

Two children were loitering beside Casinelli's booth, a boy of about six, a girl of seven, both well dressed ;

they were talking of God and sin. I stopped behind
them. The girl, who seemed to be a Catholic, held that
the only real sin was to deceive God. With childish
obstinacy the boy, who seemed to be a Protestant, asked
what, then, it was to deceive human beings or to steal.
" That's a very great sin too," said the girl, " but not
the greatest, the greatest sins are those against God ; for
sins against human beings we have the confessional.
When I confess the angels are around me again in an
instant, but when I commit a sin the devil comes behind
me, only I don't see him." And tired of being in half
earnest, she spun round light-heartedly on her heel and
said : " Look, there's nobody behind me." The boy
spun round too and saw me there. "Look," he said, without considering that I must hear him, or perhaps without
caring, " the devil is standing behind me." " I see him
too," replied the girl, " but that's not the one I meant."

* * *

He does not want consolation, yet not because he does
not want it—who does not want it ?—but because to
seek for consolation would mean to devote his whole life
to the task, to live perpetually on the very frontiers of
his existence, almost outside it, barely knowing for whom
he was seeking consolation, and consequently not even
capable of finding effective consolation, effective, not
real consolation, for real consolation does not exist.

* * *

He fights against having his limits defined by his fellow-
men. No man, even if he be infallible, can see more than
that fraction of his neighbour for which his strength and
kind of vision are adapted. He has, however, like everybody, but in its most extreme form, the longing to limit

himself to the limit of his neighbour's eyesight. Had Robinson Crusoe never left the highest, or more correctly the most visible point of his island, from desire for comfort, or timidity, or fear, or ignorance, or longing, he would soon have perished ; but since without paying any attention to passing ships and their feeble telescopes he started to explore the whole island and take pleasure in it, he managed to keep himself alive and finally was found after all, by a chain of casuality that was, of course, logically inevitable.

* * *

" You make a virtue of your necessity."

" In the first place every one does that, and in the second, that's just what I don't do. I let my necessity remain necessity, I do not drain the swamp, but live in its feverish exhalations."

" That's the very thing you make a virtue of."

" Like every one, as I said before. But I only do it for your sake. I take injury to my soul that you may remain friendly to me."

* * *

Everything is allowed him, except self-oblivion, wherewith, however, everything in turn is denied him, except the one thing necessary at the given moment for the whole.

* * *

The question of conscience is a social imposition. All virtues are individual, all vices social. The things that pass as social virtues, love, for example, disinterestedness, justice, self-sacrifice, are only " astonishingly " enfeebled social vices.

The difference between the " Yes " and " No " that
he says to his contemporaries and those that he should
actually say, might be likened to the difference between
life and death, and is just as vaguely divined by him.

*   *   *

The reason why posterity's judgment of individuals is
juster than the contemporary one lies in their being dead.
One develops in one's own style only after death, only
when one is alone. Death is to the individual like Satur-
day evening to the chimney sweep ; it washes the dirt
from his body. Then it can be seen whether his contemporaries harmed him more, or whether he did the
more harm to his contemporaries ; in the latter case he
was a great man.

*   *   *

The strength to deny, that most natural expression of
the perpetually changing, renewing, dying, reviving
human fighting organism, we possess always, but not the
courage, although life is denial, and therefore denial
affirmation.

*   *   *

He does not die along with his dying thoughts. Dying
is merely a phenomenon within the inner world (which
remains intact, even if it too should be only an idea), a
natural phenomenon like any other one, neither happy
nor sad.

*   *   *

The current against which he swims is so rapid that in
certain absent moods he is sometimes cast into despair by
the blank peace amid which he splashes, so infinitely
far has he been driven back in a moment of surrender.

He is thirsty, and is cut off from a spring by a mere clump of bushes. But he is divided against himself : one part overlooks the whole, sees that he is standing here and that the spring is just beside him ; but another part notices nothing, has at most a devination that the first part sees all. But as he notices nothing he cannot drink.

* * *

He is neither bold nor thoughtless. But neither is he fearful. A free life would not alarm him. Now he has never been granted such a life, but that too causes him no anxiety, for he has no anxiety of any kind about himself. There exists, however, a Someone completely unknown to him, who has a great and continuous anxiety for him—for him alone. This anxiety of this Someone concerning him, and in particular the continuousness of this anxiety, sometimes causes him torturing headaches in his quieter hours.

* * *

A certain heaviness, a feeling of being secured against every vicissitude, the vague assurance of a bed prepared for him and belonging to him alone, keeps him from getting up ; but he is kept from lying still by an unrest which drives him from his bed, by his conscience, the endless beating of his heart, the fear of death, and the longing to refute it : all this will not let him rest and he gets up again. This up and down and a few fortuitous, desultory, irrevelant observations made in the course of it, are his life.

* * *

He has two antagonists : The first pushes him from behind, from his birth. The second blocks the road in front of him. He struggles with both. Actually the first supports him in his struggle with the second, for the first wants to push him forward ; and in the same way the second supports him in his struggle with the first ; for the second of course is trying to force him back. But it is only theoretically so. For it is not only the two protagonists who are there, but he himself as well, and who really knows his intentions ? However that may be, he has a dream that some time in an unguarded moment—it would require too, one must admit, a night darker than any night has ever been yet—he will spring out of the fighting line and be promoted, on account of his experience of such warfare, as judge over his struggling antagonists.

THE WARDEN OF THE TOMB

Small workroom, high window, beyond it a bare treetop.
PRINCE (*at writing table, leaning back in chair, looking out of window*). CHAMBERLAIN (*white beard, youthfully squeezed into tight jacket, standing against wall near centre door*).
Pause.

PRINCE (*turning from window*): Well?

CHAMBERLAIN: I cannot recommend it, your Highness.

PRINCE: Why?

CHAMBERLAIN: I can't quite formulate my objections at the moment. I'm expressing only a fraction of what's on my mind when I quote the universal saying: Let the dead rest in peace.

PRINCE: That's my opinion, too.

CHAMBERLAIN: In that case I haven't properly understood.

PRINCE: So it seems.
Pause.

PRINCE: Perhaps the only thing that disconcerts you is that instead of going ahead with the arrangement, I announced it to you first.

CHAMBERLAIN: The announcement certainly burdens me with great responsibility which I must endeavour to live up to.

PRINCE: Don't speak of responsibility!
Pause.

PRINCE: Let's see. Hitherto the tomb in the Friedrichspark has been guarded by a warden who lives in a lodge at the park's entrance. Was there anything wrong with this?

CHAMBERLAIN: Certainly not. The tomb is more than four hundred years old and has always been guarded in this way.

PRINCE: It could be an abuse. But it isn't an abuse, is it?

CHAMBERLAIN: It is a necessary arrangement.

PRINCE: All right then, a necessary arrangement. I've been here in the castle quite some time now, have gained some insight into details which hitherto have been entrusted to strangers—they manage fairly well —and I've come to this conclusion: the Warden up there in the park is not enough. There must also be a guard down in the tomb. It probably won't be a pleasant job. But experience has proved that willing and suitable people can be found for any job.

CHAMBERLAIN: Needless to say, any orders issued by your Highness will be carried out, even if the necessity of the order is not fully understood.

PRINCE: (starting up): Necessity! Do you mean to say that a guard at the park gate is necessary? The Friedrichspark belongs to the castle park, is entirely surrounded by it. The castle park itself is amply guarded—by the army, what's more. So why a special guard for the Friedrichspark? Isn't this a mere formality? A pleasant deathbed for the wretched old man who is keeping watch there?

CHAMBERLAIN: Formality it is, but a necessary one. A demonstration of reverence for the illustrious dead.

PRINCE: And what about the guard in the tomb itself?

CHAMBERLAIN: In my opinion this would have a police

connotation.   It would mean a real guarding of unreal things beyond the human sphere.

PRINCE : For my family this tomb represents the frontier between the Human and the Other, and it's on this frontier that I wish to post a guard.   As for the police connotation, as you call it, we can question the Warden himself.   I've sent for him.   (*Rings a bell.*)

CHAMBERLAIN : He's a confused old man, if I may say so, already quite out of hand.

PRINCE : If that's so, all the more reason for strengthening the guard in the way I've suggested.

(*Enter servant.*)

PRINCE : The Warden of the tomb !

  (*Servant leads in Warden, holding him tight round the waist to prevent him from collapsing.   Ancient red livery hanging loosely about Warden, brightly polished silver buttons, several decorations.   Cap in hand, he trembles under the gentlemen's gaze.*)

PRINCE : Put him on the divan !

  (*Servant lays him down and goes off.   Pause.   A faint rattling in Warden's throat.*)

PRINCE (*again in armchair*) : Can you hear ?

WARDEN (*tries to answer but fails, is too exhausted, sinks back again.*)

PRINCE : Try to pull yourself together.   We're waiting.

CHAMBERLAIN (*leaning over Prince*) : What could this man give information about ?   And credible and important information at that ?   He ought to be taken straight to bed.

WARDEN : Not to bed—still strong—fairly—can still hold my end up.

PRINCE : So you should.   You've only just turned sixty. Granted, you look very weak.

WARDEN : I'll pick up in no time—feel better in a minute.

PRINCE : It wasn't meant as a reproach. I'm only sorry you aren't feeling well. Have you anything to complain about ?

WARDEN : Hard work—hard work—not complaining— but very weak—wrestling bouts every night.

PRINCE : What d'you say ?

WARDEN : Hard work.

PRINCE : You said something else.

WARDEN : Wrestling bouts.

PRINCE : Wrestling bouts ? What kind of wrestling bouts ?

WARDEN : With the blessed ancestors.

PRINCE : I don't understand. D'you have bad dreams.

WARDEN : No dreams—don't sleep.

PRINCE : Then let's hear about these—these wrestling bouts.

WARDEN (*remains silent*).

PRINCE (*to Chamberlain*) : Why doesn't he speak ?

CHAMBERLAIN (*hurrying to Warden*) : He may die any minute.

PRINCE (*stands up*).

WARDEN (*as Chamberlain touches him*) : Don't, don't, don't ! (*Fights off Chamberlain's hands, then collapses in tears.*)

PRINCE : We're tormenting him.

CHAMBERLAIN : How ?

PRINCE : I don't know.

CHAMBERLAIN : Coming to the castle, having to present himself here, the sight of your Highness, this question-ing—he no longer has the wits to face all this.

PRINCE (*still staring at the Warden*) : That's not it. (*Goes

*to divan, bends over Warden, takes his little skull in his
hands.*) Mustn't cry. What are you crying for? We
wish you well. I realise your job isn't easy. You've
certainly deserved well of my family. So stop crying
and tell us all about it.

WARDEN : But I'm so afraid of that gentleman there——
(*Looks at Chamberlain, more threateningly than afraid.*)

PRINCE (*to Chamberlain*): If we want him to talk I'm
afraid you'll have to leave.

CHAMBERLAIN : But look, your Highness, he's foaming
at the mouth. He's seriously ill.

PRINCE (*absent-mindedly*): Please go, it won't take long.
Exit Chamberlain.
Prince sits on edge of divan.
Pause.

PRINCE : Why were you afraid of him?

WARDEN (*surprisingly composed*): I wasn't afraid. Me
afraid of a servant?

PRINCE : He's not a servant. He's a Count, free and
rich.

WARDEN : A servant all the same, you are the master.

PRINCE : If you like it that way. But you said yourself
that you were afraid of him.

WARDEN : I didn't want to say things in front of him
which are meant only for you. Haven't I already said
too much in front of him?

PRINCE : So we're on terms of intimacy, and yet today
is the first time I've seen you.

WARDEN : Seen for the first time, but you've always
known that I (*raising his forefinger*) hold the most important position at Court. You even acknowledged it
publicly by awarding me the medal " Red-as-Fire."
Here ! (*Holds up the medal on his coat.*)

PRINCE : No, that's the medal for twenty-five years' service at Court. My grandfather gave you that. But I'll decorate you, too.

WARDEN : Do as you please and grant me whatever you think I deserve. I've acted as your tomb Warden for thirty years.

PRINCE : Not mine. My reign has lasted hardly a year.

WARDEN (*lost in thought*) : Thirty years.

Pause.

WARDEN (*remembering only half of the Prince's remark*) : Nights last years there.

PRINCE : I haven't yet had a report from your office. What's your work like ?

WARDEN : Every night the same. Every night till the heart beats as if it were about to burst.

PRINCE : Is it only night duty, then ? Night duty for an old man like you ?

WARDEN : That's just it, your Highness. It's day duty. A loafer's job. There one sits, at the front door, with one's mouth open in the sunshine. Sometimes the watchdog pats one on the knee with its paws, and then lies down again. That's all that ever happens.

PRINCE : Well ?

WARDEN (*nodding*) : But it has been changed to night duty.

PRINCE : By whom ?

WARDEN : By the lords of the tomb.

PRINCE : You know them ?

WARDEN : Yes.

PRINCE : They come to see you ?

WARDEN : Yes.

PRINCE : Last night, too ?

WARDEN : Last night, too.

PRINCE : What was it like ?

WARDEN (*sitting up straight*) : Same as usual.

   Prince stands up.

WARDEN : Same as usual. Quiet till midnight. I'm lying in bed—excuse me—smoking my pipe. My grand-daughter is asleep in the next bed. At midnight comes the first knock at the window. I look at the clock. Always to the minute. Two more knocks, they mingle with the striking of the tower clock, but I can still hear them. These are no human knuckles. But I know all that and don't budge. Then it clears its throat outside, it's surprised that in spite of all that knocking I haven't opened the window. Let his princely Highness be surprised ! The old Warden is still there ! (*Shows his fist.*)

PRINCE : You're threatening me ?

WARDEN (*doesn't immediately understand*): Not you. The one at the window !

PRINCE : Who is it ?

WARDEN : He shows himself at once. All of a sudden window and shutters are opened. I just have time to throw the blanket over my grandchild's face. The storm blows in, promptly puts the light out. Duke Friedrich ! His face with beard and hair completely fills my poor window. How he has grown throughout the centuries ! When he opens his mouth to speak the wind blows his old beard between his teeth and he bites on it.

PRINCE : Just a moment. You say Duke Friedrich ? Which Friedrich ?

WARDEN : Duke Friedrich, just Duke Friedrich.

PRINCE : Is that the name he gives ?

WARDEN (*anxiously*) : No, he doesn't give it.

PRINCE : And yet you know—(*breaking off*)—Go on !

WARDEN : Shall I go on ?

PRINCE : Of course. All this very much concerns me. There must be an error in the distribution of labour. You're overworked.

WARDEN (*kneeling*) : Don't take my job away, your Highness. Having lived for you all these years, let me also die for you ! Don't wall up the grave I'm struggling towards. I serve willingly and am still strong enough to serve. To be granted an audience like today's, to take a rest with my master—this gives me strength for ten years.

PRINCE (*putting Warden back on divan*) : No one's going to take your job from you. How could I get along without your experience ? But I'll appoint another Warden, then you'll become Head Warden.

WARDEN : Am I not good enough ? Have I ever let anyone pass ?

PRINCE : Into the Friedrichspark ?

WARDEN : No, out of the park. Who'd want to come in ? If ever anyone stops at the railing I beckon to him from the window and he runs away. But out ! Everyone wants to get out. After midnight you can see all the voices from the grave assembled round my house. I think it's only because they are so closely packed together that the whole let of them don't burst through my narrow window. If it gets too bad, however, I grab the lantern from under my bed, swing it high, and with laughter and moaning these incredible creatures scatter in all directions. Then I can hear them rustling even in the furthest bush at the end of the park. But they soon gather together again.

PRINCE : And do they tell you what they want ?

WARDEN : First they give orders. Especially Duke Friedrich. No living being could be so confident. Every night for thirty years he has been expecting me to give in.

PRINCE : If he has been coming for thirty years it can't be Duke Friedrich, for he has been dead only fifteen years. On the other hand, he is the only one of that name in the tomb.

WARDEN (*too carried away by his story*) : That I don't know, your Highness, I never went to school. I only know how he begins. " Old dog," he begins at the window, " the gentlemen are knocking and you just stay in your filthy bed." They have a particular grudge against beds, by the way. And now every night we have the same conversation, he outside, I opposite him, my back to the door. I say : " I'm only on day duty." The Duke turns and shouts into the park : " He's only on day duty." Whereupon all the assembled aristocracy burst out laughing. Then the Duke says to me again : " But it is day." I say curtly : " You're wrong." The Duke : " Night or day, open the door." I : " That's against my orders." And with my pipe I point at a notice on the door. The Duke : " But you're our Warden." I : " Your Warden, but employed by the reigning Prince." He : " Our Warden, that's the main thing. So open up, and be quick about it." I : " No." He : " Idiot, you'll lose your job. Prince Leo has invited us for today."

PRINCE (*quickly*) : I ?

WARDEN : You.

Pause.

WARDEN : When I hear your name I lose my firmness. That's why I have always taken care to lean against the door which is almost the only thing that holds me up. Outside, everyone's singing your name. "Where's the invitation?" I ask weakly. "Bedbug!" he shouts. "you doubt my ducal word?" I say: "I have no orders, so I won't open, I won't open, I won't open!" —"He won't open!" shouts the Duke outside. "So come on, all of you, the whole dynasty! At the door! We'll open it ourselves." And a moment later there's nothing under my window.

Pause.

PRINCE: Is that all?

WARDEN: All? My real service begins only now. I rush out of the door, round the house, and promptly run into the Duke and there we are, locked in combat. He so big, I so small, he so broad, I so thin, I can fight only with his feet, but now and again he lifts me up in the air and then I fight up there, too. All his comrades stand round in a circle and make fun of me. One, for instance, cuts open my trousers behind and they all play with the tail of my shirt while I'm fighting. Can't understand why they laugh, as until now I've always won.

PRINCE: How is it possible for you to win? Have you any weapons?

WARDEN: I carried weapons only during the first years. What good could they be against him? They only hampered me. We just fight with our fists, or rather with the strength of our breath. And you're in my thoughts all the time.

Pause.

WARDEN: But I never doubt my victory. Only sometimes I'm afraid the Duke will let me slip through his fingers and forget that he's fighting.

PRINCE : And when do you win ?

WARDEN : At dawn. Then he throws me down and spits at me. That's his confession of defeat. But I have to go on lying there for an hour before I can get my breath back properly.

Pause.

PRINCE (*standing up*) : But tell me, don't you know what they really want ?

WARDEN : To get out of the park.

PRINCE : But why ?

WARDEN : That I don't know.

PRINCE : Haven't you asked ?

WARDEN : No.

PRINCE : Why not ?

WARDEN : It would embarrass me. But if you wish, I'll ask them today.

PRINCE (*shocked, loud*) : Today !

WARDEN (*knowingly*) : Yes, today.

PRINCE : And you can't even guess what they want ?

WARDEN (*thoughtfully*) : No.

Pause.

WARDEN : Perhaps I ought to add that sometimes in the early mornings while I'm lying there trying to get my breath and even too weak to open my eyes, there comes a delicate moist creature, rather hairy to the touch, a late-comer, the Countess Isabella. She runs her hand all over me, catches hold of my beard, her whole body glides along my neck, under my chin, and she's in the habit of saying : " Not the others, but me—let me out." I shake my head as much as I can. " I want to go to Prince Leo, to offer him my hand." I keep on shaking my head. " But me, me ! " I can still hear her crying, then she's gone. And my grand-daughter appears with

blankets, wraps me up in them, and waits with me till
I can walk on my own. An exceptionally good girl.

PRINCE : Isabella ? The name's unknown to me.

    Pause.

PRINCE : To offer me her hand ! (*Goes to window, looks
out.*)

    Enter servant through centre door.

SERVANT : Her Highness, m'lady the Princess, awaits
you.

PRINCE (*looks absent-mindedly at servant. Turns to Warden*) :
Wait till I come back. (*Exit left.*)

    *Chamberlain enters at once through centre door, then the
    Lord High Steward (youngish man in officer's uniform)
    through door on right.*

WARDEN (*ducks behind divan and flourishes his hands as
though seeing ghosts.*)

STEWARD : The Prince has gone ?

CHAMBERLAIN : Following your advice, the Princess
sent for him.

STEWARD : Good. (*Turns suddenly, bends over behind
divan.*) And you, miserable ghost, you actually dare
to appear here in the princely castle ! Aren't you
afraid of the great boot that'll kick you through the
door ?

WARDEN : I'm—I'm——

STEWARD : Quiet, first of all keep quiet, don't utter—
and sit down here in this corner ! (*To Chamberlain*) I
thank you for informing me about the latest princely
whim.

CHAMBERLAIN : You inquired about it.

STEWARD : Even so. And now a confidential word.
Purposely in front of that creature there. You, Count,
are flirting with the opposition.

CHAMBERLAIN : Is that an accusation ?

STEWARD : An apprehension, so far.

CHAMBERLAIN : In that case I can answer. I'm not flirting with the opposition, for I don't know it. I can feel the currents, but I steer clear of them. I still represent the open policy that prevailed under Duke Friedrich. At that time the only policy at Court was to serve the Prince. This was made easier by his being a bachelor, but it should never be difficult.

STEWARD : Very sensible—except that one's own nose, however reliable, never points the right way all the time. This can only be achieved by reason. But reason must make decisions. Let's assume the Prince is on the wrong track : does one serve him better by following him down or, with all due respect, by chasing him back ? Undoubtedly by chasing him back.

CHAMBERLAIN : You came here with the Princess from a foreign Court, have spent a mere six months here, and you already think you can tell the difference between good and evil in the complicated conditions of this Court ?

STEWARD : He who blinks sees only complications. He who keeps his eyes open sees the eternal truth in the first hours as clearly as after a hundred years. Admittedly, in this case, a sad truth which in the next few days, however, may take a decisive turn for the better.

CHAMBERLAIN : I cannot believe that the decision which you wish to bring about and which I know only from your announcement will be a good one. I'm afraid you misunderstand our Prince, the Court, and everything here.

STEWARD : Whether understood or misunderstood, the present situation is unbearable.

CHAMBERLAIN : Unbearable it may be, but it is founded on the nature of things as they are here, and we are prepared to bear it to the end.

STEWARD : But not the Princess, not I, not those who are on our side.

CHAMBERLAIN : What do you find so unbearable ?

STEWARD : Just because the decision is imminent I want to speak frankly. The Prince has a dual nature. The one, concerning itself with government, wavers absent-mindedly in public, disregarding its own privileges. The other nature admittedly searches very painstakingly for a strengthening of its foundations. It searches for them in the past, delving deeper and deeper. What a misunderstanding of the situation ! A misunderstanding which doesn't lack greatness— although its defectiveness is even greater than its appearance. Can you fail to see that ?

CHAMBERLAIN : It's not the description I object to, it's the interpretation.

STEWARD : The interpretation ? And to think that in the hope of getting you to agree, I have judged the situation with more leniency than I actually feel ! And I'm still withholding my verdict in order to spare you. But just one thing : in reality the Prince does not need a strengthening of his foundations. If he uses all the power at present at his disposal, he'll find it sufficient to bring about everything that the most extreme responsibility before God and man may demand of him. But he shies away from the balance of life, he's on his way to becoming a tyrant.

CHAMBERLAIN : He with his modest character !

STEWARD : It's the modesty of the one half, for he needs all his energy for the second half which scrapes together the foundation needed to build something like the Tower of Babel. To hinder this work should be the sole policy of all those who are interested in their personal existence, in the principality, in the Princess, and possibly even in the Prince.

CHAMBERLAIN : " Possibly even "—you're very candid. To be equally frank, your candour makes me tremble at the imminent decision. And I regret, as I've recently come to regret more and more, that I'm devoted to the Prince almost to the point of helplessness.

STEWARD : Everything is clear. You are not flirting with the opposition. In fact, you are even holding out a hand. Only one, which is commendable for an old courtier. And yet your only hope is that our great example carries you along.

CHAMBERLAIN : Whatever I can do to prevent it, I shall do.

STEWARD : It doesn't frighten me any more. (*Pointing to the Warden.*) And you who've been sitting there so quietly, have you understood everything that's been said ?

CHAMBERLAIN : The Warden of the tomb ?

STEWARD : The Warden of the tomb. One must probably be a stranger to size him up. Isn't that so, old boy, you little old screech-owl, you ! Have you ever seen him flying through the forest in the evening, out of any gun's reach? But by day he ducks at the slightest move.

CHAMBERLAIN : I don't understand.

WARDEN (*almost in tears*) : You're scolding me, sir, and I don't know why. Please let me go home. I'm really not evil. I'm just the Warden of the tomb.

CHAMBERLAIN : You mistrust him.

STEWARD : Mistrust ? No, he's too insignificant for that. But I want to keep an eye on him. For I think —call it whim or superstition, if you like—that he's not just a mere tool of evil, but an upright, active worker for evil.

CHAMBERLAIN : He has been serving the Court quietly for thirty years—possibly without ever having been in the castle.

STEWARD : Oh, moles like him build long passages before they emerge. (*Suddenly turns to Warden*). But first of all, away with this one ! (*To servant*) Take him to the Friedrichspark, stay with him, and don't let him out until further notice.

WARDEN (*very frightened*) : I'm supposed to wait for his Highness, the Prince.

STEWARD : An error.—Off with you.

CHAMBERLAIN : He must be treated with care. He's an old and sick man, and for some reason the Prince sets store by him.

WARDEN (*bowing low before Chamberlain*).

STEWARD : What ? (*To servant*) Treat him carefully, but for God's sake get him out of here. Quick !

SERVANT (*about to grab him*).

CHAMBERLAIN (*stepping between them*) : No, we must get a carriage.

STEWARD : It's the air at this Court. I can't taste a grain of salt anywhere. All right then, a carriage. You take the treasure away in a carriage. But now, out of the room with you both ! (*To Chamberlain*) Your behaviour shows me——

WARDEN (*collapses, with a little scream, on way to door*).

STEWARD (*stamping his foot*) : Is it impossible to get rid

of him ? Pick him up in your arms if there's no other way. Can't you understand what's expected of you !

CHAMBERLAIN : The Prince !

SERVANT (*opening door at left*).

STEWARD : Ah ! (*Glances at Warden.*) I should have known that ghosts cannot be transported.

PRINCE (*enters with quick steps, behind him the Princess, dark young woman with teeth clenched, stops in doorway.*)

PRINCE : What's happened ?

STEWARD : The Warden felt ill, I was about to have him taken away.

PRINCE : I should have been notified. Has the doctor been sent for ?

CHAMBERLAIN : I'll have him called. (*Hurries out by centre door, returns at once.*)

PRINCE (*kneeling beside Warden*) : Prepare a bed for him ! Fetch a stretcher ! Is the doctor on his way ? He's taking a long time. The pulse is very weak. I can't hear the heart. These miserable ribs ! How worn out this body is ! (*Stands up suddenly, fetches a glass of water, stares about him.*) One is so helpless. (*Kneels down again, moistens the Warden's face.*) Now he's breathing better. It won't be so bad. Healthy stock, the kind that doesn't give up, even in extremity. But the doctor, the doctor ! (*While he glances towards the door, the Warden raises his hand and caresses the Prince's cheek. Princess turns her head away, towards the window. Enter servants with stretcher, Prince helps to lift Warden.*)

PRINCE : Handle him gently. Oh, you with your great claws ! Lift his head a little. Nearer the stretcher. The pillow further down his back. His arm ! His arm ! You're all bad, bad nurses ! I wonder if you'll ever be as tired as this man on the stretcher ?—There we are—and now with slow—slow—steps. And above all, steadily. (*Turning in door to Princess*) Here then is the Warden of the tomb.

PRINCESS (*nods*).

PRINCE : I had intended to show him to you differently. (*After taking another step*) Aren't you coming along ?

PRINCESS : I'm so tired.

PRINCE : The moment I've talked to the doctor I'll come back. And you, gentlemen, who wish to make your report, wait for me.

STEWARD (*to Princess*) : Does your Highness require my services ?

PRINCESS : Always. I am grateful for your vigilance. Do not abandon it, even if today it was in vain. Everything is at stake. You see more than I. I am always in my rooms. But I know it will get more and more gloomy. This autumn is sad beyond belief.

FRAGMENTS OF "A REPORT TO AN ACADEMY"

WE all know Rotpeter, just as half the world knows him. But when he came to our town for a guest performance, I decided to get to know him personally. It is not difficult to be admitted. In big cities where everyone in the know clamours to watch celebrities breathe from as close as possible, great difficulties may be encountered ; but in our town one is content to marvel at the marvellous from the pit. Thus I was the only one so far, as the hotel servant told me, to have announced his visit. Herr Busenau, the impresario, received me with extreme courtesy. I had not expected to meet a man so modest, indeed almost timid. He was sitting in the anteroom of Rotpeter's apartment, eating an omelet. Although it was morning he already sat there in the evening clothes in which he appears at the performances. Hardly had he caught sight of me—me the unknown, the unimportant guest—when he, possessor of highly distinguished medals, king of trainers, honorary doctor of great universities, jumped up, shook me by both hands, urged me to sit down, wiped his spoon on the tablecloth, and amiably offered it to me so that I might finish his omelet. He would not accept my grateful refusal and promptly tried to feed me. I had some trouble calming him down and warding him off, as well as his spoon and plate.

"Very kind of you to have come," he said with a

strong foreign accent. "Most kind. You've also come at the right time, for alas Rotpeter cannot always receive. Seeing people is often repugnant to him; on these occasions no one, it does not matter who he may be, is admitted; then I, even I can see him only on business, so to speak, on the stage. And immediately after the performance I have to disappear, he drives home alone, locks himself in his room, and usually remains like that until the following evening. He always has a big hamper of fruit in his bedroom, this is what he lives on at these times. But I, who of course dare not let him out of my sight, always rent the apartment opposite his and watch him from behind curtains."

When I sit opposite you like this, Rotpeter, listening to you talk, drinking your health, I really and truly forget—whether you take it as a compliment or not, it's the truth—that you are a chimpanzee. Only gradually, when I have forced myself out of my thoughts back to reality, do my eyes show me again whose guest I am.

Yes.

You're so silent suddenly, I wonder why? Just a moment ago you were pronouncing such astonishingly correct opinions about our town, and now you're so silent.

Silent?

Is something wrong? Shall I call the trainer? Perhaps you're in the habit of taking a meal at this hour?

No, no. It's quite all right. I can tell you what it was. Sometimes I'm overcome with such an aversion to human beings that I can barely refrain from retching. This, of course, has nothing to do with the individual human being, least of all with your charming presence.

It concerns all human beings. There's nothing extra-ordinary about this. Suppose, for instance, that you were to live continuously with apes, you'd probably have similar attacks, however great your self-control. Actually, it's not the smell of human beings which repels me so much, it's the human smell which I have contracted and which mingles with the smell from my native land. Smell for yourself! Here, on my chest! Put your nose deeper into the fur! Deeper, I say!

I'm sorry, but I can't smell anything special. Just the ordinary smell of a well-groomed body, that's all. The nose of a city-dweller, of course, is no fair test. You, no doubt, can scent thousands of things that evade us.

Once upon a time, sir, once upon a time. That's over.

Since you brought it up yourself, I dare to ask : How long have you actually been living among us ?

Five years. On the fifth of April it will be five years.

Terrific achievement. To cast off apehood in five years and gallop through the whole evolution of mankind ! Certainly no one has ever done that before ! On this racecourse you have no rival.

It's a great deal, I know, and sometimes it surpasses even my understanding. In tranquil moments, however, I feel less exuberant about it. Do you know how I was caught ?

I've read everything that's been printed about you. You were shot at and then caught.

Yes, I was hit twice, once here in the cheek—the wound of course was far larger than the scar you see—and the second time below the hip. I'll take my trousers down so you can see that scar, too. Here then was where the bullet entered ; this was the severe, decisive wound. I fell from the tree and when I came to I was in a cage between decks.

In a cage! Between decks! It's one thing to read your story, and quite another to hear you tell it!

And yet another, sir, to have experienced it. Until then I had never known what it means to have no way out. It was not a four-sided barred cage, it had only three sides nailed to a locker, the locker forming the fourth side. The whole contrivance was so low that I could not stand upright, and so narrow that I could not even sit down. All I could do was squat there with bent knees. In my rage I refused to see anyone, and so remained facing the locker; for days and nights I squatted there with trembling knees while behind me the bars cut into my flesh. This manner of confining wild animals is considered to have its advantages during the first days of captivity, and from my experience I cannot deny that from the human point of view this actually is the case. But at that time I was not interested in the human point of view. I had the locker in front of me. Break the boards, bite a hole through them, squeeze yourself through an opening which in reality hardly allows you to see through it and which, when you first discover it, you greet with the blissful howl of ignorance! Where do you want to go? Beyond the boards the forest begins. . . .

(Beginning of a Letter)

Dear Herr Rotpeter:

I have read the report which you wrote for the Academy of Science with great interest, indeed with a beating heart. Small wonder, since I was your first teacher, and since you have found such kind words with which to express your memory of me. With some consideration it might perhaps have been possible to avoid mentioning my sojourn in the sanitorium; I realise, however, that your whole report and the frankness which characterises it could not omit this small detail once it had occurred to you while writing, although it does compromise me somewhat. However, this isn't really what I wanted to talk about here, I have other things on my mind.

FRAGMENT OF "THE GREAT WALL OF CHINA"

THE news of the building of the wall now penetrated into this world—late, too, some thirty years after its announcement. It was on a summer evening. I, ten years old, was standing with my father on the riverbank. In keeping with the importance of this much-discussed hour, I can recall the smallest details. My father was holding me by the hand, something he was fond of doing to the end of his days, and running his other hand up and down his long, very thin pipe, as though it were a flute. With his sparse, rigid beard raised in the air, he was enjoying his pipe while gazing upwards across the river. As a result his pigtail, object of the children's veneration, sank lower, rustling faintly on the gold-embroidered silk of his holiday gown. At that moment a bark drew up before us, the boatman beckoned to my father to come down the embankment, while he himself climbed up towards him. They met halfway, the boatman whispered something in my father's ear, in order to come quite close he had embraced him. I could not understand what they said, I only saw that my father did not seem to believe the news, that the boatman tried to insist upon its truth, that when my father still refused to believe it the boatman, with the passion of sailors, almost tore the garment from his chest to prove the truth, whereupon my father fell silent and the boatman jumped noisily into the bark and sailed away.

Deep in thought my father turned toward me, knocked his pipe out and stuck it in his belt, stroked my cheek, and pulled my head toward him. That is what I liked best, it made me very happy, and so we came home. There the rice-pap was already steaming on the table, several guests had assembled, the wine was just being poured into the goblets. Paying no attention to any of this and having advanced no further than the threshold, my father started telling what he had heard. Of the exact words I have of course no recollection, but owing to the exceptional circumstances which cast a spell even over the child, the meaning became so clear to me that I venture nevertheless to give some version of what my father said. I am doing so because it was very characteristic of the popular point of view. My father said something like this : An unknown boatman—I know all those who usually pass by here, but this one was a stranger—has just told me that a great wall is going to be built to protect the Emperor. For it seems that infidel tribes, among them demons, often assemble before the imperial palace and shoot their black arrows at the Emperor.

THE CONSCRIPTION OF TROOPS

THE conscription of troops, often necessary on account of the never-ending frontier wars, takes place in the following manner :

The order goes out that on a certain day in a certain part of town all inhabitants—men, women, and children without exception—have to remain indoors. Usually at about noon the young nobleman in charge of the conscription appears at the entrance of that part of town where a detachment of soldiers, both infantry and cavalry, have been waiting since dawn. He is a young man, slender, not tall, weak, carelessly dressed, with tired eyes, waves of restlessness continually passing through him like the shivers of a fever. Without looking at anyone he makes a sign with a whip, his sole equipment, whereupon several soldiers join him and he enters the first house. A soldier, who knows personally all the inhabitants in this part of town, reads out the list of the inmates. As a rule they are all present, lined up in the room, their eyes fixed on the nobleman, as though they were soldiers already. It can happen, however, that here and there someone, it's invariably a man, is missing. In this case no one will dare to utter an excuse, let alone a lie, everyone is silent, all eyes are lowered, the pressure of the command which someone in this house has evaded is almost unbearable, but the silent presence of the nobleman keeps everyone nevertheless in his place. The nobleman makes a sign, it's not even a nod, it can be read only in his eyes, and two soldiers begin the search for the missing man. This is not difficult. He is never out of the house, never really intends to evade military service, it's only fear that has prevented him from turning up, yet it's not fear of the service itself that keeps him away, it's the general reluctance to show himself, for him the command is almost too great, so frighteningly great that he cannot appear of his own accord. This is why he does not flee, he simply goes into hiding, and on learning that the nobleman is in the house he even leaves his hiding place and creeps to the door of the room where he is promptly caught by the soldiers in search of him. He is brought before the nobleman who seizes the whip with both hands—he is so weak he can't do it with one hand—and gives the man a thrashing. Having inflicted no great pain, he drops the whip, half from exhaustion, half from disgust, whereupon the beaten man has to pick it up and hand it to him. Only then may he join the line with the others ; incidentally, it is almost certain that he will not be recruited. But it also happens, and this is more frequent, that a greater number of people appear than are listed. There, for instance, stands an unknown girl, staring at the nobleman ; she is from out of town, from the provinces perhaps, the conscription has lured her here. There are many women who cannot resist the temptation of a conscription in another town, conscriptions at home meaning something quite different. And, strangely enough, it is not considered disgraceful for a woman to surrender to this temptation ; on the contrary, in the opinion of many, this is something women have to go through, a debt which they pay to their sex. Moreover, it invariably takes the same course. The girl or the woman learns that

somewhere, perhaps very far away, at the home of relatives or friends, a conscription is going to take place ;
she asks her family for permission to undertake the
journey, which is granted—it cannot very well be refused
—she puts on her best clothes, is gayer than usual, at the
same time calm and friendly, no matter what she may be
like at other times ; and yet behind all the calm and
friendliness she is inaccessible, like an utter stranger who
is on her way home and can think of nothing else.   In
the family where the conscription is going to take place
she is received quite differently from an ordinary guest ;
everyone flatters her, she is invited to walk through all
the rooms in the house, lean out of all the windows, and
if she puts her hand on someone's head it means more
than a father's blessing.   When the family is preparing
for the conscription she is given the best place, which is
near the door where she has the best chance of being
seen by the nobleman and can best see him.   She is
honoured in this way, however, only until the nobleman
enters ; thereafter she begins to fade.   He looks at her
as little as at the others, and even when his eye rests on
someone, that person is not aware of being looked at.
This is something she has not expected or rather she
certainly has, for it cannot be otherwise, yet it wasn't
the expectation of the opposite that had driven her here,
it was just something that had now definitely come to an
end.   She feels shame to a degree which our women
possibly feel at no other time ; only now is she fully
aware of having forced her way into a foreign conscription,
and when the soldier has read out the list and her name
is not on it and there comes a moment of silence, she
flees stooped and trembling out of the door, receiving in
addition a blow in the back from a soldier's fist.

Should the person not on the list be a man, his only desire is to be conscripted with the others although he does not belong to this house. But this too is utterly out of the question, an outsider of this kind has never been conscripted and nothing of the sort will ever happen.

FRAGMENT OF "THE HUNTER GRACCHUS"

IS it true, Hunter Gracchus, that you have been cruising about in this old boat for hundreds of years?

For fifteen hundred years.

And always in this ship?

Always in this bark. Bark, I believe, is the correct expression. You aren't familiar with nautical matters?

No, I never gave them a thought until today, until I heard about you, until I boarded your ship.

Don't apologise. I'm from the interior, too. Never been a seafarer, never wanted to be one, mountains and forests were my friends, and now—most ancient of seafarers, Hunter Gracchus, patron saint of sailors, Hunter Gracchus—the cabin boy shivering with fear in the crow's-nest in the stormy night prays to me with wringing hands. Don't laugh.

Me laugh? Certainly not. With a beating heart I stood before your cabin door, with a beating heart I entered. Your friendly manner has calmed me a little, but I'll never forget whose guest I am.

You're right, of course. However it may be, I am Hunter Gracchus. Won't you drink some wine? I don't know the brand, but it's sweet and heavy, the master does me proud.

Not just now, I'm too restless. Later perhaps, if you can bear with me that long. Besides, I wouldn't dare drink out of your glass. Who is the master?

The owner of the bark. They are excellent men, these masters. Except that I don't understand them. I don't mean their language, although of course I often don't understand their language, either. But this is beside the point. Over the centuries I've learned enough languages to act as interpreter between this generation and their ancestors. What I don't understand is the way the masters' minds work. Perhaps you can explain it to me.

I haven't much hope. How could I explain anything to you, compared with whom I am but a babbling babe ?

Don't, don't talk like that. You'd do me a favour if you'd be a little more manly, more self-assured. What am I to do with a mere shadow of a guest ? I'll blow him through the port-hole into the lake. I need several explanations. You who roam around outside can give me them. But if you sit trembling at my table here and by self-deception forget the little you know, then you may as well clear out at once. What I mean, I say.

There's something in that. In fact, I am superior to you in some ways. So I'll try to control myself. Ask away !

Better, far better that you exaggerate in this direction and that you fancy yourself to be somehow superior. But you must understand me properly. I am a human being like you. I'm as many centuries more impatient as I am older than you. Well, let's talk about the masters. Listen ! And drink some wine, to sharpen your wits. Don't be shy. Take a good swig. There's another large shipload there.

Gracchus, that's an excellent wine. Long live the master !

Pity that he died today. He was a good man and he went peacefully. Healthy, grown-up children stood at his deathbed, his wife had fainted at the foot, but his last thought was for me.   A good man, a Hamburger.

Heavens above, a Hamburger !   And you down here in the south know that he died today ?

What ?   I not know when my master dies ?   You're really a bit simple-minded.

Are you trying to insult me ?

Not at all, I do it without meaning to.   But you shouldn't be so surprised.   Drink more wine.   As for the masters, it's like this :   Originally, the bark belonged to no one.

Gracchus, one request,   First, tell me briefly but coherently how things are with you.   To be truthful : I really don't know.   You of course take these things for granted and assume, as is your way, that the whole world knows about them.   But in this brief human life —and life really is brief, Gracchus, try to grasp that— in this brief life it's as much as one can do to get oneself and one's family through.   Interesting as the Hunter Gracchus is—this is conviction, not flattery—there's no time to think of him, to find out about him, let alone worry about him.   Perhaps on one's deathbed, like your Hamburger, this I don't know.   Perhaps the busy man will then have a chance to stretch out for the first time and let the green Hunter Gracchus pass for once through his idle thoughts.   But otherwise, it's as I've said :   I knew nothing about you, business brought me down here to the harbour, I saw the bark, the gang-plank was down, I walked across—but now I'd like to know something coherent about you.

Ah, coherent.   That old, old story.   All the books are full of it, teachers draw it on the blackboard in every school, the mother dreams of it while suckling her child, lovers murmur it while embracing, merchants tell it to the customers, the customers to the merchants, soldiers sing it on the march, preachers declaim it in church, historians in their studies realise with open mouths what happened long ago and never cease describing it, it is printed in the newspapers and people pass it from hand to hand, the telegraph was invented so that it might encircle the world the faster, it is excavated from ruined cities and the elevator rushes it up to the top of the sky-scraper. Railway passengers announce it from the windows to the countries they are passing through, but even before that the savages have howled it at them, it can be read in the stars and the lakes reflect it, the streams bring it down from the mountains and the snow scatters it again on the summit, and you, man, sit here and ask me for coherence. You must have had an exceptionally dissipated youth.

Possibly, as is typical of any youth. But it would be very useful, I think, if you would go and have a good look round the world. Strange as it may seem to you, and sitting here it surprises even me, it's a fact that you are not the talk of the town, however many subjects may be discussed you are not among them, the world goes its way and you go on your journey, but until today I have never noticed that your paths have crossed.

These are your observations, my dear friend, other people have made others. There are only two possibilities here. Either you conceal what you know about me, and do so with a definite motive. In which case let me tell you frankly ; you are on the wrong track. Or you actually think that you can't remember me, because you confuse my story with someone else's. In that case I can only tell you : I am—no, I can't, everyone knows it, and of all people I should be the one to tell you! It's so long ago. Ask the historians! Go to them, and then come back. It's so long ago. How can I be expected to keep it in this overcrowded brain?

Wait, Gracchus, I'll make it easier for you, I'll ask you some questions. Where do you come from?

From the Black Forest, as everyone knows.

From the Black Forest, of course. And was it there, round about the fourth century, that you used to hunt?

Man alive, do you know the Black Forest?

No.

You really don't know anything. The helmsman's little child knows more than you, probably far more. Who on earth sent you here? It's fate. Your obtrusive modesty was indeed only too well justified. You are a nonentity whom I'm filling up with wine. Now you don't even know the Black Forest. And I was born there. I hunted there until I was twenty-five. If only the chamois had not led me astray—well, now you know it—I'd have had a long pleasant hunter's life, but the chamois led me on, I fell down a precipice and was killed on the rocks. Don't ask any more. Here I am, dead, dead, dead. Don't know why I'm here. Was loaded on to the death-ship, as befits a miserable dead man, the three or four ministrations were performed upon me, as on everyone, why should they make an exception of the Hunter Gracchus? Everything was in order, I lay stretched out in the boat.

POSTSCRIPT
TO THE GERMAN EDITION
BY MAX BROD

THE unexpected discovery of the story which provides the title of this book lends an unforeseen
form to the present Volume V. of Kafka's collected
works.—I had assumed *Description of a Struggle* to be
lost, for although it had been in my safe-keeping for a
long time I remembered returning it to my friend in
exchange for the manuscript of *The Trial*. It was this
exchange alone which at the time prevented Kafka from
destroying the manuscript of *The Trial* and enabled
me after his death to publish that novel as the first
sample of his rich, posthumous work. I deplored
Description of a Struggle as lost ; this however turned out
to be an error of memory. Apparently on some other
occasion I had succeeded—probably as a reward for one
of the frequent minor or major, serious or jesting,
services of friendship that we rendered one another—
in begging back the manuscript of *Description* of which
I was particularly fond. For now, in August 1935,
during a thorough examination of my library, I stumbled
upon it. This discovery is all the more important since
Description of a Struggle is Kafka's earliest extant work and
among his literary remains the only manuscript to survive
in a complete and fair copy. In the folio containing
Description lay drawings by Kafka, letters to me, drafts

for minor works (reviews), and the unfortunately rather sketchy beginning of a novel entitled *Wedding Preparations in the Country*, which I had also suspected of being lost. Several of these discoveries will find their way into Volume VI.

In the present volume fourteen short and longer stories as well as one complete Act of the drama *The Warden of the Tomb* are published for the first time. The additional pieces have been taken partly in a revised version from the posthumous volume *The Great Wall of China* which I edited in 1931 in conjunction with Hans Joachim Schoeps. Schoeps deserves high praise for the careful arrangement, dating and editing of these manuscripts. Unfortunately, philosophic differences of the most serious nature, gradually extending also to the interpretation of Kafka's work and in this context becoming even more pronounced, prevented me from continuing this association.

Later on I found an efficient assistant in the young poet Heinz Politzer, to whom I am indebted for a zealous and successful co-operation. It was he who conscientiously revised the first four volumes in their definitive form and who sifted part of the material for Volumes V. and VI.

In the Postscript to *The Great Wall of China* (written in conjunction with H. J. Schoeps), I commented on the distribution of material for Volumes V. and VI. and on the method employed in the editing of these books. I should like to point out here that in broad outline Volumes V. and VI. of the collected works correspond to Volumes I. and II. of the posthumous edition. Only the aphorisms were reserved for Volume VI. At that time we wrote : " From the vast wealth of long and short stories, notes and fragments, written partly in a highly personal, almost indecipherable shorthand, but partly also in fluent longhand, and on exceptional occasions in partial or complete fair copy, the editors have chosen for this first posthumous volume of shorter pieces all those stories that have been completed or completed to a certain point. When faced with Kafka's work the word ' fragmentary ' takes on a meaning that deviates from the traditional connotation. Even the three long novels edited out of the posthumous work (*The Trial, The Castle, America*) have not been completed in the conventional sense. And yet no perceptive reader can miss the essential idea unfolded in them ; for just this unfolding in continually new directions of a unique human and spiritual predicament is already anticipated with full intensity and lack of ambiguity in the very early stages of each novel. The same is true of the stories in the present volume in so far as they too are not quite completed in the literal sense. Thanks to Kafka's original technique (provided this term can be applied to something pouring forth from the depths of a soul), the human predicament in these stories stands out quite sharply from the very beginning ; the manifold variations of Kafka's basic attitude become clearly visible even if the ' action ' of the story is not always carried through to the end.—Any writings not continued to this immediately recognisable point on which the author's intention and the different versions of his basic problem become clear, we have relegated to Volume II. But this volume too will of necessity present only a carefully sifted selection of the posthumous work which, on account of its abundance, cannot be published in its totality. But it will be guided by different criteria. In Volume I. we made *artistic unity and completeness* our criterion ; Volume II. will be dominated by *philosophical and biographical significance.*

" As for the rest the editors were fully conscious that they could not and must not carry out their task in accordance with the usual methods of philological-critical editions ; for they were dealing not with papers and manuscripts destined for publication, but almost without exception with writing to which the author had not as yet put the final touch. Thus for instance there frequently exist two versions of sentences or even whole paragraphs, and the editors had to let themselves be guided by intuition as to which version was the better or more in keeping with the author's intention. Or on closer inspection it happened repeatedly that passages deleted by the author turned out to be indispensable for the whole context, or at least of such relevance that we decided to include them. A future ' Definitive Edition ' will no doubt have to employ conjectures, separations, and different versions of the text ; we on the other hand were concerned with producing a readable whole coming as close as possible to Kafka's hypothetical intentions. That in so doing the original text was considered with the utmost care and that nothing has been changed (except for some punctuation, necessary divisions of paragraphs and correction of obvious errors) goes without saying. There are incidentally long passages in the text —a result of Kafka's inspired manner of writing—which are perfectly clear and almost without correction, thus lightening the responsibility of the editors ; other passages admittedly had to be carefully deciphered and constructed from fragments ; these fragments in turn had to be lifted from many insertions relating to other themes.

For the following Notes, so far as they concern stories

from the volume *The Great Wall of China*, I have also
partly used Notes composed by H. J. Schoeps and myself
for the 1931 edition.

Description of a Struggle. This story is the first work
Kafka read aloud to me. I would therefore date it as
having been written during 1902 and 1903. Two small
fragments of the work appeared in 1909 in the periodical
Hyperion, as mentioned in the Postscript to Volume I. of
the collected works (*In the Penal Settlement*). Here I
should like to correct a printing error : the title of the
first of these fragments should be *Conversation with a
Supplicant*.—Both pieces are reprinted here because of
their context, though in an unabridged form which does
not coincide in every detail with the publication in the
periodical.

The story itself exists in two versions, both written as
fair copies. The first, in a copybook with black covers,
shows the Gothic script so characteristic of Kafka's early
youth ; only this first fair copy is complete. Like most
of Kafka's manuscripts, it is written on both sides of
107 pages, which in itself proves that it was not meant
for publication. An exception to this rule is the second
fair copy of *Description*, composed in Roman script,
proving that it is of a later date. It is written almost
calligraphically on one side of loose quarto pages. Both
fair copies show very few corrections, sometimes for
several pages not a word is changed. The first copy has a
few cuts ; the second unfortunately breaks off on page 55.

So as far as words are concerned both versions coincide
for short periods, for longer ones at least as to content ;
nevertheless they reveal considerable divergencies.—
When publishing, I kept predominantly to the second

(later) fair copy, and only when this came to an end was I forced to resort to the first. However, I retained several characteristics of the first version as essential—for instance, the title, the motto, the subtitles, the strange divisions into I., 1., a, b, which are so reminiscent of " German homework " and may conjure up for the reader that peculiar youthful-melancholic atmosphere on the threshold between school and college, the period of the first dancing lessons—in short, the whole atmosphere of the story. The first version is also somewhat clearer, cruder. For this reason I have added the end of the (framed) chapter I of the first version. I'm referring to the last paragraph of this chapter.

Chapter III. of the second fair copy coincides word for word with the prose-piece *Children on a Country Road* from *Meditation*. (*In the Penal Settlement*, pages 19–23.) This is preceded by the following lines : " I slept and with my whole being slipped into the first dream. I tossed around in it so much in fear and pain that it could not bear it, neither did it dare wake me up, for I was sleeping only because the world around me had come to an end. And so I ran through the dream that was split in its depth and returned as though saved—having escaped sleep and dream—to the villages of my native land.—I heard the waggons rumbling past the garden fence, sometimes etc."—In other places too the reader may recognise short pieces from *Meditation* which Kafka later on may have discarded as a whole but which in isolated passages remained dear to his heart, as may be deduced from their publication in his first book, *Meditation*.— Instead of reprinting the already known episode *Children on a Country Road*, I returned at this point to the first version. From it I lifted the end of the chapter *Excursion*, following it with chapter 3, *The Fat Man*—a) *An Address to the Landscape*. Beginning with chapter 3b both versions tally again. 3b of the first copy corresponds to IV. of the second. But since the second copy breaks off in the middle of chapter IV., I kept to the first version as being decisive in the context of this chapter.—The inspiration for chapter 3 came from an old Japanese woodcut (Hiroshige) which was popular at that time as a picture postcard and of which my friend was extremely fond.

The Great Wall of China was written during the years 1918-1919. Several signs suggest that the fragment had originally been completed but that the final version was burned by the author, a fate shared by many more of his works. The present version was found in a small notebook,[1] written hastily in pencil.

The fable embedded in the second part of the story had been published by itself in 1919 under the title *A Message from the Emperor*, in the volume *A Country Doctor*, but it reveals its full meaning only at the proper place in the context of the story.

The Refusal and *The Problem of our Laws* as well as *An Old Manuscript* (in the volume *A Country Doctor*) belong to the story-cycle (or idea-cycle) of *The Great Wall of China* ; but owing to the time at which they were written we cannot look upon them as preliminary studies, because they were found in a bundle of random papers which probably date from the years 1920-1922. The fragment *The Conscription of Troops* (Volume VI. of the collected works) was presumably written later.

The City Coat of Arms. One motive among others for writing this fable may have been that Kafka's native town Prague bears a clenched fist in its coat of arms.

[1] *Skizzenheft*.

On Parables was found in a quarto copybook dated 1922 which served its owner partly as a diary and partly as a notebook.

The Hunter Gracchus was in the same octavo copybook as the three above-mentioned fables.

The Knock at the Manor Gate is in atmosphere very reminiscent of *The Trial*. Date : 1919. (The first draft of *The Trial* was written during 1917-1919.)

The Bucket Rider was found among other sketches published in this volume in octavo dated 1918–1919.— *The Bucket Rider* was originally intended to be included in the volume entitled *A Country Doctor*, but was then published by the author as a feuilleton story in the *Prager Presse*, issue 25. XII. 1921. Background of the sketch is the coal famine in Prague during the winter 1917–18.

The Married Couple can no longer be precisely dated. Faced with two versions of more or less equal value, we decided on the one evidently meant for a fair copy.

My Neighbour is also from the octavo copybooks of 1918–1919.

The Burrow is dated 1923–1924, the last year of Kafka's life. It was written in Berlin-Steglitz, inspired by a new apartment and a household of his own. Many of the words in it were used by him in daily life (for example : the beast=the tormenting cough ; Kafka died of tuberculosis on June 3, 1924.) The work was completed. In the manuscript which has come down to us, not much is missing until the concluding scene describing the hero taking up a tense fighting position in expectation of the beast, and the decisive struggle in which the hero succumbs. (For this information we are indebted to Dora Dymant, Kafka's companion during his last year.)

In content the story follows clearly the trilogy of

loneliness formed by the three novels. But the reader should pay attention to the important passage (page 191) where the author, usually so careful to avoid any abstract statement, lifts the veil a little and hints that *The Burrow* means more to him than mere security : it means a home and a life founded on honest work—in short, the very things for which the Surveyor K in *The Castle* searched in vain.

The Giant Mole can no longer be precisely dated, but we may assume that it was written during the postwar years since the fragment (which incidentally was not completed) shows, apart from a more balanced description and calmer mood, the signs characteristic of the author's last period : in it he turns to super-individual connotations (in this case the interest for " science ") which lends to his struggle a greater objective validity without diminishing its personal problems.

Investigations of a Dog is probably the last story from Kafka's pen. In any case, it was written after *The Hunger Artist* which appears a few pages before *Investigations* in the same quarto copybook. But whether *The Burrow* was written still later cannot be established for certain. As far as page 238 the text has been revised in accordance with the first beginnings of the author's fair copy. Although the story was apparently uncompleted, it gathers together once more all the leading themes of Kafka's production : the insecurity and uncertainty of canine—i.e. human—existence ; the failure of all search for truth, however painstaking (apparently characteristic of a certain type of dog), a failure due to the fact that mankind has been annihilated as a result of some catastrophic error preceding the life of this dog—a fact that has changed the conditions prerequisite for a true canine understanding of existence and has turned them into a new but untrue reality ; the bizarre humour in the endurance of desperate situations, so typical of Kafka ; irony as a means of describing paradoxical circumstances ; the unrelenting, indefatigable search for truth, and in the end the dog's Being-beyond-Himself achieved by fasting and privation, by a complete renunciation of life. Then there is the strange sound of music coming as it were from another sphere and implying the theme of redemption which alone enables the dog to endure its life. It is this theme of redemption which—as a never-achieved but, despite every uncertainty and doubt, ever-present goal and meaning of Kafka's strivings—fuses his life and work into a great unity that becomes representative of the search for truth in our God-estranged epoch.

I would like to include here a passage erased by Kafka (perhaps because he found it interrupted the flow of the story unnecessarily) on account of its personal quality and the psychological light it sheds :

" At first I considered only the spectators. Their attitude has changed in the course of time. As long as I was still a child my activities were ignored. A child up to foolish pranks, what does that matter ? One passes it by with a reproving glance and hopes for improvement in the future. Now in reality I was no longer a child at that time, rather in my great precociousness I behaved quite deliberately in a manner that appeared rude, but it's true that my deliberate behaviour achieved no more than the harmless playing of children, and it really required an uncontrollable temper for an old dog —as sometimes happened—to butt me with his head, to roll me on my back (no doubt to make me appreciate his height), bite my shank till it bled, and give all this the name of education. And yet he was right (if one can talk of right in this connection) ; and as I grew older I used to nod to him in acknowledgment of the reasons for this behaviour while he was mistreating me, except that I took his brutality not for education but for what it was : the self-defence of a dangerously threatened creature who is so vulnerable and fundamentally so helpless that he is even afraid of children ; for altogether education probably only means two things : first, a warding off of the ignorant child's vehement attack upon truth, and second the gentle, imperceptibly gradual initiation of the humiliated child into lying.—And things got worse and worse as I grew up and refused to give in."

He—*Notes from the Year* 1920 were found, most of them in succession, in an octavo copybook dated 1920.

The Warden of the Tomb. The original manuscript of this dramatic fragment exists in three different versions. The complete handwritten version was in one of the blue octavo copybooks. In addition there was a type-written copy corrected by Kafka himself. This manuscript shows some alterations as well as cuts. The handwritten version, for example, begins with the words : " Narrowest stage, open at top." Then " Adjutant " stands for " Chamberlain " ; " Mausoleum " for " Tomb." The type-written copy is clearly a later treatment, the beginning of a fair copy. The original script as well as the fair copy lack a title. I myself added the title *The Warden of the Tomb.* The fair copy comprises six closely written sheets, the backs and right halves of which are unused. The sixth sheet breaks off with the words : " If he has been coming for thirty years it can't be Duke Friedrich, for he has been dead only fifteen years. On the other hand, he is the only one who——" Since the sixth sheet ends on the last line, we may assume that the fair copy did continue, but the sequel can't be found. In order to resume, resort had to be made to the blue octavo copybook which carries on clearly as far as the Isabella episode inclusively. (Second stage of the text.) Beginning with the entrance of the servant who summons the Prince to his wife, the text in the blue octavo copybook is erased and is followed by several versions which partly overlap (Third stage of the text). This concluding passage can be reconstructed only by combinations and conjectures and by arranging the existing fragments in such a way as to avoid contradiction. The kind of task I have undertaken here can never be completely successful, but a verbatim reproduction, even a photostat of the contradicting versions that are crossed out and show within the erased sections even more definite erasures, would not provide a satisfactory solution. As a result, the publication of this fragment (like many others among the posthumous writings) almost becomes itself one of those never-ending problems, one of those " Chinese Walls " that play such a predominant and recurrent rôle in Kafka's work.—The blue octavo copybook marked I by Kafka himself contains incidentally a number of prose fragments in narrative form. Of the content of these, two (*Torn Dream* and *The Grandfather's Story*) show connections with *The Warden of the Tomb*, another is reminiscent of *The Warden* as well as *The Hunter Gracchus*. These pieces which, like so many fragments that have not progressed beyond the suggestion of a situation, I have not included in the present volume ; in this case too I am aware of an insoluble, or at least never completely soluble, task.